THE ODDS

OTHER BOOKS BY KATHLEEN GEORGE

FICTION

Afterimage

Fallen

Taken

The Man in the Buick (STORIES)

NONFICTION

...ythm in Drama

Playwriting: The First Workshop

Winter's Tales: Reflections on the

Novelistic Stage

THE ODDS

KATHLEEN GEORGE

MINOTAUR BOOKS

A THOMAS DUNNE BOOK

NEW YORK

A THOMAS DUNNE BOOK FOR MINOTAUR BOOKS.
An imprint of St. Martin's Publishing Group.

THE ODDS. Copyright © 2009 by Kathleen George. All rights reserved. Printed in the United States of America. For information, address St. Martin's Press, 175 Fifth Avenue, New York, N.Y. 10010.

www.thomasdunnebooks.com
www.minotaurbooks.com

The Library of Congress has cataloged the hardcover edition as follows:

George, Kathleen, 1943–
    The odds / Kathleen George.—1st ed.
        p. cm.
    ISBN 978-0-312-54999-2
    1. Abandoned children—Fiction. 2. Ex-convicts—Fiction. 3. Drug dealers—Fiction.
4. Police—Pennsylvania—Pittsburgh—Fiction. 5. Pittsburgh (Pa.)—Fiction. I. Title.
    PS3557.E487033 2009
    813'.54—dc22

                                                                        2009007909

ISBN 978-0-312-57323-2 (trade paperback)

First Minotaur Books Paperback Edition: July 2011

10 9 8 7 6 5 4 3 2 1

For Vivian, Richard, and Janet

ACKNOWLEDGMENTS

I have many people to thank. Since this book was long in the making, some of these people may not remember me, but I remember them. There was, as always, enormous help from retired Commander Ronald B. Freeman of the Pittsburgh Police Major Crimes Division. Another policeman, an undercover Narcotics detective who must remain nameless because of the nature of his job, patiently answered a million questions about heroin distribution in the Pittsburgh area. To him, many thanks. Janice Gore of Family Service of Western Pennsylvania and Amy Ross of Children, Youth, and Families were enormously encouraging; they see many children who aren't cared for properly and they engaged with passion about helping me tell the story of the fictional Philips children. Dr. Gary Gruen, an orthopedic trauma surgeon, answered my calls and, with grace and enthusiasm, helped me through the trauma part of this plot. John Bishop and other staff pharmacists at the University of Pittsburgh gave me crucial information about pharmaceuticals, and Vivian Preston gathered for me information about chemotherapy.

Anna Rosenstein, Diana Calderazzo, and Sharon Yam proofed the manuscript at various stages. The University of Pittsburgh supported my efforts and granted me help through the Richard D. and Mary Jane Edwards Endowed Publication Fund. Parts of this book were written at the MacDowell Colony, heaven on earth.

Writers Nancy Martin, Rebecca Drake, Lila Shaara, Heather Terrell, and Kathryn Miller Haines provided, and continue to provide, wonderful friendship and camaraderie.

My husband, Hilary Masters, read this manuscript many times and responded with patience and wisdom. For his support, I am eternally grateful.

PART ONE

ONE

MEG HAD BEEN SLEEPING
when something woke her, something slight as the scratch of a
mouse. She came into the kitchen to find her stepmother standing at
the stove, writing a note. It was the middle of the night, and there
was only the stove light on. Meg wondered how Alison could write
in the dark or why she wanted to. Slowly she took things in: Alison's
shoulder bag was hanging on her shoulder; she was fully dressed; in
her left hand under the purse, she dangled car keys. Meg thought, I
shouldn't have said there wasn't enough money for the pizza. Why
did I tell her?

Alison said, "I just wrote you a note. Should have guessed you'd get
the vibrations and wake up."

Meg felt embarrassed because she wore only a thin T-shirt. She
reached for the note and crossed her arms over her chest while she read.
The pose made her feel even shyer. She didn't want to cry.

I have made up my mind and I am going for good. Here is what you need to do:

Meg stopped reading. "But you just got back. Susannah said you were going to start work again."

"I came for some things."

"Oh." Meg saw there was luggage piled by the front door. She turned back to the note.

For old times sake give me a couple of days start and then you go to the school authorities and tell them you need foster care.

Meg's heart sank. "Where will you be going?"

"I can't tell you that. Someone might get it out of you."

"For how long? Is this about a job?" Meg asked, but she saw by Alison's face, it wasn't about a job.

Alison said, "I have to get going. I didn't want to get into it."

"But—" She wondered if there was something terrible she didn't know. "Why go in the middle of the night? Why not start after breakfast?"

"This is best."

Her stepmother moved toward the suitcases—two big tweedy things plus an ample weekender and a smaller satchel, all of which looked like the kind of luggage rich people carried. And a cardboard box. In the satchel, the round hairbrush was sticking up. Funny. Meg had heard the note-writing, not the packing.

"You might change your mind," Meg said gently. It had happened before.

"No."

"We could wait a bit before doing anything."

Alison hesitated. "I don't know. I made up my mind. I'm no good at this. I'm not cut out for it. I never counted on it when I met your father. It was bad enough there were four of you to worry about. I don't know why I stayed so long."

Maybe Alison had loved them a little, in spite of herself, Meg thought, even though the initial staying had more to do with their father's insurance and the house they'd owned—until Alison sold it—than it did with them.

"I wouldn't wait much past three days, you hear. Get yourselves some foster care. Okay? Just wait a little for my sake."

"You'll call?" Meg asked. "Just to—" She didn't say the rest about being sure before they did anything.

"Best we forget we ever knew each other," Alison said softly.

Meg sat down on the kitchen chair, hitting harder than she intended. The hard jolt the chair gave her spine seemed the mark of some sort of defeat.

Alison took the note from her, crumpled it, and began to throw it in the trash. Then she paused and put it in her purse. "They'll ask you questions. Just keep saying you don't know. You could get me in a whole bunch of trouble, so just say the last you knew I met somebody, I left, went you don't know where. That's the simplest. I did well by you guys; I tried, anyway." Alison fumbled to get her checkbook from her purse. She searched for a pen, finally found one, and wrote a check.

Meg looked at the tan mules her stepmother favored, toeless and with a narrow heel. Alison wore a short brown clingy dress with a little black sweater. She always tried to look like a kid. Their father had wanted to get them a mother, but he ended up getting them a person who was trying to be a teenager.

Alison put the check on the hall table and came back to the kitchen. Suddenly there was something that passed for a hug and kiss. Meg threw her arms around her stepmother and held on tight. There'd been plenty of tension between them. Even she couldn't explain the hug. It was just that anybody she ever knew, she *kind of* loved. "Will you be okay?" Meg asked.

Her question started Alison crying. "Don't . . . don't. I'm counting on you to do the right thing. You understand? Let me be and then get yourselves some parents."

Meg would have liked to be angry with Alison, but the truth was, she understood her. Alison hadn't bargained on any of this, four kids and, the last two years, no man in her life. She'd craved romance and got hard-knocks reality. Alison was going to meet a man—that was clear from the high excitement and triumph underneath her apologies.

Alison broke the embrace and picked up the luggage—enough luggage to hold just about everything she owned.

Meg went to reach for one of the tweed bags, but Alison said, "No. My God. No. You can't do that, too." Meg stood helpless as her step-mother went to the car once, then twice. Finally Alison put the last piece of luggage and the cardboard box in the trunk. She kissed her fingers in farewell, got behind the wheel, and started up the car, but she didn't start out right away. The moment stretched to three minutes.

Meg watched, thinking, I've done it, I've turned her around.

Alison put the old Civic into gear. Still she didn't move.

The stars were visible, and a half moon washed the closely parked cars in an eerie light. The car motor made its familiar coughing sound. Suddenly, the car and its driver were gone.

The night was chilly. Meg didn't put on a robe or a sweater. She didn't go back to bed. She sat still at the kitchen table for a long time, hearing the memory of the car driving away and understanding why Alison went in the night. License plate. Alison wanted to get far enough away that nobody could find her if Meg rebelled and called the police.

Meg thought about how to tell the others in the morning that their stepmother had come back for a few days only to take off again and this time it was for good.

The check sat on the "hall table"—it was really just redwood out-door furniture, although it was nicely made—nearest the front door used for schoolbooks and mail. Meg was the one who found the table outside Keystone Plumbing, on sale for ten bucks, and she thought it could substitute for one about the same size her stepmother had sold when they downsized from a house in Greenfield to this little saltbox. "Only ten bucks, and sturdy," she'd come home saying, and Alison told her she sounded like an old woman.

The comment stung. Meg did not want to be an old woman, but she supposed she was. She'd always been the caretaker of the other kids, but in many ways, too, of her mother when she was alive, her stepmother, and even her father. She wanted to be like . . . not like her classmates, exactly, but like *some* kids her age. Pretty, laughing, music-playing kids. *Old woman.* Her schoolbooks were stacked neatly. Her class was giving book reports. She was doing *A Tale of Two Cities* tomorrow, one of her father's favorite books. She was finished preparing, had been for a week. Math done. Geography done.

Meg got up and looked at the check. Forty bucks. She could make it on that for a long time. Alison had no sense of money—she had told Susannah to call for a pizza today, and all she had to pay for it was five dollars and something. The man had been nice, letting them have it.

She put on the television so low, there were no discernible words, only a murmur. Some kind of community-access talk program. She tried to guess what they were talking about so earnestly. Then a movie in which people raised their eyebrows every time they spoke, but she couldn't hear the words of that either and couldn't read the lips and didn't turn up the sound. After a while she let the light of the television flicker over her like firelight. She had the idea that if she concentrated on the thought hard enough, her stepmother would turn around and come back. She was gone three days the first time she left, almost a week the second time. Meg's vision was clear, a dream with a sound track. She'd hear the unmistakable sound of the cranky used has-been car, and she would go to the window and welcome Alison back.

At about half past four in the morning, she took her school copy of the Dickens novel from the table and read certain sections all over again, just because she liked them.

She read all night, letting the book take her again.

THE NEXT MORNING, MEG SAT

in her English class, floating, looking out the school window, thinking: She was a *good* caretaker; if only some agency would give her money, she could keep the family going just fine. She had to get after Joel sometimes, but when she tried to imagine being without him, any of them, she couldn't stand it. She knew exactly how Susannah's hair curled when it dried, she knew Joel's moods, she knew when Laurie's eyes would close in front of the TV. And they wouldn't be okay without her, they just wouldn't.

"It's a story of human *frailty*," the English teacher was saying. Ms. Blair liked to be dramatic. She had matte black hair that she always pulled back tight into a knot. Most days she wore scarves and big earrings.

Images of her own mother came to Meg. Little bits. The way she had moved, as if she were onstage. Lighting a cigarette, blowing out a long stream of smoke, putting the cigarette down in an ashtray. Fingers through her hair, a hip out, her sassy pose. And pretty, kind of like Alison, but with a lot more attitude. "Troubled," her father had said once, when they talked late into the night. He never said *crazy*. Troubled, unhappy, those were his words. Joel remembered her. Laurie hardly did. Susannah didn't. Brilliant. Their mother was brilliant, everybody said so. Read all kinds of things, was always in a fever, and not too nice to their father who was plenty intelligent but not smart enough for her—not brilliant.

Well, their mother had given them brains, anyway. Their father had given them kindness. He used to say something of the sort, sitting up at night, talking with Meg. She had to agree about her father anyway. He had had pained, gentle eyes, a soft voice. He never hurt anyone.

"Did you see that in it, the humanness?" the teacher, Ms. Blair, was asking Jordan Zugaro, the boy who had done the first report.

His answer was an unpleasant snorting laugh meant to let his classmates know how stupid the teacher's questions were.

"What do the rest of you think? Rob? Pete? Any answers? John?"

The boys rustled in their corrals, kicking at chair bottoms and book bags.

The teacher said, "I give up. Meg? Let's have your report now."

Meg stood and went to the front of the room. She wasn't sure her voice was going to work. On top of that, her report was eight times longer than anyone else's. But she began and she persisted, explaining the plot, reading sections, and then telling her reaction to the novel. When she looked up, the sea of puzzled faces threw her. She wanted to say something else, something different. *I'm Meg. I'm falling apart here.*

Ms. Blair turned to the class. "What did you think of Meg's report?"

"Long!" one boy said, and several laughed.

Then there was a tangle of voices saying that they did not want to be expected to match it and that it was more than they thought they were supposed to do.

"It was excellent," Ms. Blair said quietly. "You liked Sidney Carton? Why? Because he sacrificed himself?"

"I liked him even before he sacrificed himself."

Ms. Blair smiled.

Finally class was over and everyone hurried out to lunch. The teacher called Meg back into the room. "Look, Meg, you can't stay in this school system next year. It's ridiculous. You're so far ahead of the others. You need AP classes."

"Well, maybe, I guess."

"I have to intervene," Ms. Blair said with all the drama she could muster. "I can't stand the waste. Have your mother call me."

Meg nodded slightly and left. Then she stood at the fringes of the cafeteria line, stretching, looking at the free meal, hoping Joel and Laurie and Susannah would listen to her and eat *everything* coming to them so she could stretch that forty dollars for as long as they needed. In front of her, thick brown gravy sat like mud over ground meat. Memory conjured the taste of cheap beef and salt and fat, making her mouth water and her stomach heave at the same time. She chose it because the other choice was tubes of pasta with red sauce, and they ate pasta all the time.

She ducked toward a corner booth and opened a book because she wasn't in the mood to talk to anybody. If she talked, she might cry; she ate her lunch, pretending to study, while other kids played the game of constantly shifting seats.

She managed to make it through lunch and was passing the main office on her way to Algebra when the counselor, Ms. Stephanyak, leaned out, chomping on a carrot, and called her over. "How's your mother doing?"

Meg tried to hit a level, ordinary tone of voice. "Okay. Working hard," she said.

"I'll try calling again. I haven't been able to get hold of her. You don't have your answering machine on."

"We don't have one."

"Ms. Blair was just talking to me about you. You're doing very well. Time to talk to your mother about some options."

She imagined herself blurting it all out suddenly. *You need to report that we need a foster home.* Instead she said, "Thanks. I'll have her call you. I have to get to class right now." Why couldn't things just go on and on? They always had.

A voice behind her said, "They got nothing better to do." It was Patrice who caught up with her. Patrice was large and black, with soft eyes and oiled-down hair. She was good in school, as Meg was. "Can't wait to get out of here."

"I don't mind it, I guess." Meg looked at the old walls and lockers, wondering where she would end up, where her siblings would end up.

Then she and Patrice were at the Algebra classroom and they parted to take their assigned seats. Somehow Meg answered correctly what a fulcrum was, and replied, when asked, what result she'd got on certain workbook problems. Which, it turned out, she'd done correctly. The other half of her mind was on how she would catch Laurie after school, have Laurie walk Susannah home slowly while she rushed over to East Ohio Street to cash the check and ran back to catch up with them. She worked out shopping lists in her head. Forty dollars. A math problem of sorts.

Finally school was over. Finally she got to the bank.

The only available teller, a tough-looking woman with a cap of nappy hair and a jacket with epaulets, looked at Meg suspiciously, turned the piece of paper over a couple of times, and took on a very official tone. "You tell this person with the account—I remember her . . . Is she your mother?"

It wasn't exactly true, but Meg managed a nod.

"Tell her to come in. She has a low balance in the account and if she wants to get money out she needs to be the one to cash it because it would close out the account. And it needs to be signed here. You tell her to come in."

Meg said, "Thank you. I will."

She left the bank without anything. For a moment on her way home, she thought she heard her stepmother's car. But when she turned to look, it was just another rattletrap.

Meg took her backpack into the bedroom and changed out of her school clothes. She heard Joel come into the house, his sounds. Good. She had to sit them down and talk to them.

Nothing in the cupboards. No, not quite true. Three slices of old bread, a pat of butter. It would have to do.

"Are you changing clothes?" she called out.

"Yeah," Joel called back.

"Good."

Laurie came up from the basement and began sweeping the kitchen floor. "For once!" she said, "he remembers to change his clothes." She was three years younger than Meg. She had reported earlier that detergent was low. Laurie's glasses slipped down on her nose all the time and they perched there now, giving her a quizzical look. "We're out of everything."

"There's a half inch of dish detergent in the bottle," Meg suggested. "You could make that go far."

Laurie sighed and nodded.

"Where's Susannah?"

"She's sitting on the basement steps, drawing."

"Good."

They heard Joel come to sit in the living room.

She went into the living room and saw his two books on the table in front of him, saw that he was far down in spirits, as if he knew already. He opened one of his books and sat back, reading.

"I need to talk to everybody," she said. "Could you get Suse? Could we all come in here?"

"Susannah!" Laurie called. Susannah clattered up the steps. It was clear to Meg they were all expecting something. They knew, but they didn't want to know. Laurie sat on the couch and Susannah scrunched up next to her.

"Did you eat a lot at the cafeteria?"

They all said they had.

"That's good because . . ."

"There isn't anything," Laurie said. "Nothing."

Meg looked at them evenly. "Things are bad. Things are real bad." They waited. "Alison left for good," she said at last. "I was thinking she was going to stay this time. But she only came back to get her things. She's gone."

"Where?" was all Joel asked.

"I don't know."

"She'll be back," Laurie said miserably. "Even though we don't want her."

Meg paused. "She took all her clothes. Really everything."

The other three waited patiently for more. They did not seem particularly surprised.

"I'm glad she's gone," Laurie said. "I don't miss her at all. She's a whacko."

"Well, I know but . . . here's the thing. One way or another, she brought a little money into the house. We're stuck without that."

"She sold our house," Laurie muttered. "Where's all that money?"

"It's gone."

"What does she expect us to do?" Laurie asked.

"I tried to cash one of her checks today, but it didn't work. She never did understand money. What Alison said . . . she told me we need to turn ourselves in. She wanted me to do it in a couple of days, but I . . . could go to the school office tomorrow if you all want."

Joel had put down his book at the phrase *turn ourselves in.*

Laurie asked tersely, "How?"

"I suppose we could go to the police, too. If we hang on through tomorrow, as she wants us to, we could call the police anytime on the weekend."

Joel said, "No. There has to be something we can do."

Susannah's lip was trembling. Laurie soothed her by smoothing her hair and saying, "Shh. We'll figure it out."

Joel muttered, "She spent all our money. She could have gotten something for us, welfare, why didn't she?"

Meg said, "I don't know. She didn't like agencies."

Laurie said, "We're better off without her," but she said it mostly to Susannah.

"Well," Meg explained, "she was right about one thing. We need help. We can't make it for long."

"But we don't *want* foster parents," Joel said.

"I know," Meg said.

"Do *you?*" Laurie asked. "Want to end up with strangers?"

Meg said, "Nobody ever does. Ever. No, I don't want it."

"Don't want it," Joel said, raising a hand, as if voting.

"Don't either," Laurie said, raising her hand. And of course Susannah followed them.

"We're fine the way we are," Laurie said brightly. "Alison never did anything except smoke and look for boyfriends."

"We have no money," Meg cried out. "And we need food."

Joel went silent. Laurie, on the other hand, was energized by the problem. "School is out in three weeks, right? We could babysit nights for now and babysit all the daytime in summer. I could. Add it up. We don't need to give ourselves up."

Meg felt herself falter. She'd been thinking, if she lied about her age, she could possibly get hired somewhere. She looked straight at Joel. "What do you want to do?"

"We all have to get work," he said, "something, at least until school is out, right? That's only three weeks."

"There's rent," Meg said. "And utilities."

"We can try it. We can try for a couple of days anyway, can't we?"

They did the dishes and tidied the house until six.

They sat and read, all in the same room. At seven o'clock, when the hunger was fierce, they made three pieces of toast and split each piece four ways—twelve pieces divided by four.

They were watching television at eight, but the volume couldn't disguise Susannah's stomach growl. Meg suddenly couldn't stand it and she sprang up. "Be back in a minute," she said.

She crossed the street to the pizza shop. Yes, the same man was in there. Cleaning things up.

"I'm so glad you're still here," she said breathlessly.

"Just turned the ovens off. Sorry."

To her great distress, she felt herself starting to choke up. "I need to get a job. I can learn anything. I can cook, clean. I could definitely make pizza or work the counter. A couple of hours even would help."

The man started looking around. He took a drink from a bottle of beer. "I can't," he said. "You're too young. Some rough people come in here. How old are you?"

She wanted to lie. But she told the truth. "Almost fourteen. I won't tell. I noticed you work long hours and I thought maybe you might want a break."

"You hit that right. I was sneaking out early tonight."

"I could work for you," she said breathlessly.

"The job isn't mine to give."

A trick of the light made him look like he might cry. He had beautiful eyes, a light blue, and they seemed to open up like the sky. She turned to the door.

"Here," he said. "You're in luck. This has been sitting around for hours. Never got picked up."

Her eyes widened. Was he just giving it?

"And, just a second. Here's some dough. Some cheese. You'd know what to do with these? Your parents would?"

"Yes. Oh, yes, thanks. When I get some money—"

"Are you kidding? These are throwaways."

Meg ran home. She hadn't gotten the job she most wanted, but there were other places she could try tomorrow. As soon as she entered the house, she felt the other three dive toward her.

"Food!" Joel said.

"We can just have it?" Laurie asked. "What did you *say*?"

TWO

NICK HAD PUT THINGS AWAY

and was cleaning up after the girl left. He usually closed at ten, but he was cutting out early because Marko had told him to give himself a break. Marko didn't care if the shop turned a profit or not. Yet somehow Nick found himself taking everything about it seriously. Flyers on the counter. Fresh ingredients. Cleanliness.

It was quiet now. The refrigerator unit kicked on with a loud sound that made him jump. Because the machine grunted and sweated, he felt, every time he wiped it down, like a boy on a farm grooming a horse.

When the door opened again, he was hardly surprised to see Carl, the kid who came in four or five times each day. He was one of Marko's street runners—Nick had figured that out after the first couple of weeks. Because of that other connection, Marko didn't want the kid coming around. Yet Carl kept showing up, and he never ordered anything. He was using, so he was never much for eating. The kid had confided to Nick a day or two ago that he was getting straight. Nick supposed they all said that. But then Carl added, "I heard one guy on the radio, wrote a book about it. I went to the library, but they didn't have the book. People have done it. Got off it solo."

"I never got on it," Nick told him.

Carl had leveled him a look. "Booze, that's your poison."

Carl was a funny kid, eighteen, with a big thick head of curly dark hair and big eyes. He was tall, skinny, and sometimes appeared younger than his years. Tonight the boy looked like he had the flu, eyes looked sick.

"Buy you dinner," Nick said now. He quickly finished up in the shop and he told himself the whole time he picked up stray napkins and swept the floor that he couldn't wait to be done with Marko, to pay off his debt and be gone. But the truth edged in that he actually liked the simple humble pie of the job. Hot water, yeast, dough, and an accounting for each of his hours.

THE MODERN WAS ALMOST empty when they went in. He chose a booth away from the other customers. Carl slipped into the seat across from him.

A large-boned woman, proprietary, probably the owner, came over to them. "What'll it be?"

"Burger?" Nick asked Carl.

"I'm talking drinks. You got a card?" the woman asked the boy.

"No," Carl said. "Maybe like a Coke."

Nick looked up at the television. The baseball game was on, but it was only the third inning because the Pirates were out of town.

"Double whiskey. Seagram's VO. You okay with a Coke?"

The boy nodded curtly. His face was furrowed for a moment; then he asked, "What do *you* do for K? How are you in it? I don't get you."

"Me, I just work the shop. It's one of his businesses. I'm not into your end of things."

"You don't seem to be."

"I'm not. What happens after you get straight? I mean, what, you'd leave town—"

"Maybe. Yeah."

"I wish you luck, then."

"Couple of days, I'm going to be ready. I have a plan."

"Like in the book you told me about?"

"Yes. Weaning, then cold turkey. Why, you planning to tell K what I'm saying? Snitch?"

"No. He'll find out sooner or later. When customers are looking for you."

"I'll be long gone. K can always find somebody to sell."

Their drinks arrived, and they took a moment to order burgers from the woman.

"How do you know K, then? Huh?" Carl asked. The boy was studying him, not meanly, but with unwavering attention that amounted to suspicion.

"From ages ago."

"He's older than you, right?"

"Yeah. Kind of a substitute father. When I didn't have anybody."

Carl nodded. "But you came here from fishing."

"Right. Fishing. New Jersey coast."

There was a pause as Carl watched him. "They have you driving to Philly yet?"

"Philly?" Nick felt uncomfortable. Carl knew more than he did, it seemed, about Markovic's operation. "No. So far I just run the shop. Favor to—" He caught himself in time. "—K."

"You don't seem cut out for this," Carl said. He took a drink of his Coke. "Sugar," he said, tapping the glass. "A drug. Addicts gravitate toward addicts. Addictions come in twos and threes. I have to fight sugar, too, if I'm going to get healthy. See I know one or two things."

"You know a lot of things."

"Did I tell you I went to college for a year?"

"I thought you were only eighteen."

"Right. I went when I was seventeen. I was fucked up, couldn't study. Very nervous all the time. But—I couldn't flunk math no matter what I did. Had a British prof. *Maths*, he kept calling it. All the girls liked him. Whatever. I was really good at math. Even if I missed two weeks, I'd go to class, catch up."

"Hmm," Nick said.

"You ever hear of Wole Soyinka?"

"No. He one of your friends?"

Carl's large brown eyes widened. He choked out a laugh. "Maybe. Maybe in a way. He's a famous guy. Writer. Never met him."

"Never heard of him."

"I saw this thing about him on TV. He was cool. He told about being in prison and giving himself math problems to keep himself from going, you know." Carl tapped his head to illustrate.

"I never pegged you for a college guy."

"Neither did the dean," Carl laughed.

Nick watched the game for a bit. The players couldn't hit anything tonight.

"So you just run the shop, that's all?"

"Yeah."

Carl pretended to watch the game, too, then. He said, "Baseball is very mathematical. I can't explain it. I just know it is."

"You mean the score?"

"I'm talking deeper than the score."

They both watched TV for a while longer. "What happened to your friend you were worried about?"

"BZ . . . is nervous. K thinks he's stepping on it."

"Is he?"

"Nah."

"I always heard everybody did."

"I don't do it. I'm telling you that, and I'm telling you to pass that on," he said tensely.

"Well, I wouldn't be too surprised if you did."

"I don't. And I don't want to be killed for something I don't do. You know about the guy named Carson ran the shop for a while? Your job?"

Nick said, "No."

"They'll find him in the river one day. K favors the river as a way to clean up."

Nick went still, trying to figure out if he believed what Carl was telling him.

"He told me once if I screwed up, he'd make me want to die."

A large clang came from the kitchen. Nick looked in that direction and then back to Carl. His heart was suddenly tumbling and falling in his chest.

The boy's face was narrow and sad like a saint's face. Nick felt an unwanted wave of sympathy. "You want to quit, you should hurry up and leave town, cut your losses. You have someplace to go?"

"Nah." Carl stared into his Coke, then looked up at Nick suspiciously.

Through his sidelong glance, Nick saw two women come into the bar and sit on the stools up front. Nick watched them shake their hair and take out cigarettes and look around and then begin to talk to each other. He saw one of them catch his eye and then toss her hair and whisper to her friend. The hostess went to the women to take their orders and started back to the kitchen. When she passed Nick and Carl, Nick signaled that he wanted another drink.

The hostess came to them with their burgers. "Get you your drink," she said.

For a while, Nick concentrated on his food, slopping mustard and ketchup onto the burger and taking big bites. When his drink came, he polished it off quickly. When he looked up from his food, Carl was still watching him. "You selling me out?" Carl asked.

"No," he said. "No." He rose up in the booth and excused himself. He went into the men's room and ran cold water over his hands, then cupped some in his hands and splashed his face. Marko was where he owed his allegiance. Marko had saved his life.

When he got back to the bar, Carl was staring at his untouched hamburger. It sat in a paper basket with a heap of fries. "Can't you eat?" Nick asked.

"No." Carl took one of the fries and swallowed hard. "It won't go down."

Nick put down money for the burgers. "Let's get it wrapped. Try later. You have to eat." Carl shrugged an assent.

The woman who waited on them brought them a bag and some foil and let them wrap it themselves. Then they went out to Nick's old Pontiac.

"Which way you live?" Nick asked when they reached Brighton. "Left, right?"

"Thought of something. Let me walk. I'll be okay."

Nick inched along, watching Carl go up the hill.

CARL SLIPPED INTO THE OLD house where he sometimes met Mac and Zero, two of his customers. Better to give Nick a red herring, let him see *this* place instead of the right place, *his* special place.

He had liked Nick and that was stupid. Nobody could be trusted, especially not some old pal of K-man's.

For a while he sat in the old house on the second floor in the dark. He almost didn't have the energy to go back downstairs, fit in the plywood plug. There was a hole in the roof; moonlight spilled in, enough that his eyes adjusted after a while.

Carl's secret place where he was going to hole up was a charred house seven up the street from this one—awful looking from the outside, but better inside than anyone could guess. He'd found it five weeks back when he ducked into a yard avoiding K's van. Before he left the yard, he noticed an outdoor tap dripping water. Every window was boarded up. He felt above the door for a key. Nada. But the trickle of water had his attention. He started looking under stones, bricks. To his astonishment, he found a key under a brick. It was corroded and it threatened not to work, but a push, a tug later, and he was inside the fire-damaged house. There was, of course, dirt from the fire, but other than that, it was usable because most of the fire had been on the second floor. Gingerly, he tried the kitchen tap—water, very rusty, but it was water and it hiccoughed its way out. A person could survive here. He'd known that one day he would need the place, and he didn't tell anyone about its existence.

He visited it about once a week, thinking, dreaming. He made sure the giveaway outside tap was turned off tight.

Tonight, after another hour of sitting in what he thought of as Mac's and Zero's shooting-up place, he went outside and made his way down the hill again. He knew this neighborhood like nobody knew it. He noticed things—who worked when, which cars belonged to which houses.

When he passed the house where Nick had his apartment, the Pontiac was parked outside. A fifteen-year-old car. Not worth much. Pennsylvania plates. Inexpensive apartment. Carl catalogued it all. Was Nick in there reporting to Marko?

They'd be fishing Nick out of the river someday, too.

He headed back to his apartment on Veto. When he got inside, he could see someone had been there. He went straight to his mattress. His two hundred dollars was gone.

For the better part of an hour, he stood listening. He peered out the window. Something was coming down. This wasn't random. He knew, suddenly, how unsafe he was. And Nick—watching him, asking about BZ.

BZ *was* stepping on it, and heavily, too. The kid had laughed earlier today and said, "I got to get mine, you know?" BZ had moved his fingers as if sprinkling powder, dust.

He should try to warn BZ again.

He began to gather things: two large jugs of water, an old coffee can, soap, towels, loaf of bread, peanut butter, pills. He looked outside. It had just begun raining.

THREE

detectives on Homicide sat around talking. Their commander was in the hospital. The news about Christie had spread quickly last night, as bad news does. Colleen Greer had been one of the ones to visit the hospital, to stay and listen. Then she went home, where she sat at her computer most of the night. Now she was an expert on different kinds of leukemia, prognoses, treatments.

Last night Christie asked his young doctor what was the longest anybody had lived with it. The doctor said the average was five years. Some made it to ten. The bad-luck version was two. But there was a story about a guy who lived with it for forty years. "That's what I want," Christie told the doctor. "Forty."

Colleen told him to go for forty-five, fifty *at least*. And also, she requested that he never retire. She'd made Christie laugh to think of himself, hobbling around the city at a hundred, cleaning up crime.

The detectives traded stories about people they'd known who had had leukemia.

"He'll fight it," said McGranahan.

"Rotten luck. And with young kids." That was Coleson.

"And he was a clean-liver, too," Hrznak grunted.

"Christ, you don't have to bury him yet," Potocki grumbled.

"Who's in charge?" Nellins asked. "He tap any of you?"

"He's orchestrating from the hospital," Colleen said testily. "It's good for him. To keep working."

"You going to be okay?" Potocki asked her in a low voice when they moved aside from the group.

She knew her eyes were red-rimmed. She loved Christie, and to see him being brave . . . worried about his kids . . . Well, it had hit her hard. "I was just up late."

A siren sounded in the distance. She sat at her desk and stared at the litter of papers.

She was aware of Potocki taking a phone call. "C'mon, partner," he told her moments later. "We got one."

She got up from her desk. "What is it?"

"Drug overdose. Very dead. A young kid."

"Let's go, then." They started down the steps for the parking lot. Work was the only cure.

"You talked to Boss a lot last night?" Potocki asked.

"Yeah, I did."

"Chemo's the worst of it. My mum had it. You might as well be a drug addict. I hate chemo." Potocki went around to the passenger seat of the fleet car, a Monte Carlo, and let her take the keys from Pete. "Up to Garfield Street," he told her when she'd started the car up.

"Boss *has* to do the chemo. He doesn't have a choice. He has a family."

"Oh, I know."

It was still raining some, but the day was supposed to get nice—birds singing, sunlight. She put on the windshield wipers and started out.

Soon enough they were climbing Garfield, where an ambulance and a patrol car sitting outside led her and Potocki right to the aluminum-sided small frame house. The rain had lightened to almost nothing, just mist.

"You can take it," Potocki said. "The lead. If you want."

Potocki was not his usual self. He hadn't made a joke all morning.

An old man with light brown skin and very white hair met them at the door. Colleen showed her credentials.

The patrol cop appeared from the back of the house. He was about twenty-five, white, gaining weight, face already florid. "Just an addict," he said, shrugging.

Just was a word Colleen found dangerous. Just this, just that. People said it when they didn't care. To the cop, a needle in the arm meant the kid did it to himself, suicide by accident, suicide by error.

"Show me," she said to him.

"It's around back. A back entrance."

Everybody, including the old man, trooped around back. The old man was saying, "I don't know. He musta done something. Drugs or something. I don't know about what he was up to. He seems dead. Is he dead?"

Don't know, don't see, don't want to see.

Colleen went into the single room, leaving Potocki just outside to quiz the old man. Inside the darkened room, the EMS guys who were on their phones and writing things up stepped aside so she could see the body. In the center of the floor was a boy, a dark-skinned black boy, about fifteen, sixteen. The needle was still in his arm. He'd gone fast, never knew what got him. There was nothing fun in the room—no basketball, no posters, no portable CD or MP3 player, even though there were some CDs tossed around. All through the mess, there was powder, either heroin or what he cut it with.

She could hear Potocki outside getting the name of the old man—"Lee Evan Bodance."

"Mr. Bodance, what relationship did you have to the boy?"

"He just rented from me."

"And tell me his name again."

"Something like De-Mott Roi. Something like that."

"You never saw it written?"

"Never did."

"How did you find the body?"

"Some little kid knocked at my door. He was on his way to school. Said he saw the door open and peeked in, just curious."

"Where is this kid?"

"I don't know."

"Who is he?"

"I don't know."

"You ever see him before?"

"Nuh."

"What age?"

"Six, seven."

"What did the kid say?"

"He said, 'You better call an ambulance. He's either bad or he's dead.' Then the kid run."

"You think he was buying?"

"Oh, I don't know."

"Okay, where did your tenant go to school?"

"He didn't go to school. I never knew him when he went to school."

"Why don't we go around to the front and sit down, Mr. Bodance," Potocki was saying. "How well did you know your tenant?"

Tenant. Such a polite word for this rattrap.

Colleen got herself a ziplock and picked up the used stamp bag. She used another one for the powder she began to scrape up. Looking some more, she thought she saw, in a shoe wedged under the body, another bag. She was right. And it looked different from the first. This one was filled and not bordered in blue ink. She took it, put it in another ziplock.

She stooped down and studied the kid's face. He was bruised. And there were a couple of cuts. He'd been in a fight. She stayed there, looking, because it's what Christie would have done. She'd seen him do it. The time, the attention paid, signaled the patrol boys, even

Forensics, they could joke all they wanted after they took a tiny moment to remember this was a kid, a person, someone who had died too young. Period. Never got the chance to turn it around, have a life. And so she studied him.

The more she looked, the more certain she felt the case wasn't simple or routine. She got out a digital camera from her big purse and snapped several pictures—of his face, of the evidence around him. Two bags, one plainly stamped, one with a blue ink border. One full, one not. Powder spilled. Everything a mess.

She'd get the bags looked at, tested. She'd get a team here.

She walked around to the front of the house, ducking under the yellow tape that was going up. She heard, "What am I to live on now? I got my food by renting out the place."

Potocki caught her eye. He asked the man a few more questions about when he'd last talked to the boy while Colleen called for the cars she needed to take further evidence and to get the body to the morgue for an autopsy.

"He's got some scratches, some contusions," she told Potocki on the front steps. "Fresh. He was in a fight. Maybe it means nothing, given the life he led. But I wouldn't mind finding out who hit him as a start."

"I don't think it was Bodance. How many hundreds of possibilities are out here?" With a wave of his arm, he indicated the street and beyond. He looked around.

"After we get the team here, we can go to the schools. Somebody can possibly tell us when he dropped out."

They started back to the small room where the boy lay dead on the floor.

CARL WALKED THROUGH THE

park to the library. The building was beautiful, made of some kind of light stone in large blocks, peaks and towers, formal looking. He stood outside, looking at it, then sat on one of the benches, watching kids go to school. Because he had to wait for the library to open, he slinked to a corner of the park that was secluded and waited. He slept for a little while. And then it was time.

At the hexagonal stand of computers, people tapped away. Finally one of them was free.

Standing there, his legs aching, Carl searched out the chat room he'd been in yesterday. At first he'd thought he wouldn't join in. They aren't like me, he thought, the people who chat here. They misspell every other word. Yet he'd read on. And after a while he was used to them, the way they sounded, their spelling. He'd typed in his own entry. *I have been reading your stories. I want to get off H. I have started weaning myself and was having some success, but I'm having trouble yesterday and today. Terry, did you really do it cold turkey?*

He hadn't signed his real name—just Carl, the addict. He wasn't Carl at all. He was Matt. He kept Matt protected, inside him.

Today he found that people had written back to him. It was sort of exciting.

Oooohh, Baby, a person named Beautiful wrote. *You're doing it the hard way, thinking to make it easier on yourself. I have quit so many times and finally the only thing that worked was cold turkey. Look for Terry. Terry really did cold turkey, I know that. But Baby, you just keep logging on and we'll be there with you.*

Terry, who dropped apostrophes, not to mention vowels and consonants, had answered, *Carl, Dont let nobody tell you Methdone. It sucks. Its the wors. Dont do Methdone, hear me. You do on your own. First two days is good, easy, you say you can do it. Third day is the hump day you fuckup on the third day, back to hell. Dont do gradul, just cold turky. I'm serious. Got a job and all, listen to old Terry.*

He kept reading. He learned methadone had worked for a person named Simplesolutions.

He didn't want to be like the guy who wrote, *Bad day, bad day. Went and got some. Amen.*

He was going to do it. He started up the street to say good-bye to BZ.

COLLEEN HAD JUST DRIVEN A

block down the street and was about to turn the corner when she and Potocki both became aware of a kid with a mop of dark curly hair coming toward them, turning onto Garfield. Both detectives saw his eyes register the police cars. The kid turned and started walking back the way he'd come. Colleen sped up to catch him, and Potocki flew out of the car as soon as she stopped. "Whoa," he called. "Just a minute. Hold on. Police." He jogged toward the kid and overtook him. Colleen got out of the car and trotted alongside them to hear the boy ask, "What's this about?"

"You were looking for something," Potocki said.

"I was just walking up the street." He dropped his arms, his head. "Oh, shit, I was just walking. Why am I being stopped?"

Was it going to be this easy? Was he the one who'd done it, come back to look at the crime? She took in his long sleeves, the look in his eye. He was on it; he was probably dealing it. She saw him look around, eager to dump something, eager to run again. "You don't have to run," she said. "We just want to ask you a question. Just help us make an ID, if you would."

"What? What kind of ID?"

But his face showed he had guessed.

"You know this kid?" Colleen showed the photos in her camera.

"No." But the kid was already crying.

"I can see you do."

The boy looked around helplessly. "Oh, my God."

"What name did he go by on the street?" The boy swiped at his eyes, but didn't answer. "Look. You know we could take you in. It's clear what you're up to. Why don't you help us out, just tell us what name your friend went by?"

"BZ."

"And his real name?"

"I never did know it."

"We need to get your name. Can you show us some ID?"

"I don't have any ID."

"Your name?"

"Carl. Metzler."

"Where were you last night?"

"Around. At my apartment."

"And where is that?"

The boy gave them an address. Sweat had broken out on his forehead, but Colleen thought he looked sorrowful, the first person who seemed sad about the other boy's death.

"When did you last come by BZ's house?"

"The house? A week ago."

"Did you see him anywhere else last night?"

"No."

"You hesitated. Why?"

"I saw him yesterday, earlier in the day."

"Where?"

"Up the street. Just . . . we just sat."

"Can you be more specific? Could you show us?"

"Yeah."

"Let's get in the car. We have some nosy neighbors around here."

The boy hesitated again.

"Calm down. We're not taking you in," Potocki said. "Just turn and let me do my thing. I got to do this." He patted the boy down, looked at Colleen with a shrug that communicated there were a couple of stamp bags in the pockets, but no gun.

They put the kid in the passenger seat. Potocki got into the backseat and Colleen took the driver seat. Potocki spoke. "We're working Homicide. We're too busy to make a Narcotics arrest. What we need is information. Did your friend make somebody mad lately?"

"Nah."

"Who'd he work for?"

"Don't know."

Potocki nodded. "Where do you go to school?"

"I don't. I'm eighteen."

"Where did you go?"

"Not here. I come from Chicago."

"What are you doing in Pittsburgh?"

"Just . . . trying to figure out where to be."

"You have any family?"

"No."

"How come?"

"Mother died."

"What was her name?"

"Sarah Metzler."

"Show us where you met BZ."

"Two blocks up."

Colleen drove and a minute later they all looked at the stoop of the apartment building Carl pointed out.

"We sat there sometimes," Carl said.

"Before we leave you, we'll need some addresses. Where you and your mother used to live. We'll need your cell number." Potocki nodded toward the kid's pockets. "You have a cell phone."

"Okay." Carl wrote addresses and phone numbers down. When he finished, Potocki took the phone from him and checked the number, then wrote down a few numbers of callers.

She said, "You must have liked BZ. Tell me something about him."

"He was funny. Made me laugh."

"I'd like to help you, Carl. I don't want you to end up like your friend." His moist eyes met hers, and she knew, as she took out her card to give him, she had made a connection.

Her phone rang. Christie. "It's Boss," she told Potocki before answering. "Hey, Boss."

"Hey, yourself. Look. Can you and Potocki come up here to the hospital? Now. Seems you have a victim our Narcotics people are interested in. There's a boy you're talking to—you're supposed to let him go."

"Someone knows this already?"

"Yes. Eleven o'clock meeting. Farber is on his way."

"Oh. Okay. Just a minute." She turned to Carl. "Where do we drop you?"

"I can walk from here. This is fine."

"We'll have to be back in touch. You understand?"

They watched him walk down the street. She got back on the phone. "We were just about to go to the schools . . . to get the identity of the young kid who died."

"Give the photo—you have a photo?"

"Yeah. I have to print it."

"Give it to . . . I'd say Coleson and McGranahan. Let them do the schools."

She noted the time and hung up. "We have to stop at the office, make the photos, then go meet Christie. Something to do with Farber," she growled.

Potocki laughed. Nobody liked to muck with Farber, Narcotics.

"And also, on the way, I want to get these bags over to the lab. See if they say anything beyond what I'm guessing."

"Which is?"

"One ordinary Pittsburgh dose. One very intentional hot shot."

FOUR

ON FRIDAY MORNING, WHEN
Ms. Stephanyak, the school counselor, called Joel into her office, he got
a stab of fear. Had someone reported them? Stephanyak, a short, round,
worried-looking woman, was saying, "I called . . . but we didn't get a
reply from your family about the Honors Assembly."

"Oh. Sorry. It's . . . no, nobody can come."

"Your mother can't come?"

"She's working."

"That's a shame. They want to make a big fuss over you. Does your
mother understand what an honor it is? She ought to see if she can get
out of work."

"I'll ask again, but I don't think she can."

"Joel?"

"Yes?"

"Is everything all right at home?"

"Yes."

"Good. No, don't go yet, there's more news. There's a woman from an association, well, it's charitable, and they want to give a scholarship to someone for Shadyside Academy. They're taking names from about seven schools. All your teachers put in your name."

He couldn't think what to say. Shadyside. "How would I get there?" he asked finally.

"Either your mother'd drive you or you'd take the bus. Transportation can be worked out. It would be a great honor."

"I don't know. I wanted to have a job next year."

"You're a little young for a job. Joel? Is everything okay with your family?"

"Oh, yes."

"These are all honors coming to you. I hope your mother understands that. I'll put her on my list for a visit."

"She's just really busy."

"Joel? Why are you half out the door?"

"The bell already rang; I'm late."

"Oh, just tell Mr. Harper you were talking to me."

He escaped and was walking fast when he ran into his friend Ryan coming out another doorway. Ryan said excitedly, "Police are here. Did you see?"

"No. What about?"

"I don't know. I think some kid who used to go here died. I was trying to listen, but I got called to the nurse for my allergy shot." Ryan made a big wheezing sound. "You? You in trouble?" Ryan looked toward the principal's office, where Stephanyak had a corner.

"No."

"More gaga slobbering over you?"

"Kind of."

"Get out. I don't even want to know somebody like you, gets teachers all hot and bothered. Creaming their jeans over your IQ."

"You're gross."

"I am gross and that's why people love me. Guess what? Your pals, the future criminals of America, have a shitload of cash on them."

"Do they?"

"They ever give you anything good to try?"

"No."

"I've seen you with them. Is that your new crowd now?" Ryan raises his eyebrows in an almost compliment.

"They want me to write their homework."

"Well, they can pay, that's for sure. They're in the money. Hey. Meet us tomorrow up at the court? If you're not too busy with the fast crowd."

"Yeah, sure."

Ryan made a pantomime of playing basketball. He dribbled, backpedaled, leapt up to touch a spot over one of the classroom doors. Everybody in class looked out into the hall and Ryan shouted, "In!" The boys in the room laughed and the girls giggled; the teacher instructed them to keep their eyes on the blackboard. Joel's friend called himself Ryan the Crazy Cracker. He even told teachers to call him that. Joel liked Ryan pretty well, even though they had just about nothing in common.

FIVE

detectives arrived at Christie's room in the hospital, Marina, Christie's wife, stood in the doorway. She wore black pants and a black sleeveless turtleneck and some kind of dazzling earrings that glinted through her thick hair. It was bad enough that she was beautiful and exotic, but she had to be talented and *nice,* too. Everyone said so, Colleen thought irritably. It was hard not to hate her a little.

"I'll just be in the hallway," Marina said.

Franklin Farber was already at Christie's bedside.

Christie smiled. "Have a seat." Colleen and Potocki took the chairs on the other side of the bed.

"We have a situation," Farber said. "As I was saying to your commander, we need to come to an agreement before he's carted down the hall."

Carted down the hall. What did that mean?

"We're shorthanded," he continued. "We're in the middle of something significant. So we're borrowing the two of you." He pointed to Colleen and Potocki. "I'll brief you myself. We're close to making a large bust, and we need reinforcements."

"This is something to do with our case?" Colleen asked. Christie shot her a look. "Because he's just a kid—and it looks like a hot shot. Could be a homicide." She looked to Christie for support.

Christie bit his lip.

Farber said, "Okay, let's just say it's a homicide. If it came from higher up, we need to step carefully. The organization we're looking at, it's complex." He entwined his fingers. "We need information. Relationships. I'm out of undercover guys, but—" He turned to Christie with a challenging look. "We've rattled the cages and we're borrowing you two."

It was unfair. Christie was too exhausted to say, no, no, no.

Farber continued. "We have a pizza shop that we know is dirty. Chief wants us to move forward with this. It's priority. Chief wants me to have a couple of extra people undercover, soft cover, every which way. I'm going to need you."

Colleen's heart jumped. A Narcotics operation with surveillance and stings could take two years. She looked away from Farber, trying to get her bearings. Outside the hospital windows, the trees were a fresh lime green, blossoms hung off the boughs. Everything was damp, but the day was turning sunny now. Spring in Pittsburgh was gorgeous.

Potocki asked Farber, "Who do we answer to? What are we?"

"One captain on a ship. For the next week or weeks or months, you'll report to me." Then Farber said, "Detective Greer would be very good to send into that pizza shop. The new guy who runs it is a good-looking fellow, seems to live alone from what we can tell. He might be susceptible to her." He turned to Colleen, who thought her face must be very red by now. "I heard how you got the confidence of that guy last year."

Colleen knew he meant the Washington and McCall cases.

"So you go in, soft cover. You're a detective on the case with the overdose. Just a very friendly detective. Who breaks a lot of rules and is, you know, single, friendly."

Just then an intern came into the room. "Mr. Christie? We're ready for you now."

"Give me five minutes?"

The intern winced a small disapproval. "Okay."

"They decided to start the chemo today," Christie said.

Colleen seized on the chemo issue, partly to avoid Farber. "On a Friday?" she asked. "That's odd. I mean sequencing. I read a little about it. They usually want to do a series in a row."

Christie shrugged. "He said they have some medical staff on weekend shift, so they're starting. They told me I was going to be pretty punk and not want to be making decisions after today. So . . ."

"You'll want to, Boss. I know you."

Christie smiled. In the hallway Marina paced.

"Back to you," Christie said to Farber.

Farber lowered his voice. "Okay. This is top secret." He produced a legal pad and started making a rough map. "Pizza shop is called Dona Ana. Way over here in Morningside is an auto repair shop with a rent-a-wreck component on the side. Cell phone shop in Squirrel Hill. These businesses essentially belong to the same two guys, a man and his brother-in-law, names are Stile and Petrucci. We don't have the identity of the guy who regularly visits the pizza shop and reups the street guys. Goes by the street name, K. Also goes by George White and George Victor. Neither one checks out as legit. We know he's living pretty high. The shop can't make that kind of money. We do know he goes to the Morningside shop a couple of times a week, picks up a different car each time, and presumably takes it to Philly. Two days ago, our men found him on the Turnpike on his way back. They were able to tail him to Pittsburgh. He drove to an apartment in Oakland and carried some stuff inside. My guess—I'd put it in the Tide detergent box. Giant size. So we can see the machine working, parts of it. Questions so far?"

"How big is the Pittsburgh part of it?" Potocki asked.

"We think he keeps on four boys, give or take, in each area he supplies. We have four areas so far that we know about. East Liberty. South Side. Wilkinsburg. North Side."

"That's a big operation," Potocki said.

Farber nodded, swallowed hard with excitement. "Our guy lives in a fancy house owned by a Melissa Thomas. She's some kind of ghost-owner. He's the only person who ever goes into it."

"He uses mostly black kids?" Potocki asked. "Like this BZ?"

"Black and white. Completely integrated business. Equal opportunity. What else? Cell phones, yeah, he has a few kids on cell phones, not all."

"I thought cell phones were out these days," Colleen said. "Because of tracing."

"This operation is old-fashioned in national terms. A few still use them."

To their surprise, Christie stepped in. "This scum—K, whoever?—apparently has a talent for finding kids who are loners. He either finds them or imports them. Runaways, nine times out of ten."

"That would explain our OD. Nobody so far knows who he is."

Farber said, "He likes them dispensable." With that, he reached into his pocket and put an empty stamp bag on Christie's hospital table.

"Whoa, watch it!" Christie joked.

"This is what we see most often." He pointed to a stamp bag that looked like the one Colleen had taken from BZ's shoe. "This one has been stepped on pretty good. It's down to seven percent or so. It makes the users crazy of course. Whoever steps on it marks the bag with the littlest dot in the corner. Otherwise it tends to look like a lot of others. We see a couple of brands. Power Times Three, Cuban Special, and Kong are the most frequent. The other ones that look like it without the dot on them come in at around twelve to fifteen percent."

"The bag BZ shot up was different," Colleen said.

"I'm not surprised. You two are canvassing on the homicide. Here's what I want. Greer, you'll include the pizza shop, even though it's not that close to where the kid was found. Make it believable. Get friendly with the guy if you can. We have our Janowski living at the Y for three days. He's going to establish himself, go up to the shop with others from the Y, eventually hang there when he can."

Janowski was a nice guy, good-looking, forthright, clean-cut. A family man. Colleen liked him from the academy days, and she'd noticed how scruffy he was looking lately. Undercover at the Y made sense of that.

The intern came back for Christie, saying, "No excuses this time."

They had to leave the room with hurried good-byes. *Carted down the hallway*—Farber's phrase—infuriated Colleen. Marina gave them all a small wave and went back into the room, her face full of worry.

They walked to the elevators with Farber and rode down together. Farber asked, "Walking out?"

"We're going to stop at the coffee shop," Colleen said. "Didn't get any this morning." It was a lie, but it got rid of Farber.

Colleen led Potocki to the coffee shop, explaining, "I know the way. I ate here last night." She poured coffees for both of them while Potocki paid. They met up at the service table with the sugar and Splenda.

"What an assignment. I'm supposed to make a pass at some guy. I think I'm out of practice."

Potocki stirred cream into his coffee. "When an attractive woman hangs around and acts friendly and a man has a normal ego, he thinks it's a pass."

She knew he was right.

He sipped the coffee. "Not very good."

They started down the hallway, moving slowly so as not to spill the bad coffee.

"So you get to do some acting, huh?"

"Such as it is. You know I had a conversation with Christie's wife about acting. You know she's a professional actress?"

"I know."

"She told me she would have liked to become a detective. Funny, huh?"

"It means she understands the work. Better than most wives, that is."

"I guess," Colleen said, feeling a small tug of disappointment that Marina continued to get high grades. "She told me if she ever did join the force, she'd want to be undercover."

"Very interesting. Could work."

"All I know is musicals in high school. But I keep getting acting detail."

"You sang and danced?"

"I didn't do any of it well."

"It's fun to think about."

"What is?"

"You being bad at singing and dancing."

Colleen swatted him, lightly enough not to spill his bad coffee.

It had turned cloudy outside again, just like that.

Her phone rang. "Aha, the lab," she said to Potocki.

"How do you do it?"

She listened as the guy at the lab told her the cutting agent was baking powder, that the full bag was cut with it down to about 7 percent heroin and that the residue in the other bag was as pure as he'd ever seen, something like 90 percent.

"Fantastic. Thank you so much. And . . . you haven't seen this ninety percent around?"

"I sure haven't."

"Ninety percent," she murmured to the tech. "Can you do any further tests on it, try to see where it came from?"

"I'll try."

She ended the call as Potocki shook his head, saying, "You flirt."

"Did you hear me flirting?"

"That's what's so tricky about it. It's in your voice. I'm not condemning. I'm admiring. So. Let's get you to the pizza shop."

SIX

THE CLATTER OF GURNEYS

and the intermittent interruptions of the PA system over the voices of the nearby doctors and nurses seemed a comfort. Christie tried to breathe steadily.

An aide came in, creeping up toward the bed in a kind of deference. Christie sensed her first in his peripheral vision, then turned to her. She was large, sweet-faced. "I heard you was here. I seen you on TV a lot of times. How you doing?"

"Doing okay."

"That's the way. We're going to get you started. They give you some reading about it?"

"Oh, yes." Diarrhea, chills, nausea, weakness, vagueness, the whole ball of wax.

They had a TV playing in the treatment room. The voices bothered him. The next time somebody came in, he said, "I don't want news."

Instead of turning the thing off, the new aide just changed stations. "There," she said.

He watched a wounded cowboy crawling into a barn. A lovely woman came in, touched his forehead, brought him water and food, wrapped him, and watched over him.

Marina entered. "They're going to let me sit with you." She took his hand and sat waiting with him for the hard part to start, the needle in the arm, the poison.

CARL HAD MOST OF WHAT HE
needed in an abandoned grocery cart: soap, towels, can, jars of tap water, two blankets, sheets, pillow, extra clothes, bread, peanut butter, three books, radio, broom, pills—Tylenol, valerian. He made himself move slowly, as the homeless always did.

He passed Mac's and Zero's place, kept going. Seven more houses. When he got to *his* place, he quickly rolled the cart around back of it. The key balked again, and it took forever to work it. But then he was in. Complete darkness.

He needed to buy flashlights. And extra batteries. And more food.

For a while, he worked at chipping an end off a thin piece of wood on a kitchen window. He did the same in what had once been the dining room. The openings let in only the smallest bit of light, but the light would eventually save batteries.

He was shivering and sometimes crying again. Somebody had killed BZ. He concentrated on how Wole Soyinka, in solitary confinement with absolutely nothing, found a way to make things. When he had no ink, he made ink out of dirt. When he had no paper, he used toilet paper. Soyinka counted everything to keep himself from going crazy, and that led to doing math problems. He didn't *learn* math, he *created* math, invented it. Carl piled up the textbook and workbook from the course he'd never finished. He had to work at tasks. Every day. Like a regular person with a job.

It was going to get bad, he knew that, especially two days from now or three. The weaning had given him a preview of the main feature: *goose bumps, dilated pupils, watery eyes, runny nose, yawning, loss of appetite, tremors, panic, chills, nausea, muscle cramps, insomnia, stomach cramps, diarrhea, vomiting, shaking, chills or profuse sweating, irritability, jitteriness.*

Like the flu. Maybe worse.

Think of good people, good places, he told himself. His friend Tracy who'd left Pitt because she was homesick. The lady detective who told him to get himself together.

SEVEN

COLLEEN WALKED INTO THE
pizza shop. The guy working the counter looked up, gave a shy flash of
a smile, then went back to waiting on an older woman who was having some trouble making up her mind about toppings. He displayed
peppers and loose sausage to the old lady with the patience of a loving
grandson.

"Take a seat. I'll bring it over when it's ready," he told the old
woman. He turned to Colleen. "What'll it be?"

"Same as she's having, sausage, peppers."

"Size?"

"Small."

She watched him slide two shells toward him and begin to spoon
on sauce. Then slivers of cheese wiggled through his fingers onto the
dough.

What could she learn about the place? It looked clean. The green peppers were very green; the cheese did not look at all dried out. How could she get the guy interested in her?

"How long have you had this shop?" she began.

He tossed the green peppers on. "Oh, it's not mine. I just run it. The shop's been here couple of years, I think."

"Different managers."

He smiled, nodded.

Colleen went to the soda case and got herself a Diet Coke. The guy had the pizzas in the oven and was adjusting one of the oven settings. She watched him as well as she could. He was strong-looking, but his hands moved delicately, carefully. Pianist, guitar player . . .

She sat and waited, trying to find her moment.

And . . . let's face it, she thought, the man behind the counter was extraordinarily good-looking—almost exotic. Olive skin, dark hair, blue eyes. He had a jaw that slanted forward ever so slightly, but somehow it was just right. Broken nose? Slightly off. But the whole thing together was . . . distinctive. And the eyes. Not just blue. An unusual, alarming blue. It almost hurt to look at them.

He delivered the two pizzas at the same time, and the old woman left.

Positioning herself so that she could seem to be simply looking out the window, she opened the box, wiggled a wedge of pizza out, and began eating. It was delicious. Certainly not a bad assignment so far.

She took a second bite of pizza. "This is fan*tas*tic pizza."

"Thanks. I do okay." He put the radio on and seemed about to say something else to her when suddenly the door to the back room opened and a man came out just past the frame. He was somewhere between fifty and sixty, dark, muscular, with short hair. "You have a minute?"

The two men went into the back room, and the older one closed the door.

Colleen looked about, but there was nothing to see. A minute later, the handsome younger one came back into the shop.

She took a drink of her Coke, pointed to the radio. "You like jazz, huh?"

"I don't know much about it. I just like music. In the shop I generally flip back and forth between jazz and country."

"Me, too," she said. "Either 90.5 or 107.9 on the FM dial. Even though they call it 108. Right?"

"Right." Something clicked in him, a gear shifted.

She tossed her Coke can into the garbage. "You ever go to hear jazz on the South Side?"

"I see the ads all the time, but I haven't got there. I keep meaning to."

"You should. I'm going tonight. With some friends. Blues Café. You'd be welcome to meet up with us if you'd like."

"Maybe I will," he said. "Maybe I will."

"Good. We're just a bunch of friends. They're fun." Colleen had eaten two pieces of pizza and thought she could manage a third. "This place has a nice atmosphere. Did you always do restaurant work?"

"No. I tended bar for a while. That's as close as I got."

"Where was that?"

"Kansas City. Couple of years." He came around from behind the counter. "Mind if I sit?"

"Not at all. Kansas City, huh? You were born there?"

He paused, then said, "Yes."

He was lying—interesting. She would have sworn he sounded like a local boy, someone from Western Pennsylvania. "I'm from nearby," she said. "Never went too far. I was guessing you were from around here, too."

He shook his head. "You work in the neighborhood?" he asked.

"Kind of. Headquarters is a couple of blocks away on Western. I'm on a job today in the hood. Canvassing. I'm police." She'd said it as casually as possible, but she knew it might frighten him. In fact, he leaned over and started cleaning up stray pieces of paper and napkins.

"I'm trying to get an ID on some kid, but I badly needed to take a break," she continued. She dug around in her bag.

He paused in his movement, crumpled the napkins in one hand.

"Here. This is off my assignment. Arch was my last street coming this way. But you can tell me if you recognize him at all."

She showed the picture of BZ, watching the man's face as he looked.

He angled the picture close, far. "No. I can't say he seems familiar. What happened?"

"Drug overdose. We need to find his family." She reported simply, "The kid may end up in potter's field."

"Crummy."

"It is. Very. Surely somebody somewhere cared about him."

He shook his head.

"By the way, my name is Colleen." She dug out her badge and let him read it. It provided her last name, Greer. "I never got your name," she said lightly. "I'll tell my gang you might join us."

"Nick." He hesitated. "Banks."

The truth? She couldn't tell. She gave him her best smile. "Hi, Nick. You got yourself a regular customer. The pizza's wonderful."

"Thank you."

"So maybe tonight at the Blues Café?"

"I'm going to try."

Nick Banks, Nick Banks. He reminded her of someone. She was rapping her brain with it as she walked down the street. The way he moved, the whimsical smile, the nervousness. Damage, damage, and all that in a beautiful package. She saw Potocki waiting, standing next to the Monte Carlo.

"How'd you do?" he asked.

"I think I got myself a date for tonight."

He raised his eyebrows. "You see anything going on?"

"Nothing we can get our hands on. Only one other player of interest, the guy in the back room, surely this K we heard about. I'd put money on it."

"Who's your date with?"

"The front-room guy. Here. Eat. It's cold. But good."

She remembered who Nick Banks reminded her of. It came into focus bright and clear as she heard again the rhythm of speech and thought, the natural self-deprecation. Her brother. Sweet, messed up.

"I want to show you something," Potocki said when they got back into the car. He drove a few blocks in the opposite direction from Headquarters and parked in front of a row of fairly new town houses, clean and modest.

"I'm going to be living here," he told Colleen.

She thought it looked small from the outside. He had a wife and kid. Judy and Scott.

"What I'm saying is—Judy and I are separating."

"Oh. I'm sorry. I had no idea. You've been keeping it very hidden."

"I didn't want to bother people with it. She took Scott to Florida so I can move this weekend. A couple of the lighter things myself tomorrow. The rest on Monday. You're my partner. I thought you should know."

"I'm so sorry. I'll help you move if you want."

"That's very decent of you. Hard for me to say no."

EIGHT

went seven blocks over to the neighborhood McDonald's to put in an application. It wasn't very busy, but none of the workers seemed to have time to look up. When she finally got the attention of a boy not much older than she was, he went into the back for almost five minutes before he came out with an application form. "You sit here, fill it out," he said.

After wiping away a smear of ketchup from the booth table, she put down the application form and began writing. It was only the year of her birth she put down falsely. Making herself three years older struck her as almost true, as if you could age by saying it. She used her correct name, address, and Social Security number.

A big girl, big as Patrice, squeezed into the seat across from her. Was this the boss? The name badge of the young manager said LEAH CRANE.

"What are my chances?" she asked Leah.

"We might need part-time starting in summer. Can't say for sure."

"How many hours—if you have something?"

"We start small, like eight, ten a week. We don't have anything now, but we might."

Some food money, then, but not until later in the summer. It wasn't enough.

She stopped at Subway and put in an application. They told her they had a waiting list of college students wanting jobs. She asked at the 7-Eleven; a man told her she was too late, he'd just hired somebody. Wendy's had nothing. She ran back home because she hated to leave the others unsupervised for too long. She found a note from Laurie: *Went to ask about babysitting. Took S. with me.*

She changed clothes to her oldest sweats, sat on the edge of the bed, and looked at her father's picture. "What should I do?" she asked.

He seemed to say, smiling all the while, *Stick together.*

"About food."

Her father kept smiling.

She heard somebody at the door, then the two voices of her sisters. "Whazzup?" Laurie asked her, standing in the bedroom doorway.

Meg nodded toward the picture. "He was nice, wasn't he?"

"Except for dying."

"Where's Joel?"

"Oh, who knows. Hopefully getting some car washes."

JOEL CUT OVER TO THE ALLEY

behind California Avenue, then the other smaller alley, looked left, right, darted through the high grass that obscured most of the first floor of the abandoned house, and got himself to the spot behind the propped piece of plywood that was wedged in the door of the building. He popped the plywood out, listened. Couldn't tell if Mac and Zero were in there.

There were flies all around the back door and his shoes had picked up mud from the overgrown yard. The rain last night woke him up, so the swampy wetness of everything around him made sense; he didn't question it, even remembered there were periods like this in late spring other years. "Spongy earth," people called it. He climbed in, fitted the plank back in, and listened. Somebody was whispering upstairs. A fly dive-bombed his neck. He swatted it away, but it came back, again and again.

His jagged breath signaled him to be afraid of the place, every time. Lots of wall and floor were torn away. Most of the skeleton of the place was still there, the muscle and flesh gone. The stairs were rotting, but Mac and Zero climbed them anyway because they used the upstairs—that's the part they liked—to mess around with the dope. There was an intact floor in much of the second story, and what had *been* on the walls was partly there, too—window, fireplace, closet. Joel was fascinated by the place. There was a back wall of what had once been a closet, one of those shallow ones like the one in his own room—a couple of hooks and not enough depth for a hanger even if you put a rod in. You could tell how things had been, even with the place ruined and torn up.

He topped the steps and there they were. They were busy, shooting up.

Mac said, "Get out. Go away."

"Leave him alone," Zero said.

"Wait, then," Mac said.

Joel had never seen them do it. He knew it was dangerous. He thought maybe it was a good idea he was there. He could help if something went wrong. Did they carry Adrenalin? They were supposed to. But they weren't very smart.

Now they were just sitting slack-jawed, eyes drifting almost shut. Zero laughed a little and let himself lie down, kind of like a doll, falling to the side from a propped-up position.

"Don't talk," Zero said.

Joel waited. The dope made them happy. He'd heard it didn't last, so what was the use?

Finally they started sitting up, looking at him. "You want?" Mac said. His smile was nasty, condescending.

Joel shook his head. "I don't have money. I need money." They started coughing and coming to attention.

"We're meeting somebody," Zero said. Then he turned to Mac and shrugged. "We were planning to ask—"

Mac reached over and swatted Zero, "Fucking shut up, shut up."

Zero said, "He was just asking, he don't mean anything. He's Curious George."

Mac said, "Shut it."

Joel thrust his hands in his pockets and walked around in a circle.

Mac muttered, "Kid like him wouldn't know fuck about this, couldn't handle himself."

Zero had once been friends with Joel, and so he couldn't seem to help himself, still talking. "H, you know what that is?"

Joel recited as if in school, "Called *boy*, called *horse*, called *H*. It has a couple of names."

"See that," Zero laughed.

"Geek," Mac scoffed. "Who calls it that shit?"

Joel tried to humble himself. "I'll do your reports. I'll do your homework."

Mac coughed so hard, Joel thought he was going to die. "I have to take a piss now," Mac said. "Let him try it if he has ten bucks."

Zero looked less certain when Mac went downstairs. "Want to come back tomorrow? I could get him to change his mind. He gets mean sometimes. Come back tomorrow."

"How dangerous is it? Selling it on the street?"

"Not bad. We never sold it to strangers yet, just some of the kids at school, but we never had any trouble buying."

"Who sells it to you?"

"Some guy. Carl."

Joel felt a nausea come up in him. He couldn't do it. He kept hearing his father's voice telling him no.

But just then Mac shouted up the steps. "Tell him to get the fuck out of here! He's a baby. He's making me nervous."

I'll wash cars, Joel thought. So much for making decent money.

Zero muttered, "I don't know how much room there is, you know. We have to watch out for our own stake. You understand? Meet you up here tomorrow, okay, maybe then." Zero's face showed Mac was coming back up the steps.

Mac said, "Hey, read my lips, punk. *You* aren't coming back here anymore. Stay away." Mac unzipped a backpack and looked inside, zipped it back up. "What are you looking at?"

"Nothing," Joel said.

Suddenly Mac shoved him. Joel went back two steps, looked around to see that he wasn't going to fall down the steps. Mac laughed, then started pushing Joel down the stairs, saying, "You getting the message? No room on the mountain. And hey, do you know how to shut up?"

Joel went the rest of the way down the rotting stairs and out. It felt good to be outside. He walked slowly for a while, then began to run.

Finally, closer to home, he began tapping on doors and asking the people who answered if they needed a car washed. After lots of knocking, he had only two yeses.

When he got home, Meg called them all into the living room. "I didn't get a real job yet. The question is, should we keep trying," she asked, "to make it for a little while?"

They all said yes, including Joel.

Laurie announced that she had three babysitting jobs lined up, but not until next week, Tuesday, Thursday, and Saturday, but she would check with the people again about this weekend. She counted out loud, "Six dollars, ten dollars, and maybe another six dollars." She looked bright. "Good, isn't it?"

"It's great," Meg said. "Twenty-two dollars for food. And I got two people to say they'd let me clean."

"Where?" Laurie asked.

"I talked my way into the apartment building on the corner. But nobody needed me until after school next week. Tuesday and Thursday. People cancel and change their minds, so . . ." She looked at Laurie to prepare her for that eventuality as well. "We can't completely count on it. But if we're on, I ought to bring in another twenty."

"You're doing it too cheap."

"I am, but it's how I got them to say yes."

Joel blanched. "I got two car washes. I told them I'd be back. I have to get going. Do we have soap?"

Meg mopped her brow. "Not much. Just a little dish soap."

"Well, I have to get some somewhere. I only charged three bucks for the car washes. I tried five, but nobody said yes to five."

"That's the message all right. Low wages. But we'll have food at least. If we get you soap, we have six dollars we didn't have. People must be waiting." She went to the kitchen calling, "On Tuesday and Thursday, you need to stay with Susannah since both of us are going to be busy after school. Okay?"

"I figured that."

They went silent, calculating what they could buy at the grocery store for six dollars. Whatever it was had to last until Tuesday.

"Maybe the pizza man would give us food again," Susannah said.

Meg came back with a couple of rags and two buckets, one of clear water, the other with a haze of soap in it. "This is the best we can do. You better go."

Joel went off to wash cars. One person didn't answer the door, no matter how many times he knocked. The other paid him three bucks after he worked for an hour on the car. He tried knocking on more doors. Three bucks was not enough. Period.

Meg bought pasta with the three dollars. She said she would not go up to the pizza shop to beg, not without trying other things first.

NINE

HE HAD BOUGHT A COUPLE OF
bottles of whiskey and now had one under the counter. About four
o'clock, he had a double and he started to feel better. He turned his
mind to the woman who had come on to him. She had that interested
look in her eye, but what was he going to do? He couldn't go messing
around with police. He couldn't tell her anything real about himself.
He couldn't actually meet her later. Yet he kept thinking of just that.

When Marko had burst in, he'd asked a lot of questions—where
was Carl, had Nick seen him?—and then gone to make rounds for a
second time. Marko in his distraction had not paid attention to the detective, Greer. That was good, that was luck.

And Nick sure didn't ask if the kid who overdosed was one of
Marko's customers. Chances were, yes.

There wasn't much business in the late afternoon. He was listening
to the radio when he heard a car stop. Markovic came into the shop

from the front, angry, agitated. Nick busied himself chopping peppers. Unfortunately there were no customers as buffers. Markovic
paced. "Want a drink?" Nick asked.

Marko said, "You better hide that shit good. Yeah, I want one.
Make it quick. You seen Carl today?"

"No." Nick poured. He poured himself one.

"Little shit. He didn't make our meet." They both downed their
drinks and Nick washed the glasses and put the bottle back under the
counter.

"You're gonna get tested tonight," Marko said. "A job."

Well, that was that. So much for hoping the moment would never
come.

"You fuck me up, I will never forgive you. You have to follow orders." Marko paced a little. "I vouched for you, you understand?"

Nick felt himself not breathing. He said, "I think so."

"Do better than thinking. Just follow orders. Plain and simple."

"Whose orders am I following?"

"A guy we use. Earl. He'll come get you. He knows how to do these
things."

"When?"

"Tonight. Later. When you close up. You don't follow directions,
you won't live to talk about it."

"What, throw me in the river?"

Marko's head jerked up. "What are you getting at?"

"Things I heard."

"Just remember, get it straight, the person who told you that is a
fucking cunthead worthless shit."

"We all are."

"We all are. You got that right."

Marko left.

Nick took another drink. His lives receded and seemed not to be
real. Boyhood, Marko, fishing, marriage, gambling, trouble, prison,
fishing, here. There was only here. Only now.

Numb felt good. Not moving felt good. Dead wouldn't be so bad either.

The bottle of whiskey under the counter wasn't quite tall enough for what Nick needed—a way to skate past tonight and maybe tomorrow until he could get out of this mess.

TEN

fetch the kids and bring them to the hospital. Eric's and Julie's expressions when they entered their father's room were half bravado, half curiosity, eyes quickly taking in bed, table, IV stand.

"Did they bring you dinner yet?"

"Not yet."

Marina told them, "If you stay out of the nurses' way, they'll let you stay. Go on, you're allowed to hug him."

Eric and Julie hesitated, looking at their father for a sign, before they went to him. Julie, who had a surprising, stringy muscularity, went for his neck and clamped. Eric did a quick brush of a hug.

"Let's go for a little walk," he said, pointing to the hallway. "Um, I smell food." He tried to make it sound cheerful, but Marina wasn't fooled.

When he stood, the blanket he'd been using around his shoulders fell to the floor.

"Were you cold?" Julie asked.

"Just my little security blanket." He tossed the blanket, with a show of panache, to the visitor's chair.

They led him toward the hallway. He caught himself giving into shuffling and worked to lift his feet.

Marina told him, "We're not going to stay too long. They just needed to see you. I'll take them out for dinner. Something fun."

A huge cartful of trays came rattling toward them.

"Damn," he said as nausea hit him again.

"What?" Julie asked.

"The smell. My body doesn't like the smell of food anymore."

"Do you think you'll always hate the smell?"

"Oh, no, no, no, I'll like it again when I feel better."

"How long do you think?"

"When they're done pumping medicine in him," Eric informed his sister. Whose harsh phrase was that? Their mother's? Marina flushed with anger.

He shuffled back to his room. An aide had just put the tray with its warming tin on his rolling table. She lifted the lid with the flourish of a French waiter. She was the one who liked him, his fan. "There you are, baby," she said.

Carrots, beans, chicken, rolls, pudding.

Marina hugged him because she knew he couldn't look.

ELEVEN

NICK WAITS UNTIL AFTER closing time, but the man hasn't come for him. He starts to breathe again, locks up, and walks the few blocks home, thinking about a shower and wondering if he is sober enough to go meet the woman detective at the Blues Café. His luck has held. Plenty of liquid courage in him and no need for it. He's home and just about to pull out the keys to his place when he hears someone behind him. An unfamiliar voice says, "Let's go."

This moment, this, feels more like his life. When he hesitates, the man says, "Move it. We got a job tonight."

Nick pockets his keys and turns. The two men walk in silence toward a Ford the man is pointing to; Nick tries to look at his companion, the bad luck that has come after all. Short man. Long hair and long sideburns, a face that looks as if it has weathered several beatings.

"What's your name?" Nick asks.

"You don't need my name."

"Well, you better be Earl. Where's Markovic?"

"Who? You don't learn too good. You aren't supposed to use his name ever. Huh? Or mine. You don't need names."

Nick wants to haul off and hit the guy. The drink has given him that anyway, the loosening of the arm hinges. He wants to keep drinking. It helps. He has a nice bottle in his apartment.

He looks longingly back toward his building. "Where we going?"

"You ask too many questions. Get in."

Nick gets into a small Ford, an Escort, an old thing that has something you rarely see these days, rust. This guy's job doesn't pay much, he thinks.

The guy's face becomes a little clearer. Profile, if you could call it that, well, the guy hardly has one; it's a smashed-in face framed by hair that's brown, long, and greasy. The sideburns aren't shaped as muttonchops or anything intentional; they're just long growths that go the length of the face. The guy wears a T-shirt under an open threadbare shirt, jeans, shitkickers.

It is starting to move from warm to chilly. The light has been gone from the sky for almost two hours. He hopes whatever he has to do goes fast. He hopes for luck.

They drive only a couple of streets. The man parks the car. It occurs to Nick that Carl lives somewhere in this direction, but the fact of it doesn't adhere to any other thought. His brain sends up signals—cut, run, remember—but the signals are weak, and for that he is almost grateful.

"Walk the rest of the way," says the hairy fellow. His sideburns have the look of something dripping down to his chin, Nick thinks, and he laughs.

"What?"

"Nothing. Just amusing myself."

"You get to have a lot of fun in a little bit."

"I don't have a gun."

"I know that. I got you covered."

Will the gun Marko promised him be presented later as part of his test? Or is tonight a matter of fists and threats? Which? He shakes his head to banish resistance. He doesn't care. He doesn't care. Whatever happens will happen.

The other guy is moving fast now, and Nick has the impression he's been scanning the street. They go to a house, they go around back, the man takes a ring of keys out of his pocket, chooses one with a piece of black tape on it, jiggles the lock for a full minute, and they're in.

"Shit. Fuck," the guy explodes. "He was here again. He must have been here minutes ago, because I was . . . I missed him. Missed the fucker."

Who? Nick wants to ask. But a part of him knows; it's coming to him who it is, and he doesn't know what to do with the knowledge. He looks around. The place is skimmed down, not bare, but spare. It was probably fairly clean to start with, but now it's a mess.

"We're going to find him."

"Just wait here for him, might be better," Nick offers.

The other man adjusts his T-shirt over the gun he carries as if to let Nick see it. "Just do what I say. Huh? Just do what I tell you. You know where he went?"

Nick doesn't ask, *Who?* He just says, "No."

Then they go back to the car and start up the hill. To Nick's dismay, they see someone up ahead, a tall kid who walks like Carl, and he's carrying something.

TWELVE

COLLEEN PAYS THE COVER

charge at the door to the Blues Café. She's been home to change—her best skinny jeans, a little tank, a lacy jacket, heels. She feels kind of good. She's all ready to say the speech about how her friends couldn't come after all, and she even has an image of these friends she's supposed to meet. They're John and Judy Potocki—in her mind, back together again.

He isn't here yet. Nick. Banks. He liked her. He'll show.

She feels hot, alive, interested, interesting.

It could be the jazz. That helps.

She takes a seat at the bar because it seems wrong to tie up one of the tables on a gamble. She watches the bartender working. When he gets to her, she orders a scotch, rocks. She tries not to direct her attention to the door, but can't help it and looks up just in time to see Potocki come in. He maintains a bland expression, doesn't flinch or react or even look toward her, but pays his fee and takes up a spot far away.

The tenor saxophonist is blowing a storm and the rest of the band seems to want to follow him, so she listens to the music for a long time as if it's what she came for.

The menu chalked on a board tells her the bar serves fried provolone, fried onion rings, fries. She decides fries; she didn't have much dinner. By the time she gets the waitress's attention, it's close to eleven thirty. She has to shout over the music what she wants.

"They already closed down the kitchen. They probably still have some fries, though. I'll see."

Still no Nick. A man comes up next to her and starts a conversation with, "Hard to talk in here, isn't it?" He wears his hair in a long ponytail and tattoos appear everywhere his skin is visible.

Cacophony is good for something. "Very hard," she calls back.

When she looks at her watch, the man asks, "Waiting for someone?"

"Kind of. Yeah." The saxophone is whimpering now, very nice, very nice.

"Let me buy you a drink."

"Thank you, but I'm going to pace myself for now."

The bass player is having his say—which makes the room vibrate with a low almost nasal thrumming. Next in rotation, the drummer sends the tables to a quiver.

Something, she's not sure what, maybe just imagining Christie imagining her here, makes her think of him. What is he doing? Up watching TV, sleeping, beating down nausea? Tomorrow she'll call early to check on him.

The fries arrive. Soggy, salty, and somehow satisfying. A coda later, the music quiets down to a low background pulse, a signal, a prelude to the bass player coming forward to announce a break. His amplified voice is a bit of a shock; the piano player has started up doing an underlining riff while the bass player introduces the members of the combo. A couple of people cheer. One guy bangs at his table, and suddenly, it's calm again.

"Now we can talk," the man says. Suddenly she wonders if Nick has sent the guy. She looks up to the front of the bar long enough to see Potocki wink at her.

"What do you do?"

"Police. Homicide."

The man's eyes glaze. "Not really?"

"Yes. Truly." She orders another drink and gets no argument when she pays for it herself.

The man drifts away.

The next set lasts half an hour, a little more. She has a third drink. By the time it's done, she is pretty sure Nick isn't going to show. Potocki must be sure, too, for he's come up to her. "Sorry I'm late," he says, winking again. "Buy you a drink?"

"This was my third."

"When you're ready."

"I was trying to nurse it so I could concentrate and . . . and speak if he came." She looks at her watch. "What the hell, huh?"

"That's what I say. You got stood up."

"I guess I did."

"Well, you snagged a biker anyway."

"And I wasn't even trying. That's the way."

"What drove him away?"

"I told him what I do. Same thing I did with Nick Banks." She groaned. "I blew the charming part, I guess."

"Don't think about it."

"Right. So. Maybe Farber won't want us. And wouldn't that be nice. We could be who we are. Do what we do."

Potocki buys her her fourth drink, which makes its way quickly into her bloodstream, making her feel reckless. "You have to move tomorrow morning," she says.

"Some things. A few things."

"I'll help you. Like I said."

"If you're up to it tomorrow. See how you feel."

The music turns mellower in the set that begins close to one o'clock.

When she gets up to go to the john, Potocki takes her elbow to steer her the first couple of feet. She falls back into him and he kisses her brow before sending her on her way.

The whiskey floats her toward the sink in the ladies' room. Makeup is faded, hair needs a fluffing. What a mess. She applies a little lipstick, tries to make the "pieces" of her hair take the right, jaunty shapes.

She plucked four grays this morning. They're coming in faster than she can pull them. She has two distinct laugh lines at each eye. And not enough laughs to account for them. Wishes: taller, thinner thighs, lose ten pounds so that *all* clothing will look great—it does on sylphs, why is that? Five-five and curvy in a world that values tall and skinny.

She gives herself a hard look in the mirror. I'm getting old, she reminds herself. I'm fucked up. Potocki is my partner.

PART TWO

THIRTEEN

SATURDAY MORNING JOEL headed up the hill toward the playground where Russell and Ryan played basketball. On the way up the hill, he passed the house he knew Mac and Zero crashed in. His heart pounded adrenaline anger up to his head when he thought of the way Mac treated him. Zero was nicer. Tried to be.

He didn't really believe Zero would come to the house to meet him. But he couldn't help himself. He slipped into the backyard anyway and found the door not quite in place. Ha. It meant they were in there early. Or maybe Zero was.

The ground was wet from Thursday and yesterday. There were flies everywhere even though the weather had cleared.

He let himself in.

Flies, a smell, yes, it smelled different. They were up to something.

He drew in a deep breath and climbed the stairs. They were up there. He could sense breathing. Dirt got on his pants from the banister that was torn down and just hanging there. Meg would kill him. It meant he either had to wear dirty pants to school next week or . . .

Joel surfaced on the top floor, heading toward the little bit of light.

At first he couldn't take in what he was seeing. But he knew he was in the middle of something bad.

There was one man to his right, almost behind him now as he lurched forward. The man was lying against the wall with a lot of something all around him. Tar. Blood. He knew it was blood. He could hardly take in that sight because a second man, five feet in front of him, to his left, lying curled up, held a gun on him. The man didn't move and his eyes seemed half closed, but still Joel felt pinned to the spot. He saw the clenched jaw. He saw the glittering eyes. Suddenly the man grunted and made a terrible face.

"I . . . was looking for my friends," Joel said. His voice went high, embarrassing him. "Please don't—?"

The man jumped and shifted forward, seemed to relax the gun downward. Was that a trick? "Wait. Wait. Who's coming here, did you say?"

Joel didn't want to say their names. He shook his head, tried to break the gaze of the man. He wanted to back away, but he didn't know how long it would take to aim the gun again or how far back the stairway was. Now he could see there was a lot of blood around the dead man. And that the man who held the gun was curled awkwardly over his leg and there was blood there, too.

"Come here."

"No." He looked around him. He wanted to run, but not—not slipping in the blood.

"You have to or I'll—"

He came a couple of steps closer.

"You're just a kid." In one move, the man leaned forward and grabbed his leg. He heard the gun bump against the floor and the man made a terrible sound as Joel toppled and fell forward. Judo, martial arts. There were answers to how to get away. He tried to remember something—kicking under the chin, something. He fell across the man's body and onto the other side of it. The man shouted again, a terrible sound, but the vise-hands didn't let up squeezing his leg.

"Let me go." Everything in him flailed—arms and legs, head, torso. "Oh, man. Stop. Fuck. Stop."

He kept kicking. The man screamed and let go. Joel managed to get up on one knee, but he couldn't right himself and the sounds the man made frightened him and pretty soon the man grabbed and he was down again.

Joel's shoulder hurt. He was not breathing right. He gulped for air from his lying-down position.

"Listen. I been in this place maybe twelve hours. What time is it?"

"Like ten thirty."

"I'm not going to make it out of here without help. Listen to me."

"Let me go. I'll go get you help." Joel began to get up slowly, an inch at a time so as not to scare the man. He could see the gun was on the floor, two feet away.

"No police. No ambulance or anything like that."

Joel went still, he didn't mean to, but he did and the man felt it.

"No police. You can't tell anybody. You understand?" He reached over and slid the gun closer as he asked, "Is anyone else with you?"

"No." Joel wished he had said yes.

"What day is this?" the man asked.

"Saturday."

"Okay, under twelve hours then. I need you to listen to me."

Joel wondered if he ran whether the man would shoot him in the back like a coward.

"I can't stay here. I'm going to need to move. And I can't walk. Are you listening? I need water real bad. And a bandage and alcohol. My leg's torn up and I can't walk. But if I could get to my car . . . I'm going to need food, too. You're the only one can help me get out of here."

"I don't care. You killed that guy."

"Listen to me. You don't know what happened here. It isn't what you think. The thing is, listen, you tell the police and I know some people would kill you and your family on the way to killing me, that's how they are. If you don't believe me, it's going to be bad for both of us. My leg is shot." The man looked straight at him, then seemed to collapse. "I can't move. That's what I'm saying."

"You want me to look at it?"

"You know what a bullet hole looks like?"

"No. Yeah, I do, from pictures." Joel looked toward the leg. He wanted to see it. He wanted to be able to look at anything.

"Go on, then, take a look." The man's voice was raspy, almost a whisper, and the more he talked, the more Joel got used to his voice and the less scared he was. "You aren't afraid of things, huh?"

He was. He looked around behind him to see if the other man moved at all.

"One shot and it killed him. I was lucky. He got me once and I'm still here."

Joel looked toward the other guy for a few more seconds. Not a twitch.

"He's dead. For sure," the man said.

Joel nodded.

"I need you to reach in my pocket. Go on. I don't want to hurt you. I don't even want to hold you down, but you're a kicker. Pull out my wallet."

Joel did this gingerly. He thought his own right leg might never move again and he now had blood as well as dirt on his clothes. His hand brushed the plaid hunting shirt the man wore and it reminded him of something good. His father. Maybe that's what broke him down. He stopped fighting and tried not to cry while he waited for directions.

"Open it up. Take out a twenty."

Joel did this. He saw another twenty in there and maybe more behind it, but he took only the one. It's what he'd come in for after all, money. Got it one way if not the other.

"That's for peroxide, bandage, water, food maybe, and some kind of stick to wrap my leg. But hurry."

Water was the most important thing, Joel knew, the crucial thing, but if he said it, the man might take the money away.

"Good boy. Good boy. I'll take anything. Peroxide, alcohol. Whiskey would be a treat. Anything you can find in the way of yardsticks, rulers, rags, bring them. I have to splint my leg and figure out how to walk. You're going to do this for me?"

He felt now how hot the man's hands were as, sweating and shaking, the man reached out to retrieve his wallet.

He looked back to the leg, wondering how the bullet went in.

"Anybody can see it's . . . it's bad," the man said.

Close up, the bullet hole was a spirally burn right through the man's jeans. And the shape of the lower leg was funny looking, but maybe it was just the angle the man was in and the blood on the pants. No. It was a compound fracture, that's what they called it.

"You have to let me call an ambulance."

"No. If you believe in anything, no. They'll kill me."

"The doctors?"

"Other people. I'm telling you, don't call. You'd be killing me. Just get me what I need."

"Okay."

The man let him go.

MEG WAS CLEANING THE
kitchen when she heard Joel come into the house. She was planning a family meeting to be held at the kitchen table during lunch when she served the macaroni again. The food, if they ate small amounts, would get them to Sunday noon. The four of them had decisions to make. "Did you play basketball?" she called after him.

"Some. Ryan didn't show. I went to Russell's house for a while."

She started up the steps and saw him turning the corner. "Did they offer you food?"

"No. I was just using his computer a while."

"Are you changing clothes again?" she called out.

"Putting old clothes on," Joel called back.

"Should have done that to begin with." She never knew what Joel was going to do, never could guess. "You going out again?"

His voice was muffled, but she heard, "I don't know." His answer was a surprise. He might be getting sick. Something was off. She knew for sure something was off when she heard his footsteps on the way to the basement. She flicked on the little radio that sat on the kitchen windowsill. Some talk program was on, and Laurie, who was sitting at the kitchen table said, "Not that. I want music," but Meg didn't feel like working the radio to get another station in clearly. Even with the radio talk, she could make out the sound of water going through the pipes. Joel in the basement.

Laurie caught her eye. "Again?" she asked. "With what?"

"I don't know."

The next surprise was that Joel slipped into their living room and put on the TV. It was nice outside today. He had an hour before lunch to be out in the sunshine. Meg went in and looked at him. "Did you throw up on your clothes or something?"

"Yeah."

She felt his head. "I can't tell if you have a fever or not." After that she went into the kitchen and poured water into the tallest glass they owned. "Here. Drink this. All of it."

"Okay."

"Best medicine in the world."

"Yeah, I *know* that. Do we have rubbing alcohol?"

"I don't think so."

"Peroxide?"

"Maybe some, I don't know. Why? That's for cuts. Do you have a cut?"

"Nope."

"Why are you asking all this?"

"Ryan wanted it for something. School project or something."

"Tell him we have nothing to spare. He's a freeloader. Lunch is at twelve thirty. We're having a meeting. Serious meeting."

He made a *huh* sound that signified he'd heard.

"Do you have anywhere to get soap? If you could borrow some from Russell, you could try car washes again. I don't think bar soap would do it."

Joel slapped a twenty-dollar bill on the coffee table. "How long can we eat on that?"

Meg stared at it.

She thought the answer. A week. She was a good quartermaster, her father had always told her. He had smiled at her and told her she was peerless. Peerless had its pros and cons. People tend to need peers.

"Where did it come from?"

"I found it."

Meg wrestled with herself. She determined to get to the bottom of her brother's lie, but later, later. She grabbed up the money and started out for the Giant Eagle.

She bought ten boxes of a cheap pasta that was on sale, two for one. She bought cheap bottled sauce (one jar), bread, bologna, milk, juice. They would want cereal. One box of generic was all she could afford. She had done the math in her head. When she checked out, it came to $20.23. She was about to put back one box of pasta when the man behind her gave her a quarter. "Keep the change," he said winking.

"Thank you." People were so nice. Luck. She'd always had luck.

"It's nothing."

The bags were heavy to carry—she had to keep rearranging—but it was going to be summer soon, and for a while they had food.

JOEL WATCHED TELEVISION

with Laurie and Susannah while Meg was gone.

Laurie asked him, "What are you thinking about?"

He said, "Nothing," but his mind was spinning. He told himself no way was he going back to that place. Mac and Zero would go up there eventually, let them help the guy. But he *knew* all kinds of things, things Mac and Zero wouldn't know—how to clean the wound, how to prop the guy so he could walk.

He couldn't go back.

But if he waited, there might very well be two dead guys up there. He should just go ahead and call the police.

He jumped up suddenly, and when he did, Laurie sprang back in fright on the other end of the couch. Susannah didn't react.

"What happened?" Laurie asked.

"I have to get my pants."

She said, "I'll hang them for you. You always just toss them over the line." She slid off the couch, halfway crouched over, like the little old lady in some fairy tale, then inched herself upward as she went to the basement door. Susannah watched her go.

Joel began to suppose. If I got water for him, what container would I use? If we didn't have peroxide, what would I substitute? The television program was just stupid, with people walking into rooms and making faces and talking about sex, sex, sex. On the screen was a series of gestures and possibilities he had already internalized. The "Oh, no!" The "I'm sorry." The repetition was a kind of sedative. Surprise still looked on Saturday the way it had looked on Tuesday.

Laurie came back up from the basement and asked, "What did I miss?"

"Nothing," he said. He had no idea or interest in what was happening on the tube. His sisters were different. Laurie and Susannah seemed to be able to look at each episode as if it mattered and as if something fresh would be revealed if only they stuck with it.

Meg came home with food, saying, "Sandwiches for lunch." She began to put groceries away. She seemed happy.

Before lunch, Joel roamed the house and located a little bit of peroxide in the brown bottle under the bathroom sink, a very little bit. In the basement, pretending to check on his pants, he found a gallon plastic water bottle that had once held distilled water, something Ali-

son must have had. He took the lid off and smelled for bleach, insecti-
cide, couldn't smell anything, filled the bottle and tucked it away next
to the dryer. He looked in the back of the cabinet under the kitchen
sink where Alison occasionally kept whiskey. Yep, a quarter of a bottle, still there. So he *could* do it, if he had a mind to.

"What are you looking for?" Meg asked.

"Thought there might be dish soap we never found."

"Sorry. I got food. Try . . . shampoo. There's a little bit."

"Oh. Good idea."

He went out to the backyard and tossed a small blue ball at the
basketball rim that hung on the garage, no basket. Partly what kept
him going was the neatness of it, that he knew what he would do *if* he
did it. He liked problems. In this neighborhood, you could get into a
lot of trouble being good at stuff. Russell and Ryan (not to mention
Mac and Zero) counted his successes against him.

Meg had bought sandwich makings. He could make two to go. With
mustard. Adults favored mustard. If he went. If he took rags and a
bucket and some soap, Meg and Laurie wouldn't question why he was
going out. He could take a lot of water that way. Maybe sneak in the
sandwiches, whiskey, peroxide in a bag of rags.

And a saw. He needed a saw. Because he remembered exactly a program he'd seen on the education channel about World War I injuries
and how they were treated.

If he knew how to do things, wasn't that a sign that he should?

AFTER LUNCH, MEG HAD THE
windows open in the kitchen and she was singing. She had the impression Joel wanted something; he seemed to be hanging around as if
about to ask a question. "I'm sorry I didn't have enough for detergent.
As it was, some guy gave me a quarter. It was nice of him. Funny how
people are, sometimes, just generous."

He didn't say anything, so she kept talking, more to stay connected
with him than anything else. "Laurie went over to the Coles' house

because she called them again and they said they'd use her a little while this afternoon. She's a hustler. I'll go shopping again."

Joel grunted. "I'm going to do car washes again, if that's what you're trying to say. I'm not a good hustler, okay?"

"What's the matter with you?"

"Nothing."

"Tell me where you found the twenty," she said. "I'd feel better if I knew."

"It was just blowing on the street."

"Don't lie," she said sharply. "If you stole it, we have to return it."

"I'm not lying." After a while, he said, "I found it in the park."

"Oh, well," she laughed in spite of herself to imagine money just blowing toward them. "That's a good trick. I wish I had that trick of needing something and it just comes to me."

"You do," he said. "The guy gave you a quarter."

She nodded. "I do feel something sometimes. I'm going to concentrate on getting a job."

He went upstairs for a while. She wondered again if he was sick. When he came back down, she said, "I don't want to fight. We need to stick together."

"Right. I know."

She went out into the yard to check a couple of items washed earlier in the residue of dishwashing detergent and now drying on the line. It was amazing how little detergent you really needed. Most people were wasteful.

The house they lived in was an odd little thing, set back from the street a little. On either side of her were larger houses that had been split into apartments. She didn't know any of the neighbors on either side. She doubted any of them knew her or noticed the absence of Alison. Still, as she moved about the yard, she tried to look purposeful and content so as not to raise suspicion.

Since it was still a little damp out, the clothes hadn't dried. Meg turned in the small yard to look back at the house. It was hard to see inside, but she thought she made out Joel opening the refrigerator.

And then she thought she saw him tie up the bread bag, dive down low. Did he feel he had to be sneaky about it? Was he that hungry? If so, their provisions wouldn't last a week, and she was wrong to let the others talk her into staying, living on nothing.

She toed the ground. Their little patch of grass was more weed growth than anything else. Dandelions, though. You could eat them, she knew about that, but she wasn't sure how to cook them.

It was nice out. Really spring. Her heart lifted. She didn't want to argue with Joel, so she took up the broom and swept at the sidewalk, trying to be a good role model, always busy. When she got back inside, he wasn't there. Quickly, she looked in the fridge and determined he'd taken enough for a couple of sandwiches at least. It was those shitheads he hung out with, then! There his sisters were with almost *no money* and he was feeding other people. Anger took hold—her head started to pound from the blood rushing to it. Partly she felt stupid, conned. There she'd been, feeling concern for her brother when he was basically stealing from his sisters for those no-good boys who were her age and bad news, worthless, worthless.

She ran out the front door without even taking a key and saw Joel way up the street, cutting through an alley that went over to Brighton, a pail of water slopping at his side, a whole sack of things in his other hand. He was headed for the really bad section. He didn't look back and he walked fast. He was carrying more than he needed if he was really planning to wash cars. She became aware of the mechanism of him, the way his body propelled itself.

She guessed where he was going—that empty house those boys played in that she'd forbidden him to go to. There had to be rusty nails in there, dirt, an invitation to disease in each corner. There was no choice but to reverse things before he got in with those kids. She'd take on Mac and Zero, let them laugh at her, let her brother hate her for it.

She passed houses that were broken up into apartments and houses that were tiny like theirs—little narrow two-story frames with four rooms, two up and two down, cut by a central stairway. All of them were over a century old. It was a historic area; Joel knew all about it.

Some houses were renovated and others untouched, like theirs. The house in Greenfield that Alison had sold out from under them was more ordinary, but larger.

Meg followed Joel up to the bad section where most of the houses were abandoned, hundreds of them, maybe even up to the thousands. Bums and addicts came here. You could never guess for sure which were occupied, who was where. It gave her the shivers.

She almost told herself, Let him go today, have it out with him later. She watched him slipping into the door of the house she'd feared he was going to.

She walked through high weeds to the back door, her stomach churning. As she geared herself to step through the door, she thought about how it was all coming apart and she wasn't going to be able to act as mother and father both. She'd end up in a fight with Joel; the other boys would make fun of her. She was shaking, thinking, she'd ask for foster care on Monday at school. Somebody else could take over, bad or good. They wouldn't be starving.

Flies buzzed, droned, came at her. She waved them away, slipped in.

"Shhh," she heard.

With a sick heart, she climbed the steps in the semidark. She knew something was terribly wrong even before she got to the top. The heat, the smell, the insects told her that.

She screamed when she saw all the blood, the dead man. Over in the corner to her left was Joel.

Joel. Bag. Man. In that order. Joel, bag, man.

"Who's that?" the man said.

Everything stopped. The square of light glanced off his hair. She saw who he was.

He was hurt.

She couldn't take her eyes from his—startling blue eyes, beautiful eyes. Quickly, she managed to take in the rest: his dark hair, his scowl, the way he leaned over his leg, the dirt, the surroundings.

"Oh," she said. "It's you."

"I'm hurt pretty bad," he said. "Your brother was trying to help me out."

Meg, trying to make herself breathe, looked at the dead man and back to the other. "You killed that man?" she asked. Her voice was a whisper.

"Accident. He tried to kill me."

"I'll . . . I'd better call the police."

"No, please, no. If you could just help me," he cried. "Just help me get out of here." He breathed hard. He met her eyes. "If you—please believe me."

"But you're hurt."

"It doesn't matter. I need to get to my car."

"That's what he told me, too," Joel said. "There's somebody after him."

"I don't understand. If you didn't. . . ."

"It's because . . . I didn't do what they wanted and . . . They're going to kill me. That's what they do."

"But wouldn't the police—?"

"No. They wouldn't." He took the smaller bottle of water and drank. He drank the whole thing down without stopping. It seemed he wasn't going to be able to breathe when he put the bottle down. He gasped and winced. "You better get out. Don't tell anyone. I'm going to try to move on my own. Just go."

"You can't," she said.

"I can't stay here."

"But—"

"There's no way you could understand what I'm up against."

Joel said, "I tried to talk sense into him, too."

Meg moved forward and put an arm around Joel, who shifted slightly but didn't shrug her off. "You didn't shoot that man, then?"

"I turned the gun away from my own heart. You ought to go. It's dangerous." He closed his eyes for a second, but when he sank back to lie down, the movement seemed to hurt his leg.

"His leg is shot, and it's fractured, all out of line," Joel said. "I think I could fix it so he could move."

The man's eyes flickered with hope. "How could you?"

Meg tried to read the man's eyes. She kept a hand on Joel. "He's good at stuff like that."

"Then, how—? What's this?" he pointed to the bag.

"Whiskey and sandwiches," Joel said. "Some other stuff." His voice sounded proud.

"Your parents? Would they be able to—? They know where you are?"

Meg and Joel looked at each other, but didn't say anything for a moment; then Meg said, "They're away, I'm afraid."

The man opened the bag and took a long drink of whiskey. Then he doused some, not a lot, on his leg. He winced and held the expression for a long time.

Joel said, "No. Water. You should have used water."

The man shook his head. Meg watched, fascinated—it was like something she had seen in a cowboy movie when they used to have the channel that did old films. Then the man tore into the sandwiches. His face was all contorted and he swallowed without chewing. It reminded her of an animal eating.

"How should his leg be cleaned?" Meg asked Joel.

The man looked up.

"Water, I know that much. Then setting it."

"Could you do that?"

"Maybe. I think. If he went to the hospital, it would be pins, all that, but there are other ways."

She moved forward and touched the man's foot. "Let him try."

He groaned and lay back down.

"He has a fever," Joel said.

"Do you?" she asked.

"I think so," the man whispered. "Sorry to waste your food." He coughed and laughed.

"Do you have any money?" Meg asked.

"Sure, take it, the wallet." He gestured to his back pocket and put his head down, making a jagged moan. There didn't seem to be any way he could move that didn't hurt him. Then she saw he had a chip of wood, a bit of floorboard tied to the back of his leg with a handkerchief, intended to hold on the pathetic piece of wood.

Joel leapt forward and grabbed the wallet and leapt back to her. He opened it and took out two twenties. "That's all there is," he said, handing her the wallet as if for verification.

She tilted the open wallet toward the light that came from the hole in the roof. Nicholas Banks. Picture on a driver's license. Nicholas Banks. She dug around in all the pockets of the wallet.

"Won't buy much," he said.

"I have to try to cut some wood for your leg," Joel said.

Nick Banks nodded. They started to move away. "If anybody sees you," he said, "it's too late. If somebody sees you, don't come back."

Joel grabbed up the bag, a burlap bag he'd found in their basement. He and Meg went down the steps.

On the way out, Meg saw she had blood on her from something, and her stomach heaved. But she didn't stop, just looked left and right, back and ahead. "Keep going," she said to Joel. They kept walking. Out of the grass, out of the alley, out of the other alley, and up the street proper into an even worse section. She let Joel lead.

Joel asked, "See anything? Anybody?"

"No." But she couldn't tell for sure if anyone had been watching them. "I looked, too."

He told her haltingly how he went up there and found the man in trouble. He explained the man had asked for food and water, and that he wasn't going to take anything to him, just keep the money, but then he changed his mind and took supplies up. Then Meg arrived.

"You recognized him. How do you know him?" Joel asked now.

"He's the pizza man."

"Oh. You think we should turn him in?"

"I don't know." Meg couldn't catch up with her own mind. She picked carefully through what she was feeling, questions about whether she would help the man if she didn't owe him anything. Or if, like Joel, she didn't recognize him. "It could have happened the way he said, I guess. I don't know. I feel sorry for him."

"See all that blood?"

Viscid, she thought. Viscous. She had looked at the other body on the floor and not fainted—surprised herself. "How much did he bleed?"

"Some. Mostly it was the other man's," Joel said.

Meg kept walking. Joel was taking her away from the direction of home and she kept following.

"So you believe him?" Joel asked.

"I think I do."

They were headed up to a wooded section—scrub woods, dumb old woods, not pretty, but thick with junk and trees.

"I have to find two branches. I have to guess at the size."

She didn't know what Joel was going to do, but she knew he would be good at it, that she knew.

They went up into the woods and looked around. Joel chose a tree and climbed it. She handed up the saw.

FOURTEEN

COLLEEN'S HEAD HURT. SHE
gave sidelong glances to Potocki as he worked at his desk. They'd made
it through moving his clothing and cooking utensils to his new place
without mentioning last night's flirtation, and then they sat tight at
their desks for three hours.

He tapped, tapped, tapped at his computer keys. She'd told him to
find her any Metzlers outside of Chicago, to try variations on the name
BZ and also the De-Mott variations and then to run Nick Banks again.

Colleen could never get over how much faster he was than she at
digging through Internet sites. She looked at her watch. It was time to
head for the pizza shop. "So I'm ready to try Nick Banks again," she
told him. "Give me a lift? You should take a break."

He left his computer reluctantly it seemed. She was perfectly happy
to leave hers. They asked for one of the Narcotics cars, the LTD, but
Pete said, "Sorry. It's reserved." He handed them the keys to a Century.

"A grandmother car," Potocki teased.

"It has a good sound system," Pete said.

Colleen put on the radio. Might as well enjoy the big sound. She chose jazz and sat back. "Grandmothers might have a point. The seats are comfortable."

"They are. Made for when your butt gets all bony."

Potocki looked nice in light cords and a dark blue shirt. His slightly long hair, light brown, had probably been blond in his youth, but now showed a trace of gray. He wore glasses sometimes, sometimes not. He had a broad Eastern European face, friendly and open. There were a lot of such faces in the city. Blue eyes, but not a bright blue, not like the startling eyes of Nick Banks.

She'd seen the inside of his life this morning—yellow kitchen walls, tomatoes on the windowsill, cartons of pots and pans.

He drove her past the shop, intending to drop her three blocks farther on. They both craned their necks on the way past the pizza shop. The Dona Ana wasn't open. She and Potocki just looked at each other.

Potocki said, "He must be as hungover as we are."

"Right. Let's get lunch somewhere else and come back later. Pastrami or something. Western Avenue." She pointed back over her shoulder. She had a terrible headache.

AFTER LUNCH, THEY CHECKED
the address Carl had given them. It didn't exist. Nope. Number and street did not go together. For a while, they looked for Carl on the street and in the park. They didn't find him in those places either.

And then they went back to the Dona Ana. It was still closed.

"Don't say anything," she said.

"About what?" He was all innocence.

She started to laugh at how largely she was rejected. "My God," she said, "he probably left town! There goes my career."

"Not if you solve a homicide."

"How close am I to doing that?"

"We'll do it. We need real names and addresses. Such a small thing."
He smiled whimsically.

"I liked him. A lot. Nick."

"Huh," said Potocki. "Yeah, you said. And where's K, George White,
George Victor, and whatever else he goes by?"

Colleen shook her head. They started back to Headquarters.

A kid lugged a bucket up the hill. Industrious.

MARKOVIC DROVE PAST THE
Dona Ana several times with Billy in the passenger seat. He knew something had gone bad the night before, but he didn't know what. Earl
had never disappeared on him.

Billy had proved himself utterly useful today—first at Carl's place
on Veto, where he jimmied the lock. The place was completely torn up.
"Earl was here all right," Billy said. Next they'd gone to Earl's little
apartment, where Billy jimmied another lock. The third place they
stopped was Nick's apartment; the Pontiac was parked out front.
Markovic was thrilled to see the car, but it didn't make sense that Nick
was just sitting inside, waiting for them. They knocked. Billy had to
work hard at that lock. Finally they got in. The place was neat. Laundry folded in a pile. No Nick.

Markovic started looking in drawers. Right away, in the top drawer
in the bedroom, he found money. "Fuck, look at this." He started counting. "This is five hundred bucks. Start looking," he told Billy. "Money.
Rings. Anything of value." He felt like he was going to explode or have
a stroke. Where the hell could Nick be? The guy owed him forty thousand; five hundred and an old car were not going to cut it.

Billy said, "I can't get the sense of this. Leaving the money. He must
be dead."

Markovic called his cousins at the auto shop and Stile answered.
He tried to keep it positive. "Yeah, Billy's good. Yeah. He got in
everywhere—Carl's, Earl's, Nick's. It's coming along. We have Nick's car."

Stile wasn't buying it. He started in on why the hell Marko had brought Nick into things to begin with.

When the tongue-lashing was over with and he'd hung up, Marko said simply to Billy, "Stile said to get the Pontiac over to the shop, pronto. He'll probably have one of us watching this place. So let's go. I need you to hot-wire the Pontiac. We have to be quick, nobody seeing us."

"No need." Billy held up a car key he'd found right on the dresser. It had a string around it and appeared to be a spare.

"Way to go."

So Billy drove the Pontiac over to Stile with Markovic following in his van. They watched Stile look into the Pontiac cursing, then kick it hard. There were no clues at all to tell them where Nick might be.

They left and drove up and down alleys and streets again.

Finally Billy said, "There you go. Up the street."

Marko looked and saw Earl's Ford.

Nobody was around to see Billy break into it except an old man who shuffled by without taking his eyes off the pavement.

FIFTEEN

ONCE MORE, NOW, HE TRIED to pull himself up by hanging on to a door that was propped against the wall, but the pain traveled the whole way up his body, exploding into his head, his ears. The door began to slide. Crying, he let himself back down to the floor and reached for the gun. If someone came to finish him off, he would use it.

The gun felt heavy in his hand; it was only a 9 mm, but it had managed to cripple him. He put it down.

His face went tight with a sob he tried to stifle. He'd never get out now, he'd made too many mistakes. He lay down, the gun in his hand.

He tried to get his mind right, but ideas came and went, and he couldn't get any of them to hold still.

His shirt, the blue plaid shirt, very light wool, had once been among his favorites. He looked at it sorrowfully, knowing he wouldn't make it far without attracting attention. It was crusted with blood.

He went still, trying to think. His car was parked on the street. He needed to get to it. No . . . no. By now they would have sent someone to his apartment, started a lookout for him on the streets in this neighborhood, the shop. Getting to his car was risky. Did he have a choice?

He realized he was waiting for the boy to come back. The boy had got him what he asked for; the girl made less sense to him, not afraid somehow, stooping down to touch his foot.

Of all the mistakes he had made in his life, the biggest one was calling Markovic.

How it had happened last night, he thought he knew, but there were parts he wasn't sure of. He tried to remember beat by beat. But what he felt like now—mixed up, thoughts careening—is what he felt like last night, too.

They'd gone to Carl's place on the first floor, just a bed, some kind of old couch, kitchen table and chair, livable, but everything was turned inside out and Carl wasn't there. Okay.

They stood in the single room, yes. The toilet was running. Suddenly Nick understood nobody else lived upstairs in the building. The man with the sideburns said, "I shoulda waited here. He got away."

Then they were driving. When Nick saw Carl walking up ahead, he didn't say anything about it; he pretended to be fixing his shoe, said, "Marko wants it this way? You sure?"

"K. K. You don't learn fast, do you? Yeah, he does. He wants a cleanup. And he wants all the money there is. There's more stashed somewhere."

At that point, no, he didn't know for sure, but he *thought* it was Carl walking up the hill. Nick kept hoping, if it was, Carl would cut in somewhere, but he didn't, and the man said, "There's the bastard."

Nick remembered he wanted to slow it all down. The guy with the sideburns fingered his gun, and Nick wanted to distract him. Stalling for time. "I know where he's going. Somewhere around here is a house he uses." And Carl was near that house, only a couple of buildings away from where Nick had seen him go last night. "Maybe he stashes there. We could look."

"Okay. Better than the car anyway, for what we're gonna do." The man pulled over and jumped out of the car. "Move it. C'mon. Fast."

Seconds later they were on top of Carl, and the other man had the gun in Carl's side. Carl didn't run; he just stopped dead, dropped a bunch of books.

"We know what you done," the man said. "You're going to take us into your place. Which is it?" he asked Nick.

Carl had looked to Nick, panting.

Nick tried to nod very slightly to Carl, to give him a sign. He said to the boy, "Take it easy." To the other, he said, "It's that one. He goes around back."

They marched the kid up there, around the back, through the weeds, and nobody saw, nobody saw. They made the kid open the plywood door. Nick thought, Slow it down, something will happen, some lucky break, if I can slow it down.

"Fucking dark in here. This where you keep the rest of your money?" the man asked, " 'cause Marko wants it."

"Get it," Nick said. "It's just money. Let them have the money."

Carl looked at Nick. His face, even in the dim light, was awful to see. Betrayed me, the face said, you betrayed me. "I don't have any money," he said. "I had a little. Someone stole it out of my place."

The man put his gun to Carl's temple. He talked to Nick. "We're going to hog-tie the bastard. You're going to help me with that. Then you're going to start slicing his balls. He'll talk. They always do."

The downstairs of the place was mostly rubble. And dark, really dark.

"You have anything stashed upstairs?" Nick asked Carl, buying time.

"I have nothing."

"Let's see about that." The man kept the gun at Carl's temple, pushed the kid to the banister, telling him to hold on to it, both hands on it, then saying to Nick, "Empty his pockets."

Nick hurried to do that. He tried to let Carl know he was looking for a way out for him. He tried to give Carl a look that said, *I'll try to help.* In Carl's pockets he found a ten and some ones. A tissue. A pen. A key. Two keys. Nothing else.

He put the things back in and said quietly to Carl, "Just tell."

"Up the stairs," the man said. "Show us this beautiful place."

Carl said, "Honest to God, I don't have anything."

But somehow they moved up the steps, gun still at the boy's head. When they got the kid up against the wall near where the closet had been, the man moved away. He reached into his pocket and took out a knife. He threw it to the floor in front of Nick. "Pick it up."

Nick moved toward it, thinking he must find some way not to pick it up, but he got there and he did it, because he didn't know what else to do and he thought if only he could get the man calmed down, they could work it out. He held the knife loosely away from his body. He said, "Give the kid a break. Just talk it out."

The man hissed, "What's the matter with you, pussy mother-fucker? Do what I tell you."

Nick went toward Carl. He had the knife held out, but he knew what he was going to do with it. Where there'd been a closet, it was just a hole in the wall now. He said in a low voice, almost not moving his lips, "When I move, run." He pretended to move toward Carl; he dropped the knife in the hole. Carl ran for the steps as Nick ran at the man with the gun. The gun went off. The bullet hit the floor. He felt Carl stop. He said, "Run. Go." The gun went off again.

The second shot shattered his leg. The third was aimed at his heart, but he was a madman by then, twisting it away from him and, in the end, he had switched it around to the heart of the man with the drippy sideburns.

He could remember that part clearly. He'd watched the man die. He even laid him down as it happened. The gun fell out of the man's hand as he cursed and groped and gave up. Nick's leg gave way and he passed out.

He tried to move again now, but the pain zinged the whole way up to his ears. He lay down, trying to stay awake, but he couldn't. In his dream he began running in place, but running nonetheless, and whoever was chasing him just kept coming. He couldn't tell who it was, then something slid into place and he was awake, but the dream continued. It was real. Someone was coming up the stairs.

Something in the rhythm of the sound of the voices told him it was not the police.

It didn't sound like the boy and girl either.

Two boys he had never seen before stood at the top of the stairs, squinting, muttering, "Holy shit." He didn't know where the gun was.

One had bleached blond hair, short and tight to his head, an earring, and a black plastic jacket. The other was taller, had dark hair, buzz cut, and a denim jacket. "Holy shit," the tall one said again.

Nick tried to find the gun. His brain was mush. He wondered if these two had a car and if they could carry him down the steps, then drive him someplace.

"Who sent you?" he asked.

"Nobody. We were just coming to mess around." The blond was the one who spoke. The two looked more closely at the other body, and the taller boy looked terrified, but the other did not. He looked excited.

Nick wasn't sure what to ask them for. "Gun," the taller one said. "He has a gun."

Their hands went up.

The blond one spoke again. "Mister. We aren't going to tell anyone anything. We were never up here. You hear? What you did, we don't care about that."

"Who are you?"

They didn't answer. Their eyes shifted from the other man to his gun to him.

The blond one said, "Run."

And in an instant, they were backing down the steps.

His hands shook as he held the gun on them. "I need help," he said.

Did they hear? They must have understood he wouldn't shoot, because they turned from him and ran. He could hear them hurrying to get out. His ear was sharp. They left the plank off the door.

His heart pounded. These two would talk to somebody, sometime, soon, and he had to get out before they did.

JOEL RAN DOWN TO THE BASEMENT
to clean up the two branches. "Hurry," Meg said.

Laurie had left a note that she had managed to get Saturday work after all and was off babysitting for the Coles. She would come home with maybe six bucks for watching three little kids for two hours. It was something, Meg thought, not much, but something. Susannah was sitting alone in her bedroom, drawing.

Meg said, "Sweetie, you know that bag where Laurie keeps clean rags in the basement? See if there are any in there."

Susannah said, "Where were you?"

"We won't leave anymore, well, just one more time. I'll make it up to you, honestly I will."

Susannah nodded and went.

Meg searched through the medicine cabinet and, shaking, saw it behind the aspirin. The bottle was empty. Twenty-four capsules on the refill were allowed. Not the strongest stuff. Alison had needed it for all her dental work. Twenty-four was better than nothing.

Meg looked up the Coles' number and dialed it. One of the Cole babies answered and eventually, after a lot of talk, put Laurie on the phone. Meg told Laurie to look in the medicine cabinet for prescription medicines with an *illin* or an *icin* on the end and if she didn't find any, to bring whatever else she could grab, even if the bottle was empty.

"You mean, *take* it?"

"Have to. I'll explain. We'll put it back. Also, anything that says, " 'For pain.' Anything."

"Is Joel sick?"

"I can't explain now," she told Laurie. "I know it's wrong. Don't get caught."

The little house they lived in didn't harbor a lot of useless junk because Alison had moved them with only the basics, never really making a home. She'd even sold some things off. Meg was in a fury to find *things*—spare things, good old junk—she could use to help the man with the raspy voice and the startling eyes.

THE NEXT TIME HE WOKE UP,

he thought it was the two boys again. He tried to reach for the gun. He was aware of the play of a flashlight in the dark. "It's us," a light voice said. "Put the gun down." Then they stood before him, the boy and the girl. She handed him a small bottle of water and some pills in an envelope. "Here," she said. "Take these." She used a flashlight to show him.

"It smells bad up here," the boy said to her.

She nodded.

First she spread a bedsheet on the floor and instructed him to use his upper body to climb onto it while she and her brother held it straight. He tried not to scream, but he had to scream once as he did what she said. Then they trained two flashlights on his leg, and the two of them began. They put something funny looking, looked like a crutch but it wasn't, under his right arm and something else, looked like a little crutch, right in his balls. The girl had strips of rags she kept wrapping around him, even his chest. She told him to drink the rest of the whiskey while Joel rolled up the left leg of the jeans and she cut into the blood-stiffened right leg of the jeans with a scissors, snipping slowly and with difficulty until most of his leg was exposed. The boy studied both legs for a while, then murmured, "We have to get that part to line up with— It's going to hurt," he told Nick.

Nick screamed three times as the boy moved his leg around. The girl held a cloth to his forehead. She said, "I know what we're doing is tearing some tissue, but we have to try." After a while, something seemed right, to her, to her brother. They nodded to each other and held the tree branches steady—he saw that's what they were, tree branches that had forks in them—while she wrapped the branches to his legs with old cloths and tied one piece of cloth after another.

"How'd you know to do this?"

"It's pretty primitive, but you weren't doing any better by yourself. And it's the only way to get you out of here." She sounded smart, word-smart. The boy put a crosspiece between the two branches under his foot and lashed it to the side pieces. All the while, the girl focused on keeping the branches straight. Her brother seemed to have patience and a certain amount of physical strength, too. "That's good," the boy said from time to time. "It's good. It's working." After a while, the girl cut strips of some kind of tape—mailing tape, maybe—to hold a few things in place. Nick was so scared he couldn't talk, but his question must have hung in the air because she continued to answer it. "My brother saw this on a program. Some soldiers from World War One."

Nick watched the girl's hair fall toward her face as she worked. She blew a strand away, bothered by it.

"Some campers know about how to do this kind of splint, too," Joel added. "That's what they said on the program."

"I'm going to be able to walk?"

"Not yet. I mean, try not to. We have to lift the sheet. If we can support you, we will. If you can use your arms and your upper body going down the steps . . . try. We might make it."

He didn't understand at first.

They lifted and his leg didn't feel worse to him than before, but they put him down. "We can't do it," she said. "He's too heavy."

The boy said, "Switch sides. Let me take the front." By that the boy meant the legs.

"Be careful. He can't be jostled."

Jostled, Nick thought dreamily. It was a word he didn't use.

Together the two dragged him to the stairs and started descending. He put his arms down step by step, like a crab. He weighed 175 and they were kids, but they kept going, lifted and relaxed, lifted and re-laxed.

"Now we have to get you out," she said.

"Where to?"

"You told us it's dangerous here."

He nodded.

"Then . . . we scouted a place a couple of doors away. You'd be out-side till dark. It's not raining."

"My car. If I could get to it. I . . . I still have the key. You know someone who can drive?"

"We'll have to find someone."

He told them, "A Pontiac silver Sunbird. Black seats. It's old, '94. License is DCG 2465." He tried to reach for his pockets, but he needed help because the tree limb was in his way.

The boy and girl looked at each other. "Get the key out," he told them. He was lying on the ground just inside the doorway. They were getting ready to carry him out.

The boy reached into his pocket and got the key. He put it in his own pocket.

Nick thought, They aren't going to pull it off. They have to tell someone about the car, that person will balk, call the police. If they try to drive it—he almost laughed to think of them being pulled over, trying to explain. They didn't look like the typical car thieves.

The boy went back up the stairs for the sack of things he'd brought, and when he got down, he put the sack right on top of Nick's belly. Before Nick knew what was happening, they were lifting him and carrying him out the door, through the weeds, across the alley, down two houses, to a garage. He thought their arms wouldn't hold out. He thought he heard voices, music. The garage they approached looked boarded up. Even so, he imagined they were planning to put him *in-side* it, and that felt safe. He was wrong.

"There's no way in," the girl said, reading his thought.

They took him around to the back of the garage, away from the sight lines of the alley, and they put the sheet with him in it, down on the ground.

"I'm sorry," she said. "It's the best we can do."

"The gun. I need it."

The kid hesitated. He took the sack off Nick's belly. He reached in and brought out a bottle of water, a bottle of juice. These he put on the ground near Nick. Next came the envelope with the pills. "Keep these. In case we don't get back in time. You have a watch. Take the rest at ten o'clock, midnight the latest." Then the boy reached for the gun and handed it over by the butt, careful to point it away.

"Midnight," Nick said. He didn't tell them he could never wait that long. He'd be hobbling along somewhere on his own by then.

"We need dark for the next part," the girl said.

THE PONTIAC WASN'T THERE.

Meg and her brother walked up and down the street; they tried a street over, then a street over in the other direction. Then they went back to the street Nick told them to search and looked harder, studying every license plate, since he might have got part of it wrong. There was no Pontiac of any kind on Sherman and nothing with a license plate remotely similar to what he'd told them.

"Can't do anything until dark," Meg said. "So we might as well . . ."
"What?"

"Figure out the next step. No car. We have to put him somewhere. He needs more pills. He needs . . ."

"I have to set the leg more firmly. Disinfect."

They let a silence go by, understanding what they were saying to each other.

"We need more information. Patrice's mother has a computer. Maybe I could go over there."

"Russell has one. He's on the Internet all the time."

"Russell then. You go there. I need you to look up the prescriptions Laurie found. I know. I'll go to the emergency room and see if I can get anybody to talk to me."

"How?" Joel looked incredulous.

She shrugged an answer. Trying. Trying anything. They had at least five hours until it was dark enough to move him.

SIXTEEN

"He's in his room, doing something or other."

Russell is sitting at his computer, playing golf and eating a large candy bar. When Joel comes in, he jumps to hide the candy before he sees who it is and takes it back out of the drawer he dumped it in. "My mom gets mad," he says. "I got another one. You want it?" The invitation is grudging, but Joel says yes anyway. Russell's room is comfortable, with a desk-and-bureau combination, posters of Tiger Woods and Randle El up on his walls. An athlete is what Russell would like to be, but he's not going to make it; he doesn't like to move fast, and he is already overweight by twenty-five pounds. But here in this room, it all seems fine; he's loved, cared for. The bedspread is puffy, quilted, a medium brown color. At the foot of the bed is a Steelers quilt. "I can't go out. We got my aunt coming to dinner in half an hour. You want to stay if my mom says okay? She might say no. She gets mad sometimes if I ask."

Joel manages to say no. He smells something good. Roast beef or something like that.

"What's up?"

"Wondered if I could use your computer."

"I just want to finish my golf game."

"Okay. Finish it." Joel would rather go to the library, but on Saturday it closes early. This is the best bet.

Russell hits a few more balls. Joel watches a ball roll slowly toward the hole on the screen, then go in. "Yay," Russell calls out. "I can do this game. This is a game I'm good at. So, you want a turn?"

"I was going to look up some other stuff."

Joel's friend moves off the chair reluctantly and plops onto his bed. "Like what?"

"Just stuff my sister needs for a project she's doing."

"Like what?"

"Guns. Kinds of guns."

"What kind of project?"

"Something she's doing for school. A report."

"Cool."

Joel pounds keys as fast as he can, almost cursing with impatience. He kills time looking at guns, waiting to transition to *gunshot wounds*. If only Russell would be called to dinner and leave him alone for a few minutes. He opens the candy bar and breaks off a bite for himself. The gun he handed to Nick is possibly a .45, or no, a 9 mm. He thinks, the latter picture is the weapon that made the wound.

"Cool gun."

Joel grunts.

"You taking notes?"

Joel points to his head. "Memory. You got anything good to eat downstairs?"

"Cheese and crackers. My mom gets mad when I eat before dinner, but maybe I can get some." He slides off the bed, hesitates, and finally leaves the room.

As fast as he can, Joel types in *GSW compound fracture*. A bunch of pictures comes up, but he's going through sites as fast as he can. He tries, *treatment*. And *shin,* then *tibia*.

It is the tibia, and it is broken—and he has set it, but not firmly enough. Now he studies the text of medical journals and other sites. *Neuropraxic, paresthesias*. New words come at him, words he likes. His heart pounds as he reads on. He has done right. He was right.

Russell comes up with some crackers and cheese and a couple of cartons of juice. "She's mad," he says. "I took these anyway."

The part of the candy bar Joel ate has awakened his hunger. He grabs handfuls of crackers and cheese, eating, going so fast on the Internet highway that Russell, who wants to be interested, can't catch up.

IN THE WOMEN'S ROOM AT the hospital, Meg splashes cold water over her face, extracts a comb from her backpack. Her breath is still ragged from rushing. She mustn't look like someone who's been scrambling around in the weeds all day. Her light brown hair is shoulder length and straight, her bangs long. She looks . . . ordinary. She takes a deep breath and walks out and down the hall to Emergency.

"I'm here to talk to someone about my research project," she explains at the intake desk. "I need to do an interview with a trauma doctor. Physician."

The receptionist rakes up some incredulity. She's a black woman with severely straightened hair, very orderly, and she says, with affront, "This is an emergency room!"

"That's what I'm supposed to write about. Trauma units. Specifically, treatment of gunshot wounds."

"I'm afraid I can't let you talk to the doctors. They're busy."

"It's important. It's for the nationals of the science fair, a big prize." She says all this while scrambling to put together a story. "It's the project I proposed as a finalist. All the teachers approved it. They told me this hospital was famous for trauma." She catches her breath, opens her notebook as if that will help to persuade this woman.

"Where do you go to school?"

"Allegheny," she says quietly. "Is there a nurse I could talk to?"

"Please sit in the waiting room."

Meg hesitates, but decides to risk it. Is the receptionist calling the police? She tries to watch what the woman does as she chooses a green plastic chair, like all the other chairs, this one away from people who appear to be sniffling and coughing. Most of the other people waiting look really sick. Some are reading magazines, some looking at the TV, but most stare ahead or clutch an arm or hold out a bum leg that has something wrong with it. If the police come for her, she will have to tell the truth. But her heart squeezes to imagine Laurie and Susannah looking shocked as other, different, police come to take them away.

People look at her curiously. No parent, no visible illness, just a kid with a backpack. She almost gets up, almost leaves.

Finally a nurse sits down beside her. This nurse is a solid blonde with a skeptical smile. "This is a school assignment?" she asks.

"It's for a science fair. A contest. There's a . . . a prize. Two hundred dollars. I think my project is pretty good."

"What is it?"

"I need to show treatment of a GSW."

The nurse raises her eyebrows. "You talk the talk."

"Well, I've done the part I could do on paper," Meg says. "I've done some research. I chose tibia. Broken bone. Compound fracture."

The woman is amused, all right. "I like head wounds myself," she says. "So much possibility for drama with the trauma. Lots of blood."

"I thought a lower leg wound was kind of interesting. Not a lot of blood, I mean no danger of bleeding to death or any of that, but a broken bone and nerve trauma and an inability to walk and possible infection. I have to construct a dummy to show what happened."

"What are you going to use?"

"Clothes stuffed with newspaper and a couple of sticks so I can show the broken bone."

"Neat."

"Here's what I have so far. Wash the wound. I need to show how to do that. But what is the current . . . cleanser?"

"Water. Primarily water. We also use surgical cleansers."

"What are they?"

"You know, professional products. Phisohex is one."

"Phisohex." Meg writes it down. "Do you have an empty container I could use? Or maybe something almost empty."

"Can't you just say the name of it?"

"Well, we act it out. And we show everything. We make a whole scene, kind of a stage set. Kind of like theater."

"I see. I'll go look. What else?"

Meg tries to speak quietly since two men across from her are watching her, listening to everything.

"Splint. Sticks at first."

"No, no, mostly we get 'em into X-ray right away. Then we call our carpenters with the surgical nails." The nurse smiles, pleased with her little joke.

"No. I forgot to explain. It's an outdoor, outpost, amateur kind of thing. An accident, far from a hospital."

"Oh. A hunting rifle, then. That'd pretty much blow the leg off."

"Hmm," Meg says. "No, that ruins my project. I didn't want to blow the leg off. I mean, this is supposed to be an emergency procedure first. Hospital later. And a regular gun."

"Handgun. But out camping?"

"Yeah . . . Couldn't that happen?"

"Sure."

"So, say it's an accident and . . . there they are, two friends, with just about nothing to use and the wounded guy can't move."

"Well you can forget the Phisohex then until you get your victim to a hospital. And he would get a tetanus shot once you get there, too."

"Okay." Meg makes a pass at writing the part about tetanus. But she is dashed. X-rays and cleaning solution and tetanus vaccine she doesn't have and can't get. "And, what if . . ." Meg feels herself losing power fast. "What if the guys made a splint? Would it hold for a while?"

"Not really. Too tricky. We tend to nail the bone. Without that, a victim would have to lie still for a long time. Six weeks, no movement."

"Couldn't move at all?"

"Upper body very carefully. Major risk of reinjury. Mega-complications."

She can feel sweat popping out on her forehead. Does the woman notice? "My brother and I saw a splint in a war movie," she says. "Maybe it wasn't realistic. I would have paid more attention if I'd known I was going to do a project. What about antibiotics?"

"If there's infection, absolutely necessary. It's done anyway as a matter of course, prophylactically, with an open wound. Prophylactically means—"

"Yes, I know. I'm definitely going to make infection a part of it. Fever. That's more dramatic, I think. What kind of antibiotic is best?"

"Well, you're out in the sticks."

"Yes. Part one, anyway."

"Anything you have. Irrigate the wound. Water is the best, believe it or not. *Copious irrigation* is the recommendation these days." It's what Joel said. He knew that already. The nurse continues, "It's not the bullet that infects. That's sterile. It's whatever the bullet carries with it."

"Material from the pants?"

"Right. Exactly. Once you get to the hospital, they're going to administer penicillin G or clindamycin. Different docs, different drugs."

Meg keeps making notes that the nurse reads over her shoulder.

"Usually six hundred milligrams a day for a week. At least. If the infection is already progressed, even more than that at first."

She has done right, then, in giving him a heavy dose. "I see. I need samples."

"We can't give out samples."

"Old outdated pills?"

"Oh, no, no, no. Not pharmaceuticals. For one thing, we don't keep old pills around, honey. This is a hospital emergency room. Why are the pills so important?" The nurse leans back a few inches to direct a good long look at Meg's face. "You could use a Contac capsule. Who'd know?"

"I guess I was being too literal."

The nurse looks toward the admission station and back to her. "I'm going to need your name."

"Catherine," she says, her middle name, not the largest lie in the world. She might be one of those people who prefers her middle name. And then "Charles" pops out, her father's first name.

"I'm going to ask you a question. Do you have a boyfriend, maybe played rough, got himself in some kind of trouble?"

Meg's breath quickens. "No."

"If you know anyone who needs help, you must make that person come in, do you understand? We could be talking about something very serious here."

Meg bites her lip hard. "Yes. But no, this is a project," she insists, her voice light, whispery.

"I'll see if I have anything you can use."

The woman is gone for a quarter hour. The door to the inner workings of the emergency unit open and shut; each time Meg catches glimpses of men and women in white coats, sitting around, laughing. The nurse returns, walking swiftly. She hands over a virtually empty bottle of Phisohex, a card with pictures of six pills, and a sheaf of papers she's taken off the computer. The tiny type at the top says they come from a trauma unit Web site.

Meg streaks home.

SEVENTEEN

SOUND. HE IDENTIFIES CAR
radios playing through open car windows far away, the crunch of tires on broken cement, closer, one set of footsteps going down the alley. Each time he hears a car, he thinks it might be another of Marko's men come to find him.

Twice, he tries to stand up, thinking, I just need to get myself to the alley, flag someone for help; but his body rebels, shaking so badly that he falls back down.

The three houses behind him, the one belonging to the garage and those on either side, are boarded up, but there might be someone there. And that person might see him and pick up a phone. He studies the three yards, trying to determine how long the junk in each has been there, and he watches the windows for signs of life. Nothing changes at all, except the sounds.

When the sun begins to dip, he realizes it's going to be cold soon.

The ground is damp from the rain of two days ago. No. No, that was only yesterday.

He tries to work out how, when he gets to his car, he's going to drive it. His right leg is useless, but there might be a way to prop the right leg up and move his left under it, working the pedals. He needs the kids for that, to figure it. They're good at figuring.

Suddenly there is a noise of footsteps on dirt coming close. He tightens his grip on the gun.

To his surprise, the boy appears again and quickly dumps three things on the ground. Half a candy bar, cheese, a carton of juice. "Here," the kid says. "Can't do anything else yet. It's too light out." And he is gone.

The sight of the little bit of food next to him gives him unreasonable hope.

Eventually he hears sounds again, an organ? He realizes it's the baseball game about to start up—a mile away, stadium sounds. He eats and tries to stand once more and can't.

CARL LISTENS TO THE RADIO.
There is nothing on the news that tells him what he needs to know. Did anybody die when the three shots were fired?

Last night, after Nick let him go and he flew down the street, grabbing up his books from the pavement, he kept expecting to die, but he kept moving and made it to his hideout, where he rocked himself all night in the dark, waiting for the dawn. He shivered all night, too, and he cried most of it, but when morning came, he began his routine. Breakfast, seven to eight. Radio, eight to nine. From nine to ten, jogging in place. Then, ten to twelve, reading and working out problems. And making journal entries.

Lunch and then the same routine again. Then dinner, radio, jogging, reading and working for two more hours, and hopefully sleep soon with the help of valerian. Three chunks to the day. Three meals. Three physical workouts. Three work sessions.

He keeps changing stations, but there is nothing about what happened last night. He settles on music, popular songs, and plays the game of trying to be always a mini—split second ahead of the singer. *You said you love me but we all know a liar, I'm not sorry for the things I—* It was going to be *said* or *done.* Said.

He puts out two valerian waiting for night to fall.

Somehow he's made it to evening of the first day. The radio is at the lowest volume he can tolerate. He continues to search for the news. When he finds it, he hears about auto accidents and Memorial Day festivities, but nothing about Nick or a murder just down the street.

Nick betrayed him, came after him— And yet, and yet Nick was the one who helped him get away. Carl goes over it, trying to figure it out. Nick emptied his pockets, but put back his key and his little bit of money. What was that about? He can't figure it.

Carl is shivering much more now. He tries other stations. The radio seems to be whispering to him. Even the baseball announcer on the sports station is murmuring. It's nice, like people in the other room talking when you're a little kid. You don't care what they're saying, only that they're there.

EIGHTEEN

MEG HAS DONE THE PASTA
this time with just butter and a little cheese. The four of them sit in the
kitchen, eating, but her sisters are angry.

"I have a lot to explain. I know that," Meg says.

"I thought you weren't coming home," Susannah says. She is now
plastered next to Laurie.

"I'm here," she says. "Always. My goal is . . . keeping us together. I
don't want us to ever be apart."

Even Laurie, who is usually afraid of nothing, looks frightened.
"Where were you?" she asks in a tight voice. "You made me steal. And
Susannah was here all by herself."

"I know. We have to do this one thing to help this man."

Laurie says, "We don't have to. You *want* to."

"I do."

"I don't get it." She looks to her brother. "Why?"

Joel gives the stage to Meg with a glance.

"It's the pizza man," Meg says finally. "I kind of know him."

Laurie's jaw drops. "Oh."

"I got us into this," Joel says gamely.

Meg hastens to press her advantage with her sisters. "We're just doing what we have to do. We owe him. This food is bought with his money."

She knows Joel's reason is different. For him, it's work, challenge, being a doctor.

"After today, we'll talk again, after we do what we know to do for him. Nick is his name. He's scared. Remember when Joel found a bird and wanted to fix it, but the bird was so scared, remember? If it tried to fly, or hopped on the ground, it would get killed. So Joel saved it, remember?"

Susannah's face becomes soft with the memory.

"Same thing going on here," Meg explains. "We have to try to calm him down. If he seems to get worse, well, I'll give it all up and call the ambulance." She has them, for now. "Please eat. If you're in with me, we have work to do."

They all eat faster now.

As small children, they all used to pretend each slippery strand was a worm. The memory shadows them every time they eat pasta. Meg pauses, takes two strands with her fingers, and tilting her head back lowers them into her mouth. "Slithery worms," she says, winking to entertain Susannah.

"Is the pizza man hurt bad?" Laurie asks.

"Yes. His leg. He can't walk. But he's also messed up in his thinking. We need things. The pills you got us. Crutches—we still need to find crutches. And something to set the leg."

Joel nods.

"Think of it as a job we're all doing—for pay." She is certain Laurie will point out the food came before the job, but for now Laurie is thoughtful. Meg is sorting some of the pages from the hospital while she's eating.

"What are you reading?"

"About fractures."

Susannah asks, "Doesn't he want a real doctor?"

"Doctors call the police. He's afraid of the police."

Fork clinks against bowl. A truth blossoms in the middle of their dinner. Life without the criminal bird is less dangerous, certainly, but also less interesting.

After dinner, Meg has them call around to a few of their friends, asking do the friends have a set of crutches their older sister could borrow for a school science project? Nobody they know has crutches. By then it's after seven o'clock.

She and Joel hurry to the small table they use as a desk in the living room. The two of them trade information. Laurie has volunteered to do dishes, but she's too curious to stay away from their work. She is fascinated by the pictures and hands them on to Susannah, who studies them as if she understands.

"Let's get to the pharmacy before it gets any later."

"What can I do?" Laurie asks.

"Boil a big pot of water. Let it cool."

"Susannah will help me. Won't you?"

"Yes."

"Come here, sweetie," Meg says. "Promise me you won't tell anyone." She enfolds Susannah. "You understand?"

Her sister says, "Yes," and strokes Meg's hair. Meg feels relief that she's won her over again.

"There's one thing here—" Meg shuffles among the papers. "It's about braces made of polyester foam and straps. If only we had something like that for him. No, what am I thinking? Those things get put on *after* surgical nails."

"Right," Joel says. He takes the pages from her hands and considers them as if he were an engineer. "On the Web it said a person could use rolled newspaper for a temporary splint," he tells all of them. "But I want something firmer that hugs the leg and isn't temporary and looks okay. He can't go anywhere with tree branches hanging off him."

Susannah is hugging Meg very hard, and Meg is hugging back even as she's saying almost breathlessly, "We've got to get moving, but if you could all just keep thinking . . ."

"We have to give him all kinds of bad news," Joel says.

Meg nods, but this is where she really needs to get them on her side.

"What?" Laurie wants to know.

"Well, see, he's supposed to be immobile for six weeks. Tricky problem. In any circumstances."

Laurie says, "He's going to need a lot of books."

"And he . . . his name is Nick. . . . See, he thought he had a car, but the car is gone."

"We can keep him for a couple of days," Laurie says gamely. There is a crackle of silence as they all consider this and allow it to sink in. "What will you use instead of that stuff?" Laurie points to the papers.

Meg lets go of Susannah, saying, "It's going to have to be with something we can find. We need the right lightweight materials and we have to replace the branches. The thing is, I didn't even have time to wrap the branches very thoroughly. We can do better. With time and light. And good tape. We ought to buy duct tape at the supermarket," she tells Joel.

"With what?" Laurie asks.

"He gave us a little more money."

Laurie whistles.

Joel paces like an old man. "For the splint, I don't have an idea yet."

"We can cut up Tupperware or something," Laurie volunteers. "How would that work?"

"Too inflexible. Wrong shape."

"We must have something around here?"

Meg looks at her watch. "Okay. We still have time before the pharmacy closes. Five minutes, even ten. Look around, see what we might have that . . . would work."

It's like a scavenger hunt. They all run. "I'll take the basement," Laurie cries. But Susannah goes with her. Joel takes the second floor, Meg the first.

In the kitchen closet, she finds some Styrofoam from liquor Alison once bought, just a few little chunks of a reverse mold, but it makes her wonder if she could cut it up and carve it effectively to the right shape. No. Too small, too narrow. She rejects it, puts it on the kitchen table. After she's combed the kitchen for anything else—Tupperware, even though it's too unyielding—the lids to things, the cardboard from the roll of paper towels, seeing everything in a new way, according to durability and shape, Joel comes into the kitchen. His eye lights on the Styrofoam.

"Too small," she says, defeated.

And it's Saturday night. The Salvation Army and the Goodwill are closed tonight; tomorrow is Sunday; those places will be closed tomorrow and Monday because Monday is Memorial Day; and so the world will come to a stop, has already *begun* to grind to a stop. It's the worst time to *need* things.

But Joel is handling the Styrofoam, saying, "The right size would work. We have to find places where they throw things out."

"The Giant Eagle?" she tries. "The Dumpster behind the Rite Aid?"

"Maybe. We'll look."

This is what she loves about them. Joel has not given up. The other two have come in and are eager to help, Susannah patting Meg's arm with encouragement.

NINETEEN

POTOCKI ASKS, "YOU HAVE plans tonight?"

"Um. I was going to hop up to the hospital. Visit Commander. You . . . want to come?"

"I don't feel right about seeing him when he's down. Just a personal thing. If you want to get something to eat after your visit, I can wait."

The two of them have had quite a few meals together today—after the pastrami wore off, they split a falafel at Janet's Middle Eastern, all the while cracking up about the skinny flatiron building a block away that had a worn-out sign saying TERMINAL LUNCH. For a while it had been Brad's Terminal Lunch. Then Rita's Terminal Lunch.

Truth is, dinner with company sounds good. "You could eat as late as nine?"

"Sure." He brightens.

So, the nut of it is, she runs home, showers, changes into a new pair of linen pants she's been eager to wear and a lacy stretch top, zips over to the hospital, arriving at five minutes after eight. Through the maze of hallways, familiar now, she speeds toward the elevator that takes her up to his room.

Marina is there.

Christie looks horrible. His eyes are vague, his lids keep closing. It's all she can do not to gasp.

"It's just the chemo," he says. "My body isn't liking it."

"Does the nausea go away after a while?"

"They tell me yes." He motions to Marina to continue.

"They're trying different antinausea drugs," she explains.

There is a silence. "Solve your boy's identity?" Christie asks finally.

"Not yet."

He smiles.

She feels ridiculously intrusive and forces small talk for a few minutes to soften her early exit. All the way down the elevator she beats herself up for coming at all.

Outside the building, she calls Potocki to say, "Meet me at Tessaro's."

They get there around nine and they order gazpacho and drinks to start.

"How's Commander?"

"Brave. Miserable. Way out of it."

"Shit."

"I can't imagine things without him. Can you?"

"No."

At Tessaro's, the ball game is on TV. Everything seems easy, friendly, chatty, and at one conversational turn, Potocki is telling her, "Judy and I went into therapy two years ago. It didn't fix anything."

"Was it police work?"

"In a way. Any case I was on, she accused me of infidelity."

"Police work, then."

"It took us a while to figure out she wanted to see someone else, so she projected that onto me. She was interested in the idea of it—having a lover—even before she cast the role. It was in everything she said. I didn't hear it at the time, but I heard it later, you know, in retrospect."

Colleen is grateful when her grilled scallops arrive. Hearing about another woman's infidelity is unsettling.

It is almost eleven when they leave the place. He kisses her on the eye before they part to go to their separate cars. The eye. He was aiming for her forehead but missed. Sort of funny.

Now she sits in front of the television, not really watching, Nick and Potocki and Christie all dancing in her head.

TWENTY

THEY ZIGZAG UP THE HILL,
trying to look casual yet purposeful, so that no policeman will stop
them, two children out at midnight. Meg pretends to be talking to Joel,
walking ahead of him and facing backwards toward him, just a kid, rag-
ging her brother. She's scanning the streets. Joel is watching everything
from the other direction. "Anybody looking at us?" she asks.

"No. Just a minute."

"What?"

"Look what I found," he says.

She turns to see he's looking at a shopping cart up ahead. Wheels,
yes, oh, they need wheels all right, but how to use it?

"We need to go into the alley," Joel says. "Find something to fill it
with."

"But how—?" Meg asks. How do the two of them lift a heavy body
up to the basket, no matter that it's filled, maybe even harder when it's
filled. They both look at the lower rack, where people put crates of

soda, laundry detergent. Maybe the bottom of the cart could work. When they get into the alley, to test it, Joel climbs onto the lower section and backs up until his leg is supported. He has to squeeze his body through the space in back and then hold on to the basket in a sitting position. Meg says, "He's a lot bigger."

"Fill the basket, in case we need to lift him up." They scout garage areas.

"This is taking too long," he says.

"There. That's a box. Grab it."

"Couple of these—"

"We might have something at home."

"No, keep going. I don't want to lose more time." They pretend to be cuffing each other, goofing around.

By the time they get to the alley where they have hidden Nick, they have managed to fill the cart with four boxes inside each other for strength and a couple of small stray pieces of wood.

A quick look up and down the alley, then they duck behind the boarded-up garage. He's still there. Asleep. Like a little baby.

The man's eyes open. They search Meg's face. It looks as if he is going to cry. Like this, when he's not angry, this is how she likes him. She feels his head. Warm. Not so hot as it was.

"We have to get you onto this," she whispers, tapping at the cart.

"Oh," he says, despondent. "I can't. It isn't possible."

"You have to try."

"How will we get down the street?"

"Fast," Joel says.

The man almost laughs. A good sign?

They try to wedge the cart with their feet while lifting him onto the bottom. But the cart keeps moving.

"It isn't going to work," he says.

Meg nods.

"We have to put him on top," Joel murmurs.

He tugs at the cart until he's tipped it over so it's lying on its side. "We have to get him in it this way, support him, then lift it up."

The pizza man closes his eyes. Is he praying? Dying?

For twenty minutes, the kids angle things this way and that, until finally they manage to get him in while the cart is down. It takes some doing to right the cart. But they do that, too. Then they arrange the sheet around Nick, covering his legs as well as they can. "What a shame this isn't one of those carts that opens in the front," Joel says in that voice that made Alison call him an old man. Nick is wincing with pain, biting into his hand. They've jostled him after all.

Meg reaches into her pocket, searching for the pain pills she's gathered. She swishes around the juice carton, but it's empty. "You have to take these." She hands him four pills. "I don't have any liquid. Try to swallow anyway," she says. "It isn't aspirin, don't worry. We know about aspirin and bleeding."

He rolls the pills and looks at them. "What are they?"

"For pain."

"Maybe four will kill me."

"We looked up all kinds of things. He did." She points to her brother. "You're going to need those when we get to work on your leg. They'll put you to sleep."

He looks at them again. "Whiskey? How about a lot of whiskey?"

"We don't have any more. We gave you what we had."

His face is so . . . distraught. He wants to believe in them, but doesn't quite. "What are you going to do now?"

Joel answers in that adult, old voice. "I'm going to clean the wound again, more thoroughly. Then check the bone and if it's not right, reset it better, with something firmer and clean. If I can be sure it's stable, you'll be able to do about anything a person with a broken leg can do. Which isn't much, but still, way better than where you are now. I'm not sure it will work, but I think I know what to do. You still want me to try?"

He nods. He takes the pills.

And then they start out, down the hill. They act as if it's just a merry ride down the hill. Just a game. In case anyone asks, Meg is prepared to say, "Our uncle got drunk again."

They use alleys. They search ahead and behind them. The pills are starting to work, and yet he tries to look around. He's scared.

They keep a pace without ever running.

When they get to their own alley, they go in past their garage toward the back door. They get the cart up to the back door, and Laurie comes running outside, Susannah behind her, very sleepy.

"Susannah, hold the door open. Laurie. Lift a corner. Move him as little as possible." The man groans. Laurie grabs a corner, and they get him inside, where they put him down gently on the kitchen floor.

"What's happening?" he mumbles. He tries to look around, but he is already doped up. His eye lights for a moment on the sink. Things are lined up, ready to be used. Meg, trembling, puts one more pill on his tongue and gets it down. He sinks back and gives himself over to them; it reminds Meg of Susannah when she stops fighting to stay awake.

There is a second pot of water boiling on the stove in case they need it. That's Laurie, thoughtful, always, about things like that.

Laurie's eyes are almost shutting. Susannah is asleep on her feet.

"If you two could stay in the living room until we need you—"

The two younger kids hold on to each other as they leave the kitchen.

It's still humid out, has been for a week, so the steam that's coming from the boiling water is not very welcome. When Meg lifts Nick Banks' hand, it falls back down, dead weight. "He's out," she says. Joel loosens the rags they used to wrap his leg. "Easy," she whispers toward Nick. "Everything is all right."

The hard part is cutting his pants off the rest of the way up to the waistband and through. At first he stirs and tries to complain, but he gives up. His near nakedness is unsettling at first, but then, surprisingly, it seems like nothing.

For a long time, Joel cleans his leg.

It's almost two in the morning when they're ready to do the hard part. Laurie has done everything they asked her to do. She's made holes in the Styrofoam they gathered earlier, and she's done it carefully, with a skewer.

"Air." Joel explained when he gave instructions. "The wound has to have air."

Meg wishes she could be like Laurie. So regular and competent. Or like Susannah. Trusting. Now her sisters are asleep on the couch.

Joel looks worried. "When we lift the leg, it'll wake him up—"

"I know."

Because of the way the bullet went in, Joel is able to do the first step of washing entrance and exit wounds without having to move Nick's leg. Now he's still using a magnifying glass, dipping tweezers in boiling water, searching for and removing what looks wrong. One thing he identifies as a small dot of cloth. Finally he nods. The two of them irrigate the areas one more time before they bandage the wounds, entrance, exit, both sides, with clean gauze. Then they have to face the job of lifting the leg to get the Styrofoam underneath it. Joel's job is the engineering. "How?" she asks.

"My hands. I kind of wish we had the branches on again. It was pretty steady with them. It's a shame to have to move him at all since the position looks good."

"If he's to have any mobility . . ."

"I know, I know. I just hope I get it right again. One picture I saw on the Net . . . showed a soldier whose leg healed with the bones every which way so that his one leg was shorter than the other. But it knitted anyway. And he walked."

"Amazing."

Joel grunts thoughtfully.

The murmur and hum of working together shifts into silence. They pause, almost freeze, before moving forward.

Then Joel lifts carefully, pressing from knee to ankle while she slides the foam splint underneath; Nick moans only a little. Does it mean Joel has kept the bones steady?

Meg begins the process of filling in the shell of foam with small pieces of crumpled newspaper, so it will be tight. Earlier she and Joel and Laurie went over and over what to use: rags would not be clean enough, and gauze—they didn't have enough, couldn't waste it. Newspaper. It had to be newspaper, because as Joel said, if people used it for birthing babies . . . Not perfect because it's going to be uncomfortable when he sweats, but it might just make the Styrofoam pipe secure. When she has fitted the paper in tightly, she fits the top pipelike piece on. It will be lightweight, anyway. Joel holds the Styrofoam in place while she tapes. He adds a foot-piece to secure it—what he learned from the tree branches routine. The two of them tape everything carefully. "Good job," she keeps telling him. "Way to go."

Once the work on his leg is done, it seems wrong to leave him in the dirty bloody shirt. She and Joel prop him up and begin to take off the plaid shirt. He groans from deep within his stupor, trying to hold it on him, but eventually they get it off. The activity is waking him. While he is on the verge of half awake, Meg makes him swallow more antibiotics. She wants to fetch warm soapy water, give him a bath and a shave, but tomorrow, tomorrow is soon enough. She checks his upper body for wounds, wipes him quickly with alcohol, and puts a blanket over him.

Almost without words, they lift him and carry him to the living room where they have placed on the floor the cushion that belongs to their only good lawn chair, the one Alison always sat in. It makes a bed of sorts.

There are problems to solve. The only bathroom is on the second floor. They don't yet have crutches.

The more immediate problem is that she has made him drink lots of water. By now his bladder must be full. What will happen if he wakes in the night, distressed and disoriented? What if he tries to stand up? She has to do something. Rattling around in the cupboards, she finds a large jar. "You have to help me wake him a little," she tells Joel. She puts the blanket over Nick and begins to whisper to him to pull aside the flap on his briefs, use the jar. "It's okay," she keeps saying. She knows urine is sterile, so if he does have an accident, it won't be a terrible thing, but he was clean-looking, well put together. She knows he won't want to wake all wet.

"He isn't going to do it," Joel says. "Man, I'd hate to be in his shoes."

Suddenly they both laugh. Shoes.

Meg keeps at Nick. "Go on, use the jar. That's what it's for."

He is still mostly out, but the power of suggestion finally works. After a timid start, he fills the jar.

"Good, good," she says.

Joel grimaces, looks around for a joke, gives up.

Meg asks, "Can you watch him for a minute?" She takes the jar, which is heavy and warm, and swiftly heads upstairs, where she dumps the contents into the toilet. He'll need it again, so she takes it with her as she hurries back downstairs.

They cover him with two more blankets and stare at their work. What will tomorrow bring?

She wakes Laurie and Susannah then. It's after three in the morning. They put on the television. The four of them sit on the couch with narrow columns of space between them.

Laurie asks, "Is he all right?"

"Better than he was before," Meg says. She looks to Joel and feels the odd feeling of seeing him for the first time. "Joel did it. He's going to be a good doctor."

Nobody is looking at the TV. They're watching Nick sleep. Susannah's eyes close again.

"We have to get to bed," Meg says.

But they don't move for a while.

"He looks like Dad," Laurie says.

PART THREE

TWENTY-ONE

MARKO HAS BEEN SITTING outside Nick's place for hours. He calls Petrucci, who has been waiting next to a phone all night, waiting for word. Markovic says levelly, "He hasn't showed."

Petrucci breathes into the line. Marko lights up another cigarette and waits him out. It's after four, almost morning. He reaches for the bottle he keeps under the driver's seat and takes a drink. It's been a very long day. And tomorrow, *today*, he's supposed to get the pizza shop going again and find more substitute runners for the North Side; and he somehow has to be rested enough in a little more than twelve hours to do the Sunday-night drive to Philly.

His fat cousins don't think. They sit, stomachs hanging over their groins, legs spread. They look like brothers. Bald heads and girth. Working the phones is about all they do. They don't do the hard stuff.

Petrucci says, "You brought Nick into this, you brought this on us."

"I get it."

"Because you were soft on Nick. All that rigmarole about the guy killed a man once, we can trust him—what was that all about?"

Marko had liked Nick. He had liked going to the shop and belly-aching to him and just sitting with him. He felt betrayed. That was bad enough without having it slammed to him.

"I hope you have your head together about this. Your mistake."

"Yeah, I do."

"Go home. Sleep and get ready for later. Go home."

TWENTY-TWO

THE SUN SLANTING IN MAKES
a pattern on the counter and the kitchen table. She opens the windows
to the sounds of church bells. The others are sleeping and may not
wake up until late. The brewing coffee, something she learned how to
make at an early age for her father (and drank at times because it made
her feel older), smells so good to her, she can hardly wait for it. She
will have a little today. The aroma conjures a memory of her father
coming up out of sleep; she wonders if the smell will awaken Nick
Banks. She peeks. His chest rises and falls, his breath makes a noise
going in and out, his hands clutch at the blanket.

She stands at the stairway to the upstairs. It provides the wall, the
barrier between the kitchen with its eating area and the only other
room downstairs. Considering him from that little distance, she tries
to determine, does he look like her father? She'd thought more like
someone in a photograph she'd seen. An actor. A ballplayer. A writer.

She tiptoes back to the kitchen where the sounds and smells of morning envelop her. Birds singing. Coffee.

They were in the middle of a crime—aiding and abetting it would be called if they were hauled in. Last night, as the four of them got themselves upstairs, Laurie asked her, "We know nothing about him, right?"

"Not facts, anyway."

"Joel said he scared him at first."

"I can't make myself believe badly of him." She didn't mention the dead body up at the house. Joel hadn't either. But it would come out sooner or later.

Last night she learned she was not afraid of the grit and dirt of nursing him, she was not squeamish. This surprised and pleased her. She had thought she would be.

She slips to the basement, where she has stashed the wool plaid shirt and the remains of his pants in a cardboard box inside a large plastic bag. The gun is wrapped in a towel for now. She has considered soaking the shirt—he might want it or need it—but if he wears it, he might be recognized. It would be easier to throw it all away, not give him the choice. Yet if he turns himself in eventually, or if he is caught, the gun, the clothes, are evidence. Blood, his and someone else's mixed, could be crucial. If he's telling the truth . . . For a moment she tilts with a real vertigo, uncertain. Her mind leaps to a garish image of water in a basin rusty from blood and swirling down the drain.

The thought of the dead man up at the house makes her grip the edge of the sink. If Nick Banks is lying . . . She gets a startling flash of the picture of the other man, whom she hardly looked at, but in her mind's eye there keeps coming back an image of an odd man who, in death, looked like a sack of something bunched up, old scatter-rugs tangled in a pile.

She has seen only one dead person before, and that was her father, stiff, in a suit, "presentable" as Alison put it—the violence of the car crash wiped away.

She puts the gun, in its towel, in the box inside the bag and folds down the top of the garbage bag again, wondering what to do with it all. Finally she carries everything to a far corner of the basement. She will decide later.

If the splint Joel made works, and if they find crutches, Nick could be gone in a few days or a week. It will seem this whole episode has been a dream. Her mind creates a scene she will play years later—her telling all this and no one believing her. In her imagined scene, she says, "We never told anyone and we lived on our own for four years," and everyone she tells is skeptical. "How?" they ask.

Because we were good at it.

She climbs the basement stairs, trembling, and looks into the living room once more; there he is, stomach rising and falling, still alive.

She sits in the kitchen, drinking coffee and trying to read another Dickens. The school she goes to is substandard. None of the other students do anything challenging. Nobody else has read anything one-tenth the length of *A Tale of Two Cities*. So her teacher told her, if she liked *A Tale of Two Cities*, she should read *Great Expectations*. And the teacher handed over a copy and promised to get her one of *Oliver Twist*. Meg didn't tell the teacher they have these books at home because her father liked them.

Her father. She can almost feel him in the room. He was a "fine" man, the minister said at the funeral. But the minister didn't even know her father. He was just there to make fifty bucks, Alison explained, for saying a few words. The word *fine* is so . . . clean. It is the thing itself, slender and simple. A fine gentleman, Dickens might have called her father. A fine gentleman has patience and knowledge while a brute is all impatience and blunt instruments. Self-control and kindness. Yes, that's how her father was.

She repositions the book before her on the kitchen table. Because it's a book about miracles, it manages to seduce her for a few minutes from the man in the living room, who himself is a story to rival the one in print.

Twenty pages later, she gets up and tiptoes again to look at him. Nick opens his eyes. Her heart jumps, *she* jumps, and a little sound escapes her. He looks startled, too.

"Where am I?" he asks.

"Here. In our house. Our living room."

They both still themselves. His electric eyes flash with fear, then soften.

"What happened—?" He feels for his leg, and his hand hits the Styrofoam, making a muted thump. He gets up on an elbow and reaches for the blankets that cover him. "Is my leg o—?" he begins.

"Don't move. You're okay. Don't you remember? I gave you pain pills, then my brother reset it. Well, he checked the setting and recast it."

"Recast? This is a cast?"

"A splint. A made-up one."

"What is it?"

"Styrofoam."

"That works?"

"It's working, we think."

"You set my leg?"

"Yes. My brother did, mostly."

"I don't feel too good."

"In what way?"

"Weak. Hard to think."

"That would be normal after what you've been through."

"How long have I been out?"

"Just last night. It's Sunday."

He nods.

"Do you drink coffee?"

"Coffee? Yeah."

"I'll get you a cup." She hurries to the kitchen and pours so fast, she spills some of the coffee and has to slow herself down and wipe things up. When she returns, he has peeled the blanket back and is looking at his leg.

She puts the cup of coffee beside him on the floor.

He is up on one elbow still, learning his surroundings. "How did you move me?"

"We carried you in the sheet again. Into the kitchen, then from the kitchen to here. You don't remember?"

"I remember now. The kitchen. I was on a couple of pills, right?"

"Yes. We couldn't work on your leg without pain pills. . . ."

"Why did you do this for me?"

Meg tries to find the right, the most accurate answer. "My brother and I thought we knew how, that together we could figure how."

"But you're kids."

"We studied what we should do. It's temporary anyway. A hospital would do it better."

He falls silent. He brings the mug to his lips, sips, puts it back down. He says slowly, "I don't get it. I'm grateful. I don't get it though. I asked for whiskey and a stick or something and you did all this."

"You were kind to me. Twice."

"I was?" He blinks rapidly.

"At the pizza shop. Alison had a flyer. She called and ordered wrong. I didn't have enough money and you gave the pizza to me anyway. That was the first time." He doesn't remember.

"Who's Alison?"

"She used to live here."

He lies back and rests for a minute.

"And then you gave me some food."

"I remember that."

Meg comes closer and lifts the coffee cup. In the hospitals they give patients straws that bend so they don't have to move. She will have to pass through McDonald's and filch a couple.

He raises himself up again. "My clothes," he says.

"I saved them, but they're no good. I have to get you something else."

"Your father's?"

"If . . . if there is something that would work." She and Laurie had snatched a few of their father's things when Alison was giving them away, but only things they thought they could use for cleaning, sleeping in, just clothes that allowed them to feel close to him still. Was any of that going to be usable?

"I don't get it," he says again, eyes narrowed. He takes the cup from her hands and swallows some coffee. "How did you study"—he nods toward his leg—"about my injury?"

"Internet. And I went to the hospital and asked some questions."

His eyes widen.

"I think I did it okay. I said it was a school project."

He takes another drink of coffee and tries to put the cup down on his own, but trying to find the level space on the floor is too intricate a move, and she has to take it from him.

"Joel's going out to find crutches today. For when you feel up to it. No hurry."

"How am I going to get out of here without clothes?"

"I'll buy you something, but not until Tuesday."

"What's today?"

"Sunday."

"Oh. That's right. You told me."

"And tomorrow's a holiday." His face is strained, trying to remember what holiday. "Memorial Day. We can't afford to go to a real store. We have to wait till the thrift stores open. I don't think you're strong enough to do anything much yet anyway. Give it a couple of days."

"In here?"

"Yes. Well, probably better upstairs."

He looks around, getting the lay of the land. "Will I be able to walk?"

"I don't know."

"It hurts like hell."

"I think it would." She is getting used to the shifting expressions on his face. "There are only four more of these little buggers—pain pills. After that, you have to start on Advil, which isn't very strong. It's all I could find. Try not to worry. Try to get some rest."

"What about whiskey?"

"You don't have enough money. Unless you have more somewhere."

"I had some money in my wallet."

"You only had another forty. We used some already and we're going to need more supplies."

"What's going to happen when whoever takes care of you finds me here?"

"It'll be okay."

"Why don't I believe that?"

"It will."

"Where are they?"

"They . . . work. They might not be back for quite a while."

It got quiet for a moment. He was figuring he was going to need the jar or the bathroom, one or the other, soon enough. She isn't afraid of anything having to do with taking care of him, but by the way he pulled the covers over him even when he exposed his leg, she knows he has modesty and some pride. Up and down the steps on crutches if they manage to find them is possible eventually, but more than he can handle today. Up the stairs on his bum *might* be possible.

Better to say it all out loud, deal with it. "We probably will have to put you upstairs where you can have a bed that's a height you can get to from standing. And our bathroom is up there."

He swears under his breath as he lets himself down again. He turns slightly to look at her. "What'd I do last night?"

"Jar."

"If I had a pair of crutches—," he says.

"Right. We just have to find them."

"How?"

"My brother will go out after breakfast. Until then, the jar. It's okay. It's no trouble."

After a while, he asks, "Who was here last night?"

"My brother, my sisters, and me. Nobody else saw, if that's what you're asking."

From upstairs comes a small noise, someone getting out of bed.

Laurie, from the light footsteps. The sounds that are utterly familiar to Meg make Nick go tense.

"It's my sister. Try to rest. It's only us."

He tries to rest. He's only pretending.

First Laurie comes down the stairs, then minutes later, Joel and Susannah. They slide into the room and stand, awed, looking at their captive.

"Don't stare at him," Meg says.

"I'm the Christmas tree with all the lights on," he mutters wryly.

Meg urges them toward the kitchen. "Let him rest a bit." Before she vacates the room herself, she asks him, "Would you like TV? I'll put it on. For company?"

His eyes move along with the TV for a minute or two and he is asleep again.

TWENTY-THREE

COLLEEN GREER AND POTOCKI
hadn't been long on duty on Sunday morning when Colleen heard on
her radio the 911 call for a patrol car. The operator was saying, "We have
a call from a pay phone. A kid's voice. Says there's something up at a
house on this street called McCandor. The kid thinks it's 822 or something, green paint. Said there might be a dead person or maybe a murder on the second floor. I couldn't keep him on. That's all we have to
go on."

Colleen got on the phone and identified herself. "We're Homicide on
duty. We can be there in ninety seconds. We're right at Headquarters."

She waved to Potocki. "We maybe got another one."

Farber would see they were needed in Homicide.

Disappointment leaked into the voice of the policeman who'd also
just answered the call. He said, "Oh. Okay, yes, Detective." Patrol cops
wanted to make their mistakes among their own rank with nobody
scrutinizing, nobody seeing if they accidentally stepped on evidence.

"I'm on it, too," a voice came from a second patrol car.

Nellins and Hrznak, two old homicide detectives who were also on duty, looked up as if the tornado that swept around them was kicking dust into their faces. They squinted as Colleen flew past them.

Colleen could hear a siren starting up in the neighborhood. Those guys loved their sirens—sometimes needed them to get through traffic, but mostly it amounted to yelling yahoo. She and Potocki hurried through the parking lot to the car they were using. "Could be nothing," he was saying.

"Could be something."

Potocki drove today, and he drove fast, laughing. "Go get 'em, girl. Nothing lazy about you. You're stepping on their heels."

Colleen tried to remember something. There was a phrase for *stepping on the heels of.* Out of Shakespeare. *Hamlet.* She could almost grab hold of it, but it eluded her. She could distinctly remember her teacher talking about it. Couldn't remember the phrase. "Damn, damn," she whispered.

"What?" Potocki asked.

"Oh, nothing." She told him what she was trying to remember.

It seemed 822 McCandor didn't exist anymore, but 826 had green painted external shutters on some of the second-floor windows. Two patrol cars were out front.

"Oh, look. They waited for us. They did."

"Your voice," Potocki said. "The sound of your voice. Very authoritative."

"That and they're chicken." She and Potocki got out of their car.

The two patrol cops from the first car came around from the back. One and Two, she named them. "Point of entry seems to be a plywood plank. My guess is you just push it to go in, you pull it by some of the nails to board the place up."

"It was in place, boarded up?" Colleen asked. Two more patrol cops came up to them—Three and Four.

"Yeah, but we messed with it and it's partway down."

She said to the first two, "That means whoever called this in possibly went to the trouble of boarding it up—"

All six tromped around to the backyard—if you could call it a yard, smaller than a postage stamp. A tree, two overgrown bushes, and some wild weedy grasses would have blocked a lot of the view from anyone across the alley in what looked to be other abandoned houses.

Potocki said quietly, "Two of you go out front to make sure nobody escapes that way." He gave Cops Three and Four a few seconds to return to the front door. "Come on, guys."

They all drew their guns. The plywood door went down easily, and all four of them smelled death.

"Shit."

"Yeah."

Potocki and the two cops went in while Colleen covered them from the doorway. They plastered themselves against the walls downstairs and swept the space a couple of times. Then Colleen went in herself. Their feet crunched glass, cardboard, nails, and other noisy debris as they moved.

There was nothing to see downstairs. Guns still drawn, they climbed up to where the smell was.

There were flies clustered around the body of a man who looked at first glance like a deadbeat. Tangled hair, clothes none too tidy, aggressive facial hair, the face of the borderline personality. Shot straight through the chest, straight to the heart.

They took a moment to stand back and survey the mess. The chaos would talk eventually, but Colleen couldn't read it off the bat. She moved forward to examine the dead man's pockets, but before she tiptoed through the clearest part of the mess, there was a new siren outside—and soon after, more sounds, a shout, and a "Hold on."

Stepping on their heels was Franklin Farber.

The head of Narcotics was banging up the steps, saying, "Wait, wait, wait. Just hold up. Greer and Potocki, move back." Farber looked at the body, reached forward to pull up the long sleeves covering the man's arms. There were no tracks.

Potocki said, "Commander, I have to ask you to stop. You're interfering with a Homicide investigation."

"Well, the two of you are needed for a Narcotics investigation. I thought I made that clear."

Potocki lit into him. "We were first on the scene. We got a Homicide call."

"For a while, you privilege Narcotics."

"But Homicide can't take a backseat to Narcotics. Anywhere. Any time."

Farber looked around at the cops and the detectives gathered. "But I have clearance to use you two the way I want to; there are other people on duty to take the Homicide cases."

"Who?" Potocki asked, even though he knew the answer.

"Nellins and Hrznak are twiddling their thumbs back there while we have a big case to build in the next couple of weeks. I called them. They'll be here in a minute. They told me the two of you *leapt* at it." Farber took a big pause and summoned some diplomacy. "I think we didn't get all the directions clear yesterday. You've already started in on work for me— You want to talk to your commander?"

Greer and Potocki watched as Farber pressed a couple of buttons on his phone. "Hey. Farber here. How you doing? Yeah, I know you started it. Can you talk? Okay. Here's the thing. I want your two people on my team, not jumping at other cases, but— Yeah, yeah, yeah, but I happen to have the chief by the balls on this one."

Colleen laughed inadvertently.

Farber gave her a dirty look. "Well, I have clearance," he said into the phone. "Because this is going to be big and juicy, and it'll put us all in good graces."

And you'll be famous, Colleen said to herself. Franklin Farber, defender of the city.

On the way out, she gave a polite wave to Hrznak and Nellins, who were on the way in.

HRZNAK AND NELLINS WEREN'T

fast moving. They had reached retirement age without eating any farms;

for reasons, possibly financial, they were content to bumble around for a while longer. Together, they and the patrol cops cordoned off the house and yard and waited for the lab to come over and get pictures, footprints, the usual. "This sure didn't just happen," said Hrznak, the more talkative of the two. "Advanced stink."

"He doesn't look like much," Nellins said, inclining his head toward the body.

"Somebody was eating up here."

"Him, probably." Nellins, getting whimsical in old age, imagined a loaded submarine sandwich from Peppi's.

"Him or whoever killed him. The crumbs don't seem all that dry."

Whimsy was about all they could do to make the case appealing. Murders that happened in dirty, out-of-the-way places with victims that looked hapless—this one was hairy and ugly—didn't interest Nellins and Hrznak.

There was no ID in the man's pockets, but they did find some cash, about sixty-five dollars. They put that in a plastic ziplock.

They jotted a few notes out of sheer duty while the lab took samples of this and that. They murmured jokes about their commander getting a hospital vacation in clean white sheets while they stepped through muck.

They went outside for air and, after a few minutes, ordered food from Lindo's and sent a patrol cop to get it. Hrznak took sixty of the dollars out of the bag and counted out thirty for Nellins, pocketed thirty for himself. "Buy lunch today and tomorrow." There had to be some luck in this job. Some.

LATE THAT SUNDAY MORNING,
when Peter MacKensie finally woke up, he tried to remember again if he and Zero had left anything up at their hideout that could get them in trouble. Fingerprints, maybe. But the police could never find them just like that, right? He needed to talk to Sean Zero again. That meant either a phone call to Zero with his father hanging over

him or else getting dressed and going over to Sean's place. He got dressed.

If the man with the gun remembered him, would he come after him? Maybe the guy was dead by now. One way or another, the house was off-limits. He'd liked that old place because he'd found it, because it was his. It made him angry that he had to give it up.

He shuffled into the kitchen where he poured a bowl of cereal and sat down to eat it. While he ate, he watched his father in the living room doing what he did best: watching TV and smoking. When his father went to the cabinet where he kept his cartons of cigarettes, Mac knew the explosion was coming. He started running some water in the sink.

"Get over here, you little fuck."

"I'm doing dishes."

"How many packs you steal? Two, three? Three. What the hell good are you, huh? Get in here."

"I'm doing dishes."

So his father came into the kitchen and hit him on the side of the head with the half-filled carton. It didn't hurt. He didn't mind it. He summoned his good spirits, his cutting-up spirits. He said, "My head is hard as yours. But my dick is harder." He scrambled and scampered upstairs, locked his bedroom door, listening for footsteps. He was good at the sounds of the house. Wait long enough and he could run. He shoved his portable CD player onto the floor. He wanted modern things, not this old shit he was using.

When he heard his father go to the can, he opened his door and flew down the stairs and out of the house to Sean Zero's place.

Zero was up. He had a guilty look on his face, Mac saw that right away.

"Let's go out," Mac said.

Zero said, "Um. All right. Where we going?"

Mac said, "See if we can find Carl."

They walked for a while, up toward Federal, and Zero said haltingly, "Don't get mad, but I called, um, you know, 911."

Anger flashed in Mac. "Why the hell would you do that?"

"That guy was hurt up there. He was calling for help. See, I kind of told my mother. Not everything. Just that we used to play up some place, that's how I put it, and I thought maybe there was a guy hurt, but I didn't want to get involved. She said the only thing to do was call. She was pretty upset, asking me questions, but I didn't say anything else, honest. She handed me the phone, but don't worry, I told her we don't want the police coming around the house, and she agreed with that. So, I went to a pay phone. Called from there."

"When?"

"This morning."

"Shit. We're the first people they're going to look at. That was really stupid, asshole."

"Why are they going to look at us?"

"I don't know. If they find us, I'm going to kill you."

"What were we supposed to do?"

"Nothing. That's what. Nothing. Let the people up there work it out for themselves. I want to find Carl, get our subcontract going. Only, what if he did it? He knows we go up there. What if he was the one?"

"Carl?"

"Yeah, Carl."

Zero kicked a few fences, frowning.

Mac hit Zero on the side of the head. "Think," he said. "Think. I don't want to tell you how bad you fucked up." He lit a cigarette and sucked in smoke. God, it felt good. Smoke in his lungs gave him courage. How could it be bad for you when it felt so damned good?

"Give me one."

He handed the pack over, saying, "Don't know why I should."

After a while, Zero asked, "You have anything good on you?"

"Two bags. If you weren't a fucking idiot . . ."

"We got to find someplace to do it."

"Yeah."

They've heard all the hullabaloo about heroin grabbing you until it didn't even feel good anymore. But some people manage it, some people use it like cigarettes.

HEADQUARTERS IS PRACTICALLY

empty. Tomorrow, Memorial Day, basically the whole force is taking the day off. For most divisions, the holiday has already begun. Almost nobody *except* Farber and some of his men have shown.

Farber, gritting his teeth, says, "Potocki, try to get a home address on the guy who used to work the pizza shop. Greer, we can have you call him or call on him at home. Work on building that relationship. Plus keep after any other computer searches Potocki is in the middle of."

Farber goes back to his office. Greer is about to tell Potocki she might as well go roaming, searching for Carl, searching for Nick, when she is interrupted by Potocki's radio reporting another 911 call has come in, this one much more specific. "A kid again calling about the disturbance on McCandor," the dispatcher says. "This time he gives the address. Says it's 826. *This time* the caller says there's a dead man on the second floor."

Colleen calls back the dispatcher. "Same kid?"

"Can't tell."

"You have the phone number this one was called in from?"

"Pay phone on Arch Street. That's all we have."

"Where did the first call come from?"

"Pay phone over on Cedar near the hospital."

"I have to hear those tapes, both of them. I'm coming over." Without a word to Farber, and only a small punch on the shoulder to Potocki, she's out of the office. Problem. They will need an hour or two to get the tape pulled, and it will take her only fifteen minutes to drive to the call center on Lexington Avenue. But she's out of the office. She can do what they call the "slow drive." How to explain to Farber why she's following up the 911 call is another problem.

Because she wants to.

She could look for Carl and for Nick in the meantime, two of her assignments.

She's not very obedient. Her car isn't either. With a mind of its own, it detours and drives right up to McCandor. As she parks, she scans the street for kids who might have made that call, but sees none watching. The scene is casual enough. Hrznak and Nellins are out front eating—not that she can cast stones about eating on the job. She breezes past the two old guys and inside to where the Forensics team is working. Because of the holiday, it's two of the youngest and least experienced workers, easier to intimidate. "I need lots of scrapings. Everything you see here. And I need to borrow your kit. I want to do a presumptive test for heroin. I'm virtually certain there are drugs on this one."

"We're scraping. Planning to. There's a trace of powder in the corner, there."

"Well, let me do the presumptive myself."

"So that Hrznak guy isn't in charge?"

"It's okay. I'm working the case, too, from the Narcotics angle."

"Oh."

Battery-operated lights have been set up, so the scene is now easier to see.

"The footwear is interesting," says one of the men, pointing. "Various people were up here and the shoes are not all adult size. Most aren't."

"Interesting," she says, her mind going to the phone calls she intends to trace. All the while she's gathering residue from the floor, she moves carefully so as not to disturb those child-size shoe prints.

As she's stooping, scraping up the little bit of powder—could be, could be heroin—she watches the workers. With their inexperience and the boredom projected by Nellins and Hrznak, something could easily fall through the cracks. "This *is* a Narcotics case," she tells old Farber in her mind.

She thinks. The dead man got it right in the heart. Would have been quick. So what are all the other blood smears, the one close to the wall? The bits on the stairs?

"I suppose Hrznak told you to be careful to keep the blood from different areas distinct, right? It's going to be interesting to see how many people bled in this place. I'd say more than one person was hurt up here."

One of the young guys grunts, says, "I thought so. I've been keeping it separate."

"Good going."

The other has handed over his kit for the presumptive test.

Colleen sends up a small prayer, uses the dropper to add solution to the powder she's gathered, closes her eyes, opens them again.

Good. Good. Almost certainly heroin. Let the lab people go at it. She can tell Farber . . . What will she say about why she was back here? Someone on the street said it was a drug house, so she's following up. That's it. Some kid, she'll say. Some kid who said it to her and ran. Too bad, but she has no name for him.

Downstairs she tells the two old fellows, while she looks enviously at their egg-and-bacon wraps, "I'm working Narcotics now, and this one is related. I'll be checking with you on everything. We need to coordinate. I'll be very eager to hear what you get on the evidence. Shoe prints, fingerprints. Dead man's got ten good fingers, so we ought to know who he is soon."

They look up, dazed.

"Unless he's homeless," Nellins says.

"What was in his pocket?"

Hrznak swallows a bite of his breakfast. "A key. Five bucks. A snot rag."

"Why did whoever killed him not take his money?"

Hrznak shrugs. "In a hurry?"

She leaves the two old detectives and drives over to Lexington, where she listens five times to the tapes. The second is definitely a different kid. Smarter than the first. More responsible and more specific.

There is no way Christie will want to leave the case to the tired old grandpops who just want to take it slow.

TWENTY-FOUR

MEG AND JOEL LIFT HIM UP,
not an easy task since they are smaller than he; he has to bend his left
knee and keep his right leg extended; Laurie fits the crutches in under
his arms; slowly he adjusts to an upright position.

"How did you find . . . where did you get these?"

"Salvation Army shelter. They're used—I mean left behind by someone. I said my sister needed them for a school project, and some woman
went and got them from a back room," Joel explains. "Okay. Does your
leg feel any worse upright?"

"It hurts either way."

"But not worse?"

"No."

He moves a little, a few steps, but then he stops, wavering. When
he wobbles, he curses.

"We might be moving too fast," Joel says. "You could just wait a day
to use these."

He doesn't have a fever this morning, but he is weak, panting after only a few steps. They all look at each other, wondering how to calm him.

"I want to go upstairs," he says.

"You can't," says Joel testily. "I don't think anybody could the first couple of days—well, maybe an athlete."

"Here," says Meg. "Sit down. Use the couch. Keep your leg straight." She and Laurie support him as he lowers himself to the couch. "There."

He lets the crutches drop next to him, propped against the sofa. His face is a mask of defeat. "What am I going to do? I can't move."

"Not yet. Little by little." Meg motions to Laurie to take Susannah into the kitchen. The two of them are reluctant to go; they look at him the whole way out. He's drinking them in, too.

"If you want us to make a bedpan, we will." He snaps to attention. "I'm not a squeamish type," Meg says.

Joel sounds firm, but not particularly friendly when he says, "If you decide you want to go upstairs, we need to get you on your butt and you need to use your hands, and one of us has to be around to support your leg. There is no other way."

He closes his eyes, opens them again. "You think I can get up the steps on my butt?"

"Yes," Joel says simply. "With help."

They get him standing again and to the stairway where he lowers himself to sit, landing on the third step. Joel has two hands under the splinted leg. "It's going to take hand and arm strength. If you don't feel up to it, say so. You're probably going to knock yourself out in one trip, because—"

But Nick has begun to hoist himself up, crawling backwards like a crab, Joel crawling forward attached to the crab. Meg follows with the crutches. She senses behind her the other two have drifted back to the bottom of the steps to watch.

When Nick gets to the landing, Meg climbs up and over him in order to get him standing again and positioned with the crutches. He looks like a fallen bandit, like a collapsed rock star—whisker growth, tousled hair. Meg says, "I'm going to put out a towel and soap and a razor. I know that's probably the last thing you care about right now, but when you're ready, you'll have them."

Laurie and Susannah creep up the stairs, not wanting to miss anything.

The four of them stand crowded in the hallway, listening, while in the bathroom Nick pees for what seems like years.

"Kidneys are working," Joel says.

They manage to stifle a laugh.

Laurie suggests they read for a while before the Sunday house-cleaning in order to let Nick sleep.

Joel agrees. "He needs to sleep."

"So long as we clean," Meg says.

"And have TV time," Susannah adds.

"He better stay upstairs, huh?" Laurie asks.

"Definitely," Joel says.

"Are you giving him Alison's bed?"

"Yes." Meaning Meg is giving up the space she enjoyed the last three nights. Space—and she was able to keep the light on into the night. "Back to the bunk bed," she says, equal with them once more.

The bathroom door opens.

"In here." She points Nick toward the bedroom. "In here you can really rest."

It takes him a long time to get from the bathroom to the hallway and then to position himself at the bed, and finally to figure out how to pivot so he can lie down. The kids lift his leg up slowly while he tries to help. The effort clearly exhausts him.

Joel is frowning. "There are ways to do this. I'll work them out. A strap would help. And . . . I think there's a way to use the left leg to lift the right." He scratches his head, an engineer working out the mechanics, while Nick looks even more defeated.

Meg lets Laurie put the crutches in the bed where Nick can get to them, but she tells Nick to call if he needs to get up. "Don't try to do it alone yet." She turns to Joel. "Right?"

"Right."

Susannah, without being told anything, has brought him a glass of water from the bathroom.

"Not likely," he says, looking at it, bleary eyed.

Joel says, "You have to."

Meg adds softly, "Water is the best thing. Can you sleep, do you think?"

He grunts, nods. Outside a thunderstorm threatens. At first it's just wind, but the clouds come in darker and darker. He is looking toward the window, where the shades are drawn.

They all four retreat and go downstairs.

In the next moments, they can hear him sobbing. For three hours after that it's quiet because he's sleeping again.

They do everything they are supposed to do, the lunch, the homework, all the while waiting for some sound from Nick. They dust, sweep, clean in a quiet hush of concentration but stop short of using the vacuum. Finally it's time to turn on the television, and Meg is heading toward it when Joel speaks.

"I didn't tell you one thing," Joel says. "We're supposed to clean the wound and dress it—two or three times a day."

"Two or three *times*? Why didn't you say?"

"I'm trying to figure out how to do it. We don't have enough gauze. We need clean bandages, something sterile to wrap around the whole wound. Where do we get the money for all that? And we'd have to take off the splint to do it. Put it back on."

The others listen intently.

"I didn't know," Meg said. "It makes sense now that you say. Of course. If we have to, we have to. We can take the splint off, put it back on."

"It's the best guard against infection."

"We should have done it this morning, then."

"Yeah."

"Tell me what kind of bandages?"

He makes a circling motion with his hands. "Ideally they circle the leg. They're wrapped around. Well, that's what I was reading. Do we have any safety pins? The bandages are supposed to be clean each time. You dip them in clean water. It's good to keep them on tight. You can use an Ace bandage for keeping them on."

"We have to buy gauze, I guess," Meg says worriedly. "We have an Ace. It was Dad's, remember? It's in that drawer in the bathroom."

Laurie still has nine dollars from babysitting all Saturday afternoon. They have enough gauze and mailing tape to get them through until tomorrow. "We have to ask him for money," she says.

"We have to," Meg agrees. "But he might not have an easy time getting it. There was just cash in his wallet, no bank cards. And we used all the cash."

"I know what," Laurie says. "We have bleach. If we took an old T-shirt and washed it in bleach . . . and then boiled it and then cooled it, would that work?"

Joel nods. "That wouldn't be bad at all."

"Maybe," Meg says, "when he's not so scared, he'll . . . want to go to the hospital after all." Although she doesn't say it—none of them do—if he does the right thing, they're in trouble.

Laurie goes to the basement to make the bandages. At four in the afternoon, they hear a thumping sound. He's trying to get up. "Damn," Joel mutters. Meg flies up the steps, Joel behind her. They catch him from behind, support him without a word, get him into the bathroom, and retreat to wait in the hall.

They hear a gruff, "Okay now," and they help him back to the bedroom.

The bandages are boiling on the stove. They have to wait until the water cools, then all four of them tromp up to the bedroom. He looks at them with dazed eyes as they explain what they will have to do—three times a day—the undoing, the irrigating, the fresh bandaging.

"Who are you?" he asks. And of course he means *what are you?* Spirits, demons, dream figures, odd little creatures who don't fit in the world.

HE CAN'T BELIEVE THEIR existence. He woke up thinking he dreamed them. He needs to know things. What they have in mind, when he'll be able to get out, whether they're likely to rat on him.

When they gather around his leg, he says, "If you want money, I'm afraid I'm going to be a big disappointment to you. You got what was in my wallet."

"That isn't it," the oldest girl answers.

The boy jumps in with, "Why should we lie about it?"

"We *need* money," she says, turning to her brother. "Okay, that's the truth, but he's asking why you took him food to begin with. He wants to know why."

The boy says angrily, "I don't know why."

They start to do things to him once more. They put plastic on the bed and move his leg over it. The littlest girl has carried up a pot of water and she stands in the corner guarding it. The middle girl holds a bucket of rags.

What kind of thing has he fallen into?

"Are you hungry?" the oldest one asks.

"A little."

"That's a good sign. Lie back. Concentrate on something else. We have to irrigate the wound again. Really, lie back."

He starts to look around. A plain room, a bureau. A chair.

"Where did you get the Styrofoam?"

The boy tells him, "Rite Aid. The Dumpster. In a box that held an industrial vacuum cleaner. We were lucky. We tried the Giant Eagle and the liquor store, and we thought we weren't going to find anything, and then we did."

"So, after you do this whatever, I'm good to go?" There is a long silence. "When? What are you saying?"

"It's just that we need to do this a couple of times a day. Either us or a hospital. It's very important."

He lies there looking at the ceiling, trying to work it out. If he limps through the street, will one of Marko's men find him? If he stays here, is he actually safer? His car is gone, so that means someone is staking out his apartment. That means his cash is gone, too. Almost certainly. "What do you need money for?"

"Food, more bandages, pills."

"What pills?"

"Antibiotics. We have almost enough, not quite. We should refill again."

"How much does all that cost?"

The older girl is helping her brother uncover the leg. "The newspaper's going to get wet," she murmurs. She begins to take bits of it out, warning him, "Whatever you do, don't move."

"How much?"

"Say about twenty-one or twenty-two dollars for supplies. Then food."

"And you have how much?"

"Nine at the moment. We're okay for today."

"The parents or whoever get back when?"

"Don't know. We'll think of something. But if you had a bank card, well, that would make it easier."

"I'm sorry. I was living without cards," he tells them. He sees the unmistakable flicker of suspicion cross their faces.

The boy pours water on the wound; the middle girl mops it up. "If it stings some," the boy explains, "it's because I put a little salt in. Saline is good in a case like this."

He almost laughs. These kids are so odd, he wonders how they make it in the world.

"Well, you say I can't move. I had some cash at my place, but . . . it'd be gone now. And people watching. I still have a key to the pizza shop."

"It's got a sign posted that it's closed for a couple of days."

Nick thinks about it, the likeliness that one of them could get in and out without being seen.

There is a still silence in the room.

If Marko sees one of them and follows . . . "Maybe you better nix that idea," he says into the silence.

"Earlier today," the older girl says, "we thought about it and we decided against it."

"It's stealing," the middle girl says. "We don't intend to do that if we can help it."

"What are you going to do for food?"

"We have jobs. Little ones. We're going to look for more."

When they leave the room, he looks around again. His breath comes quickly, in little panicked bursts, when he realizes how hard it is for him to think clearly. Who lives in this room? There is almost nothing in here. And only one other room upstairs from what he can see when he hobbles to the bathroom. He wonders how long they've been alone. He tries to remember the downstairs—couch, chair, table and chairs. Bookcase, lots of books. Otherwise, it's a sort of bare house down there, too. It runs in his mind that poverty usually equals clutter, but even though this is the other way, not cluttered, even clean, he can see poverty.

The kids don't act as if they owe obedience to anyone. What a wild place he's landed in. He tries to get his brain to cough up a solution to the money problem, but everything he thinks of is impossible or dangerous.

The middle girl brings him a book and turns on the lamp. He thanks her, but he doesn't look at it. He isn't a reader. He doesn't have time to tell her because she leaves again, busy.

Strange. Strange. Better than jail, but not unlike it. A bit more space, a bit.

The middle girl returns eventually with a bowl of pasta. "Kind of boring, but it might go down okay."

He eats a little and feels himself moving toward sleep again. At six he wakes to a sound like cannonballs. He goes still, listening. Thunder and rain. The kids are all downstairs. He can hear them in the kitchen.

After a while the boy comes up. "It's a storm out there." He goes to the window and pulls up the shade to show how bad the rain is. Yeah, it looks bad, all right. Nick tries to figure out where he is exactly. "Is the pizza shop near?" he asks the boy.

The boy points. "Just across the street at the corner."

In the boy's open hand are two pills that look alike and one different one.

"What is all that?"

"Antibiotics and pain pill."

He takes them down with a glass of water. Trust. What choice does he have?

The boy starts out of the room.

"Come here."

He comes back a few steps.

"You know two boys, one bleached hair, wears a black jacket and the other dark hair wears a—?"

"Yeah. Mac and Zero."

"That's who you were looking for up at the house?"

"Yeah."

"What do they do up there?"

"They shoot up."

"They know I'm here?"

"No. Nobody does. Except us."

"They know you found me?"

"No."

"You sure?"

"Yeah."

"'Cause if they did, it would mean . . . there could be a couple of guys come around asking questions, looking for me. It could get violent. If they ask—"

"I won't talk."

"Okay. You understand what I'm up against."

"Yeah. Killers. Drug people. Killers."

Panic hits him again; his whole body feels like electric wires connect one part to the next. He wants to leave here, run, but where?

"Tomorrow's a holiday, so we'll be here at home. After that we have school. Tomorrow it would be good to practice with the crutches while we're here to help. Don't try to make it down the steps. You won't be ready yet. When you get bored, you're going to want to, and that'll be tough."

"Sure will."

"We only have one television. We don't have cable. We were thinking of bringing it up, but it doesn't do too well in here. Still we could. If you want it—"

"It's okay."

"Better to sleep anyway."

He lets himself fall asleep again. When he wakes up, he has no sense of what time it is. He tries to listen for sounds. A faucet running, the television.

He makes it to the bathroom alone, defiant. They hear and come up to watch him making his way back to the bed, but they don't stop him. The crutches kill his underarms, but he's not going to say it.

He uses a belt the girl brought in to lift his own leg up.

They watch.

Then all four kids arrive again with the water and bandages and start on his leg all over again.

TWENTY-FIVE

IT'S THE MIDDLE OF THE
night and Meg wakes. She sits up in bed, listening.

He's trying to get out of bed. As she slips from her own bed, she realizes she should have put her mattress on the floor in his room, slept there, kept watch. She tiptoes to the hall, getting there just in time to catch him faltering, one crutch slipping. She holds on to him, steadies him. "It's okay," she whispers. "You all right?"

"Yeah. Foggy. Something woke me up."

She takes him the whole way into the bathroom and backs off to leave him alone, but she keeps the door open a crack. "Call me when you're done. This is too hard."

"I did it before."

"It's night and you're on pain pills. It'll get better."

Meg settles herself on the top step, working out how, eventually, in a day or two, Nick can get to the downstairs if they support his leg for him. She practices the moves as if it's her leg that's hurt. A person would go nuts staying upstairs all the time.

She listens to the sounds in the bathroom—the movement of the crutches, urine meeting water, sink water running. In the dim light, she spies a blanket that has fallen in the doorway of his room.

Maybe that's what made him slip. He tried to put it around him and it fell. She has to find him something to wear.

"I'm . . . I'm ready," he says in a low voice.

She opens the door and guides him back to bed. Quietly, without speaking, she helps him pivot, get his leg up, and settle back. She covers him with sheet and blanket.

"How long can this go on?" he asks. "Me staying here?"

She shrugs. She puts the small lamp on beside the bed. She looks behind her to the chair in the room. Does he want to talk? She does.

"I'm trying to learn to walk. I'm trying to get out of your hair."

"That would be foolish. You're too weak."

"But . . . what's going to happen when somebody finds that body?"

"They did. Find it. It was on the news. We . . . we couldn't let him rot up there. I mean, we couldn't just let it go."

"You called it in?"

"Yes. Joel did."

"Oh, my God. I'll be found."

"He called from a pay phone. He made sure nobody was watching. We had to do something. Kids use that place. Somebody would have found him eventually."

"The police are on it, then?"

"It was on the news. We were afraid to tell you before you were going to sleep. It was on TV and radio. We checked."

"So everyone who watched tonight knows. That's why I was awake. I sensed it." His face furrows. He struggles for a bit, hesitating, finally speaking. "There's someone I'm very afraid of."

Now she goes for the chair and brings it next to the bed. "I need to know how to help you. You told us you didn't do it, that it was—"

"I was fighting for my own life."

"Then, *why* are you running?"

"Because there is nobody in the world who's going to believe me."

"I want to. I guess it would help to have some facts."

"Why didn't you call the police on me to begin with?"

"We should have. But once we got to . . . trying, we didn't. Now here we are and I don't know what to do."

"Saved me for the slaughter, huh? You could call them now. Middle of the night. Anytime. Are you going to?"

She shakes her head. It's the first time he's seemed really mean. It's a disappointment and a kind of relief in a way, but she can't explain that.

"Why should I believe that?"

In the lamplight, his face is changing again. It keeps not being the same face. But one of his expressions is just right. She knows it and trusts it and waits for it. She's trying to make it happen when the truth comes rolling out. "Because we don't have anybody here, and once they know that about us, we'll have to leave."

He works over what she has said as if he needs to take it apart, put it back together. He grunts. "You have nobody?"

"We had my stepmother, but she's gone now. She told me to call someone for foster care, but we didn't want to."

Slowly he nods, still looking foggy. "Foster care, huh? I had that. I get not wanting to bring that on yourselves."

"You were in a foster home?"

"They put me with a family from when I was fourteen to eighteen. I hated it."

"Did you have brothers and sisters?"

"Nope, just me."

"Why did you have a foster home?"

"My grandma died. It was just her and me, so no choice. Where's your mother?"

"She died five years ago. She went kind of . . ." Meg touches her head. "After my little sister was born. She was very . . . reckless."

"Reckless. I don't understand."

"Violent. My father was worried. He thought she was going to hurt Susannah. Then she left."

"She on drugs?"

"No. Just . . ."

For a moment Nick's expression is right. His eyes soften. He begins to speak several times, seems to think better of it, and finally comes up with, "She never came back?"

"Never. My father blamed himself. Then we heard she committed suicide. In Canada." Nick listens to each little sentence and does not seem surprised or shocked. This story she can't tell anyone she's told to him just like that in the middle of the night and he seems to take it in as if it's ordinary. Suicide doesn't disturb him. Some people just *want to sleep*. That's what her father said.

"So you miss her?"

"Kind of. I miss the idea of her. I miss my father more."

"What, he took off?"

She feels the anger of a blush. "He would never. He loved us. I was very close to him. No."

"Something happened to him."

She nods. "Things were fine when he took care of us. It's just that he thought we needed a mother, and things got complicated."

"With the stepmother?"

"My father didn't choose too well."

Nick smiles, almost laughs. "Join the club. People never like their stepmothers."

"I know that."

"So he's not around?"

"No."

"When did the stepmother leave?"

"Last week. The day she didn't give me enough money for a pizza and you let us have it anyway."

Nick stares hard at her. "You're the opposite of a person who holds a grudge. You hold a—whatever the opposite is."

Opposite of a grudge. She can't think of a word for that. "I guess."

"That's not so long ago. She might be back."

The room is completely bare of any trace of Alison. "I don't think she's coming back."

"Gut feeling?"

"Yes."

"Hmm. Where'd she go?"

"She told me she didn't want me to know. I could tell it was to meet a guy."

"Stepmothers almost never work out."

"We tried hard for three years. She wasn't too happy having all of us to worry about. My father was working so many jobs. He was exhausted all the time and could hardly ever be home. She had expensive tastes."

Nick says, "It happens. It happens."

Expensive tastes? Exhaustion?

Meg used to sit with her father in the kitchen late at night and they would talk. He would drink and she would keep him company so he didn't fall when he went to bed. That was up at their other house, the one Alison sold as soon as her father died, to buy luggage and clothes and to pay off her credit card debts.

Her father was sorry he'd brought Alison into it. He said as much to Meg before he died. When they talked alone, he told her he was unhappy. She tried to make him see things weren't his fault.

"Do you want anything?"

"You have a beer?"

"No."

"Whiskey?"

"No, nothing like that."

"I didn't think so. I sure could use a whiskey."

"Tea. I could get you tea."

"Tea. Hmmf. Okay. Tea."

Meg goes down to the kitchen where she already knows there are exactly three tea bags. She brews his tea down there, saving the bag. If he likes tea not too strong, she can get six cups out of the three bags.

Conserving this way makes her feel good, wise, in control. A moment later, she sinks with despair that there is so little in the house. What is she going to do? She must trick one of the old women tomorrow, say she was supposed to clean on Monday. If Joel gets two car washes and if she can manage to clean one place . . .

She doesn't put milk or sugar in the tea because there isn't much of either and he didn't ask for any.

When she gets upstairs, his eyes are closed again. She tiptoes in, puts the cup down gently, and his eyes open. "Where's your father?"

She says it simply. "He died in a car wreck." She thought she could say it without crying, but she starts to cry because of the way Nick is looking at her, pitying her.

"You miss him big-time."

"He was the nicest, kindest man you could ever meet. To everyone."

After a while, Nick says, "I'm not kind. Or good. I'm a rotten person. That's the problem. I didn't kill that guy. I was trying to save another guy and myself. But look at my record and it's rotten and that'll talk louder than anything else. Nobody is going to believe me."

"I think I do."

"But you want facts?"

She's still crying, nodding like an idiot. He takes a sip of tea.

"What are we going to do, little one? Huh? You need food in the house and I have no money. I know you hoped I did. I'm wanted by the law and they are never going to believe the truth. I'm wanted by some people that . . . let me just say, if I go to jail, they'll get me out so they can kill me."

"Why?"

"That's how they are. I'm stupid. I make big mistakes. You want to believe I'm different, I can tell that much. You're a little nuts, if you'll excuse my expression."

"Maybe you're kinder than you think."

He shakes his head. "I can't even remember your name. Or the others'."

"Meg, Joel, Laurie, Susannah."

HE WATCHES AFTER HER AS
she leaves the room, crying. Good. Grow her up some. He's landed in
a nest of babies.

He tries to imagine the report on the news—what the girl was
keeping from him. In his mind's eye he sees Markovic in front of the
big TV in his fancy basement watching the news and going ballistic.
The guy he hired, Earl, is dead. His enforcer gone, his apprentice enforcer disappeared, and maybe his target gone. Markovic never took
well to losing his bets.

TWENTY-SIX

COLLEEN WOKE EARLY ON
the holiday, did laundry, read the papers, lingered over her coffee. She
worked it out that the half of her that Farber said could take the day
off would relax, and the other half that was Homicide would go in.
There was little she could accomplish with the labs closed and everybody in holiday shutdown, but it would feel like something.

Anyway, there wasn't a hamburger or a hot dog in her refrigerator
and she wasn't in much of a holiday mood.

She went in at nine instead of eight, feeling recklessly idle. Potocki
was already there, tapping away at the computer. "You, too," she said.

"My private mover for the furniture pieces isn't coming until three.
I figured I could do a little something."

"You stay at your old house last night?" Too personal. She was sorry
she asked as soon as she did.

But he answered. "No. Why?"

"Oh. Just more comfortable."

"Yeah, it would have been. But I didn't, partly because I told Judy I was going to leave and it seemed important to keep my word. Believe me, I couldn't tell you why. These things are crazy."

He kept working and she went to her desk to make notes, hearing the fluffing sound her shoes made on the carpeting as she walked the empty space. She would try harder to find that kid, Carl, again, who struck her as someone who might know lots more than the usual.

The silence was strange. Nobody had put on a pot of coffee. No phones were ringing. No voices. Every once in a while a crackle of paper. Tap of Potocki's computer keys. Very few people around. Nellins and Hrznak were the only ones with a really hot case, and where were they? Off buying hot dogs or something.

Outside the prison-bar windows, it was a gorgeous May day.

Ten o'clock, she figured, wasn't too early to call Christie, but his cell phone rang and went to voice mail.

Suddenly she felt nervous. She decided to call the hospital.

The first thing she heard made her gasp. "We don't have him on record."

"No, yes, he's in 1017."

"Just a moment."

Her heart thumped with terror.

The operator came back on. "He's been released."

"When?"

"It says today."

"On a holiday?"

"They get them out when they can."

Colleen called Christie's house, but there was no answer. Was he in transit? She rattled around with her questions and was just about to try them on Potocki when her phone rang.

"You called?"

"Hey, Boss, they told me you were released."

"Released to outpatient chemo. We're on the way home now."

"So this is good, right, getting out?"

"You bet. Who wouldn't want to go home? I talked them into it." His energy had suddenly flagged on the last line.

"Good, good. But they're keeping up with your treatments?"

"Unfortunately. No, seriously, they're giving me a lot of . . . special scheduling. I have to be grateful."

"I was just checking in. I was going to come up to the hospital."

"Give me a couple of hours to get settled. You can visit me at home."

"Really? You're up to it?"

"Make me work my brain a little."

"But how do you feel?"

He paused. "Oh, you know, the jokes about death being preferable."

"Is it nausea?"

"That and weakness. Hard to describe."

Weakness did not become him. That was like a line from something. What? "I'll be over later, then."

Had you told her ten years ago she would end up in this job, attached to a man who didn't read, didn't love her back, she would have told you it was impossible, she was smart, she was saner than that.

HE SAT IN A CHAIR WITH A

lap rug over his knees. He was wearing a sweater. It was almost eighty degrees out.

"Greer. Come on in, have a seat."

"Hey, there you are. Boy, everybody misses you. They want you to take care of yourself."

"Thanks."

"It's gorgeous out. Don't you want to sit outside?"

"The sun is too hard on my eyes. Plus I'd see everything I should be doing in the yard. This"—he points to a thermos—"is tea. It might still be warm. You want some?"

"Sure." She didn't, but it seemed only civil. "Let me pour."

"You're still working your overdose?"

"Yeah. Spent most of the afternoon in the park showing pictures of Carl, the kid who knew BZ. A nice alcoholic couple told me they used to see Carl using the library. That's all I got, all afternoon. How are you doing?"

He fussed with the lap rug. "I'm on something experimental. Marina kicked up a fuss and they switched me. I had my first new treatment today."

"I'm counting on your forty years at least. I hope for fifty, fifty-five. I'll hobble around with you, cleaning up the city."

He laughed. "How old are you?"

"Thirty-nine."

"You're a funny kid." She nodded and he changed the subject. "How is everyone treating you over in Narcotics?"

"I'm only half Narcotics," she grumbled. "Remember I was supposed to make friends with the guy who worked the Dona Ana? I blew it. The guy was going to meet me for a drink but he never showed. Now the pizza shop is closed."

"Closed? That says something, eh?"

"It's a puzzle. He was a *nice* guy on the surface. New in town, he said, and I sort of believed him."

"The guy ran?"

"Maybe."

"You checked him out?"

"Potocki is checking. The name he gave is Nick Banks. Whoever he is, I'm supposed to keep putting moves on him."

Christie looked worried. "Are you okay? You feel danger?"

"Danger? No. . . ."

"What?"

"I feel stupid. If you'd asked me, apart from the case, I would have said he was okay. A good guy."

"You can't always untangle from the charming ones. He was a charmer."

"Yeah. Was."

Christie sipped his tea. "Glad to see you're dating!"

"Come on. I'm in a real pickle here. The thing is, all I care about are the homicides. And the new one, the one Hrznak and Nellins got—Boss, Farber just took it away from me. I'm so angry—"

"You're worried Nellins and Hrznak can't handle it?"

She gave as small a nod as she could. "I mean, I started it. And then I get in there yesterday, and they don't even have the guy's prints classified yet. I would have had results yesterday. Tomorrow, they say. I have to wait till tomorrow because it's a holiday. And . . . it's still their case, not mine. But in my mind, it's mine." She looked at him challengingly.

"Take your assignment and swallow. You're going to be a big help to Narcotics."

Although she knew perfectly well he was very politic on most days, it made her angry to think of him as being a company man—old boys, don't rock the boat, all that.

"While you're doing what you have to do, you can get very buddy-buddy with Nellins," he was saying. "Hrznak won't be so easy but—"

She interrupted, "Hrznak is the primary."

"Hmm. Nellins will talk to you. If you keep pushing the Narcotics angle, you can get in if you're clever."

"Yeah, that's what I've been doing." She added, knowing how her boss felt about children, "There are kids roaming around in these houses with the more dangerous types, and we're supposed to keep hands off? Because Farber wants big fish?"

"People want to leave a name behind," he said, not without sympathy. "But you're my kind of police, for what it's worth."

"Thank you." Colleen looked around. His kids must be with their mother. "You're not alone here?"

"No, no. Marina is upstairs reading. She wanted to be sure we had time to talk. I could call her."

"No, I was just worried you'd need something and not have anybody here."

"Are you kidding? She took off work all week, even though I told her not to. She's quite a nurse. She's making some kind of soup tonight she thinks will cut the nausea. We'll see about that."

"You have to eat."

"That's what she says. Anyway, it's just sick food here tonight or I'd invite you."

Did she sound as if she was begging for dinner? To erase that impression, she asked, "How are your kids doing?"

"Well, we talked to them about everything so they wouldn't get that feeling that there were secrets being kept. We let them know the scoop, let them ask questions. I hope that's the right way. How does a person know what to do?"

"You did right. You're going to get better."

"Am I?"

"Too many people are determined. There's power in thoughts."

"There are a few people who hate me. More than a few. Couple of them are in jail," he chuckled. "Probably cursing me."

"Visualization is supposed to be good. You should do it. First picture the bad cells swaggering, then the drug weakening good and bad both, then the bad ones looking surprised, like what's going on, and the good ones perking up and getting stronger."

"Like a cartoon."

"Right. So, I'll leave you with that and I'll get going. Thanks for the time."

"Hey, Greer, you take care."

When she got outside, she dialed up Potocki. "Just checking in," she said.

"Have I got some surprises for you."

"Really? They ran the prints after all?"

"No. They're saying they can't get a good technician until tomorrow. You coming in?"

"I could."

"You have other plans?"

"Not really. I could come into the office."

"Greer, you don't have to put in twenty-four hours. I was just—"

"I'll come in for the surprises. They better be good, though."

"Well, right now I'm starting for the old house to meet the movers.

I could use your company in two hours, say at the new place; I'd be grateful for it. And if you by any chance have time for dinner, we could order something or eat out. I don't have a grill yet, so I can't make a picnic."

She had a grill, but the thought of playing hostess was more than she had energy for. She got an inspiration. "You like fried chicken?"

"I love fried chicken. It's lethal in my family, but I love it anyway."

"I could bring over a picnic. Chicken, fixings, and I'll make a salad."

"That would be . . . great. Really, perfect."

"Okay, done. You going to make me wait for my news, then?"

"It's only two hours. Give you something to look forward to."

POTOCKI PRECEDED HIS NEWS

with a tour of the house, which now had a few bits of furniture in it. They walked around, drinking cold beers from bottles, and ended up back at the kitchen. "Nice. It's going to be nice. So, spit it out, Potocki. What do I finally get to know?"

"I cracked a couple of codes," he said, fetching a file folder from the kitchen counter and taking it into the living room.

She followed and sat on the sofa, the stiffness of which told her it was the classic studio bed that probably served for guest bed the first couple of years of the marriage.

He explained he had tried "Roy D. Mott." "Roy Mott." "Mott Roy." Then, finally, surprisingly, there it was. Dermott Roux. Detroit. Missing child. Picture of a young boy, hard to distinguish the features, but—he plunked down the picture and she stared long enough, and there he was, Dermott Roux.

The kid didn't like his name, she guessed. Messed around with an altered combination of vowels and consonants. Then took a street name, and that's how he'd disappeared. Dermott Roux. Short life.

"Family?"

"An aunt. I called. No answer."

Potocki plunked down a second photo printed on a plain old

DeskJet. Colleen took up the piece of paper and looked at a younger Nick Banks.

"Nicholas Kissel," Potocki said. "He did time for killing a man."

She whistled. She wouldn't have guessed it. "He's not very old. So it wasn't murder one." Unless he'd escaped from somewhere, which would make her really wrong about him. "Manslaughter?"

"It went down as murder two, but some lawyer got him off."

"Sheesh."

"Must have had a hell of a time in prison. Even I like looking at him. What do we think?"

So Nick Kissel already tended toward big trouble. "Was it a drug killing that got the murder rap?"

"Gambling."

"Gambling. Sheesh."

Potocki smiled. " 'Sheesh.' Haven't heard that in a while."

"I know. Paucity of words tonight." She looked at the photo some more. "I'd better know everything I can about the prior conviction, who got him off, all that."

"There's more."

"Hit me."

"He broke parole. He's supposed to be in Philly."

"Yoy."

"You're really something with the language tonight."

She nodded, wondering why her brain was handing her expressions she didn't generally use. Finally she said, "Did you tell Farber any of this?"

"Are you kidding? Call him up when I don't have to? He must think he's going to be governor or something when he makes the bust."

"Delusions . . ."

"So we got names."

"We got names."

TWENTY-SEVEN

walked into the YMCA and took out his notebook. He'd be writing all day, that was for sure. His thick hand simply wasn't made for pencils and pens, had *never* worked right, even when he was young.

"If you could just get me the list," he called after the tall woman who was too busy to pay attention to him and was walking into an adjoining room as if on a more important matter.

Nellins had once had violent impulses, but he'd learned to curb them. He sucked in two deep breaths and walked outside. He kicked at some butts on the ground, considered this might be a good time to take up smoking again.

His phone rang, and it was the new babe on Homicide telling him she'd been trying to catch up with him. "Fingerprints, shoe prints," she was saying.

"Yeah, well, Hrznak is on it. You'll know when we know."

"There were *kids* up at that house."

"I know, I know." He laughed to himself. "Kee-ripe," he had said to
Hrznak, "the wee ones did it." But he knew not to say that to Detective
Greer, who had no sense of humor.

The tigress receptionist came out the front door for him. "I'm ready
now," she said.

Who's in charge? he wondered. It ain't me.

NICK FEELS THE PANIC RISING

again. What he needs more than anything is a drink.

"When you get that panicky feeling, use the pain pills, even the
Aleve will help you sleep," she said.

He fumbles for the water and takes two Aleve. Then two more.
With great effort he persuades himself to lie still, for once in his life do
nothing reckless.

His first day alone. The television, now on the bedroom dresser, is
on, low. On the table beside him is a sandwich, a glass of water, a book,
an empty glass jar in case he doesn't think he can make it to the
bathroom—she said not to try when nobody is home. A shallow metal
bowl in case he needs a bedpan. Paper towels to cover it. It's disgusting.
And amazing. He could never have thought of all this, could he?

The flesh above the splint looks good, so he tries not to have doubts.
They came in again and changed his dressings this morning before
school. A little team of doctors. They confound him; he ends up thinking about them when they're not in the room. The boy looked straight
at him like a doctor and said he might limp if he didn't get the leg set
with surgical nails; he said he wanted to make that clear straight off.
Joel.

And Meg. Meg is her name.

Laurie. Susannah.

On the television, some good-looking women wearing little suits
sit in comfortable chairs talking about some book or other. How stiffly
they move their heads. How tightly they squeeze their knees together.
Being in front of the camera, what a horrible way to live.

He picks up the book that sits on the bedside table. Tilting the book under the light of the lamp, he attempts the first three pages. It's dark because even though it's daytime, the window shades are drawn—safer, the kids said. The window, however, is open and he can hear an occasional car, a voice, a dog barking. He reads the first three pages a second time. Nothing penetrates to his brain. He starts again and by page three he is asleep.

JOEL READS AHEAD TO THE

next chapter in world studies. Everybody hates this class, so all the kids are doing something or other, reading magazines, trading gum.

He has a secret. Yesterday he took Nick's key and walked past his apartment. There was food, money, clothing inside, Nick had admitted to him, but also told him it wasn't worth it, not safe. He had to try. His sisters were the wage earners and he wanted to do his part. But he studied the street the whole time he walked. He noticed a man in a car, just sitting, head back, radio playing. He kept walking, went around the block, and didn't come back until two hours later. The man was still there. Then he knew he couldn't go inside. He slipped the key back among Nick's things and didn't tell anybody, not even Meg.

LAURIE SITS IN HER CLASSROOM

looking out the window, again, looking for the mother who plays with her baby in the park.

Mothers. She doesn't know much about them. She sees only other kids' mothers. And substitutes like Alison. Her *teacher* is a mother. Ms. Hines. She always talks about her baby to the class. "My little Carson just loves the color blue," she'll say. Things like that. Carson Hines. It isn't a name Laurie would have chosen.

Meg got cleaning work yesterday, even though it was a holiday. She made ten dollars. So they had hot dogs cooked in a frying pan, and after school today Meg has cleaning again, and Laurie has babysitting.

So, all is well. What Laurie doesn't understand is why Nick doesn't manage to find some money somewhere, somehow. He ought to pay his way. Meg is too much of a softie.

Outside the window, she can see the school guards standing, watching the park workers drive their tractors over the lawn. People are awful, dropping all kinds of dirt on the park lawn, like it's one big garbage can.

She tries to drag herself back to her workbook to look ahead to the next lesson. Other kids smile at her when they look up. She is popular. Popular is good. Clean, good. Polite, good. Polite she doesn't always manage.

"Everybody done with your workbook?"

Noooo, they all cry out.

The teacher goes back to the book she is reading. Laurie, who is finished with her workbook, studies the scene out the window.

SUSANNAH CAN STILL FEEL HIS

hand on her hair. He touched her hair last night a little bit when she brought him water. First he said, "Come here. Just a minute. You're Susannah, right?"

She said yes.

He said, "Thank you for bringing me things."

She said, "You're welcome."

He said, "I hope to do better by you."

She wasn't sure what that meant. So she didn't answer him, just smiled. When she has time later, she is going to draw him, the way he looked when he leaned forward and wasn't angry or sleepy, just looking at her as if he wanted to know her.

"I can't move around much now," he said. "But I know how to cook. I'm a good cook."

She wasn't sure why he told her that, about cooking. She's not supposed to talk to anyone about him, ever. Meg whispered it ten times last night. She hasn't told her friends or her teacher.

Was he trying to say, when he smiled and leaned forward to touch her hair, that he wanted to live with them and cook and do some of the cleaning?

MEG STUDIES THE SHELVES IN
the library, looking for something good to read next. Hardy? The teacher thinks she will like Hardy. She chooses *The Mayor of Casterbridge*.

"What kind of a thing do you want to read?" she asked Nick yesterday. If *she* had to stay in bed, she would read the whole time.

He said, "I don't read. I'm not much of a reader."

"I do. All the time."

He seemed to find that interesting, repeating, "All the time, huh?" She had lent him her copy of *A Tale of Two Cities*.

"You study this in school?"

"Special project."

"You're smart, huh," he said, "knowing all kinds of things."

"We do well in school," she said. "All of us do."

He smiled and shook his head. "You know anything about Belize?"

"A little."

"You do?"

"I guess. Like what?"

"More like, how do I get there?"

A stab of feeling, like butterflies, hit her. People taking leave, departing—always hit her that way.

Now she sits down and begins to read the Hardy, noting the time. Lunch hour is coming soon. She will eat fast and run home to check on him and help him to the bathroom.

NELLINS IS STANDING OUTSIDE
the Y at noon, watching the street, when Hrznak calls and says, "Want to meet for lunch? Heard the pizza shop is good."

"I'm ready to take a load off."

But when they get to the pizza shop, it turns out there is no place to sit. Behind the counter, a man is training a woman to do the work. The man training the woman is thirty or so, lean and impatient. The woman is a bit older and harried-looking, lots of eye makeup and super-clean clothes and shoes. Hrznak and Nellins put in their orders and stand outside for a while.

"That Greer called me about the shoe prints up at the house being kids' shoes."

"Tell her I've been shot at by little kids."

Nellins knows that. Hrznak often tells that story.

When their food is ready, they take it down a block to the park, where they find a bench and sit. People tend to feed the ducks, and so there is duck shit all over the sidewalk.

"Bird flu," Hrznak says.

"I know. But there's going to be a vaccine."

"But who gets it first?"

"Police probably get first dibs."

"You think?"

A kid runs past them, a girl. Nellins watches her hurry up the street he's been working. "Hooky," he says.

Hrznak grunts.

Halfway through his calzone, though, the girl goes racing back the other way. "Maybe not playing hooky," he says.

"Forgot something."

"Probably."

MEG HAD COME HOME FOR A
few minutes to help him, but she was gone again. Now he looked at the glass jar beside the bed. No, he thought. He had to learn to do it alone.

Meg had put out a towel and razor and shampoo in the bathroom. If he cleaned up, he could do some of it sitting, some of it standing. He slowly, carefully, lifted his right leg out of bed using the strap, pivoted, and took up the crutches. He was up. Good, he congratulated himself. Then he thumped awkwardly down the hall to the bathroom. Stared at himself in the bathroom mirror. Sickly looking, he thought, but alive. In the medicine cabinet, he found a half-full bottle of cough syrup, two ounces of mouthwash. He took a swig of cough syrup, then finished the bottle. He sat on the closed toilet seat for a few minutes, catching his breath, letting the alcohol catch up with him.

Then he got up and moved around the small spaces upstairs, spying. Only one other room. That's what he'd thought. Small place. In the kids' room, he saw two bunk beds, all of the mattresses made up, two matching spreads, two not. One radio, one alarm clock, one bureau with six drawers. Picture of a man on the bureau top. Must be the father. Didn't look like he was ready to kick it over yet, but he had.

Nick opened the drawers to find T-shirts, polo shirts, underwear. But it wasn't much for four kids. Ditto the closet, the shallow sort, with a couple of hooks. All told, it didn't amount to much. Jeans, jumpers, shoes.

He realized he'd been standing and moving on crutches for five minutes. Good, good.

Nick limped back to the bedroom he was using. The closet was bare. Funny. One bureau. He opened the top bureau drawer and found more photos. Mostly of the kids, a few framed. Nick studied the photos, figuring out the sequence—the stepmother and backwards to the mother, before Susannah, with three children at that point, one of them a baby.

Interesting. The new wife didn't look that different from the old wife. If he had to bet on crazy, he would have thought number two had eyes that gave away an unstable personality. But you never could tell. Or he never could.

The kids in one picture after another—what was it he was looking for? Something that helped him understand them.

These kids went to school. They *liked* school. One time when he was a little kid, he'd run out the door of his school and hid under a bush.

He rested, using the bureau for support. Where would important papers be kept? With enormous effort, he leaned down to open the lower drawers. Empty. Nothing.

And where had the girl hid Earl's gun? She said he couldn't have it back. She said it was evidence and it might free him. She was a brainy one, but she didn't have street smarts. He tried to put the photos back the way he'd found them. Nick let himself drift into the idea that had been scratching at him for a day—he had to find out what the father's name was.

Suddenly he heard a big knocking at the door. Somebody must have been using the heel of the fist and pounding, pounding. He couldn't see out the window, was afraid to get too close to it, and went dizzy thinking it might be Marko.

The bathroom struck him as the best place to hide. He started toward it, shaking. One of the crutches almost slipped from his grip because he had the shakes so bad. He held on, frozen.

"Anybody home?" The knocking repeated. Nick's heart pounded so hard, he almost couldn't hear. He stood in the upstairs hallway, unable to move. His good leg went weak on him. He thought he was going to fall before he could figure out how to grab for a wall and then the bathroom door. Suddenly, he heard a repeat of the knocking, but fainter. He listened, holding his breath. The person was knocking next door.

It took him what felt like ten minutes to get himself into the bedroom again and positioned at the window so that he could see out without being seen. He watched a heavyset man in a sport coat plod up the street, door to door, stopping to write things down. Detective.

He stayed at the window, trying to figure out what it meant. Why door to door? Were they looking for him in particular? Had someone said he was on this street? And if the policeman came back? There was no place to hide in this small house.

He got himself into bed, trembling.

When he heard the front door open, he went still, not breathing at all. A key put down somewhere, sound of a package being put down. It was someone familiar.

He gasped in air. He knew these footsteps. He almost cried with relief.

The girl Meg surfaced at the top of the stairs, carrying a small plastic bag.

When he told Meg about the policeman making his rounds, she stood stock-still then went to the front window to look.

"All right, all right, let's think," she said. "You still don't want to—you know—explain it all, turn yourself in?"

"No." He felt wild, thinking she wasn't getting it yet, the danger he was in.

"I understand you think the police can't help."

"No way. I can't. . . ." He felt the life drain out of him.

She watched him. "Okay. Stay up here. I'll close the bedroom door. Without a search warrant, they can't do anything. The way he's going door to door, alone, making notes, he doesn't have a search warrant. I have to go out. I'll leave a note for the kids and explain to them not to let anybody in until I'm back."

"I thought you went back to school."

"I did. But I got to thinking about things I needed to do and I went to the nurse and got out."

"I used to do that."

Meg shrugged. "I've never done it before. She didn't give me any trouble." She lifted the bag toward him. "I bought you a couple of things at the thrift shop. They're awful, but money is pretty low." She removed the items from the bag. "The pajamas are so big, we won't have any trouble getting the pants part on you. When we have money, I'll get you real clothes. The other thing I got you is a sweatshirt, the kind with a zipper in front. That should be easier for you, getting it off and on."

"Thank you. How much did this come to?"

"Two-fifty."

"What a bargain!"

"I guess."

"What are you going to do for money?"

"Well, I have another cleaning job today. I might be able to pull off getting something else in the same apartment building."

"Does it pay well?"

"No. But Laurie has babysitting," she said. "And Joel has to watch Susannah, but otherwise he does car washes."

"You don't have anything else? Something you could sell?"

"I have a check from Alison. Forty bucks. The bank wouldn't cash it. I don't know if there's anything left in the account. I could go back and try."

"Is there a check-cashing place somewhere in the neighborhood? They take half, but still."

"I don't know of one."

She was flushed and, he thought, pretty in a way he hadn't noticed before. "We got it in our heads to finish out the school year, then see what happens. That's a couple more weeks."

"If somebody gets wind of it—"

She hesitated, made a face. His mind raced ahead, but she got there before him. "If they somehow search, I'm going to say you're our father and we were told not to disturb you because you have . . . something. I'll say a leg sprain and you've been on pain pills. They aren't going to take the splint off to look. I won't even say leg sprain unless I have to. I'll just say our father is under the weather."

Hope sprang in him. "I get you."

"It'll go way better for us if we have an adult on the premises. Even if he's a grumpy uncooperative adult."

Was that how she thought of him?

"It's going to be okay. I've always felt kind of lucky."

"Lucky?" He actually began laughing to think Meg, with nothing, could call herself lucky.

"I think you better tell me your father's name."

"My father's name was Charles. Charlie Philips. People in this neighborhood didn't know him or what happened so . . . we could make him be alive again for a while." Her long hair fell to her face. She pulled it back with both hands, twisted it, and let it fall again.

"I'll say that's who I am."

She took her leave to go cleaning.

Charlie Philips. He liked his new name. He realized he didn't know the name of his first wife yet and only just remembered the name of the second.

AT THE BACK OF THE SCHOOL

building, after school, Mac told Joel to walk up Sherman and then into the alley. "Not today," Joel said. "I have to pick up my little sister and get home."

"Oh, no, you don't. Not as much as we need to talk to you," Mac said. And Zero was along for the ride, saying, "Yeah, we have to talk." They walked up the street fast. When they turned into the alley, in a sudden move, Mac dragged Joel backwards by his shirt, while Zero, who at first looked surprised, came at him from the front.

"Don't touch me." He swung at Zero.

"Shut up and listen." Zero pressed him against the wall of a building that might have been something industrial once. "Nobody else knows about the house we use, so, fuck you, listen to me. You ever *tell* anybody?"

"No."

"You sure?"

"Yeah."

"You been up there on your own?"

"No!" Joel felt how hot his face was. He twisted away. They came at him again, so he swung back at them. Mac grabbed his arm and pushed it to the wall, saying, "Tell Zero."

He faced Zero. "No. Why are you bugging me with this shit. I never went up there."

Zero asked, "You know a guy named Carl?"

Joel swallowed hard. "No."

Then Mac jumped in. "What? You were going to say something. You *know* Carl?"

"No, you told me about him. He sold to you."

"We told you?" Mac asked.

"Zero did." Joel pried himself away from Mac's hold, but in seconds

Mac got an arm against his chest, pushed him up against the wall again. Mac was so close, Joel could feel the kid's breath on his face. He could smell it, too, salami or something.

Joel said, "Why's it take two of you to ask me a question, huh? Big and brave."

Mac said calmly, "You'd have to say right now if you know where Carl is. The guy is wan-*ted*. He's money in our pockets. You ever see the guy, there's a twenty in it for you just to tell me where you saw him. You *capisce*?"

He felt relief pour through him that it was Carl they wanted. "I don't even know what he looks like," Joel said. "I wish I did. I could use the money."

The two of them thought this was funny for some reason. They laughed for a long time.

"You guys are nuts."

"Nuts like weasels," Zero said.

Joel became aware there was blood coming out of his nose, dripping on his shirt, from the way they'd banged him into the wall. "I don't know anything about the stupid people you mess with," he spat out.

"Anybody bothers us about the house, asks us if we were ever there or anything, we're going to know it was you, you hear?" Zero said.

Joel wiped at his face and watched them walk away. It seemed their steps lightened and that they were laughing. They sashayed down the street without looking back at him. There was something in them that he envied every time, a recklessness he couldn't understand, but wished he could feel.

Slowly, wiping the blood with his hand, he walked home.

NELLINS FELT LIKE A TIRED

census taker. He'd just come from a place occupied by two guys who had a thousand plants and a thousand little vases everywhere. They had talked his ear off and given him a glass of iced tea with a mint leaf in it. Now he called to a little schoolgirl going in her front door, but she was just a little thing, too small to question.

"I was about to knock on your door."

The little girl froze.

"Are your parents home?"

"I don't think so."

"Last name, Philips?"

Then a boy came from the street, right behind the girl. He was a bit older. He was wiping at a bloody nose with a small tissue as he hurried toward them.

"I need to talk to your parents," Nellins said to the boy.

"They're just . . . still working. And then they have to go to some store. Buying food."

"When'll they be home?"

"Not for a while."

"What's your name, son?"

"Joel."

"You taking care of her?"

"Yeah."

"What happened to your nose?"

"Just a fight after school."

"Hmm. You defended yourself, it looks like."

"Tried to."

"Well, people will tell you never to hit. Myself, I always say it depends on the situation."

The boy nodded.

"Your parents come back in an hour you say?"

The boy calculated. "More like two and a half."

"I'll check back then." Nellins left, wondering how many recalls he could make without losing his mind. He looked at his phone. Call from Detective Greer, gone to voice mail. He didn't even want to listen.

IT TOOK A LOT OF THE DAY

for Colleen to find Lena Procter at home.

"You calling me about my nephew, did you say?"

"If your nephew is Dermott Roux."

"He been gone for a while. You found him for me?"

"I'm afraid I have bad news," Colleen began.

"I think I'm guessing it. It's either jail or dead."

"We found his body in the place where he was living."

"How'd it happen?" the woman said evenly. "He get beat up?"

"Drugs."

"Oh. Not really a surprise." Lena Proctor didn't sound as if she was going to cry. "Never did have any control of that kid."

"Can you come down to Pittsburgh, do an ID for us?"

"I could get my boyfriend to drive me down."

"If you have a funeral home you'd like to use, you might want to alert them. There are a couple of ways to transport the body."

"Oh, man. I didn't even think about a funeral."

"Does he have other family up there?"

"Older brother in jail."

"That's it?"

"That is it. And me."

"Maybe he had a few school friends who would want to pay their respects."

"I could put out the notice."

"I think that might be a good idea."

"I didn't think he was going to go bad, then he run away. I put in a report, but the police couldn't find him. You say Picksburgh?"

People often said it that way, so Colleen just said yes. With urging, she got Lena Proctor to say she would get down to *Picksburgh* on the next day, Wednesday. It felt like progress, but it was only a drop in the bucket she needed to fill. Questions, lots of them still.

She spent some time typing notes to clear her head. She hated to type her reports, but she forced herself to do it. Then she took out a separate list of questions she'd typed up for herself:

1. Who was the dead boy BZ? What was his name? That was solved.

2. Who killed him? Not solved.

3. Who was the dead man up at the house—now Hrznak's case?

4. Who killed *him*?

5. Who was wounded up at the house? Probably the killer, but they didn't know *who* he was.

6. Lesser, but puzzling, Where was the kid Carl, who was not on the streets anymore?

7. What was Nick to the drug operation Farber was investigating? That wasn't solved at all. All they had was Nick's real name.

8. What had happened to Nick Friday night or thereabouts, since he was no longer working the Dona Ana?

9. What kids were up at the house, and were they connected to BZ?

10. Were drugs a part of the killing of the man up at the house—as Colleen was insisting they were to keep on the case—or were they incidental?

So ten questions and only one of them answered.

The second answer came in during the day. That was the result of the statewide AFIS search. The man up at the house now had a name and history. He was Earl Higgins, his ten digits told them. He'd been in and out of jail most of his life, came from Erie. Colleen read his record. Weapons possession, theft, intent to kill—shot a guy who survived. A lousy piece of work if ever there was one. There was nobody in Erie to claim him. Potocki was working on a place of residence in Pittsburgh. Or Picksburgh, depending. This one might take Roux's spot in potter's field.

She ate at her desk, calling the morgue to ask about the powder burns on Earl's fingers and clothes. She thought about the possible scenarios.

Hrznak was not keeping her in the loop, so she called the lab herself and asked about latent fingerprints at the scene of the crime. The person who got on the phone with her was someone new, young, a woman. "I could work on that for you," the woman said. "Is this for Hrznak's case?"

Colleen gave her spiel about the narcotics part of the case and her own involvement.

"This'd be more interesting than what they have me doing."

"What were the prints on?"

"A door that was up there. They're pretty good, made with blood."

"Fantastic. You could get someone to run them?"

"Pittsburgh base?"

"Start with Pittsburgh. They don't find anything, move to AFIS state."

"If Hrznak asks me about them—"

"Oh, don't keep any information from him. But call me. Give me a heads up. I think he's busy on the street today."

She sensed the young woman was on her side by the way she said, "Either way, I'll call you as soon as I know anything."

"What's your name?"

"Ann Cello."

"Like the instrument?"

"Spelled just like that."

"Did you ever learn to play it?"

"I learned violin, actually."

"Must have heard a lot of jokes."

"Yeah. High school was the pits in every way."

"It gets better."

"It already has, some."

"Good."

By one thirty, Colleen heard news that depressed her as much as talking to Dermott Roux's aunt had. The prints came up, all right. They came up like three limes on a slot machine. The prints were in the AFIS state system. They belonged to Nick Kissel.

She thought about what might have happened, had probably happened.

She called back to Ann Cello to ask if they could work on the other blood up there for DNA as soon as possible. Nick Kissel's DNA was on record. Now she was virtually certain he had been wounded up there, had bled, had escaped. Images of him came to her—he kept smiling in the film running in her head the way he had smiled when working behind the counter—and she had to tell herself not to be stupid, not to be sentimental.

Potocki came up to her in her cubicle.

"I got news," she said. "It was Nick Kissel up at the house."

"I'm not surprised," he murmured. "By the way, I found that quote you wanted." He handed over a yellowed Penguin edition of *Hamlet*.

"When?"

"Last night. I couldn't sleep, so I was unpacking books. Look at how old this is. I used to buy used. Can you believe they once sold books for sixty-five cents. It says I paid ten cents for it. Quite a bargain."

"Well, thanks, I guess." She opened it up to where he had book-marked the quote with a Post-it. "The toe of the peasant comes so near the heel of the courtier, he galls his kibe." That was it! That was what she was trying to remember. Shakespeare had meant it as a class comment: The peasant is following so closely behind the courtier that he irritates his chilblains. Funny line, really. She looked up at Potocki and handed him his book back. "Thanks."

"So the missing Nick Kissel, aka Banks, is our perp?"

"Probably."

"You liked him."

"Eh."

"You fall for good looks. Anybody ever tell you that's shallow?"

"They told me."

"Hmf. What a world, huh?"

"Potocki," she began. She knew she had to say it. "I know what you've—what we've both—been thinking. You're a great guy. It isn't that. Did you know, it's a known fact, that a man getting a divorce needs to date for three years minimum before he knows who he is? There is so much junk to work out. Not to mention, you're my partner."

He closed his eyes briefly. All he said was, "Three years."

She made various faces and shrugged to indicate that it was a sorry deal, she understood that. He made a strained little smile and left her cubicle, and she forced herself to get back to work.

So now she had answers to more of her questions. Still didn't know who killed BZ. Still didn't know exactly what Nick did in the drug business—and the fact that he was gone looked bad. She did know he'd been up at the house and possibly injured. She started calling the hospitals.

Ann Cello called back, interrupting her. "It's getting very interesting," she said. The team found a knife at the place. It was on the first floor, dropped through from the second floor. Kissel's prints were on it, too. And the blood on Higgins's pants wasn't all his. It suggests—"

Good for Ann Cello, she was going to be good. Colleen let her say her piece.

"—that Nick Kissel was shot first and bled on Higgins and that the powder-burn pattern could mean the gun was still in Higgins's hand. Until after. When it was removed. Could be."

"You're right." Colleen felt a little glimmer of hope. Perhaps she was not completely crazy.

"And there was whiskey on the floor," Ann Cello said. "And diluted blood—"

"Whose diluted blood?"

"Kissel's, probably."

"All I can say is, keep going, keep going. You are sharp. Just the stuff I need to know."

"Thank you."

She called the Coroner's office to ask if there were any knife wounds on Higgins. There were not. Just the shot at point of contact and definite powder burns on the man's right hand. Nobody walks up and sticks a gun in somebody's chest without a struggle. If only she had the gun.

Potocki came back into her office. He'd found out where Nick Banks, as he'd signed on the lease, was living. "Should have a warrant by six," he said.

Colleen was sure Potocki was going to say something about getting a bite to eat while they waited for the warrant, but he didn't. A few minutes before six, she saw him eating takeout at his desk. Her stomach rumbled with gnawing hunger.

In the company refrigerator, she found a yogurt that was expired. She ate that and a granola bar to keep her going. But it hardly worked.

A few minutes after six, Potocki came by with the search warrant. "Let's go," he said.

They took a car over to Sherman Street where Nick Banks had rented a first-floor apartment. The landlord, Grant Bright, met them there and opened the door for them.

It was the most ordinary of places. Couch, wingback chair, old wooden tables of various sorts. There was some food mess in the kitchen. There were drawers open in the sitting room and the bedroom.

On top of the bedroom dresser was a stack of clean shirts and pants and underwear. There were other clothes in the closet. A suitcase.

The mattress was off kilter. Someone had clearly searched the place. Maybe waited here for Nick to return? She and Potocki caught each other's eyes.

Potocki started on Grant Bright. "You've been back here lately?"

"No, not at all."

"Where do you live?"

"Over on Buena Vista."

"You rent this place and the one above?"

"I bought the place thinking to turn it back to one house, but I never have enough money to do the renovations, so I've been renting it out."

"What kind of tenant was Nick Banks?"

"Never saw him. He was only here, what, two months, not even. No, just over a month. He paid his rent is all I knew. He used a money order."

"You have a tenant upstairs?"

"Single woman. Older."

"I wonder if you could come with us to the upstairs. We need to talk to her, find out if anyone was hanging around here."

They started up the stairs.

Bright said, "When I pulled up to let you guys in, there was a guy sitting in his car. He was just sitting. He drove away. Could that be anything?"

"Could, could. Tell us anything about the car?"

"I didn't notice. White. American, I think. Like Chevy or something."

The old woman who rented the second floor supported herself on a walker. She said she'd heard some noises downstairs a couple of days ago but not lately. "He'd bring my mail up for me. Missed Saturday and today, though."

"Did you talk to him much when he came up?"

"Just that kind of quick hello."

They quizzed her this way and that. She hadn't seen any strangers around. She'd never had any trouble with Nick Banks. She liked him.

It was almost eight o'clock. Potocki said he was going to knock on a few neighboring doors and see what he could find out. Colleen told him she'd return for him. She took the car and drove the couple of blocks to the Dona Ana.

The woman working the ovens and the counter was a ready talker.

"You're new here," Colleen said. "Just start?"

"I don't know about all these hours he wants me to put in. I got kids," she said, frazzled.

"Did you know the guy who worked here before you?"

"Uh-uh."

"Nick Banks?"

"Never heard of him."

"Who hired you—not Banks, then?"

"Some guy named Jim is all I know."

"He's the owner?"

"Had the keys, had the recipes. I guess so. You want anything?"

"Can you make a stromboli with some vegetables?"

"I think so."

Colleen looked at her watch, thinking, sooner or later she would have to reveal to Hrznak and Nellins what she had learned about Nick.

NELLINS HAD GONE BACK TO
the house with the little girl and the little boy who was taking care of her. Philips.

This time there were two more girls there.

"Please sit down," the oldest one said to him. He recognized her as the one who'd dashed through the park earlier. "Sit, sit," she said to the other kids.

They had books with them. They sat on the couch, lined up, and let him have the armchair.

"Would you like something to drink?" the girl asked before he sat.

"No thanks. Okay, yeah, water, actually."

She went to the kitchen for it. He was tired, crazy-hungry again (some kind of rebound reaction to the calzone he'd had for lunch from the pizza shop up the street), and he had at least fifteen more places to get to.

"Thank you," he called into the kitchen.

"You're welcome."

"Your parents? Where are they?"

"Our mother," the girl said, returning, handing him water, sitting, "is still at work. Our dad is at rehab. He had a running injury. If you can leave a card, they'll call you when they get home."

Nellins flipped the page of the legal pad. He had quite a list of people he still needed to hear from. The list wound down and around a page, both sides. "Their names?"

"Charles and Alison Philips."

"Okay," he said, writing. He considered their ages and decided the girl seemed pretty capable. "I'm going to ask you to look at this picture." He showed her the close-up of the man, crumpled upper body, pasty face, and watched her expression. Her breath caught. "I know," he said. "It's not a pretty sight. All I'm asking is, did you ever see the man before?"

"No," she said, shaking off a shiver.

Then he flashed the picture of the house at her. "This is a house. You know any kids messed around in this house?"

"No," the girl said. "Where is it?"

"Up the hill."

She shook her head.

He took the second photo over to the other kids. "Do either of you know this house?"

They looked up from their books and shook their heads. "Looks like a lot of houses," the boy said.

Nellins's phone rang. It was Hrznak, asking, "What gives?"

"Nothing," said Nellins.

"Lot of nothing. Higgins was a career criminal. Got his just deserts as far as I'm concerned. I'm done for the day."

"We still don't know who did him," Nellins grumbled in a low voice, but too late, he saw the kids were listening.

"No, but I'm for going into the guy's history. Not pounding the pavement. That Greer was at me all day. Morgue says there were powder burns on his hand and his shirt. The blood up there was definitely not all his. Greer is pushing to find out about the other guy."

Hrznak was old and crabby. Nellins was old and whimsical. Nellins had just hung up when he decided he needed a soft drink to fizz its way down his gullet. He told the kids to have the parents call him and he took his leave.

He headed up to Dona Ana Pizzeria, where he'd gotten the calzone earlier that was still living with him. Through the window of the shop, he saw, of all people—speaking of his current devil—Greer quizzing the woman who had been learning the business. Nellins was about to turn on his heel and find a soda somewhere else when she spied him. She didn't look too thrilled about running into him either. It made him curious. He went in.

She was talking about some guy.

"He was really nice. I thought he was going to come join me and my friends to hear some jazz."

The woman shook her head. "Guys never do what they say."

"Oh, every once in a while, they do," Colleen said. "I thought we connected, you know."

The woman's tight features broke into a smile. She shook her head. "I've had that experience."

"Who's the guy you work for again?"

"Jim. He didn't give me his last name. You want my opinion, he won't tell you a thing. He's a sourpuss. And he is definitely not hot."

Nellins took a can of Sprite out of the cooler. He wasn't sure he wanted to hear this conversation. He was grateful when his phone rang.

"I need a drink," Hrznak said. "*Before* we go back to sign out. By that time we'll have thirteen, fourteen hours. We're racking up some mighty good time today."

Nellins said, "Right, right. The usual place. In half an hour. For our conference. I just ran into Greer, and we need a few minutes first." He was miserably hungry, but he would wait to eat at Peanutz while Hrznak had a few. The clock above the counter said it was eight o'clock.

TWENTY-EIGHT

BY TUESDAY EVENING MAC
and Zero had met K three times. "Always be cool," Mac told his friend.
"Make him want us."

"I got the creeps, you know, the way he was driving behind us. I
thought it was, you know, one of them, wanting my butt or something."

Mac laughed. "Just be cool." The night before he had thought the
same thing when he saw K beckoning to them. He wasn't afraid of dealing with a perv, though. He went up to the car.

"I know you're Carl's friends. You want to hop in for a sec?" K had
said.

Zero hesitated, even Mac did, but then he opened the door and
climbed into the back. Zero followed.

"Some people over on Federal told me you were his friends. They
said you were asking about him, and I wondered if maybe you might
want to take over his work for a while."

Elation filled Mac—that feeling of wanting and getting what you'd wanted. "Yep, can do," he said. He hit Zero in the thigh.

They drove up the block, talking. K was saying things like, "It's not hard work, but it takes a really smart person to do it. You have to be able to read a street corner, make a snap decision. Carl has a regular business, a good business. I don't know why he isn't around, but there's good money to be made if you need money."

"Okay."

"You guys have any money on you?"

"Nah," said Mac. Don't give. Get.

"Five bucks," said Zero before Mac could stop him.

"You don't know where Carl is hanging these days, do you?"

"Nope," Mac said, "don't know."

K gave him a good hard look. He took a bundle out of his pocket and passed it before them. "You ever see one of these before?"

"Ten stamp bags," Mac said. "Called a bundle."

"What if I advance you one bundle each, see what you can do? Fifteen bucks a bag. You bring me back the money and we go from there—"

"Territory?" Mac asked.

"You go over to Federal, lean against that little grocery store over there. You have caps, wear them to the left. You have belts on, let them hang way off your pants to the left, strap hanging down. It's a real easy territory. If they ask you what brand—" He held the bundle closer to them. "What are you going to say?"

Mac read the bags. "Power Times Three."

"You in this, too?" K asked Zero, who had been silent.

"Yes."

"Way to go. Split 'em up, five in each pocket. This works, we'll have more lessons. You each bring me back one twenty-five in exactly three hours, the other twenty-five is yours to keep. We go from there. I'll be one street over from where I drop you. You want to try it?"

They said they did.

Then K said, "You ever tell anybody you saw me, talked to me, ever, it's real bad for you. Not my fault. Other people above me get violent. Talk is the one thing they won't tolerate. But it's a great business, well-run." He pulled the bundle back. "You sure you're up to this? You can shut up through anything?"

"Yeah," Mac said.

"What are your names?"

"Pete MacKensie. Mac. He's Sean Zero."

"I need to know where you live." They told him and he wrote it down. "Who you live with?"

"Mother," said Zero. "He lives with his father," he said about Mac, trying to bring himself into the conversation.

"Memorize these words: 'I don't know nothing.' Say those a hundred or two hundred times if you have to. You can do that, nothing bad will happen."

"We can do that."

"Give it a go."

They got out of the car. They could tell he watched them getting to work. Mac knew they looked natural. He started right away, walked up the street with some guy, talking. Real natural. He cut into an alley with another and came back. He gave a look to Zero—meaning, look smart, do something, but when he turned around, the van had gone. Well, they had the shit anyway.

In three hours, they went a block over to meet K and he was there. He gave them each two more bundles and said, "We're still on trial, but keep going. And one more thing. I really need to talk to Carl. You find him for me—and don't say anything to him, just tell me where he is—there's money in it for you. Can you do that?"

"No problem."

The third time they met with K was Tuesday. The selling had gone well, but they didn't have any word on Carl yet. They had hoped Joel might know something, but he didn't. When they reported they didn't have any information, K nodded sadly and looked upset, angry.

Mac said, "I'll find him."

K winked and said, "Good boy. I knew you were a good kid."

CARL OPENED THE DOOR TUESDAY
night, but he felt a terrible panic and closed the door quickly, shaking.

He breathed deeply for a few seconds, then opened the door again, slowly, a crack at a time, telling himself he had to go out sooner or later. Finally, he made himself go outside where he stood in the overgrown yard for a minute, two minutes. Anyone might see him even with the cover of night. He went back inside.

He was out of batteries. Not to mention that he was getting down to a few cans and he was out of good drinking water. He would have to go out in the middle of the night for supplies.

The last he heard when the radio was fighting to go out on him was the name of the man killed up at the house was Earl Higgins. "Anybody having information is asked to come forward," some woman said cheerfully through the static. And then the radio conked. He still didn't know what had happened to Nick.

The memory of the bright fluorescent lights at the Giant Eagle parking lot made him tremble. He had almost no money. Still, he wanted fresh bread and cheese and lunch meat. Milk. Juice. Power bars and beef jerky, tuna, soup, anything with a pull lid. He wanted new clothes, warm meals. It was good that he wanted these things.

Tomorrow, then. He could make it for another day.

He studied his journal entries. *Think of a future time when you are okay. Think of woods, house, garden. School when it was going okay. Think about Tracy. Don't panic. Keep to routines.*

He'd been religious about his routines; now he simply had to add going outside three times a day.

Before he went to bed, he opened the door again and stood just outside the back door long enough to get used to the fact that an outdoors existed.

TWENTY-NINE

WEDNESDAY—AND SO THE
kids. Christie heard the car pulling up outside.

Marina came into the house, urging Eric and Julie along. "Show him the movies you rented."

His children presented the DVD sleeves awkwardly, as if for his approval. Marina was saying, "We're having a nice simple pasta with just butter on it and a salad."

"Do smells still bother you?" Julie asked.

"Yes."

"Bummer."

"Well, the good news is I get a break for the rest of this week and all of next week, then the week after I'm supposed to be back on the treatment, but then I get a break again. Don't worry. It'll work out."

"It's nice outside," Eric said.

"Let's go out back then," he agreed. He made himself walk normally to the back door. The humid air assaulted him. It was going to rain soon for sure.

"What do you want to do?" Eric rocked a football in his hands, prompting the answer.

"Toss it to me, but easy, easy. Work on the spin, not force."

"You sure?"

"I'm sure." Already he felt better using his body. He was going to try going in to work tomorrow. A couple of hours. He needed it.

He wanted to be back at work, laughing over the insane things that came at them every day.

He wanted to be there to watch out for Potocki and Greer, who had their hands full with Farber.

The football hit him hard in the stomach.

"You hit him," Julie cried. "Why don't you be careful?"

"It's okay," he grunted, even though it wasn't, quite. How bizarre that you could walk around in your body for months, years, and not know the bad things going on inside it until the chaos reached certain proportions and the alarms went off. Then the body talked back, all right.

Later he stood in the kitchen, watching as his children set the table. They were always interesting to him. Eric remembering, with a little pantomime of knife and fork, to put the knife on the right. Julie catching Eric's almost mistake and silently congratulating herself for never having to think twice about how to set a table. Julie looking at Marina's long hair and freeing a strand that was caught under the strap of the apron.

It was going to rain again. It seemed it rained every Wednesday.

Marina said, "Dinner's on," and Christie straightened himself for the task.

WEDNESDAY NIGHT AND THE
smell of food was overwhelming, fantastic, and he was downstairs now with a lot of help from the crutches and the two older children, Meg

and Joel. He'd practiced back and forth in the small upstairs hallway. How good it felt to be downstairs, seeing a different sight. While he practiced moving swiftly to the approving gaze of the two younger girls, Joel and Meg went back upstairs and carried the TV down. They plugged it in.

"He's got the hang of it," Laurie said.

They thought of everything. They'd put a chair at the top of the stairs for him to use to support himself while lowering himself to the stairs.

Susannah took small pillows from the couch to make a space for him. "Do you want to sit?"

"I want to move. Man, I needed this."

They watched him go back and forth in their small house. The front window blinds were pulled, so the place was darker than it would normally have been, but there, they'd thought of that, too.

The smell was of chicken roasting, unmistakable. "How did you come up with the food?" he asked Meg.

"They cashed my check at Doug's Market. They said if I shopped there, they could. Things are more expensive there, but still, they had what we needed. I got milk and cereal and ham for sandwiches and bread and a chicken and some vegetables. And peanut butter. I even bought ice cream. You can get pretty far with forty dollars if you think about it. The guy was so nice, I'm going back to check because . . . if it bounces, I'd have to find some way to pay him back."

Nick got upset again, thinking about money, owing. Sometimes it seemed all you could do was cut and run.

"Anyway, we're okay for food for a couple of days," Meg said evenly, trying to read his expression. She wore a denim skirt with a knit top. Her hair looked glossy, and he thought he saw a trace of lipstick. She was acting very grown up.

Nick walked some more, into the kitchen and eating area, the only other room downstairs. If you stood at the bottom of the stairs, you could see into each room. There was a table and chairs, all set. Five places. He clomped back to the living room.

He wondered where important papers were kept in this small place. Possibly in the basement.

The two younger girls stood in the front room, watching him.

"You don't want to sit?"

"I want to sit," he said.

They hovered as he settled himself on the couch, his right leg extended.

"We had a house once. In Greenfield," Laurie said.

"Did you?"

"It wasn't huge or anything, but it was a *house*. With three bedrooms and a dining room and a kind of sunroom we turned into a book room. The good old days."

"I could use some help," Meg called.

Laurie left the living room reluctantly.

Susannah put on the television. "We don't get a lot of channels," she said.

He knew that perfectly well. Once he'd got to standing and moving upstairs, he'd tried them all. Two more days of practicing moving and he'd be ready to leave this place if he had some clothes. The sweatshirt was okay. He needed some kind of pants. And there was the problem of changing his dressings. Could he support his leg and do it himself?

Susannah watched him to see if he was watching TV. She was very cute, very . . . soft. He said, "Sorry. I was working things out."

"Okay," Meg called. "It's ready."

By the time he got himself up and into the other room, Meg was bringing a roasted chicken to the table. On each plate there had appeared a baked potato and what really surprised him—a heap of green beans. Not the shabbiest meal he had ever had, not the usual kid fare. She said, "I hope the chicken's good. It was on special."

The others looked eagerly at the bird.

"Where do you want me?"

"The end," Meg said. "You might want to sit sidesaddle a bit so you can extend your leg."

He got himself into his seat, doing as she suggested. "You kids sure keep a clean operation," he said, looking about. "Somebody must have taught you."

They all pointed to Laurie. "She's a clean-nik," Joel said.

"Are you good at carving?" Meg asked.

"Very good at carving. I'd love to carve."

They put paper napkins on their laps and waited. "You've been good to me," he said, making a neat slice at a leg and disengaging it. "I don't want you to think I won't make it up to you, somehow, sometime. Who likes the leg meat?"

Laurie's hand went up.

He sliced it in half and gave her the thigh. Meg would want to make the chicken last. "I'm not good at making speeches. You know what I mean about wanting to thank you." He held the drumstick between knife and fork. "Who gets it?" Both girls pointed to their brother.

"White meat or dark?" he asked Meg and Susannah.

Both said, "White please." He understood they were trying to give him the option of the other leg. He carefully cut white meat for all three of them. "Hey, let's get started."

Then they were eating, maybe too rapidly, all of them, and nobody knew what to say. "What grades are you in?" he asked.

Meg said, "Eighth."

Joel said, "Seventh."

Laurie said, "Fifth."

Susannah said, "Second."

"So that means you are—what ages?"

Meg answered, "Almost fourteen, almost twelve—Joel skipped a grade—and ten."

"Almost eleven," Laurie amended.

"Seven," Susannah said in that quiet sandy voice.

"And school? Nearly over for the year? You're glad?"

He half expected the usual cheer of release. But, no, they were not glad.

"More like bummed," Joel said.

Nick carefully cut into the piece of chicken on his plate. He saw with surprise that it was moist, not overdone as he feared.

While he brought a forkful to his mouth, he watched them eat. "Is it okay?" Meg asked, startling him.

"It's fine. More than fine. How'd you learn to cook?"

"Practice. My dad showed me. I used to cook for all of us even when he was here."

"How long do you think you can keep pulling this off? I mean if somebody from school calls or comes by. Or a neighbor?"

"We say something they can't check," Joel said. "We say our parents are at work. That's all they care about if they call—just not having to report something."

"Meg is going to say I'm your father—if she ever has to say something. It's okay with you if I give your father's name?"

They said it was. Other questions hung in the air.

Nick ate for a while, feeling the sting of the new silence that settled. "But when I leave . . . if you don't have food—"

"That is a problem," Laurie said. "We like food."

"So how will you get it?"

"Ask us something else," Laurie said. "Chaaaaange the subject."

Meg said, "We'll figure it out."

"I don't tell about you and you don't tell about me. Right?"

"That's the deal," Joel said.

Nick cast about for something happy to say. It was wrong to ruin a good meal with worries. "You sure have a lot of books in the other room. I was noticing the bookcases, and that's quite a pile of books on the table near the door."

"We read a lot," Meg said.

"I imagine so."

"You don't like to read?" Joel asked, and this time his tone was friendly.

"No, I never got around to it."

"Did you always do the same work?" This time it was Laurie who spoke. "Pizza shop?"

"Not at all. I used to work construction way back. Then bartending. Then for a while I was a fisherman. I mean I am a fisherman."

"Aha," Meg said.

Laurie said, "She's our Sherlock. She told us, your skin, your hands, it was something out in the weather."

"What kind of fish?" Joel asked.

"Just about everything. Over the years. Whatever swims in the Atlantic. I even lobster-trapped for a while."

"You have a boat?"

"No. Always worked for other people. But I'm good at it, good at boats."

The voice Laurie had used when she said "Chaaaaange the subject" was low, gravelly, provocative, an extreme version of her little sister's voice. Very comical. She used it now for, "Did you get seasick?" She was a kid looking for a laugh.

"Yes."

"Really?"

"Really."

"Everybody, eat," Meg said. "The food will get cold. You can talk, but eat, too."

Safe subjects. He shouldn't have said the truth about fishing. "Are your grades good? Probably are if you're readers."

"Yeah."

"A's and B's?"

After an odd little silence, Joel said, "No B's. Well, Laurie got one."

Laurie swiped at Joel. "Asshole teacher is why."

"It's not a hard school," Joel said.

"And what . . . what are you going to do with all that brain power? Besides figure out how to save my life?"

Meg said, "I think literature. My dad studied English, and I like it. I could be a teacher or a writer."

"I'm going into medicine," Joel said plainly.

"He always was," Meg said. "He knew it at age three."

Nick turned to Laurie. "What about you?"

"Not sure. Poet, architect, something fun."

"Susannah?"

"Artist."

"I saw you drawing."

"I always draw."

When dinner was over, including a small bowl of ice cream for each, Nick looked toward the windows where the pulled blinds were the sole reminder that things weren't normal. The windows said: reality, danger. But he didn't want to go upstairs yet.

"You can watch TV, it's okay. Or practice walking."

Meg started water running in the sink. Laurie carried dishes to the sideboard and fetched the cloth for drying. In moments, Joel was sweeping the floor. Susannah put things away.

He moved to the darkened living room and back to the kitchen, practicing moving fast, pretending not to notice they had an eye on him, pretending not to watch their smallest moves, all of them, as they went about whatever else they were doing.

CHRISTIE IS IN BED FINALLY,
Marina beside him, the children asleep. "Potocki's getting a divorce. Probably."

"No. Where did you hear that?"

"Greer."

"I thought he and Judy were good."

"I know."

"Does Greer have anything to do with it?"

"I don't know. Complicated, huh?"

THIRTY

NICK GOES TO BED WHEN

the kids do, sure he will fall asleep from sheer fatigue—he has gone up
and down the steps ten times using one crutch and the banister—but
it doesn't happen.

How bad would it be to stay for a while longer? After all, he has no
place to go.

After a while he puts on the light. Maybe if he chooses a spot halfway
through the book on the side table, reading will put him to sleep.

Soon she is in the room.

"You have school tomorrow," he says. "You couldn't sleep either?"

"No."

"Why not?"

"We've had you here since Sunday."

"Yes."

"It's Wednesday. I feel like I know you. I think I do. But when I ask
myself, it turns out I hardly know anything about you. I want to know."

"What in particular?"

"Everything. And no lies."

"Everything? Why?"

"I want to help you."

He can't help smiling. She has her way of angling to be in the superior position. "Are you religious or something?"

"No. Not churchgoing, if that's what you mean."

"All that honesty stuff. That and you should be very angry about your situation, but you're not and I want to know why. What is that all about, huh? Religion, I figured."

"I'm angry."

"You are?"

"A little, yes. Well, maybe I have a kind of belief in something. It would be hard to define it."

"Never mind. Well. I've been in trouble before. Is that what you're asking?"

"Yes."

"What else?"

"Everything. From the beginning. You were born where? Your mother and father were . . . who?"

"Ever hear of a town, Milton?"

"No, where is it?"

"Central Pennsylvania."

"And that's where you grew up?"

"Yep."

"With your foster parents?"

"I had a mother for a while, but she bailed when I was young."

Meg's breath catches. "Like ours." She seems almost excited by the idea.

"And I never had a father. Just the mother for a while, don't remember her much. My grandmother told me my mother had problems with drugs and drink and that she never should have been a mother. But she was. She didn't much like the job. And there I was. So I lived with my grandmother."

"And she was nice?"

"Nice, yeah, kind of out of it, though. She was old, sickly. Then one day she died. So they came and hauled me to this farm where I had foster parents—no brothers and sisters, though, just the foster parents."

"You didn't like them?"

"They didn't like me. It was mutual."

"What was the matter with them?"

"You really want to know all this?" She nods emphatically. "You're kind of like the social worker in prison. Okay, okay." He hesitates. "Well, they had this farm. They worked pretty hard. They were religious. And mean. They looked okay on paper, but there was nothing . . . nice about them. They just wanted a worker on the farm. I worked, but no matter what I did, it was never right or good enough. I guess they were a little bit—" He touches a finger to his head. "That's what I tell myself. So you think we have something that's alike, huh? But I wasn't a good kid, not like you. I got in trouble at school. I hated school. I got into fights, I skipped out when I could. I wasn't some angel. You clear on that?"

"Okay."

"What else do you want to know?"

"How you got in trouble after that. Who you're afraid of."

"Oh, man, that's a long story."

"That's okay."

"It's late at night."

"That's okay, too. I like late at night."

"You think you're going to help me?"

"Yes."

"How?"

"I don't know."

"You already have. You've been . . ." Shit. If he continues, he might cry. Stay away from the compliments, he reminds himself. When he talks soft, he becomes a puddle of mush. "There's nothing else you can do for me. I bought trouble."

She straightens herself, sets her jaw firmly. "You owe it to me to tell me. You do. All I ask is facts. We went out on a limb for you."

"Because I was kind to you."

"It seemed impossible not to. You were so scared. Of somebody."

"Still am."

"That's what you owe me. How can we not know that?"

He takes a while to think about it and decides she's right. There is something about her that pulls at him. She's pretty enough, or is going to be, and he finds himself thinking about her when she isn't there, like a man falling in love. He's wondered what his life would have been if he'd met a version of her when he was a young boy. Different. Surely.

"I'm not so used to talking."

"No fooling." She laughs. "You want tea?"

"No tea. Booze. I want booze."

"You drank all our cough syrup and mouthwash."

"You noticed."

"Of course. We don't have anything more. I looked. I really searched. Do you need it to talk?"

"No."

"Who are you afraid of?"

"A guy named Markovic. He did accounts or pretended to do accounts up at the pizza shop. He hired me. I owed him money, and he put me to work."

Meg blows out a breath as if she's whistling, but no sound comes out. "Markovic. How is it spelled? *M-a-r-k-o-v-i-c?*"

He nods.

"What's his first name?"

"George. What are you up to? You aren't going to do anything stupid, are you?"

"Nothing stupid, I promise. Just tell me how you got in trouble with him."

"By being dumb."

"I think about finding you up at the house, and I try to figure out what happened."

The clock on the bureau is ticking. He fancies he can see time moving, inching forward. After a while words come to him. The silences between don't seem to bother her. He tells her everything—Markovic mentioning cousins who had work, Markovic always being a big shot, then getting kids to sell drugs.

"But how did you come into it?" she presses.

He tells her about the forty thousand owed—well, thirty-eight now.

She whistles a long quiet whistle. "From drugs?"

When he admits to the gambling, less damning than drugs, she asks if he is addicted to gambling because a person can be addicted to that, too. There isn't anyplace this kid doesn't go, he thinks. She asks all over again about Carl, but he doesn't have an answer. He doesn't know what happened to him after that night, last Friday night, how could he know? Time keeps ticking, and he tells her his real name. "Kissel. Just a dumb farm country name."

Her face is sorrowful, but she doesn't flinch. She swings the questions to how, if the trouble happened as far away as Philadelphia, Markovic knew to conscript him?

"That's a real long story." The clock shows it's almost three in the morning. She sees him looking at it.

"School doesn't start until eight."

"Hey."

"I'll be up all night wondering. You might as well keep telling me."

"You like my stories?"

"I do. They make sense of you. Let me go make us a cup of tea."

When she comes back with the tea, it's after three. "Tell me."

"I worked for a guy who ran a gas station when I was a kid, eighteen, and looking to get away from the farm. The guy was Markovic. I was a good worker, so he liked me. I thought, I found it, finally, some luck. But. I used to go to this one bar a lot. I got in a fight, a really bad fight, with people egging me on to kill this big bruiser who was after me, but I didn't kill him and I survived it and afterwards I left town."

"Why did the bruiser want to kill you?"

"Well, he got the wrong idea about me. He thought he could have a night with me. . . ."

"Oh, he was *interested* in you."

"Right. I said no. He got mad. I was drinking. He grabbed at me, I swung back. Then it started."

"So you left town."

"I got out on the highway. Turn left or right, I told myself, just go. I turned left. What I mean is, I might have ended up in Pittsburgh. I ended up in Philly. It didn't matter to me where. For a while, I worked construction. I started crossing over the state line on the weekends going to the gaming tables in New Jersey. I was having fun. I was kind of good at cards. Either that or I got lucky, made some money anyway. Started driving a nice car, got myself a better apartment. Found some tables in Philly, illegal ones. Then everything turned the other way. I lost the apartment, lost the car. Gave up construction and went out on the fishing boats."

"So you stopped gambling."

"No. No, I didn't."

"Did you get ahead again? Winning?"

"From time to time. I got married when I was twenty-seven. Things seemed okay for a while."

He sees her breath catch again. She doesn't like the marriage part of the story.

"You . . . didn't call her when you were in trouble?"

"It lasted all of three years. I don't even know where she is now."

"How old are you?"

"I'm thirty-five. You really want to know this stuff?"

"Everything."

"All Melanie wanted was my money. The divorce was ugly and I was angry after the split because she wiped me out. I went back to the tables with this idea I was going to make back what she took from me. I owed, I borrowed to pay what I owed. . . ."

"Robbing Peter to pay Paul," she says quietly.

"Whatever. Old enough story. Then some guy shows up at my place with a gun and I had nothing to pay him back with. I mean nothing. I saw he was ready to shoot me, so I went for him. I got the gun away from him, and when the maniac was still coming at me, swinging one of my lamps at my head and then grabbing for the gun, I shot him. People heard the shot, called it in, I was arrested."

"You didn't run?"

"No, I was calling the police myself. I ended up in jail. The gaming people have the police in their pockets. That's what I found out. I got seven years."

She is shaking her head, like an old woman, shaking her head.

"What? What?"

"I feel sorry for you."

"Why?"

"The gambling and drinking."

"You want the truth? I like both things a lot."

"Why?"

"They make me feel . . . right. Like I'm going to be okay."

"Didn't anybody ever tell you . . ."

"Oh, sure. I went to AA and GA in prison. I tried to get my head straight. I had good behavior on my side. The prison officials saw that and moved me to a place more central in the state. *There's* where I ran into Marko again."

"He was in prison?"

"He was just about to get out of prison when I came in. We talked and talked. He told me, 'I'll get you out of here. I know a lawyer who can do it.' "

"It worked?"

"Yeah, the guy got me out. Markovic fronted him the money. Forty thousand. I worked on the fishing boats to pay him back. I was making payments, halfway there. Lawyer kept telling me Marko wanted me to get in touch personally, that he had work for me. I kept never calling. I was on parole, and trying to stay clean."

"Drinking?"

"Never could give that up. Gambling I gave up for a while, but then I went back to it. That's when I got in trouble and owed another roughly twenty and finally called Markovic. I knew it was a mistake.

He says, 'All you need is some new ID and they can't find you. You come to Pittsburgh, you work for me.' "

"You didn't try to get away from him?"

"I felt kind of . . . like I was half-dreaming, like it wasn't real. I told myself I'd work the dumb shop, whatever he told me to do, pay off my debt, and then I'd get out. But this kid Carl told me things I didn't want to hear. I think it showed on me."

"Things about Markovic?"

"Yes."

"Murders?"

"Yes. I figured I would just pick a day and vamoose. But then some guy comes for me to do a job. And that was the night it all happened. I never got away."

"The job was Carl?"

"Yes."

"You thought you were guilty already, right?"

He seems surprised. "Yeah."

"You can't sense yourself making decisions."

He tries to think what she means. "I don't . . . no, I don't feel I get to make decisions. Things happen to me, always have. I'm just always . . ." He puts his hands up to illustrate a man trying to say, *Whoa*. That's what it feels like.

"I'd better get some sleep."

"You hate me now?" He is almost hoping she does.

"No. No, I don't."

MEG PRETENDS TO GO TO BED
at four, but after a while when she thinks she hears steady breathing from the room next door, she goes downstairs to the kitchen table, where she begins to write. It isn't as if she thinks she will forget anything, not a word of it, but to keep a record seems wise. She dates it, puts down the hours they talked.

For a while she thought he might come to like them so much, he'd stay with them, but now she thinks he doesn't know how to do anything sensible. The Nick upstairs is a boy, a youngster, with flashing blue eyes and a smile that keeps surprising her.

Her father was a boy, too. Some fathers lead that way, hopeless and innocent, magnets for luck.

THIRTY-ONE

THE OFFICE WAS IN A TIZZY
as Christie walked through. It was as if he'd been gone for a month.
Two months. "You're back!" everyone said.

First he met with Potocki and Greer right at Potocki's desk. "Tell
me," he said.

"I've been on the computer a lot," Potocki said.

Christie pulled up a swivel chair and sat. "What'd you find Farber?"

"The other guy in the pizza shop, K, did prison time when Nick
Kissel did. Are you caught up on who Kissel is?"

"Yeah. Greer's almost date."

She groaned on cue.

"According to the prison personnel, these two guys knew each other
some before. Name of the other guy is George Markovic. He's gone by
other names. Some you've heard. George Victor. Mark Victor. Farber's
been watching him, and he's a bad one."

"Amen," Colleen said. She tapped at the picture of Markovic on the desktop and said, "I saw him. Bad vibes."

"Take it, Greer," Potocki said.

She lowered her voice. "I do talk to Nellins when I can about the Higgins case. He isn't giving me much, and I wonder about some things. For instance, he doesn't have a theory about why Higgins's pockets weren't robbed. Higgins, okay, only had five dollars on him, no loose change, but still . . . Why would the perp not have emptied his pockets? These drug guys will fight over fifty cents. Or . . . why would they empty the pockets if they did and leave a little something."

Christie had had his suspicions of the two old detectives in the past. He felt a certain satisfaction that Greer was bumping up against the same thought. "You think our boys are lifting monetary evidence?"

"I hate to say it."

"I'm going to look into it," Christie said.

"How?"

"Watch me."

Her cell phone was flashing. "Sorry, Boss. This is what I've been waiting for. There's a woman at the lab who's been just— Would you give me a minute." The flashing stopped. "Missed it." Colleen punched in a number. She gave them both a series of smiles and high signs as she listened.

When she terminated the call, she said, "It was Ann Cello at the lab. She's fantastic. We got evidence, all right. Prints for Higgins match prints we took from the Dermott Roux place. And his shoes . . . they still have some of the powder that's used for cutting heroin, so . . . gilding the lily, he was in there. A hundred to one, he killed BZ."

"Fantastic. Let me work this other thing out."

He got up and stopped at a couple of other desks on his way to his office.

WHEN CHRISTIE FINALLY GOT
to his office and sat alone for a moment, he tried to take deep breaths.

He felt awful, but he wasn't going to give up just yet. Nellins was at his desk. Now was the time to lay the trap with a tiny lie. That's all it would take. After he caught his breath, he called Nellins in to see him.

"Hey, Boss, good to see you here."

"Thanks."

"You doing okay?"

"Yeah, well as can be expected. Sit. Sit. Talk to me a little about this case you got."

"Man came up on AFIS. Career criminal. Name is Earl Higgins. Actually, Hrznak is the principal on this. You want me to call him in?"

"Eh. No, you sit tight for a minute. I'll talk to him separately." Nellins started to look nervous. "Tell me about the canvassing."

"Didn't turn up anything so far. People in the hood say they didn't see this guy. Nobody has reported anybody else using that house."

"That's hardly credible, right?"

"How do you mean?"

"Somebody would know." He wasn't sure he believed it, but he did want to keep Nellins guessing.

"Somebody somewhere, sure, but we didn't find him."

"How are the labs?"

"They're coming. Faster than usual. It's amazing."

"It is, isn't it? Somebody caught fire somewhere along the line. Tell me about the crime scene itself. What are your best guesses?"

"Two people shot. One dead, one wounded and gone. According to Detective Greer, the lab told her—don't ask me why—the cartridges are all from one gun. A nine-millimeter, it turns out. I did confirm it. She says maybe a scuffle, that kind of thing."

"Did the scene suggest a scuffle?"

"Well, you know, it didn't." Nellins hurried to indicate that the two of them might choose to disbelieve Greer.

"Drug people up there, you think?"

"Looks like."

"So what do you make of the five bucks in the guy's pocket? Who carries a mere five bucks?"

"Oh, this was a lowlife."

Christie scratched his head. "Meaning?"

"No bank cards, nothing like that, hardly any money, maybe ate a little takeout up there."

"People without bank cards usually carry cash, no?"

"If they have it."

"Well, here's the thing. Whoever killed him didn't rob him. That's super interesting, right?"

"Yeah, it is."

"And the other thing is, there's a discrepancy between how much the dead guy had on him when Greer first got up there and later. You know, she started the case, but Farber pulled her off because he needed her. What happened to the money *after*, do you think?"

Nellins colored. He began to speak, but stopped himself. He appeared to toss answers this way and that. His lips trembled. Finally he said, "I'm not sure what you're asking."

"You're sure."

"Greer checked the pockets? Before the photographers and the labs got there?"

"Yes," Christie said boldly. Straighten that one out later. "So you want to tell me where it is?"

"We might have mislaid it."

"Might have. It's evidence. How much of it did you get?"

Nellins waited for a long time. "Half."

"What'd it buy you?"

"Lunch?"

"That's it?"

"Three little meals. Boss, I'm so sorry. I should never have accepted it."

"Given to you like a gift?"

"I didn't mean that. I mean I should have refused it. The vic was such a deadbeat and . . . I'm sorry. I have no excuse."

Christie lifted the phone. "Hrznak. Christie. Would you come in here?"

They waited in silence. Hrznak opened the door.

"Nellins was just leaving. Take his seat."

Let them try to make signs to each other as they passed. He got them. For a mere—what was it going to turn out to be?—fifty bucks, whatever, he got them.

AN HOUR LATER, SUMMONING
all the strength he had left for the day, Christie picked up Potocki and Greer and walked them to Farber's office. He'd given warning. Farber looked nervous.

He started simply. "I took Hrznak and Nellins off the Higgins case. They raided the corpse for lunch money. I don't want them back on the case. So far, these two have given me more on it than those other two did, and they're still coming up with things for you, things you need to know about the drug connection. So, relax your hold. Let these two go."

"Let my people go," Colleen mouthed. Christie saw it.

Christie continued, "I want to put them back on as primary and secondary. It's only right and it's only just."

Farber lowered his head and gave a grumpy stare. "You're back."

"Just when you thought you could be rid of me," Christie said lightly.

"Robbing me again," Farber said, pretending to lightness himself.

"Other way around, if you take a look. If you see a way these two could help that they're not *already* doing, you show me and I'll release them." He sensed Farber needed a compliment about now. "How are you moving? Well, I'm sure."

Something shifted in Farber, a flash of pride. He rapped his hands on his thighs for a moment. "Okay. Very few people have the pieces of this puzzle. So far we have this K, Markovic, according to Potocki, going to Philly twice a week. We're tailing. We traced him on the Turnpike going and we picked him up again in Philly, but we couldn't go the whole way. We think he uses an area, near Temple, but we don't have the exact location and we don't know who supplies the supplier. But it's big."

Christie studied the lamp for a moment. "And you started out looking at a pizza shop. Very impressive," he said, "your work." Farber flushed. "Don't worry about our end. Anything good, these two will give it to you and they won't move on any arrests until they figure out what it means to you. But it might be time for them to step it up, put this guy's picture in the paper, you know, shake things up? Two homicides and there are kids involved."

"I . . . can't do anything to scare them and make them get careful."

"A business this big, they're not going to stop for long because of a picture in the paper."

"I want the people in Philly. Up to the top."

"Of course. We know that. You'll get that. I feel sure you will."

Farber sighed, nodded. Christie stopped short of putting a protective arm around Potocki and Greer as they left. Greer wore a smug smile as they walked down the hall.

"What?" he asked.

"Just good to watch you work."

"Our daddy is bigger and better than the other daddy," Potocki said. "And we like that."

A few minutes later, they sat in Christie's office to strategize about just how much they would leak to the media and when. They decided to use the Banks name and not to acknowledge that the man had broken parole under another name in Philly. They decided to use only a drawing and not the prison photo. Colleen insisted they account in their phrasing for the possibility that Nick Banks was hurt in a self-defense maneuver.

"This is all trace evidence or what? Your defense of the guy?"

"Labs *and* his history. The old case, he insisted it was self-defense. The man he killed was politically connected, so it went hard on him."

"You really like this guy."

"She likes him," Potocki said. "She sees a victim, not a perp."

"Sentimental, Greer." Christie shook his head worriedly. "This worries me."

"Okay, okay, I'll watch it, but my gut—"

"Says?"

"Here is a man worth a little something if he could get his life straightened out."

"I've had that thought about an awful lot of people who weren't worth it in the long run."

"I know, I mean I guess that's how it is. See, right now, I'm worried enough about what he might do if we leak his picture. He could run and get himself killed before we ever talk to him."

Christie said, "Could happen." Now he had to worry about Greer not keeping her head. The guy was handsome as hell, but she ought to know better. He said, "Order of events is going to be important. You'd better make a visit to the shop first, because if it appears in the paper and nobody tried to find him through his employers, that's going to look suspicious."

"I'll go back. I'll talk to Markovic," she volunteered.

Christie said, "Good, good."

When they left his office, he lay down on the black vinyl sofa for a nap.

THIRTY-TWO

THE SCHOOL NURSE, A LARGE
woman who'd gotten the habit of angling her hips to move through
the tight space of her office, frowned when she felt Meg's forehead. She
gave her a thermometer anyway and when she studied the result several minutes later, she said, "No fever."

"Um. I'll go back to class then." For the first time in her life, Meg
had not been able to stay awake in class.

"But if you're sick? How's your stomach?"

"A bit nauseated." None of this was true. The cot kept catching
Meg's attention. She wanted to lie down on it. Instead she sat and
waited, watching the nurse study a chart. The woman seemed kind.

"Just Tuesday you had a stomach problem. Was it just cramps?"

"It turned out to be cramps. I know we're not supposed to miss for
cramps."

"Here. I'm going to give you a couple of Midol. Then I'm going to
send you home. And you can sleep. What?"

"Just I worry about classes. Tests."

"I'll write a note so you can make them up."

"All right."

When the nurse turned away after having shaken out four pills into her hand, saying, "Two now, two at bedtime," Meg pretended to take them, slipped all four into her pocket.

With her formal release, a piece of paper in hand, she started for home. The idea of a nap was so appealing that she felt her eyes closing even as she walked home, even knowing she would have to walk back to fetch the others later. Well, she could check on Nick, anyway.

This morning, over cereal, Susannah had said Nick sang to her once. Meg wished she could hear him sing.

Chicken for leftovers tonight. They'd have to add pasta. Laurie had babysitting again. Meg's next task was to find something to get them through the weekend. She felt hopeful. She felt lucky—Nick had said they were alike, believing in luck.

When she entered the house, she knew something was different. Sounds were different. He'd come down on his own. She could hear him in the kitchen, so she hurried past the stairway to see if he was all right. He jumped. She jumped. Several of the cupboard doors were open.

"Please don't fall."

"What happened?"

"I couldn't stay awake. My English teacher sent me to the nurse."

"I'm not surprised. I heard you. You stayed up even after I went to bed."

"For a little. I was . . . still trying to take it all in. What . . . what were you looking for? In the cupboards?" Before leaving for school, Joel had changed Nick's dressings and Meg had taken him breakfast— a bowl of dry cereal, a glass of milk, a thermos of coffee—and a ham sandwich for lunch. So it wasn't food that he needed.

He held on to the sink, then to a chair back. "I'm going to need to sit for a minute."

She held the chair steady and he sat down where he had the night before, leg extended.

"Look," he said, "I was just trying to see what there was . . ."

He was being sneaky. Tears came to her eyes. "I'm sorry. I'm tired."

"I'm not what you hoped."

The sad, wistful look on his face made him closer to what she did want. His nice self. "I'm sorry," she said. "I'm sorry to hold on. In a couple of days, we'll be safe with the irrigating. You're getting good with the crutches. You just need clothes and something in your pocket."

"I can't take any more money from you, if that's what you mean."

She suddenly realized what he wanted. "I've put together what you're going to need. My father's cards. The charge cards will be expired, but you might be able to use them to open another account one day. I wrote everything down for you. I'll get them." She got up and started to the basement door. "Are you hungry?"

She was biting back tears. Then she saw he was upset, moved. She wanted to touch him. Tentatively, she reached forward and touched his arm. He took hold of her hand and squeezed. "I like it here," he said. "I think you're great. All of you. Every one of you."

"Thank you."

"You, I know the best."

"Because I talk. I boss everybody around. It isn't lovable."

"It's lovable," he said in a quiet voice. "You're fantastic. I'm sorry for any asshole thing I ever did to you."

They were quiet for a minute. She sat and made a quick dab at her eyes. "I don't want you to go. They don't, either. We can't help feeling that way. It's just . . . life."

He shook his head. "You need somebody to take care of, I guess. The thing is, you deserve better."

She liked him again. He was right again.

"You ever notice something," he said after a while. "Your phone hardly ever rings here."

"Joel has a few friends who call sometimes."

"This morning, it was ringing off the hook."

"Really? Maybe the school office," she said uncertainly. But she didn't want puzzles now. She wanted to sleep. Then to get up, buy him clothes, figure out how to make some money. The kitchen clock told her she had two, maybe three hours until she had to walk back to the school. Remembering the Midol, she dug into her pocket and handed the pills over. "This'll help you sleep," she said. "I'm going to try warm milk." She put the milk on the stove to heat and went to the basement, moving fast, so the milk wouldn't boil over. Alison had put an old bureau down there. She opened the top drawer and took out a wallet that had her father's papers in it. She held the wallet close for a moment before she went upstairs.

When she handed the wallet over, Nick didn't look inside at first. He took the pills she told him to take. He watched her pour and drink milk. Finally he opened the wallet and studied her father's cards for a long time, punctuating his thoughts with almost imperceptible nods.

MELINDA KUCHENKA, THE WOMAN

who now worked the pizza shop, looked up when Colleen came in. "Your guy hasn't showed. Honest."

"Actually, I need to talk to your boss. When does he come in?"

"Well, it's complicated. There's the older one, George, who pops in from the back room every once in a while."

"He's not the boss?"

"Well, he only does accounts. The guy who trained me works the shop at night, but the one from the back room put that sign out about hiring and he's the one who pays."

"Complicated."

"Jim is the night shift, but he wants me to stay on. Says he has other businesses. The thing is, I don't know who's in charge. Who do you want to talk to?"

"The accountant will do."

"My best guess is about three, three thirty he'll come in."

Colleen said, "I'll wait."

"You want anything?"

"Not right now." She wandered outside as casually as she could, noted the sign in the window and, making a decision, called Farber. "You have a chance to get somebody into the job at the pizza shop if you have an undercover person to spare. There's a sign in the window, the place is, you know, shaken up, and the owners, from what I can tell, are dying to hire someone. I'd move right away."

"Janowski," he said.

She agreed Janowski would be good.

"Thanks."

She paced a bit, looking at the neighborhood she used to live in. Some of the places were looking good, some not. Still, it felt like home, familiar. She went back inside and sat pretending to do her reports with a can of Coke on the single table in the place, the one she'd sat at when she talked to Nick.

She had a drawing of Nick made from the prison photo. She was going to pretend she knew only the name Nick Banks and only the Pittsburgh part of his history.

A girl came into the shop. Colleen assumed the kid was going to order something, but she heard her ask about putting in an application. Melinda handed over a piece of paper and said, "He wants name, phone number, and experience. Just jot it down. Experience, I doubt," she said, winking at the kid, "but he really needs somebody for evenings."

What was the matter with these people? The girl looked very young. Alarmed, Colleen got up and walked to the counter. "Excuse me. I think you should tell him for evenings he should have a man in here, not you or any female of any age."

"I'll tell him."

The girl, writing, looked vastly disappointed. After a while, she handed the paper over and left.

Just then, the back door opened and the same gruff man she'd seen before came out into the room.

"Oh!" Melinda jumped. "I never can get used to that door opening. This woman said she needs to talk to you."

"What? About what?" he said. His eyes darted suspiciously to her, behind her.

"Could we sit for a minute? I just need a minute of your time."

"Application for you," Melinda handed him a piece of paper.

The man Colleen knew was Markovic stopped on his way around the counter to take the piece of paper. He appeared to be glad of the interruption Melinda had provided. "We're hiring," he said to Colleen.

"I noticed your sign," she said easily. She pulled out her identification badge and showed it. "I won't take long. I need to ask you a few questions about this man." She showed the drawing.

"Don't know him," he said after looking hastily.

"Perhaps we should go into your back room," Colleen said. "If you like."

"I have nothing to hide."

Colleen said, "Fine, then. I need to get your name and some ID."

"George Victor. I don't have my wallet on me. It's in the back room."

"Okay, go get it."

Markovic got up, bristling. The front door opened again and Potocki came in.

Markovic returned to the table and showed a driver's license that said he was George Victor.

"Okay, Mr. Victor," Colleen said, writing it down. "And your position here is?"

"Assistant manager and bookkeeper."

"Thank you." She wrote. "This is my partner, Detective Potocki."

Each man acknowledged the other with a glance. She said, "Look again at the picture. Look carefully. We have reason to believe you know him."

"She's the one was here before, looking for your worker," Melinda said, surprising them all. Colleen held up a hand to caution Melinda from saying more.

Markovic pretended to take a second look. "He worked here. A couple of days. The picture is not very accurate. So. What's he done?"

"We don't know that he's done anything. We would like to talk to him. Where can we find him?"

"He lives somewhere around here. He just quit on me. No word, nothing."

"You didn't take his address?"

"No."

"How did you pay him?"

"I . . . didn't get around to paying him anything. Well, some. Under the table, if you want the truth. He seemed to want that."

"Did you try to find him?"

"No. I just closed up for a couple of days until we could rehire."

"What is this man's name?"

"Nick Banks."

"Did you know him before?"

His head wagged vaguely back and forth. "No."

"How did he hear about the job?"

"He just passed the shop, I guess."

"You know anything about him?"

"No. What's he done? I mean, what is this about?"

"We think he was present in a shooting death. We need to talk to him."

"He . . . killed someone?"

"A couple of men got into a fight, it looks like."

"I'm afraid I can't help."

"Did he say anything about where he'd go if he left? Did he leave you any clues as to where family was or anything like that?"

"Let me think. I'm trying to remember. He was from Ohio."

"Ohio?"

"Yes. He said something about a mother living there."

"Ohio is kind of big. Did he mention a city?"

"Something small, I can't remember the name. I'm sorry. Maybe if I saw a map. Since he did mention Columbus, maybe near there."

"Columbus, then. Thank you for that. By the way, just one thing before we go. I'd bet that girl that applied is too young for the job, especially for evening hours. But anyway, from the police point of view, having a guy in here at night is smarter all around."

She and Potocki walked outside, and both automatically scanned the street before they walked away. "What did you think of him?" she asked Potocki in a low voice.

"I had no trouble seeing him in prison clothes."

"We're going to have to call in the press soon. I hate to put Banks out there, picture and all. Kissel, I mean. All I know is, we better find him before Markovic does," she said.

They drove back to the office. Potocki said, "One of the prisons Kissel did time in might be the best bet for finding somebody who knows where he'd be. Tomorrow the two of us ought to go up to Allenwood."

She calculated. A three-hour drive? Four? "You think?"

"See if guards or other prisoners can shake something loose. We can start out early."

"Let's talk to Christie."

"And Farber."

"Him, too."

"Want to start out at seven?" Potocki asked.

"Sounds right."

MEG WALKED, THINKING ABOUT

whether she should make up flyers for housecleaning and distribute them along the way at the houses that seemed well kept. She found herself in front of Doug's Market. Heaving a deep breath, she went in to find the manager. "I don't know if you cashed the check yet, but I wanted to make sure it was good. My . . . aunt can be very flaky. So if it wasn't, I want to work it off."

The man gave her a long curious look. "You're a character. I haven't cashed it yet. Tomorrow. How was the roaster, the chicken?"

"Delicious."

"Hmm," he said, finally smiling.

"I'm putting in applications at a couple of places. Are you taking applications?"

"For work? Are you good at the register?"

"You want to try me?"

"I might, I might."

"How many hours a week do you need? I mean, I have school, but it's almost out. I'm looking for something more or less full-time, and I see you close at six, so—"

The man worked to catch her eyes. "I could put you on a couple of days three to six. Try you out. You want that?"

"Yes! I mean, I just have to check on another job that would be more hours. If it comes through— I'm sorry. I just need to take whatever's best."

"You don't think you're a bit young for all this work?"

"I'm old enough."

"Look, you come back if you want to try it. I watched you adding up the groceries in your head when you were buying. You brought your bill to within pennies of the check. You're good."

"It was thirty-nine eighty-two." She blushed.

He nodded some more, scratched his lip, and murmured, "If we do try it, maybe we should keep it unofficial. I don't mind getting in trouble, not for a good cause, but somebody might try to stop you working. . . ."

"I understand." She looked at the cases of food hopefully. Did employees get to take outdated things home?

"We get food stamps here. And some down-and-outs come in here. Some are addicts. Would you be shocked by any of that?"

"No. I can handle people."

"I bet you can. Tomorrow after school, then. Minimum wage is— Well, never mind. I can manage five an hour. No records. No deductions."

"Three o'clock," she said. Even if she got only one day, it would still come to three hours at five dollars an hour and maybe some food.

On the way back home, she stopped at the pizza shop again. The woman working the counter was busy, so Meg waited, sitting where the woman who interfered about the application had sat. When Nick worked here, he'd had a radio playing. It seemed friendlier.

The woman finally acknowledged her. "You're back."

"You think he's going to call me?"

"Not likely. The detective told him you were too young."

Detective. To cover her alarm, she tried to keep talking. "I don't know why it was any of her business whether I work here."

"She wasn't mean about it. Said they needed a guy here at night. I kind of agree."

"What was she here about?"

"Something about a shooting. I wasn't supposed to listen in, and I'm not supposed to talk about it. Drama in the neighborhood, huh?"

"I guess."

So the police were closer. She would have to tell Nick.

THIRTY-THREE

COLLEEN WENT TO THE GROCERY
store to fill her refrigerator, grabbing whatever looked good on the
way in—vegetables and fruits displayed outdoors. Cherries, straw-
berries, sweet potatoes. Inside she tossed lettuces and broccoli and
zucchini and tomatoes, yogurt and Coke and chicken into her cart.
The pork chops she chose would have to do, even though they weren't
of the highest quality. There, like a normal person, a few meals at
home.

Her house was hot, but she put a sweet potato in the oven anyway.
She chose one thick pork chop, zucchini, and salad ingredients. She
smeared the chop with olive oil and garlic and salt, sliced the zucchini
lengthwise, cleaned and tossed a salad. She had to go to her backyard
to fire up the grill, and when she came back, she set out a place mat on
a tray, with a dish and utensils on top. Next to it, she placed a tall
glass of wine. Light a candle, why don't you, she urged herself, but she
didn't.

She carried everything to the table in the yard. It was a sweet yard—even with the weeds popping up through the bricks. The neighbor woman with the screechy voice came out on her back deck to say, "Haven't seen much of you. Busy?"

"Real busy lately."

"You eat right, honey. That's important."

"I'll try."

"How's your folks?"

Her family had visited her only twice, but the neighbor had latched on to the idea of family. "They're doing well," she lied. Her father wheezed, he looked thin and weak, he refused to go to the doctor or to quit smoking and drinking. Her mother stuck by him, having something to drink with him every day, picking up the ashtrays, scrubbing the house clean. They loved each other. Her brother was living in the apartment over the garage. His basic activity outside his job at Wal-Mart was smoking pot. "Thanks for asking."

When she was able to make a break, she picked up her tray and started indoors.

"You didn't finish."

"No, I'm full. I think I'll go in, have an early night."

She went in through the basement, carried her tray upstairs, and, standing at the kitchen counter, fell upon the food.

THE NEXT MORNING SHE MET
Potocki at seven. They signed in and out quickly and got on the road.

"I need breakfast," he said. "Just some drive-through, whatever we see."

She'd had cereal, but she ordered again with him at a truck stop—the house special—egg, bacon, cheese on a croissant. "It's a wonder we're still alive," she said.

"My cholesterol isn't what it should be."

"You're being very bad, then."

He smiled whimsically and put on a pair of sunglasses. She found herself studying him. He wore a muted shirt that had a glaze of lilac in it, of good cotton, well laundered, and a sports jacket that was also cut well. The coat would be a forty-four average, if her guessing was good. She was just taking note of his belly—not big, simply, say, a three-month pregnancy—and he caught her looking and sucked it in. "Going to the gym is on my schedule," he announced. "For my three years of desperate dating."

She laughed. "You've always been a high achiever. Maybe you can do it in two."

When she thought, as they drove toward central Pennsylvania, how she often avoided a much shorter drive to see her parents, she got a tumble of conflicted feelings.

They got to the prison at eleven o'clock.

Soon after, they were talking to one of the guards on duty about Nick's prison life.

"Markovic," the guard volunteered. "George Markovic was always talking to him."

She practically hit Potocki with excitement.

"Their relationship?" Potocki asked simply.

"Markovic guy more or less protected Kissel. You know. From the others."

"And Markovic? Was he interested in Nick that way?"

"I might have thought maybe, but we never saw any reciprocation."

"Nick Kissel hook up with anyone?" Colleen asked.

"No, he stayed to himself."

"Who did Markovic hang out with, otherwise?"

"He talked with everybody. He was a big shot. Nick hardly talked to anybody."

"What did Nick do here? School? Reading?"

"Neither. Jobs. When there were jobs, he always went for them. Any task. Needed to be busy. He took kitchen duty for a while."

"Did his work?"

"So well he got points for it."

"That's what got him out early?"

"That and a little help from somewhere. Pretty soon there was a lawyer on his case and his record here was good, so suddenly there was a hearing and he was gone. Voom."

"Who was the lawyer?"

"We can get you that. I heard Kissel went and broke parole after all that. Stupid after getting a break."

"Real stupid," Colleen said.

From twelve to one Colleen and Potocki talked with several of the prisoners, all of whom seemed to be glad to be called away from their cells for any reason at all, like children getting out of class, getting a hallway pass. Detectives knew they'd say about anything to extend the visit. Even accounting for elaboration and invention, they didn't have much to go on. Nobody knew where Nick would go if he broke parole. They simply made the usual guesses. Family, hometown.

"His hometown is only sixty miles away," Colleen said brightly. "Let's drive there. Eat in the car?"

"Ugh. If we have to."

"Okay, let's sit down, then."

The guards advised them to go to Mary Ann's Homestyle Restaurant. Unfortunately Mary Ann and the slow-moving waitresses were like old aunties who, once they got you to sit down, simply didn't want you to leave. Colleen resorted to foot-tapping.

"I know. I know," Potocki said. "I'm sorry."

"Not your fault. You were just trying to be normal."

"I should know better when you have a head of steam up."

Finally they paid their check and made it to Milton in under an hour. The gym, hotel, and real estate offices yielded nothing. In fact, the detectives couldn't find anybody who knew Nick Kissel.

"We'd better get back," Colleen said resignedly. It seemed she would have to do the press conference after all—put Nick Banks on the TV and in the paper. Someone might have seen him, and she'd put it off for too long, hoping for some other kind of break.

The drive back was long and punctuated by Colleen's phone calls to Christie, the *Post-Gazette*, the TV stations. She set the press conference for seven, giving herself little time to get her head together. Every cell in her body was terrified she was doing the wrong thing.

"Is Christie at the office?" Potocki asked.

"Was earlier. He's home just now."

"How'd he sound?"

"Like he's trying to get his voice up to full volume and speed and just can't."

AT SEVEN, POTOCKI CAME TO her, saying, "go in together?"

"Yes. We're in the conference room."

"You go in front of the camera. I'll stay in the wings."

Two TV stations and the newspaper had sent representatives. It wasn't a hot case, so far as they were concerned. They felt they were doing the police a big favor bothering at all.

And so there wasn't much to say.

What she said was, "We have reason to believe this man, Nick Banks, might have been hurt during the shooting that took the life of Earl Higgins. We are interested in any information as to his whereabouts, and we are interested in any information he could give us."

"What do you know about him?" the reporter asked.

"Nothing else significant at this point," she said, feeling the whole world could read the lie on her face. "We have a source who says Mr. Banks has information important to this investigation. That's it."

What with lights being set up and equipment malfunctioning and needs for retakes, what with the polite seeing out the doors of the media people, the whole pathetic mess of getting her five sentences on the air took until eight when Potocki caught her elbow lightly and said, "Would you want to make it dinner, too?"

She thought of the food she'd put into her refrigerator and of her determination to make her life more normal, and yet she said, "Where do you want to go?"

"Atria's."

"Good choice."

It was so easy. Dinner led to coffee—and a drink after—until it was ten thirty.

"We should watch the news together. See how it goes," he said.

She said, "Yes." She couldn't face being alone just now. They stared at the TV in the bar for a while. Potocki said, "I'm just . . ."

"I know. Just around the corner. Let's go."

So they went in two cars to his new place, only blocks from Atria's, to put on the tube.

"I have some scotch."

"Okay."

The news finally came on. The report happened some twenty minutes into the half hour, just before sports and weather.

"You look good on TV," Potocki told her.

She shook her head.

"You do."

Potocki gave himself a little more scotch. "*Nightcap,*" he said, "is an interesting word."

"I like words."

"I know."

She plunked her glass down. "Oh, man."

"What is it?"

"Everything."

"What?"

"Kissel. Could go haywire. I'm worried I'm making it worse."

"Why doesn't he turn himself in, then?"

"He doesn't know how. He's scared. He's independent, a loner."

"How do you know?"

"I know."

She stood. Potocki stood, too, and hugged her. It was great, a hug that didn't seem to end.

"What else?"

"Commander, for another thing. You must feel it, too. You called him daddy yesterday."

"Sure. He's the father none of us ever had. Maybe the father nobody ever had. The one I'm trying to be to my son. Failing miserably, of course."

He continued to hold her. She spoke into his shoulder. "And everything else. Everything I can think of."

He ran a hand up her arm, and she leaned back for a moment, then moved forward and kissed him. He held on to her tight, kissed her. "Colleen," he said, "I know this is . . . Well, we know there's a lot between us. I just have to say I wouldn't want to hurt you for anything."

"I know. You're a good guy."

"If you don't like where this is going, just say."

"I don't know, that's the thing. It feels good. Nobody has touched me for a long time."

"I can name plenty who would have given a lot to try. I'm honored." He moved closer and pressed into her. "I'm trying to do the right thing here, but I want you anyway."

"We seem to want to do the wrong thing—both of us."

They walked up his stairs, holding on to each other.

"We should stop," she said without conviction. "It's our careers. And your marriage."

He stopped.

"I should turn around and go home."

"So long as you know I want to and you don't doubt that."

They stood in his upper hallway in a deep embrace again. "You realize we've been on these two cases only a week?" she said. "Seems like a long time."

"I know."

"Christie was diagnosed only over a week ago. And he's been down, treated, unable to move or eat, and somehow he came to the office yesterday and today."

"I was glad to see him fighting."

"I adore him."

"I know."

They walked into the bedroom and then lay down together.

"Is Judy back from Florida?"

"Yep. There's only psychological distance between us now."

She watched the way Potocki's body moved as he rolled away from her 180 degrees and turned on the radio. It was tuned into the country and western station. For a moment he didn't roll back to her, and then he did. They heard the end of an Alan Jackson cut, the very end, and then a good-bye song came on, or maybe it was *the* good-bye song, the saddest one she knew. *Lay your head upon my pillow.* Ray Price was singing it, not some new pretender, but Ray, parceling out regrets and good-byes and understanding. Potocki began singing in a small husky voice that was surprisingly tone-accurate, and she joined in as a joke. Soon they were both singing the song she might have called schlocky or laughed at on another day. Tonight it made her cry. She wasn't sure she could explain it, but old Ray had pushed some button. Potocki saw that and nodded, eyes closing a little. He kept singing softly, and then she managed to squeak out the rest of the words.

"Nobody has to know," she said finally. "We just carve tonight out of reality."

"That doesn't work."

"I know. Just tell yourself nobody has to know. We'll work at it."

He put a hand on her back and began to trace her, every part of her with the flat of his hand. His touch was full and deep. She thought, My neck? What does he get from the back of my neck? But he seemed to be investigating all of her. His hands traced her thighs; he murmured appreciatively and kept going. When he kissed her, she tasted the salty, musky flavor of his excitement. He groaned and began to kiss her neck, her breasts. Her own arousal peaked suddenly and nothing else mattered. So, she thought, slipping off her blouse, she would lose her partner, be shamed; everyone at the Branch would know she couldn't keep her knickers on. It didn't matter at the moment. He was so solid, big and solid, heated, and after her. He unbuttoned her pants and she let him—oh, it felt good.

The hairs on his chest were a light brown, almost blond. His thighs were large, all muscle. He had a hard-on a man of twenty would be proud of. "Oh, man," she said, "Oh, man."

"Say no at any time."

"Are you kidding? We're way past that possibility."

They held off for a glorious thirty minutes, but then she told him she didn't want to wait any longer. He nodded soberly and gave himself over to her.

"Please don't go," he said at three in the morning when she whispered that she had to go home.

"What do you mean?"

"You can't leave."

"I have to. I have to pull my head together. Compartmentalize. Find a different set of clothes for tomorrow."

"Maybe tomorrow we could fall off the wagon again," he said.

"Maybe tomorrow." She tried to dress subtly, half under the covers. He pulled the covers off. "Let me look at you. Let me look again."

"Pick something other than my thighs."

"What's wrong with your thighs?"

She kept dressing and he kept looking.

"Promise you won't be sorry."

"Oh, I don't like promises. I'm not trying to be coy. I just got that gotta-go feeling."

"I'll walk you to your car." He got out of bed and threw his clothes on in a hurry.

Hand on her arm, hand behind her back—oh, that flat-handed touch—he knew how to touch. Nothing tentative there. She felt herself tremble.

She fetched her bag from the first floor where she'd dropped it—gun in there, credentials.

He opened the front door quietly. He grimaced. "I have to go to a mediator early next week to figure out the rules. With Judy. You want to ask me anything?"

"No."

It was nothing, probably just sex. Two tired, horny people.

She drove home and slipped into her garage and made her way up from the basement. Dutifully she brushed her teeth, washed her face. Sleep or stay up?

Stay up. She lay down, thinking.

How odd that she didn't know herself. In seconds she was asleep.

THIRTY-FOUR

NICK HAD REQUESTED GROUND
meat, so she brought a package of it and buns and cheese home from
Doug's Market. She got several compliments on how well she'd done
at the register. She had twelve dollars in cash in her pocket and a promise of work tomorrow when the owners would set up grills and cook
out on the street—ribs, chicken, hamburgers, hot dogs—as they did
every Saturday in good weather. She was already imagining leftovers
she might get to bring home.

Nick had patted out burgers and was turning them over. "Not that I
would call this cooking," he said, "but I can stand long enough to flip a
burger." He was improving fast now. He had gone up the steps using one
crutch and the banister. In his eyes was the dream of going, being free.

He placed slices of cheese carefully on each burger. He put on the
broiler and heated the buns. The younger kids watched fascinated, as
if nobody had ever done anything so complex in their kitchen.

Meg knew she was always rushing around. She thought how attractive patience was even as she dipped to the basement and put in a load of laundry. In her head she calculated what she would earn tomorrow and what she needed to buy. She figured up what she could earn at the market full-time in summer. The astounding thing was, if they all kept at their jobs, if they got in a rent payment before the landlady got nervous, they could actually stay in the house and together. If Doug's kept her on, she would make two hundred a week; Laurie and Joel together would make between fifty and a hundred a week; that was a thousand dollars a month. They'd be together through the summer. The school year would present other problems—work hours reduced. But maybe they could save between June and September.

She'd told Nick Thursday night when they talked, late, after the others went to bed, "People don't need much. If they think about it, if they conserve."

"You need clothes and shoes."

"Well, yes."

"You need movies."

"Don't need them. They'd be nice."

"People need booze."

She got angry for a moment. There he was, looking at his stupid cup of tea.

"Who I am," he said, "is somebody who likes bars, back rooms, you know, seedy places, seedy people."

"You *like* that? Why?"

"It feels right."

"Things that feel familiar feel right," she said sharply. "You need new experiences."

"Like? You all, you mean. I admit it's sweet. I admit that. Believe me, I've thought . . . all the things you've thought of. I've imagined. In a different set of circumstances . . . You understand."

No matter what, he was going to leave. She'd gone to bed last night, drumming that into her head, angry with him. Today she couldn't remember the anger.

When she came up from the basement, he was doing what Susannah had described, singing—three lines from something she didn't recognize.

"Good voice," Laurie said to Nick. "You carry a tune."

Meg was about to ask him to sing again, but the phone was ringing. She turned the corner to hear Joel answering it. He was ashen and he was saying, "Yes." Then "Yes." Then "Just did." And "No, we're okay."

Meg knew from the look on Joel's face. "What did she say?" she asked him.

"She said she thought by now we would have turned ourselves in. I told her we didn't."

"How did she sound?" Meg whispered.

"Like herself."

"What did she say *exactly*?"

"Just, how did we keep going? And I said, we just did."

The two of them walked back into the kitchen.

"Who was that?" Nick asked, seeing their faces. He was taking the burgers out of the frying pan.

"Alison," Joel said.

"Aha! Maybe she misses you."

Laurie said, "We don't miss her."

"I don't know . . . she might be planning to turn us in—long distance."

Laurie said, "I'll kill her."

Meg said, "Don't talk like that."

"I will," Laurie said. "Honest to God."

Susannah looked thoughtful. They all sat down at the table, because Nick was serving up the burgers.

After supper, since it was Friday, they were allowed a long night of watching television. Laurie and Joel played chess. Meg combed Susannah's hair. All the while she worried that Alison might make the phone call that would end all this with a call to the authorities.

They were all awake when the news came on. They weren't paying particular attention until they heard the anchorwoman say, "Nick Banks."

Nobody spoke.

All of them stared at the TV. There was a short silent clip of the woman detective talking.

Next they heard, "in connection with a homicide a week ago on the city's North Side. Police would like to talk to this man, who they believe may have been hurt during the killing." Behind the anchorwoman was a police sketch of Nick. The drawing looked enough like him that nobody wanted to speak.

"They're after me," he said finally when the clip was finished.

"But," Meg said, "if you listen to the phrasing, it seems like they might understand what really happened. They might just want to talk."

"You don't get how police are."

"The woman detective on the TV is the same one I told you I saw up at the pizza shop."

"I met her once. She was on this case before it became a case."

"Why was she after you *then*?"

He shook his head. "Well, I tried to believe she just wanted to talk to me. Then I thought she was after me because I was . . . supposed to be in Philadelphia. Parole," he said, nodding at Meg, who knew the details. "But she was Homicide, and she was asking about a kid who died."

"Well, now that your picture is out there, it's actually safer here. It's just us. For a while. We can think this out."

The others murmured agreement.

"No. No. I have to go. That's the message. I have to go." He was clearly crazy again, running already, his thoughts all jangled.

"Let him go, then," Laurie said angrily. "People make stupid decisions all the time."

The rest of the news seemed silly, insignificant.

For a while after the kids went upstairs to bed, they could hear the television below. "If it came down to it and I got him to turn himself in, and it got us into trouble, would you hold it against me?" Meg asked them.

"Yes," Laurie said, but she used an inflection that suggested, *not really.*

Joel said he wanted to think about it. Susannah said a quiet no.

After Meg had got the others to sleep, she visited Nick, who was still downstairs. "If you want me to call . . . If you want to turn yourself in, we'll take whatever comes to us. We understand what it means."

"Thank you. No. Just no."

"Make sure you sleep on it. We're all sleeping on it."

Back in her room, it was as if she could hear his heart still pounding.

Before she left for work in the morning, when Nick was downstairs showing Laurie how to make pancakes, she slipped the twelve dollars she had earned into her father's wallet sitting on the bedside table in Nick's room.

THIRTY-FIVE

MAC COULD HEAR HIS FATHER
moving around downstairs. Bull in the house. Bellowing. That was how
he thought of the man. His father was not yelling at the moment, but
even when he wasn't yelling, you could hear the yelling. Every time
MacKensie thought of those big muscular shoulders and the head in-
clined forward, he thought of a bull. He'd made a drawing of his father like that once, when he was eight, nine years old. The teach said
it was a sin to make a cartoon of your parents, but that the drawing,
the artwork, was good.

MacKensie slipped the earphones of his headset over his ears and
pressed the PLAY button. He listened to an old song he liked. "I just
don't give a fuuuuuck." It was funny. "I don't give a fuuuuuck," he sang
along.

"You awake?" his father called. The voice came through his door
and past his earphones.

He didn't answer.

After a while, he reached under the mattress and brought out the stamp bag he had stored there. Power X 3, one of three bags left in his personal stock. Almost without thinking, he opened the bag, wet his finger, took a taste. He sat up carefully. Then, trying not to creak the bedsprings, he leaned way over and extracted spoon, syringe, lighter, rubber strap from under the mattress, everything he needed.

"Hey. You awake in there?"

The door was locked, but he was worried the sound of the rapper in his ears somehow carried out the door. He heard his father's footsteps retreat. Do it in the house with his father right there. That felt gooooood.

Half. Half for later. He prepared it all slowly, so slowly, he got another call from his father before he was finished. He wanted it so badly, yet made himself be slow and *controlled.* Strong.

He prepared his arm and shot up. It was good, good, good. Too good. He almost couldn't find the energy to put the needle and tubing away. But he did it. Then he lay there. He didn't want to move. Or for anything to interrupt his beautiful day. Sex, music, money, everything would come to him, he could feel the luck now.

"You awake yet? I got things I need for you to do."

He didn't answer right away. It was still okay, still okay.

An hour and a half later, he got up.

While Mac was eating a bowl of cereal, his father hit him on the side of the head with something, some kitchen implement, yelling, "Son of a bitch. Don't you ever stay in your room when I call you."

"You cut me. I'm bleeding."

"So's my heart. Go get a Band-Aid. Don't be a pussy or I'll hit you again." Then his father gave him a list of things to do.

After Mac swept a couple of floors, he looked for his moment and ducked out of the house. He was thinking, if Carl was around, it just might very well be somewhere close. That's the way people were; they didn't go far. He decided to just walk and look. He started up toward the house that now had police tape on it—his place no longer. He fingered the cut on his forehead where his father had hit him.

Hopeless, his father was hopeless. Why did he ever think it could be different at all? He had gone to the bathroom, cleaned up his wound a little, but hurried out of the house to see if he could give K what he wanted. He felt sick walking up the hill. His head hurt. That's when he thought he saw Carl. Then the vision disappeared. He even walked up to and around the yard where he thought he'd seen someone . . . Carl. Nothing, just a boarded-up house. With his ear to the door, he tried to hear if there was any sound inside.

He turned himself around and walked over to Zero's house, where he knocked a couple of times before he roused his friend. Zero answered the door, yawning.

"You wouldn't believe who I saw."

"Who?"

"Money in our pockets. Carl. Come with me."

"I don't think I want to mess with it. I mean, something bad might happen, right? Let's go down my basement."

"Where's your mom?"

"Out. Come on, hurry."

They shot up and got to feeling good enough that all they wanted to do was climb up to the first floor and watch television, slack-jawed, for a while.

Mac said to Zero, "I just want to find out. That's all."

Zero said, "Better we don't mess with it." He looked mellow; he was leaning back on the sofa, smiling. "We wouldn't be here, wasn't for him."

"Every time I reup, K asks me about Carl. He wants him."

"Worried about him . . ."

"No. You don't get it. Worried he'll *flip.* He almost said it. Worried he'll flip. Where would that leave us?"

"Right," Zero said, but now he was nervous again. "Better to just leave it alone."

"He's found another place. If he's not selling anymore, what's he do in there, huh?"

"You don't know for sure he's in there."

"He's been missing over a week. Let's go see."

"Not me. If we don't see, we don't have to say nothing."

"You're going with me."

"No, I'm not."

"Oh, yeah. Don't shake your head." Mac felt happy, excited, to be doing something, for all along he kept feeling there was something to be done, something to figure out and solve finally. He ran his hands through his hair and, in doing so, remembered his hair. "You think I ought to let the roots come out like this or do the blond again?"

"I don't know. I liked the blond."

"Okay. Let's go. I can't just sit here wondering."

"Just tell Markovic where you seen him, then."

"I just want to be sure before I say."

"Shit."

They left Zero's place. Ten minutes later they arrived at the fire-damaged house Mac was looking for. They skittered around the back quickly, looked this way and that; then Zero tried the door.

"It's not going to be fucking open," Mac whispered, swatting Zero. He put his head to the door. "I thought I heard something. Wait. A radio or something. It stopped. He's in there, all right."

"Let's get going."

They moved away from the door. "No. This way. Come on. I got a regular customer I have to meet first. And then . . ." He motioned to Zero to follow him.

"You want me to go with you?"

"Yeah."

"What about telling K?"

"When I have my reup later."

Going toward the meet, Mac told his friend, "K wants to split us up in a week. You take up the hill, I keep working down the hill. He must have lost somebody up there or be losing somebody."

"I don't want to work up the hill. I don't want to go alone."

"You have to. If he says."

From his peripheral vision, Mac watched Zero shambling along as they went toward Wendy's, where Mac's customer would drive by in fifteen, twenty. Zero looked dumb, depressed. They were not at the same level of cool anymore. Mac reached into his back pockets and brought out two pills. "Sometimes when you're really down, you need to get back up."

"Where'd you get those?"

"Guy in the park. He bought from me; he showed me what he had. I took one once, testing it for safety before I would let my good friend have one. I am the king's dog."

"You're too weird," Zero laughed.

"And you are the king, the king. It was pretty fun. I was wired, off the walls really, but it was a fun high. Let's go inside Wendy's—we got fifteen minutes or so—get Cokes, and have these little nuggets. I like energy. Sometimes I think I like high better than low, you know?"

Zero hesitated. Then he laughed and said, "The king says okay."

CARL ALMOST HADN'T HEARD

them. He had his radio on, and was moving it around some to get rid of the static, when a sound at the door managed to come in more loudly than the radio, which he always played very low. Without thinking, he turned off the radio, and cursed himself. He'd just given someone a signal. He was so sure it was going to be Markovic that relief washed over him at the boys' voices. But when he thought it through—they hadn't knocked, they hadn't called to him—he realized they were not his friends.

His body set up a racket of warning signals: short breath, pounding heart, weak knees. This was it. His sanctuary no longer existed. He didn't want to leave, but this was it. He managed to throw his books and notebook, his few clothes, and the last of his food into a garbage bag. He wanted the blanket, but couldn't figure out how to carry it. He looked through the cracks in the plywood.

He opened the door. Looked out. Saw no one. He took a moment to go back for the blanket and folded it over his shoulder, thinking, This is how banditos stay warm at night, by carrying the poncho over a shoulder all day. He was glad he was taking it.

He looked around again, then began walking in a direction he'd never gone—along North Avenue for a while, then down a side street until he ended up on Western. Keep going, he told himself, and see if he could hitch a ride going out Route 65. K and the people he hired wouldn't think to look for him in that direction. They'd figure bus routes and look downtown.

Yet all the while he walked, heart pounding, he let in the little truth he'd tried to keep from himself. He knew perfectly well what he was doing, who he was going to. It was a risk, a gamble, and he was going to take it.

COLLEEN WASN'T IN THE OFFICE Saturday midday. She'd gone home, taking a break, because it had occurred to her that if she ate lunch at home, she could manage to pay some bills. The case was stalled. She worried she wasn't thinking right because her head was scrambled with her indiscretion of last night and the invitation to repeat it tonight.

"Did you ever study Aristotle's theory of chance?" Potocki had asked her this morning when they happened upon the coffee machine at the same time.

"No. Never did."

"Well, he said it was the most wonderful thing that could happen. He said chance was when coincidence takes the place of intention."

"Huh?"

"Say Man A goes to the market to buy vegetables. And Man B who owes him money happens to go to the same market. Man B sees him and says, 'Glad I ran into you. I owe you money.' And he pays it. Man B is delighted to be relieved of his debt. Man A is delighted to have the money owed him. It works out as well as intention might have worked out, but there is the added thrill of its happening by chance. Think about it."

"I bought my vegetables Thursday," she said. "That's probably where I went wrong."

Potocki smiled.

"Aristotle said all that?"

"He did. He called it chance."

It sounded to Colleen like *luck*. There was probably a whole industry figuring out the probability mathematically. "Why didn't Aristotle just say luck? Did he have a concept of luck?"

Potocki looked deeply thoughtful. "Maybe it was all subconscious logic anyway—the debtor knowing deep down that the debtee shopped for veggies at a particular market. Not wanting to make a long awkward walk with money in hand to the man's house."

"And this is about?"

"Us."

"Shhh."

Her phone rang now as she ate her lunch alone at home. It was Detective Littlefield at the office with news. And the news *was* finally luck. A little of it had come Colleen's way at last. "I'll be right there," she said.

She plucked a paper towel off the roll and wrapped her sandwich for eating in the car. Was it arbitrary, pure luck, or had she planted the seeds of luck, made it? Either way, she felt hopeful that this was the break she needed.

JANET LITTLEFIELD GREETED HER.

"Where is he?"

"Room One. He had a bunch of stuff with him. We took it from him—and it wasn't easy persuading him he'd get it back. It's spread out in Room Two. You want to take a quick look?"

"Yeah. Drugs?"

"No drugs."

Colleen was glad Potocki had gone somewhere for lunch. This was hers, all hers. She took a moment to catalogue mentally what

Littlefield had already made notes on. Three math books, none of them wimpy—and one, *Mathematician's Apology*, she decided after leafing through it, that she wanted to read herself under different conditions—a journal, a blanket, some food, some clothing. Seventeen dollars and twenty-five cents. A radio. "He was living on the street?"

"He won't tell me."

Colleen opened the journal. Her eyes moved fast over the page. She saw enough to know she wanted to read the whole thing. "Wow," she said.

"He was struggling with it," Littlefield said in an even, rational voice.

"He must feel very exposed," Colleen said. "Like we took his clothes off."

"He did seem to have that attitude."

Colleen went into Room One to see Carl.

He looked up as she walked in. His hair and face were clean. He didn't look bad at all.

"I'm glad you came in," she said, "I've thought about you a lot." On the street, planting luck, she had said, "If ever I can help you, let me know." Now she had to keep her word. "They told me out there you wouldn't say why you came in. They had to write down something. They wrote down, 'Wishes to give information.' Is that right?"

"I'm not sure."

"Let's talk it out a bit. I'm sorry we have to take packages of any sort from a person coming in. If you think about it, it'll make sense to you. We have to, for safety. Hopefully we'll have a good talk and you'll have everything back."

He nodded.

"We were hoping to talk to you again. Did you come in about BZ?"

He looked honestly surprised. "No. Something else. One thing first—you said if I needed to get straight, you would help me."

"Yes."

"Well, I detoxed on my own. All on my own."

"That's what you were doing all this time?"

"Yes. And I need more time in . . . in isolation. But . . . the place I found to stay in—"

"Rehab?"

"No, just on my own. I did it on my own."

She tried to make sense of his possessions. "Did you live outdoors?"

"No, holed up. But people came looking for me there. That's why I came here. I don't have enough money to go anywhere else, but I have to get out of town. They tried to kill me."

"Who did?"

"It's complicated."

"That's okay. I'm here to listen. Who?"

"A man. He's called K." A thrill went through her. "He supplies the runners."

"We're going to show you some pictures in a little bit. Can you tell me what happened, from the beginning."

"Which beginning?"

"Any beginning you want to start with. I know it's going to take a while. Are you hungry?"

"Yes."

"You need a warm meal, don't you?"

"Yes."

"I'm going to order you something." It was terrible, what happened next; she thought she was going to cry. What a fiasco that would be. She turned to go to the door.

"The thing of it is," he said, "I would have hitched out of town, but . . . I heard on the news there was a death up at the house I used to go to sometimes. It was meant for me. They were going to kill me. And I got away. But then I heard on the news you were looking for Nick Banks. And I thought I'd better tell you he saved my life."

Then it happened before she had warning—tears in her eyes. Stupid, stupid. Was she that unstable? "Get you that food first," she said, opening the door of the interview room. "Then you tell me the whole thing." She hurried out.

Potocki had come back and was in the outer office, looking elated. "We caught a break?"

She'd have to share it.

BACK IN THE ROOM WITH CARL,

they listened to everything the boy knew. His fear was palpable. He'd been afraid for a long time.

He was able to pick out photos of Earl Higgins, George Markovic, and Nick Banks without any hesitation.

"How many shots did you hear up at the house?"

"Three."

"You never saw Nick Banks again?"

"No. I feel— I was scared, but . . . I probably should have gone to his place to see if he got home."

"You never went out of your hideout?"

"Only to the yard."

"Do you know where Nick Banks would go? Say, if he didn't go back to his place? Family or friends he talked about?"

"He never talked about anybody. Just that he used to do fishing in New Jersey for a living."

"How did he come to be hired by this K?"

Carl thought about this for a while. "Kind of knew him. There was some background. But he didn't seem connected to K either, like he didn't want to be there. Are you going to help me get out of town?"

"Yes. I'm sorry we can't let you go just yet. The Narcotics people are going to want to see if they can jog your memory about anything. After you tell them what you know, we'll figure out where to send you so you can be safe. I think I should warn you there'll be a deal. If you cooperate, tell us all you know, and agree to keep in touch so you can testify, they won't charge you with anything. They'll come up with some money to get you started somewhere. Is that understood?"

"Why would they give me money?"

"To live. If you can prove you're reliable and getting clean."

"I am getting clean."

"It's impressive what you were able to do. Next you have to do it with people around. And with talk. And counseling. That's the deal they'll make. And if you think about it, it's the right way."

"That's going to be hard."

"Yeah, it is. Try to rest up a bit. We'll get you another meal soon. Commander Farber will be coming to talk to you soon."

"Will you be here?" he asked Colleen. She was sure, then, in the way he looked at her, that she was the connection, the reason he was able to come in.

"I'll be here," she said. "We're only going out for a few minutes."

She let Potocki go to Farber.

She hurried to Room Two and opened the journal. Interspersed with Carl's writing were pages from an Internet chat room. The printed voices came at her like the voices in a play, a chorus of them, answering each other or going off on solo riffs. Even though she got through most of the journal, skimming at times to be sure she checked any references to Nick Banks, she knew she wouldn't want to give the journal up. She wanted it in her desk, for her records, to remind herself that there was sometimes hope.

"Janet?" she called to Littlefield. "Can you get someone to copy this for me?"

"The whole thing?"

"Whole thing."

THIRTY-SIX

MAC WAS WORKING HIS CORNER when K drove by, this time with another guy in the van. Mac knew the drill. He needed to go over a block and hop in. He sensed trouble from the expression on K's face. He didn't walk fast at first, didn't feel like it, but finally he pulled himself together and went up to the van. "Yeah? Carl was there?"

"Gone, it looks like. How long ago you see him?"

"Round lunchtime, no after," he lied. "We looked for you right off."

"You knock on the door?"

"No. That'd be stupid." He started to feel nervous, not a feeling he liked.

"He see you?"

"No. No way he could."

"You saw him? For sure?"

"Yeah. Not for long. Just outside the place."

"Well, he wasn't there."

The small, fierce-looking guy said, "Been there, for sure, though. Sheets on the floor, broom, this and that."

Mac said, "I figured he was living in there."

"Fucking dark in there," the little guy said. K looked angry at the interruption, but the other guy didn't seem to care. He held up a flashlight. "He left this goodie."

K turned back to Mac. "Maybe he saw or heard your pal?"

Mac wanted to sound totally convincing. "Don't think so. Hope not." His heart kicked up a bit. Zero had been stupid. A bad tip was worse than no tip at all.

"Look. You got to give me something better that this. Something. Where he is . . ."

"I don't know. Honest I don't."

"Who else would know? Who else went up to that house where the police tape is? Huh? I know people who would be real unhappy if you hold out on me. Give me something to take them."

Mac thought. "I know a kid went up the house once or twice. But, honestly, he's a nerd kid. He doesn't know Carl."

K studied Mac. "Who's the kid?"

"Joel. Nerd name."

"Joel what? Are you fucking with me?"

Mac tried to recall if he'd even known a last name. It ran in his mind it was something common. "If I knew it, I would tell you. Joel . . . Martin or something like that. I know what. He washes cars. You see a kid about ye high, carries a bucket, washing cars, that's the kid." It would turn out to be a dead end, but Mac didn't bother to say. It would occupy K for a while.

"I got other work," the little guy said. "Take me back to my car, huh?"

K looked cross-eyed with fury, and it almost made Mac laugh.

JOEL WAS TOTING HIS BUCKET.

He hadn't gotten much today, only an old Taurus.

He didn't hear the van pull up beside him.

"Hey, you."

He looked up. He thought at first the man wanted to get his car washed. "For a van, five bucks," he said.

"Oh, really. That's quite a deal. Maybe I should get it washed. Meanwhile, I want to talk. How about you get over here."

Joel stopped in his tracks. "I'm busy. There's another car I'm supposed to—"

"Come on. I can make it worth your while." He held up a twenty. He kept the car idling down the street as Joel walked. "Not, not what you think. This is just a question about somebody I need to find."

"No." Joel kept walking.

"Okay. Just wait a sec, then." The man put the car in park and got out. He was large, olive skinned, with closely cropped hair. Joel could not remember having seen him before, but he knew to be scared.

"Hey, kid, you sure got your lessons about not talking to strangers. Only, I'm not a stranger. Basically, I know people you know. See? And I need to talk to you."

"What about?" Joel asked. He hated that he was shaking and that he wanted to run.

"When did you last go up to that house where they found the body?"

Was the man police, plainclothes? "What house?"

"Don't lie. I know all about it. Carl? Nick? Where'd they go? Nick Banks?"

"I don't know. I don't know who you mean."

In an instant, everything was changed, the man was on him, twisting his arm until his shoulder hurt. "Why are you running if there's nothing wrong?"

"I'm not running. Let me go."

"Not just yet. So, you know where he is?"

"How would I know?"

The man tightened his grip. "Well, let's hope you get a little smarter, huh?"

Joel looked up and down the street, wondering where to run. He remembered people went in and out of the Lutheran Church at various times of day. Maybe he could be safe there.

"Well, I need to get hold of him. Okay?"

"Okay." He made himself stop pulling in order to give the impression he was going to settle down and talk. "Okay." But all the while he figured out what he had to do. "I still don't know who you mean. Lot of people went up to that house." He imagined himself down the alley, around the corner, and inside the Lutheran Church.

The man's grip tightened. "Lots? Plus Carl? How about the guy worked the pizza shop?"

"I don't know any pizza shop guy."

"You little liar!" The man turned him and pushed him against the van, then raised a hand as if to hit him. "You lying little shit."

Joel thought his shoulder socket would dislocate the way he had to wrench away, but he did it all at once and he ran, ran, ran leaving his bucket and brush right on the street.

He ran like an athlete, like wind, down the street, so fast, he felt unreal, or the pavement did—it was something that surprised him when he looked down, blocks of cement, one after the other, some blocks cracked, some higher than others. He saw what a sidewalk *was* as if for the first time. He ran right into the church, down the steps, past a meeting room, past a men's room, a ladies' room, and into a corridor.

He stopped. For a long time, he listened. If the man came in asking for him, he would scream until somebody listened. But when he realized what that meant, when he stopped and breathed, and the thought crowded in that there would be questions about where he lived, his family, when he realized all that, he wanted to give up. He pressed himself against a wall, gasping.

Maybe the man was a cop.

No. No, he wasn't.

Joel listened for footsteps. All he heard for several minutes was the hum of voices, people talking, and the hum seemed to be coming from a room somewhere around the corner. The first notes of a hymn were struck on a piano. There was a pause and the piano started again. Somebody who believed in playing hard was doing just that, as if to force power from the wavering voices that followed uncertainly. Joel tried to hear past the hymn. Then, the worst thing happened. He could hear people leaving. Chairs scraping and murmurs of good-bye. His heart beat wildly.

He listened for the piano. Nothing.

After about five minutes, all the voices were gone. Then, when he was about to move, he heard footsteps. Joel leaned back into a well in the corridor. Ahead was a man with long hair, walking slowly, looking as if he were in a movie playing Jesus, just contemplating the Sea of Galilee. To Joel's right was an open closet, made of wood, with thirty or forty choir robes hanging there. He slid in, plastered himself against the back wall of it. Inside he was almost laughing, almost crying. The silky lilac-colored material covered his face so he thought he would smother. He was swimming, tangled in purple robes that smelled of deodorants and perfumes.

He listened for the footsteps of the man he'd seen. The walking continued, unhurried. Lights went out, one after another. Suddenly the place was plunged in darkness. He was in a basement, no windows at all. It seemed as if night had fallen and he'd lost a day. When the footsteps were gone, he missed them. After a few moments of silence, he panicked like a drowning swimmer, batting the robes away. He turned every which way, trying to make his eyes take in some light; after a very long time, they did. He listened again. There was nothing to hear, except his heart pounding loudly.

He could stay here the night, but if he did, Meg would end up having to call the police. If he could find a phone, he could tell her he was all right. He made up his mind to find a phone. After another long wait—what seemed like an hour since he hadn't heard anything at all—he made out a voice from the floor above, a single voice. Someone on the phone? He waited a little, listening for another hint of the voice. The air around him vibrated as if a long, low organ note reverberated into eternity.

He began to look for a way out of the basement. Soon he would find a door. He stopped, trying to think what he would do if the man who chased him was outside, waiting.

Light. He caught a glimmer of light. He headed toward it and found an exit sign at the end of another hallway. He saw the door had a crash bar on it; opening it might very well set off an alarm. He stood before the door, afraid to chance it.

Then he pressed the crash bar in one quick movement. At first it didn't open. He pushed again and it did. No alarm sounded and he was tumbled outside where he came face-to-face with another person.

Before him stood the bearded man with the shiny long hair and the removed, peaceful face. For a moment, the two of them looked at each other. The man was smoking.

"Whoa," the man said. "I thought I found myself a special place." It was funny, really, how much he looked like all those pictures of Jesus—a little sad, a small tilt to his head, thin. His hair went the whole way to his shoulders. "Can I help you?" He stood very straight and seemed to protect the fall of his hair. He had a wistful smile.

Joel wanted to scan the surroundings for that other one who'd accosted him, but it seemed impolite to interrupt the slow movements of the man before him.

"You were in there. Where?"

"Downstairs somewhere."

"You live around here?"

"Yes. I . . . was hiding."

The man blinked in puzzlement.

"Someone was after me."

"Nothing bad, I hope."

Joel shook his head slightly.

"You must have been scared. I would have helped you if I'd known. How old are you?"

"Almost twelve."

"You have brothers and sisters?"

"I have a sister almost eleven and another one seven and the oldest one of us is almost fourteen."

"You could just say what age you really are."

"I guess." Joel turned his head finally. He looked behind him and around again. He didn't see anyone else.

"Does your family have a church?" The man looked longingly at the stub of his cigarette and dropped it, then stepped on it, almost sorrowfully, as Joel's father used to do with a pest he couldn't persuade himself to let live—like a huge carpenter ant.

"Not anything steady."

"Let me get you some brochures for your parents. We have a summer program. It stops at age twelve, so it's good for you and your two younger sisters. Come with me. We have to go around to the front."

Joel felt sick and his heart pounded. "That's okay. I have to go."

"No, come. I don't mind. My name is Gordon. Yours?"

"Joel."

The side of the church was windowless. There were a few beaten-down buildings across the alley from it. The whole way around the building, Joel expected to discover someone hiding, watching, ready to spring. Gordon moved swiftly now.

Without a word to each other, the two went inside the church. Joel's sneakers squeaked on the stone floor of the lobby.

"Joe?"

He did not correct the man.

"Did you see the upstairs when you were hiding?"

"No."

"Take a look."

They passed through glass doors into the church proper, where they stood behind the pews and looked at the altar with its dark wood and purple cloth up ahead. The stained glass was modern—just a bunch of triangles, not elaborate like the windows of old churches with people washing feet and kneeling in prayer.

Space. There was space here. It was calm and clean.

Gordon led him into the office to the side of the vestibule. The office was large and had a big counter in front, like a school office. From this counter Gordon plucked three brochures, which he then handed to Joel. "The Bible-school program starts as soon as school is over. There are outings. We provide lunches. Do you think you could get your parents to come by and talk to me?"

Lunches. For Susannah, anyway.

"I'll try." Joel wondered if people who went into church work tried to look a certain way or if they were born with high foreheads and intense eyes and were fated to be attracted to church work. "Do you teach the Bible school? Are you the priest?"

"I just work here. The head honcho is called a pastor here. This is a Lutheran Church."

Joel accepted the brochures. "Thank you. I'd probably better get going."

"If your friends are rough on you, avoid them."

"I will."

"And don't skip school. Learning is important."

When Joel left, he went around to the alley and stood for a long time against the side of the church before he moved on to the side of a garage. After that he darted to another building and waited, going very still, listening, searching in every direction. He stuffed the brochures in his shirt. He wanted desperately to be home, but he couldn't hurry and he couldn't at all costs end up leading the man who had chased him to Nick.

Nick had to leave. For sure. Joel understood that now.

When he finally got home, he found Nick in the kitchen cooking up some kind of stew for dinner. Susannah was sitting there, waiting for him to turn and make a chess move between stirs of the pot.

SHE AND POTOCKI WERE AT the office most of Saturday with the kid with the mop of hair and the sad eyes. Colleen was unwilling to leave him alone with Narcotics people for any length of time. Farber worked on the kid for hours, coming away with corroboration about the Wednesday and Sunday trips to Philly, about the way distribution worked. Farber asked seventy ways about the relationship between K and the street dealers, K and BZ, K and Nick, K and Philadelphia. And Colleen zeroed in on K's reputation for getting rid of people.

By eight o'clock that night, Colleen was able to shove a piece of paper toward Carl, whom she now knew was really Matt. She was trying to get used to his correct name. "If you sign this, Matt, we put in the order for someone to drive you to Atlanta. Meals on the way. We get you into rehab there. After that, if you make good, we give you start-up money. All this is dependent on you being in touch with your friend, Tracy, and with us. She's our contact beyond the rehab center. All clear?"

"Yes," he said.

"You have to trust us."

"I'm trying."

"One more thing. You know we have to go after these boys you mentioned. Anything else, any final thing, you want to tell me about them. Anything?"

"I don't know anything else. They wanted work. They were at me for that all the time. I don't have their addresses."

Eight thirty, two uniforms were assigned to take Matt to Atlanta.

"You have my card?" Colleen asked. "Keep it. And memorize my number, too. If anything feels wrong, call me."

"Yes," he said.

"Bye, Matt. I'm wishing you all the luck you can possibly use. I hope this is the beginning of something. I'm counting on it."

She watched him walk out to the car with the two uniforms.

"Atlanta," Potocki said. "You're going to get a lot of grief about letting him go to Atlanta."

"He likes this girl Tracy."

"People are going to say you're losing your head." He smiled.

"People are going to say any damn thing."

"Want to go get some dinner?"

"Yeah. Then I want to call the principal and get some addresses. Talk to these two would-be dealers."

"It's a long day."

"I know."

"You're relentless."

They gobbled down steaks at Outback, where the steaks came with more gorp and show than they wanted. They were able to get a table only because there was no home game. They saw part of the away game—innings five and six and part of seven—on the TV while they ate. Finally, they got a call back from the principal of the school with the addresses they needed for Sean Zero and Peter MacKensie. They finished up a little faster than they wanted and were on their way.

SEAN ZERO'S MOTHER HAD A fringe of badly permed blond hair. She wasn't very old, but her face was already lined.

"What's this about?"

"Need to talk to your boy."

"I think I know. He called 911. I should have never let him call. He's a good kid, he doesn't need to be defending himself for trying to do the right thing."

The woman had just solved one of Colleen's unanswered questions. "Where is he?"

"With friends."

"What's his curfew?"

Mrs. Zero looked nervous. "Soon," she said.

They waited in the house so they could keep an eye on the mother. Sean came into the house around eleven. Potocki on instinct hurried out to the street and moments later he was back, hauling in Peter MacKensie, who was giving him a viper's look. "Might as well come on in," Potocki said. "Otherwise we'll just be coming to your place." Once MacKensie was in, Potocki guarded the door with his body.

MacKensie sneered as Mrs. Zero urged her boy, "Tell everything you know about what you saw."

"A dead guy," Sean said slowly, checking with his friend.

No, MacKensie was not happy. He flashed Sean a look.

"We didn't see anything else. It was dark," Sean Zero said.

"What about another person up there?"

Sean Zero shook his head. His eyes checked with Mac again. "We didn't see nobody else."

"I don't know anything about whatever," MacKensie blurted. "I don't know what you want with me." Potocki took hold of him firmly to keep him from bolting, which he looked clearly ready to do.

"So, Sean, you made the call to 911 from Cedar," Colleen said. "Good. That was good. You were trying to help. Who made the second call?"

"Go on, tell," Mrs. Zero said.

"I don't know about any second call," Sean said. MacKensie tried to give him a sign to shut up.

"Tell us about the other guy up at the house, wounded."

There was a pause in which Zero's face showed surprise. He looked at his mother, who gestured that he should answer. "Some guy. Hurt."

"How?"

"Shot in the leg."

Colleen said, "If a kid, say your age, made the call, who would that be?"

Zero said, "Maybe a kid named Joel." He looked at MacKensie, who wouldn't look back at him.

"Who's Joel? He deals? Sells on the street? What? Uses?"

Zero almost laughed. "No, he's this little kid. Just a pest."

"Where does he live."

"I don't know for sure. In the neighborhood. Somewhere near North."

"What's his last name?"

"I don't know."

"You tell if you know," Sean's mother said.

"I don't know. Honest, Mum."

"What were you doing up at the house?"

"Nothing. We just hang out there. We saw something was going on, but we could hardly see at all. We ran."

"Mrs. Zero, I'm going to need to take a look at your son's arms."

"What for?"

"Roll up your sleeves." Sean did slowly, all the while looking toward MacKensie's feet. "Yes," Colleen said to the boy's mother. "He's got a habit. Either you knew or you didn't."

Mrs. Zero was close to fainting. "I work a lot of hours."

"I understand," Colleen said.

Generally, they would have taken both boys in and processed them for juvenile detention. But Farber had given strict orders to let them continue. There was a line from something, but she couldn't remember exactly what it was or where it came from. . . . *Let them continue in their crimes.* Something like that. MacKensie and Zero would be nervous for a day or two. They'd lose their confidence, but they'd go back into it, and Farber's men could watch them if they bothered with anyone this low down. All Colleen could do was hope the mother stepped in.

It was almost midnight when she and Potocki left. They decided to get an address for the kid named Joel first thing in the morning.

THIRTY-SEVEN

THEIR MONEY WAS ON THE
table—the forty Meg had earned that day, ten of the twelve from yesterday, Laurie's twelve, and Joel's six. Sixty-eight dollars. Like little id-
iots, they were offering it all. And hanging on to him at the same
time.

Joel got the picture, though. Joel was clued in now. "Bus is still
the best bet," the kid was saying agitatedly. His eyes were crazy from
the run-in with Markovic.

Nick asked again, "Did he see you go into the church? Did you really lose him?"

"I lost him. But he has the neighborhood. He could ask around. He
could see me again."

"Once I'm gone, even if he gets in here, even if he searches, just say
you never knew me. Okay?"

"Yes." Joel nodded. "That's what we'll say."

Meg got pale. She told her brother, "I'd rather Nick went straight to the detective. Because. If you *listened* to her, *it sounded* as if she understood. She said they wanted to *talk* to him. She didn't say he was a suspect." She turned to Nick, ready to make her speech all over again.

He didn't want to fight with Meg. You couldn't fight with her. He eyed the sixty-eight dollars, thinking what a nice long night of drinking it would buy. What he headed her off with was, "I'll take enough for a bus ride to somewhere. When I make some money, I'll send it back to you."

Meg shook her head, then said, "Okay."

He stood, pulling up the crutches. From his pocket, he took the wallet that Meg had given him, removed the twelve dollars, put it down, and picked up a twenty. That was enough. He did have some pride.

"Our basement," Meg tried one last time. "We could set something up."

He couldn't help smiling at her determination. Outside their little place, he was wanted by the police on one end, Markovic on the other, and living in the basement was not going to fix it. His heart was racing still, although he tried to appear calm for their sakes. It was time now. He was going to go.

"Look. I'll send you money when I have it, but you can't keep going like this. When I'm long gone, you have to . . . get somebody in here. If not Alison, somebody."

They all straightened up and didn't answer him.

"I wish you had more clothes," Meg fretted.

He wore the outfit she had bought him, a light blue denim shirt and a pair of wide-leg jeans. He'd caught himself in a mirror earlier and was surprised to see he looked more than respectable. He wore one of the shoes she'd scrubbed, but because of the Styrofoam block supporting his splint, he had to wear a big wool sock on the other. Still, nobody could tell at a glance what his leg was splinted with. He had taken to shampooing his hair and shaving as well as doing a couple of sink baths—whore's baths, he'd always heard them called—a day. He didn't smell.

Joel said, "One last thing. I have to cut a window into the Styrofoam, so that you can change dressings on your own."

"Okay," he said impatiently. "Okay." He doubted he'd keep at it, but saying no was not an option. Joel was his doctor.

So he sat again at the kitchen table with his leg extended. Joel said, "I'll get some things." The boy got up and went upstairs.

Meg brought him more tea. "If we had a lot of money, we'd just rent a different place somewhere."

"Move?" Susannah asked.

"Or we could rent a room for him. We could sneak over there, take him things." Susannah brightened at this idea. It was a fantasy the little girl apparently liked.

Meg knew better than to ignore the fact of Markovic out there looking for him, but she was stubborn.

A few minutes later, Joel started working on his leg, cutting into the Styrofoam slowly and carefully. "Should have done this to begin with," the kid said. "I kept wanting to look at the whole thing. Don't worry. This is going to work."

Nick watched Meg cleaning up the kitchen with a meticulous determination to account for every crumb. Finally she came to the table and looked unhappily at the money sitting there. "Take the money, at least. To give you a fighting chance."

"Twenty is enough for a bus ride to somewhere."

"And you need money for a city bus, unless you're going to take a cab. Which you probably should do."

"Cabs keep records. No, no cab."

"Almost done," Joel said. "Look. Here's how you wash it. Swab in here. Let it dry. Fit the piece back in. You need to take the tape and use the Ace to hold it all together. Okay?"

He said, "I can do that. Look. If I'm going to get going, I ought to get going. I'll gather what things I have." He stood, pulled the crutches into place.

"Wait," Meg said. "Wait. You have to time it right. You have to know where you're going. And you can't be waiting in the station where any-one can see you. You should buy the ticket just before you board the bus. And—I think they're more likely to check the population at night. That's when, you know—"

"Low-life types travel?" He shot her a smile, trying to work on her sense of humor.

"I don't know. If you rest up and you go in the light of day . . ."

"I think so, too," Laurie said. Joel scowled, but he held his tongue.

"Let me at least see about the PAT buses." She went to the phone in the living room and soon after, he could hear her part of the conversa-tion. "Travel information," she said. Then, "From the corner of Arch and North to the Greyhound Bus station."

She came back, wincing. "You have to catch the 500. It goes from North to Federal to downtown. Then you have to walk over to Fourth to catch the 56. It's a lot of walking. Too much."

"I can do it."

"Then there's getting through the bus station."

"I can do it."

She nodded. "Where will you go?"

"Erie, Baltimore, Columbus, somewhere—wherever I can."

"Isn't there someplace you want to go?"

He shook his head. But he was thinking they were right—Markovic was more likely to be roaming around at night. He sat back down. "Morning, then."

For a while everyone just seemed relieved.

"Did you like it here?" Susannah asked.

"Sure. Very much."

"We have a cap in the basement. It'll help if you wear a cap," Laurie offered thoughtfully. "I'll get it." She started for the basement.

"I can pack you a sandwich tomorrow morning," Meg said, "but I wonder if you should be carrying something to make it look . . ."

"He can't," Joel said. "He needs to keep his hands free."

"Backpack," Laurie said, stopped at the basement door. "That would work, wouldn't it?" Joel nodded. "I could let him have mine."

"He doesn't have anything to carry in it, though." It was Meg's voice, full of worry. They all looked at her.

Laurie told them, "There are the funny sweatpants and the pajamas. They're no use to us. He might as well have them."

"And the gun. Where is that?" he asked. There was a silence that told him the answer before he heard it.

Meg said, "We don't have it anymore. I threw it out with the bloody clothes."

"You what?"

The kids stopped looking at him. Nobody would look at him.

"I had to. I hate guns."

Fury came over him so strongly, he choked with the surprise of it. "How could you? You never talked to me. Don't you think that was my decision?"

"I couldn't have it in the house with children."

"I might . . . It could . . ."

"I had to."

Nick sank more deeply into his seat. Meg's face was red. He thought she was going to cry. She grabbed up all the money he had refused and put it back in the wallet. She took a key out of the kitchen drawer, showed it, and slid it next to the money. "Key to the house. In case you ever need—"

"Thank you."

No gun. Okay, okay. Better that way. A relief, really.

Laurie came up from the basement with the cap. She plopped it on his head. "Looks good," she said. "I'll go get my backpack. It's upstairs. Mine is the best." The others nodded agreement.

When she returned with her plain brown backpack, she told him, "I put a couple of things in it. See, it's going to look good, just right. You can act like a student."

"I'm a bit old for that."

"A graduate student like our father was."

"Oh."

"You'll use it?"

"Yes. Thanks."

There is a long silence. Finally Meg says, "Okay. We'd better get to bed so we can get up early."

She starts the others toward the steps.

He says, "I don't think I can sleep just yet. How about if I put on the TV again until I can? Would you mind?"

"No, of course not."

He takes his time getting settled on the sofa, pulling a blanket up over him.

Does he like it here?—Susannah's question.

With people moving around, doing this and that? The only family life he's ever really had. He can hear the little girl's voice asking him that question as he sits waiting for morning. He's gotten used to the routines, the sound of a shower running, then stopping. Wet towels drying. Dishes clacking against each other. Voices raised and hushed. A human machine in motion. He likes it all right. A dangerous amount of liking.

When Meg appears downstairs after the others are asleep, he's not surprised. He more than expected her. "Did I wake you?" she asks.

"I was just drifting."

"I'm sorry."

"It's all right."

"They're sad," she says.

"You still think I'm something I'm not."

"Please don't laugh at me."

"You must want to be a social worker." But she doesn't like it when he teases her, so he stops.

"Don't drink," she says. "Please. Don't. It will help."

He laughs, shakes his head. "You're funny."

"Please."

"I'll try. What if I say I'll try?" Maybe he will . . . who knows.

"You'd better sleep. You need energy. I'll get up early. The others, too. They'll be upset if I don't get them up."

She is hesitant to leave. He reaches out a hand to her hand, squeezes. "All right. I'll try very hard," he says.

She nods and leans forward and kisses his forehead before she turns the corner and goes up the steps again.

What he feels is terrible. An ache in his chest, a feeling of weakness, tears just behind his eyes. He blinks them away, lies back, and watches whatever the TV gives him. He keeps himself awake for three more hours, trying to be numb. When the house seems utterly quiet, he begins to prepare the leave-taking. And at every move, he fears Meg will be wakened and will be at his side.

Never could do good-byes, never could.

He puts on the sweatshirt, zips it, puts on the faded cap Laurie brought him. ABC CONSTRUCTION, it says. In the back-and-forth game they've been playing, he takes the wallet from the kitchen table and removes all the cash except a twenty, and two ones for the city bus, but he doesn't remove the key or the ID.

Quietly, he unzips the backpack, curious. A book, one of Susannah's drawings, duct tape, the pajamas, and the funny cut-up sweatpants, his right shoe. He manages to get the backpack on. He's nervous about the crutches and getting onto a bus with them, so he contemplates leaving the backpack behind. He decides, better to try it, dump it if he has to.

If anything, leaving early will make him especially noticeable—a man on crutches moving slowly down the street before five in the morning. But something tells him to make the break now, mean and clean. City transportation might not be running yet, but he can go to the park. Plenty of homeless people sleep in the park. If he burrows in, he can rest on a bench until he's ready to move on again.

He stands at the door for a moment, listening to the quiet. He opens it, steps out, closes it behind him. It's June, but it got cold last night. He thinks there are stray snowflakes in the air, pretty, drifting toward him. They're blossoms, it turns out, some landing on his face.

Hobbling down the street in the predawn, he's prepared for a gunshot to ring out. Any time, any time. After doing the better part of a block, he crosses the street into the park. No gunshot yet, but he's cold and his arms ache and he wants to rest. Fine. There's time. He chooses a bench and just sits. It'll be plenty warm in the bus. He thinks ahead to that.

He sits for a long time. Twenty dollars. A bus out of town? Or a city bus to a suburb, where he can wait for a restaurant that has a bar to open? Or go back to the kids? Or . . . call the police, and be done with it? Make them proud. So, four options.

The sky is going to be almost completely clear today. The sun is coming up and the park is nothing but pretty.

Delay. That's his decision.

People begin to come into the park. Church bells ring. He can see up ahead a few old women going into the Catholic Church—a good place to hang for a while, to think, and it's just about the distance he can handle before he needs to rest up again.

He works the crutches under his arms, walks slowly to the church to face a new challenge, a set of steps, but he manages them. Oh, man, he can't remember when he last saw inside a church. Never believed in any of it, but still it's pretty to look at, one saint after another in stained glass, the bowl of water at the back. He takes a seat. An hour or so to figure things out can't be a bad thing.

In the quiet hush, people filter in at a steady rate.

About now, he realizes, Meg will be making herself something to eat, maybe even making a cup of coffee . . . or maybe she drank it only to keep him company. She'll be weeping that he left without saying good-bye. When the others wake, Joel will be philosophical, Laurie angry, Susannah plain sad.

An old lady takes a seat beside him in the pew. She smiles at him and nods toward his leg. He nods back. She opens a missal for him, points to the correct date. Obediently he tries to follow along. The old lady appears to be a great hand at the game, flipping back and forth in her own missal like a champ.

When a woman with a sad, halting voice stands at the front, reading, the old lady points out the passage in his missal. Even with it in front of him, he can't make heads or tails of it: *When I was born, there were no oceans or springs of water. My birth was before mountains were formed or hills were put in place.* He smiles to thank her anyway. She's definitely good at church, because she speaks along with the congregation the next passage also in the missal; he reads along, almost catches up with it. A wee bit of meaning comes through. *Yet thou hast made him little less than God . . . thou hast put all things under his feet, all sheep and oxen, and also the beasts of the field, the birds of the air, and the fish of the sea, whatever passes along the paths of the sea.* Meg would understand the Bible passages. She'd be able to explain them.

When the lady with the timid voice reads again, he almost gets it—it's a message about the kids, Meg in particular. *We even boast of our afflictions, knowing that affliction produces endurance, and endurance, proven character, and proven character, hope, and hope does not disappoint, because the love of God has been poured out into our hearts through the Holy Spirit that has been given to us.*

After the service is over, he continues to sit. He doesn't know yet whether to go back to the kids, or go to the police, or go to the bus station. Does he want hope, endurance, or escape? Why did he take only twenty dollars to get out of town? It's not enough for a bus ride *or* a bender. The old lady looks at him curiously. Maybe she recognizes him from the news. Is she danger, sitting right beside him?

But she's still smiling.

"Does everybody have to leave?" he asks.

"Heavens, no. You can stay for another dose of it."

"Maybe I'll sit for a little bit."

"Going to be a beautiful day."

He watches her go to the vestibule, shake hands with the priest, and leave.

The church becomes quiet except for the puttering of a couple of workers. He studies the stained glass. Feet. Lots of saints' toes. He counts the candles burning. He sits for so long after everyone else has left that one puttering worker comes up to him. "Everything all right?"

"Is there another service?"

"Yeah, but not till nine thirty."

"Thanks."

The smell of incense, the fact of his hunger, the thump-thump of the broom keep him from sleeping, something he would very much like to do. It's almost 7:40. He thinks of his bed back at the little house where the kids live.

Meg, Joel, Laurie, Susannah.

He doesn't want to leave yet. He smiles to remember the old lady's phrasing. He wants another dose, but he doesn't stay for it.

When he leaves the church, he walks another five minutes to catch the 500 bus. By now, his armpits are sore and his ribs are sore, too, but nobody bothers him, and the driver waits patiently while he gets onto the bus.

Riding toward downtown, he tries to work out how he can pay the kids back. A job, an anonymous envelope with money sent to them every month. It pleases him to think that. He will be Charlie Philips, working quietly, sending money home to his kids. What form, what form? Cash, dangerous. Money orders—can be traced. Checks, ditto. It's going to have to be cash. A risk.

He can go back to fishing eventually, some port where he isn't known, but in the meantime—maybe another pizza shop, maybe baking, a bakery. A place where they let him rest his leg. Pop a loaf in the oven, take a sit.

So long as he gets to a town where he isn't recognized, he'll get work. He'll be Charlie Philips, bum leg healing, a man in need of a job.

PART FOUR

THIRTY-EIGHT

SHE'D CALLED POTOCKI FROM her kitchen phone, finding him already awake, sounding grumpy. "You could have come over last night, awakened me in person this morning," he said.

She almost admitted to wishing she had. But there was no time for stupidity. "See you at eight. Partner."

Coffee and a bagel later, she burst into the office.

Janet Littlefield said, "You sure seem high-spirited lately."

"Do I? How?"

"Way up on the tightrope. Really working this case, huh?"

"Making headway finally. And I'm keeping *some* kind of info going to Farber all the time."

"So you've done the miracle?"

"What miracle?"

"Servant of two masters. It's keeping you lively."

"Guess so."

She settled herself at her desk and, in spite of the hour, called the principal of the school system that Sean Zero and Peter MacKensie went to, the woman she'd made contact with yesterday. "Sorry about a Sunday-morning call," she began, "but we need to know ASAP about the frequent contacts for MacKensie and Zero. And also, especially any Joel they might know. In fact, all the Joels in the school. I'm sorry again about the hour and the day."

The woman grumbled a little. "I don't know who they hang with. I just don't know that. On the other question, I could go look. I only know of one Joel off the bat. He's our star pupil. Too young to hang out with those others."

"How old?"

"Seventh grade. Young, though, skipped a grade."

It didn't sound quite right to Colleen, but she continued, "It's a start. Last name and address." After she wrote down *Philips* and an address only blocks from where she was, she added, "If you'd look over the rosters anyway for other Joels. I'll get started on the Philips kid."

"If ever there was a kid who *wouldn't* be in trouble, it's the Philips boy."

While she gave her own phone numbers, Colleen retrieved on her computer the interview records from the files Hrznak and Nellins had typed in. Potocki came in, noted her presence, and kept going to his cubicle without stopping to listen to her half of the phone call.

She could see Nellins had interviewed the Philipses. Charles, Alison, and a bunch of kids when he was looking for information on Higgins. "Before we hang up, tell me," she said, reading her screen, "anything you know about the Philips family."

"Best students we have. Single mother."

"Know anything about the mother?"

"Not up to the smarts of her kids."

"How many of them?"

"Four."

"Four. What about the father?"

"He died a while back."

"Oh. Who is Charles to the family, then?"

"I don't know the names. I'll go into my office. I'll know more in, say, under an hour."

Colleen sat for a while reading Nellins's notes. Her head was kind of foggy. She got herself a cup of bad coffee, drank it down. Then she told Potocki, "We ought to get going."

She asked him to drive. They went downstairs and ended up with the Century again.

He asked, "Are you doing okay?"

"I'm feeling mixed up."

"It's strange, isn't it? I mean I knew I've had this crush on you—"

"Crushes," she said weakly, almost unvoiced.

"I could see all this last year your crush went in another direction."

"I don't know what you're talking about."

"Come off it. It's all over your face every time you say his name."

She didn't like Potocki suddenly and wondered how she ever had. Why did he need to embarrass her?

He kept talking. "I thought about you a lot is what I'm saying. I wonder now if Judy sensed it. I don't think I've ever felt this . . . out of control in my whole life."

That was Potocki in a nutshell. Just when she thought she could get angry with him, he baited her sympathy. Good trick. Obviously it hadn't worked with Judy, though.

Her phone rang.

The principal was saying, "Okay. I have the file in front of me. The father died two years ago. The mother is named Alison."

"Father's name?"

"Charles."

"Thank you." She hung up.

"What?" Potocki asked.

"Nellins being sloppy." She tapped at the file folder.

They pulled up in front of a small house that was set back from the street, and they went to the door. Colleen gauged the girl who answered the door to be around ten, eleven.

"Police," Colleen said. "I'm Detective Greer and this is Detective Potocki."

The girl froze.

"Please don't be frightened. We need to talk to your mother."

"She is out of town, on a job interview. Our father is out right now."

Colleen hesitated. "Where is your father?"

"Working."

"Where is that?"

"He mans the phones at Duquesne Light."

"Your father's name is—?"

"Charles. Philips."

Colleen nudged Potocki, handed him the records she was carrying. "Who's staying with you right now?"

"My older sister. It's okay. She's old enough."

"Is she here?"

"Yes. I'll call her."

Colleen got a literal foot in the door. "May we come in?"

"Just a minute."

Colleen looked at Potocki, whose eyes were scanning the pages. He looked up. Something worrisome here, all right.

An older girl came toward the door. Colleen recognized her as the kid who had been applying for work at the pizza shop. She was pretty, like the one who'd answered the door. And poised—although she looked as if she'd been crying. "Yes?" she asked. Her eyes flickered nervously when she saw Colleen.

"Hey, we've met before. Up the street? You were looking for work? And I was there in the Dona Ana."

"Oh, yes," the girl said, and it looked like a lie when she added, "Sorry. I didn't remember."

"May we come in? Talk a bit?"

"There's no one here at the moment."

"It's you we hope to talk to. And your brother Joel." Okay, okay, it was against the rules to talk to juveniles, but she felt Potocki nudge her forward. If they didn't break rules, they'd be nowhere.

"Could I see your badges?"

Colleen repressed a smile and handed over her ID. The girl hardly studied her ID. She did, however, look at Potocki's carefully. "Now may we come in?"

Finally the door opened, and she let them in. Colleen could smell toast. She and Potocki sat in the clean, poor living room. The older girl's lip was trembling. "I'll get my brother," she said. She went up the stairs and stayed long enough to make a hurried conversation. When she came down, there was a boy and a small girl trailing her. The middle girl stood back at the opening to the kitchen.

"You people are awfully young to be staying alone."

"No, we're fine. It's just for a couple of hours."

Potocki said, "We're asking because we want you to be safe. Do you understand that?"

The older girl nodded, still biting hard at her lip.

Colleen took out her drawing of Nick. "Some of your friends have told us you might know where this man is." She showed the picture. Four children shook their heads, clearly lying. She followed it up with the prison photo. They looked hard, almost eagerly, but continued to shake their heads.

"Okay. Truth time. We know you know him. We know your father isn't at work. According to school records, he passed away over two years ago. We know Joel went up to the house where there was a murder. Do you want to tell us what's going on?"

They looked at each other helplessly.

"How about if you let us look around?"

"You don't have a warrant," the boy said. It was the first they'd heard his voice. It had an adult sound.

"True. We could get one. I'd prefer that you help us without any . . . pressure."

The boy went still for a moment before he nodded agreement. The older girl looked at him with alarm.

Potocki first checked out the upstairs to be sure there was no one hiding up there. Then he came down and nodded for Colleen to look upstairs. What she found was one crowded bedroom and one empty bedroom. In the empty bedroom, there was nothing except some gauze bandages on the dresser. There were no adult clothes in the closet, no perfumes, jewelry, and, in the bathroom, little in the way of cosmetics— three mostly empty tubes of lipsticks and rouges. Where were the mother's lotions and potions? Colleen came back down and looked through the kitchen. Sparse. Very little food, no . . . stock. Some cash on the counter, okay, but something very bad was going on here.

"You need some groceries," she said mildly.

"I know," the older girl said.

"Are you . . . Meg? Your name is first on our records."

"Yes. Mary Catherine. They call me Meg."

"I'm going to send child welfare people to look into your situation."

"No, please don't. We . . . we just need to do some grocery shopping."

"Is there a basement?"

"Yes."

"My turn again," Potocki said.

He was down there for a very long time, long enough that Colleen got worried, even though the sounds coming upstairs were fairly soft ones. She called from the top of the steps. "Everything okay down there?"

"There is nobody hiding down here, if that's what you're asking, but . . . wait till I come back up."

Potocki soon did come back upstairs carrying a trash bag that held the clear shape of a cardboard box. "Got something good," he said.

"Give us a minute," Colleen told the kids. She and Potocki walked outside. He gave her a peek into the bag. "What we have in here," he said easily, "is evidence that is probably going to prove Nick Banks was here. Bloody clothes, a gun."

"Wow."

"Yeah."

"You see any evidence of an adult around here?"

"No."

"Oh, man. I'll let Christie know we need a few reinforcements." She dialed up Christie and gave him the news, explaining, "Probably one of us should drive over with the evidence and one of us should stay here. So we'll need another car eventually. There's nobody here with the kids."

"Stay there, both of you. I'll take care of this. Be right back to you."

She and Potocki went inside again, Potocki awkwardly carrying the bag that held the evidence. The kids sat on the sofa, waiting.

"We know Nick Banks was here and that he was hurt." They didn't answer. "Is he still around?" Colleen asked.

"No," the boy said quietly. He eyed his older sister, who looked distraught, but she sat forward, readying herself to speak.

"Did he force you to help him?"

"No. It was not like that at all," Meg said.

"You want to tell us about it? Are you all telling me he didn't pressure you or threaten you?"

"Yes, it was our choice," she said definitely.

"When did you last see him?"

"Two nights ago. Um, Friday, I mean."

"And it started when? A week ago?"

Joel and Meg both nodded.

Colleen addressed Joel. "What were you doing up at that house? Tell us what happened, okay? We aren't going to hurt you. You found him up there? Or he came here? How did it happen?"

Joel hesitated. "I found him. We . . . let him come here."

"But he didn't force you?"

"No."

"Where is he?"

"He left."

"You knew him before?"

"From the pizza shop," Joel said. "My sister recognized him."

"Any relationship with him?"

"I just knew him," Meg said.

"You understand we have to locate him. He's wanted for questioning."

Meg said she had to get something that would help them. She went upstairs and came back down with her school backpack, from which she dug out a sheaf of papers. "I was going to mail this to you, anonymously, with the box of evidence. I wasn't sure I could get away with mailing the gun, and that hung me up." She handed the papers over.

"How will this help us?"

"He's innocent. I tried to get him to call you, but he doesn't think anyone will believe him. I questioned him lots of times. What happened up at the house was self-defense. I saved the gun and the clothes because I thought maybe you have people who know how to read the evidence."

"We do. We have people like that."

"He's . . . I don't know how to explain this."

"Go on. Try. I met him once."

"You did?"

"Up at the pizza shop. I thought he had a nice way about him. Really nice. Kind. Is that what you're saying?"

Meg nodded. "I think he got himself in terrible trouble and can't figure out how to get out. There's a guy after him. I wrote down everything. I knew I'd need it one day."

"Let me take a moment, see what you wrote here."

Potocki said to the kids, "Let's go sit in the kitchen for a bit. I want you to tell me about yourselves. Let's just relax. We can have a second breakfast if you're up for it."

Colleen read a few lines and shook her head to clear it. What she was reading sounded professional, like something a defense attorney would come up with. It was a well-written, organized account of Nick's involvement in the killing up at the house—and more. Bit by bit the girl had tried to fill in Nick's background and how he got into trouble once, twice, and then a third time with Markovic, to whom he now owed money.

There were fourteen pages altogether.

Potocki poked his head out. "Everything okay?"

"Keep eating. I have to finish this."

There was a paragraph at the end that made her head sing. The girl had noted that the lawyer who got Nick released from prison was put on his case by another lawyer from Philly named Mickey Costanzo. And the girl had theorized—and here Colleen did laugh out loud— that perhaps Costanzo was part of the organization that included Markovic, all of them thinking to hire and use Nick for their own purposes.

The kid watched too much TV, she told herself.

But a ripple of excitement went through her. No, the kid had done their work for them. It was the closest thing to a statement from Nick Banks, Nick Kissel, that they could have. And a lead, to boot. The least she could do was run this Costanzo name to Farber, let him check it.

Colleen went into the kitchen. All six of them were gathered in the same place now. "Meg, this is very helpful, very clear. You got him to tell you all this?"

"Yes."

"How?"

"I asked a lot of questions."

"And he was willing to talk?"

"At night. I would bring him tea and make him tell me."

"Do you know where he went?"

"No."

"He left two nights ago?"

A small pause. "Yes."

"Did he mention family, friends, places?"

"No. He didn't have anyone."

"Why did you let him stay here?"

"We knew he needed help. We liked him." Meg broke her gaze and looked at her siblings as if for confirmation, which they gave by nodding.

"And he was sick," the little girl said.

"How? You mean hurt?" Colleen tapped the papers. "You made a note about his leg. How bad was it?"

"Bad," Joel said. "Fractured. From the gunshot. I fixed it best I could."

Potocki was buttering a piece of toast for the little girl. He stopped midgesture. "You fixed it how?"

"Set it."

"I don't understand. You set it? How?"

"It's kind of a long story. I . . . we lined it up and splinted it."

"You didn't do it by yourselves?"

The kids looked at each other, but didn't answer.

Colleen said, "We're going to need to learn more about your situation. How long have you been alone here?"

The kids kept catching each other's eyes, sending silent messages back and forth to stick to the same story.

"Not long. It's just Alison, our stepmother, had a job interview."

"She helped set the fracture?"

"Yes," Meg said while Joel said, "No."

Colleen sighed. "Look—"

The questioning was interrupted by the sound of a light tapping at the front door.

Both the detectives started for the front room, but so did Meg.

"Let me," Colleen ordered.

It was Christie and Janet Littlefield at the door. He put Janet Littlefield in the kitchen with the kids and commanded, "Brief me."

They gave him a telegraphic account of what they knew so far. His expression shifted back and forth between alarm and fascination.

"Go on. Go back and get this evidence in. I'll call Farber and ask to meet in about an hour."

They left as he called the kids into the living room and was saying, "This nice lady is going to get you all some lunch. She'll order in something good. In the meantime, just whatever you can tell me would be a big help."

Colleen was always surprised when she felt miffed with Christie, but it made her angry that he'd butted in this time. She was getting the dope from the kids, they were coming around. All he could do was ask the same questions again.

Potocki grunted as they left the house. "He does throw his weight around sometimes."

THIRTY-NINE

THE GREYHOUND LEAKS A
burning oil smell, sharp. He closes his eyes, brings the cap down over his
face. Hunger and the oil smell and his body moving forward when the
driver hits the brakes make his stomach lurch—and it was jumpy
enough to begin with. Images of doom keep coming to him—someone
plucking his sleeve, slipping into the row behind him, saying, "No use
trying to hide," or, "Hey, man, finally caught up with you." After about
twenty-five minutes, he puts Laurie's cap back up, hungry to see the
world.

On the right is the ramp to the Turnpike, but the bus takes the
curve of road to the left that leads to Route 22. Out the window are
people in cars and vans going to church or Sunday food shopping. It's
all so . . . He can almost reach it, the image of a life like that. He
thought he had it once, in the early days with his wife, but it wasn't a
quiet life. They argued. She wanted things—clothes and cars and

trips—and kept asking until he realized with a jolt she didn't love him.

Meg, Joel, Laurie, Susannah.

The rhythm of the bus takes over, making his thoughts less anxious. He shifts, trying to get comfortable. His body still aches from the long walk to the bus. It seems . . . nobody is interested in him. They are reading paperback books or just staring ahead. He shields his eyes once more with the cap and allows himself to sleep. Twice he wakes slightly, half aware each time that the bus stops, people get off and on, the bus starts out again. He drops into the deeper sleep he missed last night.

Finally he's awakened by a voice. "You okay, buddy?"

His heart thumps as he brings himself back up to the surface. The driver is standing over him; the bus is empty behind him. "We're here?"

"We're here."

"Might need some help getting out," he says.

"You got it." They walk toward the front of the bus. The driver reaches out to hold on to him as he descends the steps. "You need anything else?"

"Place to get something to eat here?"

"Doughnut shop. Everybody eats there." The bus driver points to a place next door.

Doughnuts. He's down to $3.75. A doughnut and a coffee, anyway. After that, who knows?

It's twenty minutes after eleven. The day is bright. He can hear a church bell in the distance somewhere.

The people in the doughnut shop—old-timers, mostly—are reading the newspaper and talking among themselves. He pulls the three dollars out of his pocket, orders a coffee, and is about to order a doughnut when something clicks; he hears Meg's voice telling him, "You don't make decisions. You let things happen, and then you blame yourself." There is one practical decision he should have made—a way to get some food and coffee free. The old lady who appears to run the place solo is already pouring a cup of coffee for him. She's a speedy one, zipping around to refill cups, grabbing sugar wrappers and used plates on the way.

"Does the phone here work?" he asks, referring to the very old phone booth in the restaurant.

"Good as new."

"I'll just come back for my coffee," he says.

"It'll be here." She smiles at him. Old and still working—he likes people like her.

In a low voice, he murmurs his request. "I'd like the number for AA."

The woman on the line tells him a number, but he has nothing to write it down on. "I'll put you through, sir."

When a second woman answers his call, he says, "I'm wondering about meetings in . . . Johnstown, Pennsylvania."

"Let's see. Ten thirty this morning at New Visions, Walnut Street," the woman says. " 'Course, let's see, you already missed that. Seven tonight in Westmont. Civic Center."

"Thank you."

He looks at his watch and goes back to the woman behind the counter. "Where's New Visions, Walnut Street?" he asks. "Is it far?"

"Four blocks." She makes a map with her finger on a napkin. "But you got crutches. You guys," she calls. "Who can give this soldier a ride over to New Visions?"

"I'm leaving now," one old fellow says. "You want to go now?"

"You don't want to get in his car," another man cracks. "It's not going to make it."

He makes a move to pay for his untouched coffee.

"You really want it? I could put it in paper," the waitress offers.

"Never mind."

"No charge, then."

"Very kind of you," Nick says. As he's leaving, he can see her consider, then pour what's in his cup back into the pot.

The man who will take him to New Visions holds the door open for him.

"Kind of you, too, to give me a ride."

"It's nothing."

He follows the geezer, who shuffles to a large Chevy maybe thirty years old.

"See, we're known as the Friendly City. Seen our billboard?"

"No, I haven't."

"Well, we're friendly. I don't know that New Visions is open on a Sunday, though."

"What is it?"

"It's medical something or other. So how come—?"

"I'm meeting someone."

"Oh, okay, then. How do you get yourself in a car?"

"Slide. Backseat. Support the leg."

"Makes sense."

The backseat has to be cleared of a gallon of windshield washer fluid and a couple of plastic bags and an empty cardboard box, but he succeeds at the new movement—sliding and supporting his leg. How visible he is . . . how memorable. He has to force himself not to think it, but instead to *feel* invisible. They drive the four blocks in almost silence.

"I was wrong. There's people coming out of there," the man says. "They are open."

Nick struggles out of the car. "I have three dollars and a quarter," he says.

"Get out."

"Thank you, buddy."

"It wasn't any problem."

He swings his crutches toward the door, where two women are stuck, talking. One is old and weathered. The other is young and strained, impatient looking. "Is it all over?" he asks.

"Except for the cleanup," the young one grunts. "You're new, right? You missed it. Try to hang on. There's another tonight. Westmont."

"How do I get there?"

"Car, bus?"

"Where's your sense?" the old one says. She turns to Nick. "You need a meal, don't you? You need a ride."

"I could give you a ride up now," the young one says. "I live up that way. Only you'd have to hang all day up there, waiting for the meeting."

"You come with me," the old one says. "We'll get ourselves a meal and then we'll work at the ride for later."

Think, decide. He chooses the old lady. She's his third old lady this morning, and they seem to be lucky for him. The young one takes her leave, shrugging them off, hurrying to her car. He looks longingly inside the building to where the meeting was, thinking he might have just missed a man with a truck and a reason to drive out of town. "So I'll get you fixed up in the food department. We have to get to my car. Over there. The VW Jetta. You think you can get in?"

"I think."

Friendly City.

AT A BIT AFTER ELEVEN THIRTY,

Colleen, Potocki, and Christie are able to walk out of Farber's office, leaving Farber salivating. Colleen played the card she had, handing over Meg's written pages, waving the name Costanzo in front of Farber; she insisted Meg knew what she was doing when she wrote all that stuff.

Farber didn't believe it at first. "Had to be the mother wrote this," he said.

But Christie backed Colleen up, telling Farber, "No. Detective Greer is right. It was the girl."

"Tiger," Potocki says, shaking his head admiringly. "You were a tiger."

Christie's expression is hard to read even now. When she asked for complete immunity for Nick Banks—should they find him, which she still hopes for, and assuming he cooperates—Christie set his jaw, but he didn't cross her. "The evidence will show it was self-defense," she told Farber. She doesn't bother to repeat to Christie, who thinks she's too easily charmed by Nick, that she sees something in him, and she's not alone. The kids adore him.

"You played hard," Christie says.

With luck, Costanzo will be everything Farber hopes for, the source he's looking for. "He couldn't wait to get us out of there," Colleen says diffidently. "He wants to get started investigating the guy. We had that on our side."

They look at her—is it worriedly?

She heaves a deep breath. "Those kids," she says now.

"*That's* the priority," Christie tells them with enough of a pause afterwards to make sure it sinks in. "All three of us are going to see the kids are safe. We have to attend to their well-being, you understand? I could have called in family services, but I want to be on this myself. I'm back on chemo in a couple of days. I might not be able to do anything then. So, in the meantime, I'm going to try a few tricks I have. I need for you to find out what you can about the deadbeat mom."

"Phone records," Colleen says to Potocki.

"Phone records," Christie assents. "We get her in here, we meet her. I got a place we can take them for today—the Pocusset Safe House. The kids don't have any relatives, so after Pocusset, we have to move to foster care."

"God, I hate to see them in foster care."

"I know it, Greer. That's why I didn't pull Family or CYS in yet. I have some ideas—one idea, anyway. I have to call in about ten favors."

"What's the idea?" Potocki asks. "Any way I can help?"

Christie lets out a deep breath. "There's a couple in Squirrel Hill I put a girl with once. Didn't quite work, but they might be persuaded to take a chance again. It's a long shot." He shrugs. "You two keep checking with me," he says. He looks at his watch. "About time to eat something," he says vaguely. Then he goes down the hall to his office.

"I ordered both of us takeout," Potocki says.

"When did you do that?"

"On the way into the meeting. It'll be here soon. Let's eat where we can talk a bit."

"Okay."

"My cubicle or yours?"

"Yours. What did you order?"

"Chicken wraps. Safe choice. Guac on one." He moves toward his desk. "It ought to be here in fifteen, twenty minutes. I'll start on the order for the phone records in the meantime."

She goes to her own cubicle, but too restless, she paces the hall. Christie comes up alongside her and paces right with her. "What is it?" he asks.

"Wanting to do everything right."

"By the kids?"

"And by Nick Banks. I feel . . . nervous."

"Sure. He's a question mark. But . . . you feel you connected with the guy." Condemnation has crept into his tone.

"So did the kids."

"Whatever you do, make sure you're thinking of what the kids need. They need somebody to take care of them. Not the other way around."

She thinks about this, fitting it this way and that. "I was thinking about their feelings."

"I know. Speaking of feelings here. Is it my imagination or are you and Potocki, you know?"

"Not really."

"Well, it happens I'm juggling assignments right now. I was thinking of scrambling things anyway. He's fantastic on computer. I'll be in and out with the chemo. He and I could both be independent for a while. You'd work . . . very well with Dolan. You could learn as much from Dolan as from me. I'm just thinking ahead say for about a year here. I thought I caught . . . you know, vibrations . . . between you and Potocki."

"Well, we got a little mixed up once."

For a brief moment, he laughs, saying, "Mixed up." Then he stops walking and asks more seriously, "You feel mixed up?"

"Yes."

"Does anybody else know?"

"No."

He smiles, thoughtful. "Couldn't happen to a nicer guy."

"Hey." She makes a mock frown.

They start walking again. "But, let's be serious here. It's a problem. You know that; I know that. He can't be your partner under the circumstances."

"It was nothing." She's sorry she broke her vow of silence, but somehow people always end up telling Christie things; they just do.

"You might get mixed up again. . . ."

"Look, I know it's against the rules."

"Rules don't work. You never did like rules anyway, Greer. You're allergic to rules."

The oddest silence comes up between them with a communication made of frowns, even a little rippling laughter.

"Does it ruin my chances with you?" she ends up saying. Her comment just bounces there between them for a moment as they walk, and it's at least as surprising to her as to him.

He laughs a little. "If you're lucky. I'm no prize package."

"I thought you were."

"Nah."

They keep walking and end up near enough to her desk that it's clear the little hallway talk is over as far as he's concerned.

"You have chemo again on Wednesday?"

He scrunches up his face. "You know it."

"WHAT DO YOU DRINK? COFFEE?"
Meg asked Janet Littlefield.

"Oh, no, that's all right. I ordered soft drinks for everybody, including me. And Chinese takeout. I hope you like Chinese."

"I think so," Joel answered.

"Let's give it a try. If you don't like it, we'll start from scratch."

"But who's paying for it?" Meg asked.

"Oh, we'll cover this one from the police funds."

"Wow," Laurie said.

"This is just a start. We intend to get you some food in the house."

Meg said, "I was just about to go shopping. You don't need to worry about us."

Janet Littlefield smiled at her with the kindest smile. "We want to worry a little. We want to help."

When the food arrived, Detective Littlefield got them all to the table, where first she opened two cartons, one large, one smaller. "White rice," she said, pointing. "And fried rice." The other containers were round foil cake-pan sizes with paper lids fitted in. The detective opened four of them. She pointed, "Okay, we have chicken, beef and broccoli, shrimp, and pork. The only one I got spicy was the pork. I hope somebody besides me likes spicy."

"I do," Joel said.

So Meg put out plates and got some serving spoons. Detective Littlefield made sure everyone got something they wanted. She portioned out generous helpings and even put a fortune cookie beside each plate. Susannah turned her fortune cookie over and over, trying to dislodge the fortune without breaking the cookie, but the strip of paper wouldn't budge.

Meg was wondering when the quizzing would start again, and then after she had her first bite of the chicken-and-rice combination, it did.

Detective Littlefield said, "We're hoping you'll tell us how long you've been staying alone."

"Not long. A couple of days," Meg said. "I thought we answered all that."

Littlefield smiled. "Maybe. It's a drag, isn't it? We're going to need an actual count."

Meg studied the crisp yellow shirt and navy blue pants the detective wore. Earrings, a yellow-and-blue combination. It all looked nice.

Decent as all the detectives seemed, they were going to question her family until they wore them down, and then they were going to put them someplace awful. All the while she ate, Meg tried to think of what she could say that would get them off the hook. She was ready to say her stepmother called all the time. Would that be enough?

They were each shoveling in their third or fourth bites of food when they heard a key in the front door lock. Meg froze, then dropped her paper napkin and got up recklessly. Nick, she thought. Nick. She had to help him not to panic. She tumbled over herself to get to the door. She could feel Janet Littlefield moving behind her. But even before the door opened, Meg understood suddenly who would be standing there. Her memory coughed up the identity of the car she'd just heard without exactly knowing she'd heard it.

And she was right.

Alison stood there dumbly with two suitcases in hand. Meg said, "Alison!" and hugged her. "Here, let me." She took one of the suitcases from her stepmother and put it near the base of the stairs. Alison dropped the other suitcase at the door.

The other children gathered in the passage to the living room.

"You see, I told you," Meg said weakly. "This is Alison, our mum. She was on a job interview."

"Um, hello. And you are—?" Alison asked Littlefield, all the while watching Meg, hoping for a cue as to what she should say next.

"Detective Littlefield. We were just having some lunch. You are just who I need to talk to."

"What's this about?"

"We'll talk," Littlefield said easily.

"Do you have identification?"

"Sure do. I'll get it for you. Then you and I can sit in here while the children finish up eating."

Alison didn't look bad—no bruises. She didn't look particularly good either. "You must have started out early," Meg said.

"Five o'clock. Why?"

"I'm just guessing the timing." She took Alison's hand and led her toward the sofa, trying to squeeze a message into it. *Hang on. Listen. Think.*

Detective Littlefield went to her handbag sitting on the end table to pull out her ID. "Detective Littlefield," she repeated, handing it over.

"I told her you had a job interview," Meg said.

Alison's eyes darted around as she tried to catch up to the situation.

"Can we sit?" the detective asked.

Alison sat down.

"All of you are going to have to leave us for a little bit."

"You want us to bring your food in?" Laurie asked.

"No. I'll get it later. The main thing is you eat."

Meg thought miserably, they were so close to safe, so close, and Alison was going to say something wrong.

"Please," Littlefield said. She looked straight at Meg. "I'm trying to do right by you, so you have to trust me."

From the other room, Meg could hear the detective calling someone on her cell phone and announcing that there was a new person to question. "Right, right," Littlefield was saying. "Yes. Yes."

Off the phone, she announced, "We have various other people coming over to talk to you. Meanwhile, just three little questions and you can have some lunch while we wait for my colleagues."

Meg wouldn't let them eat—no noise. No forks on plates or scraping of cardboard containers. They listened intently from the kitchen.

"Tell me how you know Nick."

"Nick? I don't know who you mean."

Laurie collapsed so that her chair creaked and her arms hit the table. Meg shot her a look.

Detective Littlefield was saying, "Okay. That was easy. How long have you been gone on this interview."

"I don't remember exactly."

"Try."

"Almost a week, I think."

"Could it be longer than that?"

"Maybe."

"And how did you account for the care of the kids while you were gone?"

"Meg. Meg is the most adult person I know."

"How about money, food?"

"I left money."

"How much?"

"Forty, I think."

"Forty dollars?"

"Yes."

"How often did you call?"

"I think you've had more than three questions. A lot more."

"They're all related. Just the last easy one. How often did you call?"

"Not sure. I wasn't counting."

"Well, we can get phone records, so you might as well make a ballpark count."

"Three or four times."

"Closer to which?"

"Three."

Joel put up two fingers in the kitchen. Meg shook her head in despair. Alison was hopeless, hopeless.

The detective and Alison came into the kitchen. "I'm going to let her eat with you, but just keep off the subjects we need to let Commander Christie ask about."

"That doesn't leave much," Laurie said.

"I know it doesn't." Littlefield smiled, almost laughed. She, like most people, appeared to be amused by Laurie.

"What's going to happen now?" Alison asked. "I mean, I'm here, right?" Alison looked eagerly at the table. "So does there have to be trouble?"

Littlefield turned to Alison. "Just try to hang on. We'll sort it out. What would you like? Pork, beef, chick—"

"Pork. I haven't had anything like this in ages."

Littlefield studied her closely. Meg felt itchy with nerves. Anyone with sense could see Alison was not very mature. Alison sat down where Littlefield had been sitting while the detective stood at the sink, watchful. Meg tried to send messages to the others to talk, talk.

"You know that geography project? I got an A," Laurie said.

"You already know about my Dickens report," Meg said. Alison looked blank. "That it went well."

Susannah got up from her chair and went over to hug Alison, who had taken her first bite of pork and rice. Alison looked surprised at the hug. She touched a hand to Susannah's hair, tracing the outer layer of curls, the misty aureole of soft delicate hairs that caught the light. "Your hair is getting so long," she said.

Littlefield's intelligent eyes took it all in.

Alison didn't know anything about Nick, and there was no way to feed her information. Or to remind her the rent was due two days ago. Or to reassure her with the fact that if she went back to work and brought in seven hundred a month minimum to cover rent and electricity, the kids could do the rest—Meg at Doug's Market, Laurie babysitting and housecleaning along with Meg, Joel doing cars. She didn't know anything she was supposed to know.

Not too long after Alison had finished eating and Meg was cleaning up, there was someone at the door again, ringing the bell this time. Police, then, not Nick.

It was Detective Greer without her partner. She came into the kitchen and studied Alison hard. "We have a whole army trying to straighten things out. My boss wants to know why you never got social security, food stamps."

"I didn't want those things," Alison said, trying to make it sound like a point of pride.

The truth, and Meg knew this, was that Alison stayed clear of agencies because if she wanted to bail out—which was what she wanted, basically—it was easier to do it without a legal trail.

"We're looking into what we can get you."

Meg's spirits lifted. If they were talking about food and money, they were going to work with Alison.

But then Detective Greer said, "We have to go through the courts, of course. We have to bring a case of negligence."

And Meg's spirits dived again.

"Why do you have to do that?" Alison asked. "It was only a few days. I had to look for work." Her voice sounded terrified.

"Please don't lie to us. We have evidence to the contrary." Detective Greer turned away from Alison and addressed Meg. "You," she said, "could do us all a big favor by keeping my card handy. If you hear from Nick, you need to call me. Immediately."

Meg took the card reluctantly.

"I've worked out a way to protect him, but it isn't any good to him unless I can find him."

Protect. Meg's breath quickened. "Protect him how?"

"Every which way. From jail. From the man who is after him. Call."

Meg nodded. She had the feeling Detective Greer really meant it. "All right. I promise."

"Now tell me what you guys told Commander about how you knew to set Nick's leg?"

Meg pointed to Joel, and he began to tell again how he had fitted the bones together and how his siblings had searched for something to support the broken leg. Amazement showed openly on Alison's face.

All the while, Meg was thinking of Nick out there, alone, with no money, and what she should do. Should she trust Detective Greer? Should she? Her heart plummeted. She could feel her eyes sting. She decided yes.

"There's something . . . you should know. Nick didn't leave two days ago. He left in the middle of the night or this morning before we got up."

Detective Greer went very still before she asked, "And went where?"

"Bus station, we think. But we never could figure out if he really meant to do that."

Detective Greer was already punching a number into her phone while she asked, "He took a cab?"

"He said he wouldn't. He didn't want a record."

"What time do you think he left?"

"I think four or five o'clock."

"Thank you, Meg. You did the right thing. If someone is after him, it's important that we find him first. And we need to get you away from this house. Boss?" she said into the phone. "More news."

FORTY

SUCH A DAY. THE PLANTS

virtually sparkle. Joel and Laurie, Meg and Susannah are outside in the yard at the Pocusset Safe House, talking.

Christie can see them from the window of the office where he sits with an old friend, Elizabeth, who founded this place in honor of her husband. She doesn't work here herself, but she makes sure it runs well. It's a place where kids in transition can stay for a day or two while the courts get their various acts together.

Elizabeth Ross has her own practice as a therapist—she's Christie's idea of a great place to take your woes. Warm, friendly, smart. She has wavy light hair and always looks as if she's blushing. He helped her through a bad time, best he could, when her husband, whom she adored, was killed.

He's told her the whole story of the Philips kids, everything from the fact of their father's dying two years ago to their recent adoption of

a fugitive into their lives; they definitely qualify for a respite at the
Safe House while Alison stays with a friend. But the other thing is, he
doesn't want the kids briefing Alison before court tomorrow.

"How are *you* doing?" he asks Elizabeth Ross now.

"I'm coming along," she answers. "Slowly. Grief takes a long time,
you know? You just have to give it time."

"I'll bet. I'll bet." He doesn't tell her he's ill, on chemo, and that
Marina may be in her position all too soon. To say it is to let it happen.

He says instead, "I had a heck of a time getting these kids over here.
They are all concerned about wanting to go to school tomorrow morning, so I assured them someone would drive them. The boy Joel is upset about missing exams." He chuckles, watches her, waits expectantly.

"They sound interesting."

"They are. Wait till you meet them."

"Our staff will be good to them. I got the feeling you wanted me
here for some reason. To meet them myself?"

"Actually, it's something else. A kind of long shot I was working
on." She looks at him quizzically. "I've been thinking about your
friends, the Morrises."

"No. No, Richard, they couldn't take four. Is that what you're thinking?"

"They took a wild child." Of course, it didn't work out with the
troubled kid he tried to save once, but he doesn't say that now.

"They have their names in for two children from Turkey. They're on
a waiting list for adopting."

"When does that happen?"

"I don't know. A year or so."

"Two, huh?"

"Yeah, they met another couple who got two infants, three months
apart in age. Everybody calls them the twins, but, of course, they aren't
even related by blood. It's funny, though, they *act* like twins, they even
look like twins. So Jan and her husband are going to try to adopt two at
the same time, too."

"Hmm," he says.

Elizabeth blushes. "I can't believe I walked into that. I can see what you're thinking, how you're thinking, but . . ."

"Maybe only while we get the deadbeat mom to shape up. Stepmother," he corrects himself.

Elizabeth hesitates. "How deadbeat is she?"

"Left them. Drifted back when things didn't work out. It's like putting a spacey fifteen-year-old hippie in charge of them."

She sighs deeply. "I thought hippies were long gone."

"Well, I think I've seen one."

"Drugs?"

"My guess is no. Alcohol maybe. And emotional damage of some sort."

"Half the world," Elizabeth says.

"What I'd like is for Jan and Bob Morris to . . . just meet the kids today, show them around Pitt. Entertain them."

"Today?"

"If at all possible. Give them a couple of hours. That's it. Just give them a vision of something else."

"I understand what you're angling for. But, please, the Morrises are my friends. I don't want to take advantage of their kindness."

He smiles. "When you talk to the kids, you'll see. And maybe . . . the Morrises will fall in love."

She shakes her head. "Not four. Nobody could handle four. And the Morrises end up with another big heartache they don't need."

"But isn't it better to be in love than not?"

"Do you always manage lives this way?"

"Marina says I do. She says I'm a monster."

Outside the windows is a little drama being enacted. Joel walks away from his siblings. Meg watches him. Laurie capers. Joel turns. Laurie capers some more, swings a punch at him, he's back in. Meg hugs Susannah, rocks her.

"What happens to these poor kids if they fall in love the other way around?" Elizabeth asks.

They might. They're in love with Nick. A great itch comes over his neck, his chin. He feels blood rushing to his head, agitating all his skin surfaces. He can't solve every part of it.

The day is so beautiful. The kids are floating in it, completely cut off from everything they're used to.

Elizabeth sighs, dials a number. "There's no answer," she says. "They might be away. They go to Italy when they can. I know someone I can call to find out." But when she calls the second number, there's no one answering there, either. "I'll keep at it," she promises with a wry grin.

Christie goes out to the grounds of the Pocusset Safe House. "You'll like it here for the night," he says. "It's probably just for one night. The rooms are pretty. Did you see them?"

They tell him they did. An assistant showed them around.

"And there's always food. You get hungry in the middle of the night, there's something."

"Will Alison be all right?" Susannah asks.

He nods slowly. "Yeah. She's going to be okay."

"What happens tomorrow?" Joel asks testily.

"We talk to her, we figure out what her circumstances are, what she'll be able to offer you. It might take a while. Court is never a lot of fun. I've made arrangements to have someone take you from here to school in the morning and pick you up from school when you're needed in the afternoon at court. And . . . and bring you back here or some-where tomorrow night."

"Oh," Joel says. "You've thought of everything."

"I tend to do that."

Meg steps in. "But if Alison doesn't present herself well in court, what will happen . . . you know, long-term?"

He looks at them with all the steadiness he can muster. "If that happens, the next best bet is to get some decent foster care."

"There isn't any such thing," Joel says.

"Well, let's not think about it just yet. . . ."

"Maybe you could find Nick," Susannah says. "And we could stay with him somewhere."

"That's quite an idea. A big idea. I don't know if it's the right thing for him, though, in terms of his safety. Well, while they're getting your rooms ready, let's go have a hot dog or something in the park in Oakland outside of Pitt?"

"We've done nothing but eat all day," Laurie says.

"I have someplace I have to be after school tomorrow," Meg tells Christie. "It's completely necessary."

"Well, then, we'll work it out."

"Our father went to Pitt," Susannah says.

"Did he take you there often?"

She frowns. "No. Too busy. Two jobs."

"Three, sometimes," Laurie adds.

Out in the bright sunlight, at three o'clock, a little after, Christie drives the four kids down the wide portion of Beacon near Beechwood Boulevard.

"Where are we going?" Joel asks. "This is the wrong way."

"Just for a ride first. I know some nice folks who live on this street. I was wishing you could meet them."

"They have kids our age?"

"No."

"Because we used to live near here. Over in Greenfield. But I remember driving down this street for something. Some kids from around here went to school with us."

"Oh. Good. You know the area."

"I thought we were going to the park at Pitt."

"We are. I was just spinning my wheels first." He stops in front of a house with a sloping lawn, neatly trimmed hedges, and a portico framed by two white pillars. "This is where the folks live that I wanted you to meet. They're very nice, both professors at Pitt." He can feel the kids looking at him curiously. "Let me just knock in case they were away and came home."

He gets out of the car and taps on the door, then rings the doorbell, but nothing happens. The kids watch him from the car windows. He feels a bit idiotic.

"Not home," Joel says when Christie gets back in the car. "There's a dog bowl outside and no barking. That means the dog is out, too. They should put the bowl inside when they're not home."

"I'll have to remember to tell them. Okay. Let's go down to Pitt. Hot dogs if you have any room."

AT THE CAMPUS PARK AT PITT,
there are summer students scattered on the lawn, sunbathing, book-marked texts next to them. A few little kids ride the merry-go-round. "Want to?" Christie asks Susannah.

"Okay."

She will give him that, she seems to be saying.

Her face gives in to a flickering smile when her pig lifts her up, up. There is something generous in her face already, young as she is. The light catches her hair so that she seems to glow.

FORTY-ONE

IT'S CHRISTIE, POTOCKI, AND Greer at six o'clock on Sunday. They settle in Christie's office.

He looks cheerful. "Well, I just came from Farber," he says. "He's almost out of his mind with ecstasy. He's got the Philly men on Costanzo, and—this is top secret, you understand—it looks good, good. Which is good for all of us. They found Costanzo leaving his house. His behavior suggests . . . Well, what he did was he drove his nice Lexus into this dumpy garage, stayed maybe three minutes, and drove back out of it. Huh? The garage had enough room for two cars, so after Costanzo left it, a couple of the Philly men followed him home—it turns out he stayed put the rest of the afternoon—but Farber had another couple of men watch the garage. They might be still watching it. You gave them that," he said to Colleen.

"When do you think he'll move on it?"

"He's hoping Wednesday."

"Boss, does he really have the Chief's—?"

"I think it's true. It's very flashy to make a bust like this. I said we'd hold off on our end as well as possible."

So Farber can be the big eagle swooping down. Colleen can read on Christie's face that he thinks Farber is teetering on crazy.

Let them continue, Colleen thinks. That damned line from a book, a play, a movie. Something like, *Let them continue in their crimes.* Something like that.

"Bus station was a bust, huh?"

"I showed Nick's picture, but the people on duty weren't the same ones who worked the morning shift. I quizzed drivers coming in and going out about a man on crutches. Potocki sat in the office getting the phone numbers for the other drivers who were either off-duty or on another trip. Maybe he didn't take a bus."

"People slip through cracks all the time."

She's made lists: Columbus. Cleveland. Erie. New York. Baltimore. "If he really had only twenty dollars, that would limit where he went to any city costing twenty dollars and under with him possibly getting off at an early stop on the way. That's between thirty and fifty possibilities if he took a bus in the early morning. More possibilities if he rode later. And of course, he could have gone somewhere and hitched. He could be anywhere."

"I hope Farber doesn't sit on it," Potocki says.

"He tells me he has eight guys tailing Markovic tonight. A ton of guys in Philly on Costanzo. Philly detectives."

"And still no Feds?" Potocki asks.

Christie smiles. "He thinks all they do is come in at the last minute and crow."

Colleen puts her head down right on Christie's desk.

"Greer, let's get you somebody for the bus station. You have to take a break sometime. How long you been going round the clock?"

"It's okay," she says.

"A break is good. I'll get you somebody for today. Dolan gets back tomorrow. You all can talk to more of the drivers tomorrow if you need to." He points to Potocki. "Take a couple of hours."

"Thanks. I promised my son a steak for dinner. I was going to cancel if I had to, but— He's going to have to see my place sooner or later. Might as well be tonight, then."

Colleen can imagine what will happen. The kid will explore, go up and down the steps, look into the back garden—exploring, trying to make it his. He'll like it and hate it, both.

"You're the one who should rest," she tells Christie. "Take your own advice."

"I will. I will."

They depart from each other reluctantly.

Colleen drives home, beating at her steering wheel. If she could find Nick and get him to talk, she'd be closing BZ maybe and Earl Higgins for sure; she'd have enough on Markovic to put him in jail for a long time; and she'd have a shot at protecting Nick. It's hard to let down.

When she's finally inside her house, she tries for a catnap, but it doesn't work. Her eyelids are propped open. So she vacuums; she makes herself a salad big enough for four people and forces herself to go out to grill some chicken to put on top.

While she's grilling, her neighbor comes out to her deck and says, "I watered your lawn."

"Oh, you didn't have to do that."

"Well, things were dry."

"My fault. I got busy. Sorry about that."

"I watered it good."

"Very good of you."

"Well, it needed done."

Needed to be done. Needed doing. "I'm really grateful. Let me know how I can repay you."

"Nothing. I just saw it needed it."

"Very thoughtful. Many thanks for that," Colleen says, taking her chicken off the grill before she's absolutely sure it's cooked. She eats her dinner inside in front of the TV. How familiar it feels, being utterly alone, eating in front of the TV. It erases the last two weeks somehow.

She watches a rerun of *Desperate Housewives*, deciding for the hundredth time that she needs to go clothes shopping. She watches CNN and tries to figure out how the network has managed to find so many women anchors with no lines on their faces, no shadows or bags under their eyes.

Around eleven at night, she decides she really needs to try to sleep. She drops into bed, numb, almost high, with fatigue.

THE ROOM AT THE JOHNSTOWN

Salvation Army, a kind of barracks, holds twenty cots and each is occupied. He keeps the cap over his face. His arms ache from the distance he's covered on crutches. He's waiting for the others to sleep. Then, maybe he'll go down, too.

Scared. As usual. All his life, scared.

He has a job prepping food tomorrow at a diner, a gift of the old lady who put in a word for him and who is about as royal as they come. She bought him lunch and she knew not to ask too many questions. Mo Weaver, short for Maureen. She's going to check on him tomorrow, she said, to see how the diner thing is working out. Nick will have to do most of the prepping sitting on a chair or a stool. The owner, a crusty type, hardly looked at him, just said, "So long as it gets prepped." Nick now has twenty bucks' food money—emergency money—in his pocket from the Catholic Social Services. Twenty—funny—as if his pockets somehow filled up again with what the kids gave him, magic money.

A ride out of town was his initial plan, but he owes it to the old lady to show up for work tomorrow. Because of her, he's had two free meals: soup and a sandwich for lunch, bought by her; some kind of ground-meat stew for dinner at the homeless shelter.

Hundreds of people have seen him today. Earlier, in the bathroom at the Salvation Army, he studied himself in the mirror. He'd made it out of town, possibly because he looked clean and respectable and you couldn't tell the cast was homemade. Tomorrow more people will see him. With the backpack on, he is Charles Philips, a guy, Charlie, still going for his degree. Hide the backpack and he's Charlie Philips, father of four, injured on the last job, down on his luck.

MEG LIES IN HER BED AT THE
Pocusset Safe House. Joel has his own room, but she's been given a room with her sisters. Each of them has a single bed with a thick mattress and layers of covers, the top one being a quilt made of different fabrics. They aren't quite asleep yet. Every once in a while they murmur something. Trying to remember their lines, probably, things they have to say in court tomorrow. *We missed Alison when she was gone. We're used to her. She cares about us. She was looking for a job, thinking we should move somewhere else. Because of the sad memories.*

Move to New York City, just like that? It isn't exactly believable.

Meg rehearses something that's a closer bet on a truth. *To New York because she knew a guy there and thought he could be a father to us.*

She will gag to say it. She will say it.

If Alison doesn't pull it together tomorrow, they'll end up in foster care after all they did to avoid it. She closes her eyes and sees Nick, out there somewhere, alone, uncertain.

He liked her. He did.

The covers are soft. Laurie noticed the smell—very clean. The room is decorated with curtains that match the bedspreads, a muted pink and blue and cream. Paintings deck the walls. One is abstract, thousands of colored dots. The other one is something like bits of a seashore vacation house blown by a tornado or a hurricane and reassembled as a jumble.

Her sisters seem to have adapted more easily than she to sleeping in a new place. She doesn't like this about herself, this stiffness of hers. She can remember Alison calling her an old lady, and it still stings.

FORTY-TWO

Colleen is back at the bus station, where a different ticket seller, a very tiny woman, thinks she remembers Nick. "State College, I think. Or maybe not."

"Could a person get to State College on twenty dollars?"

"No. It's more, twenty-two dollars and fifty cents."

Did he really have *only* twenty?

The neon pizza sign in the terminal winks at her. Talk about a terminal lunch. She's glad that for once in her life she isn't ravenously hungry. She takes in her surroundings. Signs in Spanish as well as English. Uncomfortable metal mesh chairs. And televisions going, of course, of course.

Somebody will know eventually. But for now, Christie is demanding she get to the office to plan for the court hearing on the Philips kids.

if she counts herself. She has half a mind to skip the hearing and take off again, but if they find her, it will mean jail or some fine she can't pay, so, sitting at the kitchen table, having the last of the coffee, Alison decides it's better to do the contrite thing, the act she's done most of her life.

She is thirty-seven, but she could easily pass for twenty-four.

She didn't obey the police last night. She didn't stay the night with her friend because the woman wasn't all that friendly, really, and the last thing she wanted to do was pack another suitcase. Badly needing something familiar, she sneaked back to her own bed, her own shower, and it helped.

If she thinks about what happened in New York, she starts to cry, so she tries not to think about it, but it edges in anyway. She was brave in a way—tried to strike out for herself for once, the way she called Juan, after all these years, to tell him she had often thought of him. How warm his voice had been on the phone. *We should get together. It should be you and me. Is it too late? Why didn't we know this?* He meant it at the time.

She said, "I'm ready to work it out."

He said, "Get here. I can't wait. Please. Come."

And she did, drove the whole way to the Bronx and got there at eight in the morning with the traffic thickening by the minute. Shaking, she drove through the unfamiliar streets to his apartment house, a huge thing, not too clean looking.

When he came to the door—and the bell brought him the whole way down to the outside door—he stood holding it open and just looking at her for a very long time. "Truth is, I never expected to see you on my doorstep."

"You said . . ."

He smiled a little. "You better come in. The thing is, I wasn't even planning to stay here. I was going to hit the road, find a place closer to—"

"What?

"Oh, where the work is."

"Is my car okay out here? There?" She pointed.

"No car is okay out here, but it's as okay as you can get."

"I have luggage in it."

"No, that's not okay. We'll have to take it in." He checked for his keys in his pants pocket before accompanying her down the street to the car. "The place is a wreck," he said.

"I won't look."

"I couldn't believe you called me. You thought about me?"

Upstairs where he lived, it was pretty chaotic. But there was no one else there. He looked at her for a long time, then pulled her to him and gave her a rough kiss. She almost laughed. It was something out of an old movie, but the truth is, it went the whole way through her body.

Why didn't she guess that he had kids of his own, five of them, and a wife? He looked like a man who would have those things. She didn't know he was a dreamer until the third day.

He'd moved some clothes off the sofa and made her sit, lit a cigarette and handed it to her, then lit another for himself. He did try to pause, she can give him that.

She tried to get used to the new lines in his face. He was still good-looking.

"I need to calm down," she said.

"You ever been to the city before?"

"No."

"I'll take you for Cuban tonight."

Her breath caught. "Sure. Okay. Sounds good."

"You wouldn't believe how good it is."

So, the strange thing started, with the gradual truth-telling and the impossible fantasies. She should have guessed it wasn't going to work when he kissed her again. The second kiss was like one from Charlie Philips. Inquiring, too soft. She needed for him to be crazy hungry for her. Then, later that morning, he was. And for a while she believed in it.

And now, as if it never happened, she's back where she started, except she's in trouble.

When she dresses to get ready for court, she chooses a baggy dress, not formfitting, and old-fashioned high heels. Her long hair she plaits into a French braid. She hardly looks like a woman who broke bedsprings in New York a week ago.

Dressed long before she is due in court, she wanders the house. They kept it neat, clean as ever. They are good kids—as kids go, but kids are certainly overrated.

When she's hungry, she opens the cabinets and the refrigerator. Leftover Chinese. No, she'll have toast and butter—little kid food, sick food, good, especially if she dunks the toast.

AT THE COURTHOUSE THEY SEE
Littlefield walking the kids into the building and talking to them. Alison is nowhere in sight. Christie keeps trying to phone those people, the professors from Pitt, the ones he thinks are a match for the kids. Colleen manages to turn in her seat enough to catch Potocki's eye. Potocki's look says, yes, their boss is pretty ragged around the edges today.

"I hope Alison doesn't show," Christie mutters. They all sit on the predictably hard wooden benches, waiting for the judge to get back from lunch.

"Boss," Potocki warns in a low voice, "they're going to say having a thirteen-year-old in the house was enough." He rolls and unrolls the phone records he pulled.

"Not with no money, no food, and the youngest one seven years old. It isn't okay."

"I know that."

"This judge, Gorcelik, worries me. Always conservative. I guess I want a visionary." Christie scratches his neck. "Whatever a visionary is. Marina's word."

Potocki smiles.

Finally Alison arrives. The appearance she makes is modest,

girlish—even in a trendy retro way, a tad fashionable. The hairstyle, Colleen wonders, or the way she holds her handbag? What is it? She looks utterly calm.

Christie asks Alison to sit on the other side of him, away from the kids. She does, but she winks and waves at them. Susannah waves back, and the others follow suit, exhibiting little real enthusiasm.

Christie sets his jaw.

Colleen and Potocki look at each other.

GORCELIK, A WOMAN OF ABOUT sixty, a seasoned judge in this court, isn't interested in anybody else's testimony, only Christie's. Colleen certainly feels like a fifth wheel. Potocki concentrates on the proceedings with patient dignity.

Christie makes his points efficiently: "Evidence at the house indicates the stepmother did not intend to come back; the children were on their own without enough food in the house for ten days; they needed or wanted an adult around, and so took in a man who was in trouble with the police and who had a criminal element looking for him; Alison Philips called only twice during that time—this was at the end of the ten days when she had decided to come back."

Gorcelik looks long at Christie before turning to the children.

"Who can answer me? Did all of you attend school during the ten days?"

"Yes," Meg answers.

"Did your grades suffer? I see in front of me that you seem to get . . . well, A and A-plus. Quite a record."

"All of us are still getting A's. Joel is going to be awarded. He skipped a grade. They want me to go to Advanced Placement, but I haven't decided."

"Why haven't you decided?"

"I don't know enough about it, where I'd go, how much extra travel time."

"But the grades haven't suffered?"

"No."

"What did you eat while your stepmother was gone? Why was she gone, by the way?"

"Looking for a job."

"She didn't have one here?"

"She did. But it doesn't pay much. Waitressing at the Park House."

"I see. Well, tell me a couple of meals."

"Roast chicken with potatoes and green beans. Hamburgers. Stew, pasta."

"Where did you get the money for food?"

"Alison left us some. We have little jobs. Babysitting and things. And we get lunch at school."

"What about this man you took in?"

"We knew him from the pizza shop. He needed a place to stay, and we knew him."

Judge Gorcelik pauses for a moment, looks straight at Christie, and says, "Let me talk to Alison Philips."

Alison approaches her.

"Ms. Philips. These are good kids."

"I know. I couldn't have gone to look for work if they weren't."

"How successful was your attempt?"

"Well, I could have gotten something, but the prices for everything were so high that I wouldn't be better off in the end."

"You looked where?"

"Manhattan and the Bronx."

"Golly. You didn't know about prices in New York?"

"I didn't know about housing prices."

"Kind of in a bubble, aren't you?"

"Sometimes I am."

"Do you love these kids?"

"Yes."

"Did you intend to come back?"

"Yes. I always intended to come back."

"Yet you quit your job."

"I can get my job back," Alison says quietly.

"These kids— It turns out they're a bit special. In the brain department."

Alison acknowledges that with a simple nod.

"Are you afraid of them?"

"In what way?"

"I mean intimidated."

"I think lots of people would be."

"I'm going to tell you a couple of things here. Now, you listen. Kids need a lot of plain hugging; they need compliments. The girls need stylish haircuts. See, these kids should have things—what other kids have. Clothes, computers, you know what I mean. You don't have much in the way of finances."

"Not at the moment."

"Hmm. That's one big problem. Please sit." She consults the papers before her. "Commander Christie? What's this you're trying to tell me about foster care?"

"That if we could find the right people, a match, the kids—who care about school a lot—could be better off in a steadier environment. I know a couple who might be a possibility. But they're in Europe at the moment, back sometime this week. I'm asking for time to look into it. The kids aren't safe in their present home. The man they took in is being hunted."

The judge takes a long time looking at all of them. She calls Christie back to her. In a not-completely-private voice, she says, "You know what kind of thing I see here all the time? Your idea about crashing the foster care system is pie in the sky; if I take these kids from their stepmother, they're going to be separated and put with people far worse than Ms. Philips."

"We can fight it."

"I have a lot of other things I have to fight for. I'm ruling for parenting classes for Ms. Philips, two full days of counseling for her right now, a family service worker assigned to the home, and I insist this family get finances in order—we can see to that. Finances are a major part of the problem here. You have a place the kids could stay for a couple of days? This Pocusset House?"

Christie says, "Yes." But he looks completely whipped.

"Commander? If you still assess the situation as dangerous, let's work together to find another place for them to live or get a policeman on duty at their home." She looks at the kids. "You want to go back home? Stay together?"

They all say yes with no uncertainty at all.

Seconds later, Alison is hugging the kids. It's a false hug; even the judge can see it if she cares to. "In a couple of days you get to come home," Alison says. "Happy?"

"I hope she takes a powder again," Christie mutters.

Colleen's phone rings. It's Dolan saying, "Found your bus driver. He identified Nick Banks. Took him to Johnstown."

"He's sure?"

"Absolutely sure. Helped him off the bus."

"You have the driver there now?"

"Yes."

"Could I—if I come right down?"

"Don't trust me, Greer?"

"Of course I—"

"I'll hold on to him."

The kids are urging Janet Littlefield to get them back to school.

"I feel like a mama again," Littlefield says. "Chauffeur."

Christie takes Meg aside. "I want you to call me or Detective Greer if there is anything you need. Anybody bothers you, you need food in the house, anything. You understand? You have my card?"

"Yes."

"Let's go," Littlefield says.

Colleen looks at her watch. After she talks to the driver, she'll pack a bag, take her own car into Johnstown, work the evening, and stay overnight with her parents, who live only twenty minutes farther on. That way, if she hasn't found Nick yet, she'll be ready to start at seven the next morning.

FORTY-THREE

NICK CAN SCRAMBLE AN EGG

as well as anyone can, but he's had to get used to how to move in the little kitchen. Business was slow this morning—which helped. The gruff owner brought him a desk chair from the nook he uses as an office, so Nick wheels back and forth in the kitchen, standing when he needs to. The owner works the counter. Dmitri Colouris is his name.

"Dmitri," Nick repeated when they were introduced.

"Means Jim."

"Charles Philips," Nick said, holding out a hand. Dmitri's calloused hand shook it. "How do you know Mo Weaver?"

"I'm in AA. She's a good soul."

An order comes in. A chicken salad sandwich is something he can make. A hamburger with fries—he can do it. He moves more and more rapidly, but his ribs and his armpits still cry out in pain from yesterday's exertions. The Greyhound terminal in Pittsburgh was like a joke. Once the city bus let him off, he had to walk another quarter mile to it, up impossible wooden ramps. It was a joke played on him; he took it, he survived it.

Mo Weaver *is* a good soul. Maureen. She's looking for a place for him to stay.

A lot of people have seen him over these two days. More will see him if he goes to a meeting. Yet he's come this far.

He works throughout the afternoon for Dmitri. It's strange. The man never smiles or cracks a joke, and yet Nick isn't uncomfortable around him. He even feels cared for by him.

Mo Weaver appears at the diner at five, just when Dmitri's son comes in to take over in the kitchen. "Got it," she says quietly to Nick. "Room for rent. You get kitchen privileges. You want to eat something here before I take you?"

"I had soup and a burger."

"Will it hold you?"

"Yeah. Would you believe I used to have a lot of money? Used to eat fancy dinners."

"No trouble believing that."

"I used to have nice things."

"I get it. It shows on you somehow. Not that it matters. We're all naked babies. That's just the dressing. You sure you had enough to eat?"

"I'm sure."

"It's just a room I'm taking you to. Nothing fancy. Fellow who's a friend of mine has rooms to rent. Don't stiff him."

"I won't."

"It's raining out."

"I'll be okay."

"Plants needed it."

GREYHOUND USES A SHOP—MR.
Simon's Barber Shop—as a depot. Next door is the doughnut shop the driver talked about.

Colleen takes a deep breath, goes into the doughnut shop, and takes a seat at the counter. "Apple pie looks good," she says, "and I'll have a coffee." A young man behind the counter nods and busies about bringing her order.

She'd rather go somewhere down the street for a stiff scotch, truth be told. Her parents expect her for dinner tonight.

The other customers in the shop eye her curiously.

She eats slowly, letting them know she likes the pie. When she finally presents Nick's picture to the man behind the counter, he shakes his head nervously. "Guy in trouble?"

"He could be helpful to us is all. I'm going to have to show the picture around some."

There are about twenty-five people eating or ordering. She shifts easily from seat to seat. *Hello. That taste good? Oh, well, I grew up close by. Seen this fellow?* By the time she gets to all of them, they appear to be used to her. But she leaves the shop without anything to go on.

For a while she just drives, getting a sense of the city, where a man might go.

At about seven, she goes into a bar and orders the scotch she wants. She shows the picture around again, but lets in the depressing thought that Nick Banks could well have hitched a ride out of town.

"Where do people go in this town when they're homeless," she asks the bartender.

"Catholic Charities? Salvation Army? The park?"

The first place she visits after the bar is the Salvation Army, where she gets good and bad news, a split second apart, delivered by a slender Calvinistic sort, a man who says simply, "Oh, he was here. Left this morning."

"He might come back?"

"Could. Might."

"Will you call me if he does? And call no one else. It's in his interest." She gives the man her number. "Any time. He knocks on your door at three in the morning, it's okay to call."

television by the time she gets in. "We ate. We couldn't wait," her mother tells her before she is the whole way in the door. "But we have some dinner ready to zap for you."

"I had work. Give me a hug."

"I don't like this work you do."

"I know."

"Where's Ronnie?"

"He's waiting for us to call him. He'll be here soon as we do. You hungry?"

"Starved."

"Atta girl," her father says. He doesn't look good. He's pale. He has a drink going.

Both parents are thin. *Frail* isn't quite the word, just . . . a hollowed-out version of thin. Metabolism. Some trick of sugar-burning their bodies learned a long time ago.

Colleen kisses each of them on the forehead. They blink up at the benediction.

"Come, eat."

Her parents hold on to her—skirt, shoulder, hands, whatever they can make contact with. It's true they neglected her most of her life, it's true they weren't looking while she and her brother grew up, and it's true that, in spite of that neglect, they love her. And vice versa. "Sit, sit," they say.

Colleen can hear the whir of the microwave.

Her father carries the bistro glass of whiskey and stands next to her, but he's interested in the program on the television, so he cranes his head to see it. Her mother brings a plate from the microwave. Her parents have their routine lives—they get ready for breakfast, lunch, and dinner; then they clean up after those meals; and, in between, they keep up on things by reading the paper cover to cover and watching the television news.

She's how they got here. They had her in the oven before they had degrees, money, or lives in order. They were both smart in college, but they had to drop out. Or wanted to. Blame me, she thinks, tucking into the meat loaf and mashed potatoes. *Blame me for it.*

They are still in love; they hardly ever argue. Instead they offer kindness to each other in a myriad of small ways. "Need that salve for your hands. I'll go find it." "I'll take your glass, save you a trip."

"I *hope* you're not doing anything dangerous," her mother says.

"Nah. Just routine work. Looking for some guy."

"Aha," her father says.

"Look, honey. If you have an appetite, we still have some chili left over from lunch. We had it with cheese and onions."

"And hot sauce," her father says.

"You want some of that, too?"

"Well . . . okay. And let's call Ronnie—"

But a noise alerts her to the fact that her brother is standing in the doorway. He's grinning. "Look no further!" he shouts.

Nobody ever guessed when her brother went out into the world that he would loop back home so soon afterwards. Some people just can't go far, aren't meant to. Of course, pot allows him some light travel in his mind. Otherwise, he travels only as far as the apartment over the garage behind the house.

Colleen gets up from the table. She and her brother hug each other hard. He backs up, hands out. "Come to arrest me, have you?"

She smiles.

And that's a life, too. Slower than hers, less "in the world." Not without merit if you count appreciating the smell of a rose from time to time.

In a way, her churning seems the shabbier choice.

"How long can you stay?"

"Long as this guy keeps escaping me."

"Well, I hope he runs for a long time," her father says.

They watch television late into the night with no calls from the Salvation Army.

The next morning, Tuesday, she goes back to the barracks just to make an appearance, just to keep them honest, and then she tries the Catholic Charities. She shows the picture, and while she does, she describes Nick as a man on crutches.

"Oh, yes!" exclaims the woman at Catholic Charities. She's about thirty, long hair, bony face. "We gave him emergency money. Charles Philips."

An adrenaline surge makes Colleen trip over herself with questions. "How did he seem? What did you think of him? Anything could be a help. Do you know where he went?"

"Um. He got directions to the Salvation Army."

"Anything else? Did he seem to be drinking, for instance?"

"I don't think so. Well, not at the moment and—if you want the truth—if I met him some other way, in some other setting, I would probably have, you know, gone out with him."

When Colleen leaves Catholic Charities, the sun is shining with decisiveness. Good. The rain is past tense. She makes a few notes, standing at her car, then drives to the doughnut shop. It's busy again. This time Colleen doesn't order anything; why add more labor for the old woman working the counter alone? She shows the picture of Nick and knows immediately she is on to something. The old woman hesitates for a good long time, looks about the shop and asks, "He do something bad?"

"No. He needs protection."

The woman nods. "Okay, then. He asked directions to New Visions. That might get you somewhere."

"What is it?"

"It's medical. An addiction place. Over on Walnut."

"Thank you. Thank you."

She calls Christie to tell him she's close. "I want to go to AA meetings and follow up with AA people for the day."

"Okay. Keep going."

"What am I missing?"

"Farber *is* going to move tomorrow so long as the tailing works out."

"Thank God."

But. There are always *buts*. How can they get everyone? In a big operation, people squeak through. Even from prison Markovic will be able to give orders about who must be silenced. What then?

IT ISN'T UNTIL TUESDAY

night—and a couple of AA meetings later—that Colleen finds a woman who examines the photo and says another woman from AA gave the guy a ride on Sunday.

"Who is she? Was she here tonight?"

"No. Don't know her last name. First name is Mo. Short for something."

Anonymous. Right. "Did this woman, Mo, know the guy in the photo before?"

"Nope. Simple case of help-your-neighbor Samaritan thing."

"I'm closer," she tells Christie by phone Tuesday night. "Give me tomorrow?"

"Take it. Call. I can't say what shape I'll be in. I'll talk if I can."

Chemo.

"And what else?" he asks.

"Nothing else. I'm seeing a bit of my family."

"Good, Greer, good. Potocki is working a drive-by. You talk to him?"

"Actually, not today."

"Well, when you catch up with him, he'll tell you about it."

"The Philips kids?"

"Don't ask."

NICK GOES OUT INTO THE

backyard wearing the large funny pajamas Meg bought him while his clothes roll around in the dryer. It's midnight and he has to be at work early, but that's okay. Work is something he likes. Order. A schedule.

He can hear his new landlord, another AA soldier, a widower, puttering around in the house. He can feel the man at the kitchen window screen, watching him. I won't stiff you, he thinks to himself; I won't take anything from you.

He fought, he gambled, he pulled a trigger. But he never did steal.

Sitting under one of the two large trees in the yard is a lounge chair, the kind made of alternating green-and-white plastic straps—a good support for extending his leg. He gets himself into the chair and sinks into a relaxation that is just on the edge of sleep. God, the night is beautiful. The aftereffect of yesterday's rain is a clear sky. Through the branches of the trees, stars he hasn't seen since nights on the fishing boat wink at him.

Whatever happens will happen.

In the back of his brain is the count. No alcohol for over a week. Not since the cough syrup and mouthwash. He still wants it.

He can hear the man at the screen, moving, worrying, even before he says, "You shouldn't sleep out here."

"I won't."

"Would you want a piece of cake? Chocolate with icing."

"I would."

"Eat it inside?"

Reluctantly, he leaves the simple beauty of the night.

That night he has a dream so real that when he wakes, he can't shake it and he forces himself back to sleep to figure out how to save himself.

Part One: He is walking down the street when he hears a motor, turns to see the van pulling up. Moments later Markovic has him by the elbow.

"Man, have I been worried about you."

"I've been laid up."

"I see that. Where you been?"

"Around."

"Who—? Who fixed you up?"

Meg, Joel, Laurie, Susannah. He doesn't say it.

"Come on. Let's get in the van where we can talk. You had your picture on TV."

"I know."

"Man, am I glad to find you. You shouldn't be out on the street like this. You need some protection. Where you going?"

"Nowhere in particular."

"God, you kill me, the way you talk. Well, get in. I can take you nowhere in particular."

"I'm not able to get in a car. I have to extend my leg."

"Backseat then." Markovic opens the rear van door. "Do you have any idea how hard you were to find? Just tell me what's been going on. Tell me how I can help you. Money, of course. Sure, I can guess that much. I can get you money, whatever you need. A place to stay where nobody is going to turn you in."

Still in the dream he hasn't moved toward the van. But if he doesn't get in, Markovic will shoot him on the street.

He wakes and wants to finish the dream. His heart is pounding so hard that for a while he can't fall back to sleep.

When he does, Markovic greets someone as the start of Part Two. Nick turns, and the man with the weird hair and sideburns is alive again. So now it's two against one. He needs a trick. Luck. He's waiting for it. Luck.

Markovic takes the crutches from him.

The man with the weird hair . . . Earl . . . pulls him toward the van.

"Take it easy," Markovic says. "We're just going to talk."

He keeps talking. He makes things up. He tells a story about a nurse who fixed his leg. Markovic nods. He keeps talking, waiting for a trick. Finally he wakes up. It takes him a while to be sure he is alone, alive.

HER MOTHER MAKES HER BACON

and eggs for breakfast.

"Wow," she says. "I'm getting the royal treatment."

The kitchen door opens. Her brother comes in, saying, "I smelled it. You have enough for me?"

"Why doesn't he just live here?" her mother grumbles, putting more bacon on.

Already the TV is going, morning news. Her father sits in front of it, reading the paper.

"Don't you want breakfast?" her mother calls.

"Sure I do. Just a minute."

Last night, her brother came over again for some TV time with the family. Colleen watched him go back to his place at one point, then return, red-eyed and bleary. She could smell the weed on him when he sat next to her. "Are you going to go back to school? Ever?" she asked as lightly as possible.

"I don't think so. I think I'm the self-educated type."

"But it isn't leading to, you know, the kind of work you could do."

He smiled. "Now, now. See, here's how *you* are: You want each day to be different. You probably like to be scared. Right? See, I'm not so dumb. *I*, on the other hand, like routine and I don't like stress. I think routine is the best thing ever invented. I like the same thing every day."

Her parents looked at each other. Was this an argument brewing?

"Some routine is good," she told him. "Everybody needs that. I just meant—"

"I know what you meant." With that, Ron got up last night and went back to his apartment. She thought she might not see him again, but here he is, sitting down to breakfast.

Her eggs are nice and runny, the way she likes them. The toast, made of bread she wouldn't choose, goes down fine, oiled as it is with butter.

"I'm not too hungry yet," her father says. "Maybe just a piece of toast."

Her mother looks confused, holding a plate full of eggs and bacon.

"I can eat his," Ron says. "I can eat double."

"What am I doing?" her mother says fretfully.

"It won't go to waste," Colleen tells her.

"Bacon sandwich for lunch," her father says soothingly.

How easily her mother is thrown. Everybody likes routine, safety.

Colleen gets a picture of the vast landscape of America, people comfortable doing the usual morning things, others frustrated because they can't for one reason or another do what they're used to, and some—people going on job interviews, auditions, something big at stake—unable to eat because they're not at home or their stomachs are throwing up all kinds of survival signals.

Ron nudges her. "I'm not angry. I just don't want you to think I'm nothing."

"I would never think that."

"I would. I just don't want you to."

A little less weed, she wants to say, but now isn't the time.

"This is like a vacation," her mother says, although she doesn't seem particularly happy. "You're staying tonight again?"

"I'm going back today one way or another." She misses her office, her house, her own bed.

"Still didn't find your man?" Ron asks.

"Um, huh-uh. Breakfast is really good, Ma."

She goes to her room, where she has already packed up and comes back to the kitchen with her overnight case.

"You aren't even coming back for *supper*?"

"I'd better not. We have a lot happening today. I need to get back."

She kisses each of them. All the hugging and hand-squeezing make her want to cry. Her brother, hugging her awkwardly, says, "You be careful."

She drives to New Visions, where—bam, just like that—she hears, "Hello. I'm Mo, and I'm an alcoholic."

IT TAKES ABOUT AN HOUR TO talk Mo into leading her to Nick, but finally they leave the coffee shop where they've gone to talk. Colleen follows Mo's car to an outlying diner.

"Let me go in first. I don't want to scare him," the old woman says.

The place has several booths, a counter with a cash register, and a doorway behind the counter that leads to the kitchen. Mo whispers something to Dmitri; he looks at Colleen; Mo whispers something more. The only two customers in the place don't appear to be paying any attention. Mo gives Colleen the go-ahead, and the three of them pass into the kitchen.

Nick is wheeling around with a plate in hand—he's saying, "pancakes, side of bacon"—and then he stops, sees Mo Weaver with Dmitri, sees there's another person behind Mo, then sees who it is.

"It's okay," Mo says in a quiet voice. "It's okay or I wouldn't have brought her."

He almost drops the breakfast.

Colleen moves from behind Mo Weaver, saying, "Nick. Take it easy. I'm here as a friend."

He moves carefully toward the counter workspace and slips the pancakes over to Dmitri.

"I'm here to talk to you. We spoke once before." She continues formally: "Colleen Greer."

"Yes." He says this quietly, with dignity, matching her tone. Good.

"I traced you as far as your friend here. I talked to her for a while this morning and she understands why I need to talk to you."

"I think she means right," Mo says.

"Where can Nick and I talk?" Colleen asks them.

Dmitri looks around, trying to help. "One of the booths?" he suggests.

"Backyard?" Mo offers.

"It's not a yard out there," Dmitri frets. "It's all overgrown."

But Colleen likes the idea of the yard. It feels right. "Is there a place to sit out there?"

"I can get you two old chairs."

"That's all we need."

Mo takes the plate of pancakes to the waiting customer while Dmitri carries two kitchen-style chairs to the yard. He plunks them down and comes back in, passing Nick and Colleen on the way.

The yard *is* terribly overgrown, but she's happy with the choice.

There is no one to overhear them and no noise except the birds scavenging for whatever crumbs Dmitri might have thrown out. She sits.

Nick takes a bit longer to get down the few steps; he sinks onto one of the chairs. Colleen watches him maneuver, still holding on to his crutches, extending his right leg. "I don't understand," he says, puzzled. "Aren't you going to be taking me in? I can't exactly run."

There. A little joke. She smiles to encourage him. "There are a couple of people looking to protect you. Mo, up there, is one of them. She's—"

"She doesn't know anything about me, if that's what you're thinking. She only just met me and tried to help me."

"She's not in trouble."

"Good."

She studies his face, wondering what they're going to do with him. He's so good looking, people are going to remember him. People are going to *like* him. "Nick, you remember we spoke before?"

"Oh yeah." For the first time in the short space that she's known him, he wears a cynical look. She thinks of cynicism in him as the punctuation or the accent, not the main part of him. "You know, I really am dumb," he says. "I thought you were coming on to me. I actually believed it."

"That's not dumb. We were both next door to meaning it. But things have happened, I'm still police, and I have to ask you about what happened up at McCandor. I think I know. Evidence talks. So if you tell me simply, I think I can help you. I want to."

"It would be hard to explain."

She takes out a legal pad from her bag. "I expect it to be complicated. Start with McCandor. Tell me about the ten days since."

He shakes his head slightly as if to say, *I don't think I can.*

"We know about the kids, if that's what you're hesitant about. We know."

Surprise is the first expression on his face, followed quickly by anger. "They called you?"

"No. We found them. They care about you—I can see you don't believe me. They do. Desperately."

"You found them?" he challenges. "How?"

She's not supposed to tell him things, but who's to know? "We were investigating McCandor. Some kids who deal drugs said Joel used to go up to the house. We knew there was a boy involved because of a 911 call, so . . ."

He doesn't react or ask about when the call was made, just takes in the information.

"Take it as easy and slow as you want. Tell me what happened."

"And then you'll arrest me."

"There's a good chance not. But you have to talk now. That's the bottom line."

"A guy was trying to kill me," he begins. "I don't know how to back this up so you understand it. I never even saw him until that night. Earl. He wanted me to slice up a kid named Carl, and I let the kid escape."

"Good, good. You're doing fine. Just tell it as it comes to you," she says easily.

It's very hard work encouraging a person. She has to wonder, if she didn't have counseling behind her, if she'd ever be able to stick to the task. She isn't naturally patient, but this one, this guy—he's a boy, really—taps something tender in her. As he talks, she studies him, puzzles over how they're going to hide a fellow like this, a handsome innocent. He's memorable. A perfect empty vessel, holder of all possibilities. Something for everyone.

An hour later, by the time he is answering questions about Markovic's operation, and he seems to be speaking more easily, Mo Weaver pokes her head out. "Is everything all right? Is he okay?" she asks fiercely.

"I'm okay," he calls up to her.

Colleen watches Mo Weaver retreat back into the kitchen. Now is the important part, the part she fought for. In a low voice, she asks, "Are you willing to become a witness? That's the main thing I need to learn from you to know where we go next. If you say yes, and I can only hope you do, we erase the parole violation, we waive the inquest on the killing of Higgins. We keep you out of jail and out of court."

He takes a moment to let her words sink in. "I'm a free man?"

"Well. That's the thing about being a witness. You're up against dangerous people. You'd have to stay hidden," she says.

"Here?" he asks hopefully.

"No. No, it has to be someplace new. We'll help you find a place where nobody has seen you before. We'll get you a new name, a new identity."

"If I don't say yes?"

"You'd have to face some charges and . . . the people who are looking for you could find you . . . with more ease." His face tightens. "It's your best chance for a new life. Do you understand that?"

"I understand that you believe it."

"I know I'm right. You're running right now. If you're running, you can't think. You can't be." There. A moment. He glimpsed something. "And I need to get you to a hospital, have your leg looked at."

"No. It's healing."

"It may be healing, but we have to be sure you are completely all right. You're under our protection."

"I'm your property."

"In a way."

"The Philips boy is like a doctor. I'm not kidding."

"Believe me, I saw those kids are not the usual thing."

"They *didn't* call you?" he asks again.

"They didn't betray you, if that's what you're asking. We went to them, Nick, that's the truth. And they tried pretty hard not to tell us anything. Don't be angry with them. They're the reason I can be here to offer you immunity. The girl, Meg, fought like a champ for you. She wrote down everything you told her. She kept lots of pages on you. Meg was basically your defense attorney."

He says gruffly, "She was good at that stuff. Words."

"Very good. And passionate about helping you."

She's almost got him. . . . Almost. "One more thing now. I want to be absolutely clear. Usually, the way this works, you get to keep your first name and your initials. But I don't know what they'll come up with in your case. For sure you have to give up the name Banks. Also Kissel. They'll make you agree to that. They'll choose you a name."

"I have a new name. It suits me. Charles Philips."

"I guessed it, though. The kids didn't tell me, and I figured— You probably have a couple of cards? Things to make an ID with? See, if I could guess it—"

"It's a good-luck name."

"I'll ask. I wouldn't count on it. But I'll try."

He leans forward, starting in on something new. "Maybe we could work something out with the kids. They need someone and—"

"They do. For sure. We have agencies involved and . . . anyway, the stepmother is back."

"They don't like her. They don't like her at all."

"I know." She starts to put her pen and legal pad away. She needs to take over, capture him physically for his own good, while she plucks stubborn fantasies from him, one after another. If she reads his mind correctly, and she's pretty sure she does, he won't want to give up the Styrofoam splint either. He knows reality. He just doesn't want to know it. "We'll get you to a hospital. We'll take care of everything. You do your part, we'll do ours."

When her phone rings, she moves away from him to talk. She even leaves him alone while she goes to the back door of the kitchen to apologize to Dmitri and Mo about having to take him away. She lets him watch her trusting him.

Finally she puts him in the backseat of her car and starts toward Pittsburgh. She says, gesturing out the car window, "Where I found you, Dmitri's diner, is close to my hometown and kind of on the way to your hometown. We came from the same neck of the woods. I felt it."

She drives the rest of the way, mostly silent, letting him get used to the idea of what he's in for.

POTOCKI IS SITTING ON HER
doorstep when she returns home Wednesday night.

"What's this?" she asks, coming up the sidewalk.

"Brought you something." He hands over a worn-looking copy of *The Mathematician's Apology,* the book Carl had, but a different edition.

She sits beside him. Collapses, really. "Where'd you find it?"

"Used-book store. I thought you might like it. I ended up sitting here reading it."

"What did you think?"

"It's kind of like reading the Bible. You feel like you're tapping into something abstract and important."

"Exactly."

He takes it from her and opens it up. "Here we go. 'In great mathematics there is a very high degree of unexpectedness, combined with inevitability and economy.'"

"Ha. Pretty, isn't it?"

"What does it mean?"

"I don't know. I'd need a context."

Potocki turns pages randomly. "'A chess player may offer the sacrifice of a pawn or even a piece, but a mathematician offers the game.' Hmm, that's probably something about seeming to lose, but really winning."

"Probably. Carl's a smartie, all right. Hey, thanks for the book."

"You're welcome. Look, I have to leave in about five minutes. So. Tell me," he says.

"I brought Nick to Pittsburgh; the others, including Boss and Dolan, questioned him in a motel room off-site for four hours before getting him to a hospital. It seemed like torture, but the idea was that with medications, he might not be as lucid. He . . . opted for staying local." Eighty percent of witnesses did. She shrugged. "This way police can get to him on a regular basis to take him supplies, to get him to physical therapy."

"For you—it was bad?"

"Just . . . No, not bad. Tiring. You know, saving-a-swimmer kind of tiring. Dolan took over tonight, getting Nick protection at the motel until we can get him into a house or apartment. That's tomorrow, hopefully. There's a line on a house on Allegheny River Boulevard.

Nick cried at the hospital when they told him his leg was healing beautifully. That was kind of rough on me, if you want the yucky truth."

"What was he like, after all the running? Not angry?"

"More . . . brokenhearted."

"Huh."

"He wants a job. Wants to work. We haven't figured out yet if it's going to be possible once he's off crutches, but maybe it will be eventually if he grows a beard. It's dangerous. He's not out of danger, no matter what. Well, you know. The usual worries." Witness protection works only if the witness can stick to rules. Most of them can't. They go somewhere they shouldn't go, make a phone call they shouldn't make. "I'm worried he's going to walk down the street one day finally feeling good and someone will drive by and— After all this, after all he's been through. He never did know how to protect himself."

"How do you know?"

"I just know."

Potocki's arm goes around her. "Who are you seeing, huh? Your father?"

"Brother," she answers.

He squeezes. His kiss lands on her eye. She laughs.

FORTY-FOUR

THE HOUSE, A-FRAME WITH
siding, is a little battered, but mainly clean. There are no neighbors,
nobody to tap on the door bearing an apple pie.

They let him look around.

In the small living room is a fairly good-looking beige sofa and a
few tables of glass and chrome. Otherwise there is only a rocking chair
in the room. Ahead, in the next room, the dining room table is a real
wooden table from the '50s perhaps, about as traditional as you can
get. The kitchen is not up to date. The sink needs to be replaced. The
wooden cabinets have been painted over a couple of times. Some ten-
ants must have scrubbed the stove so hard, they made scratches from
the work of cleaning it. Something in the rounded shape of the refrigerator reminds him of an old car. The place is okay, though; the best
part of it is that it has a backyard of sorts that looks out on the river.
He stands at the kitchen window and looks at the rectangle of crab-

grass that leads to the drop-off that leads to the water. There is a basketball hoop attached to a pole, no net.

He opens the refrigerator, closes it, opens the cupboards, closes them.
Some dishes. A little of everything. Peeler, can opener.

Food provided.

Upstairs—they wait a few steps behind while he climbs the stairs
on crutches—are three small bedrooms. A double bed, a single bed,
and two single beds. The bureaus are basic, but all the drawers work.

No job. Not for a while, they say.

Markovic's face was in the paper. Old Marko is in prison now.
Along with certain relatives of his. But according to the police, that's
no guarantee of safety.

There are footsteps coming up the stairs. Detective Greer and Detective Dolan want to know if he needs anything else.

He thanks them and tells them no.

They leave him be. He can hear their car start up, leave.

He lies down on top of the double bed and stares at the ceiling.
There's a subtle crack in the plaster that he traces for hours that afternoon, forever it seems, making it a river, then a drawing, every damn
thing. So this is it, huh? Alive. No people. No work. No drink.

MEG SITS DOWN ACROSS FROM
Alison. She says, "You look nice."

"Oh, well."

"You seem a bit different," she says.

"Well, I was the one who left this time. Maybe that was it."

"What was wrong with the guy?"

"He drank. I guess I like a drinker."

"Why?"

"Charm. Something. Charm, I guess."

"Do you think most drinkers have that?"

"Lord, no. Some are plain monsters. But your father had it, for sure."

Meg thinks how Alison would have fallen in love with Nick, but not vice versa. Nick needs to be amazed by someone. He needs to be won with kindness.

"Are you going to try to get your job back at the Park House?"

"I'll ask. Tomorrow, maybe."

"Do you want a cup of tea?"

"All right."

"I don't mean to bug you, but could you call the landlady, promise her we're coming along with the rent money?"

Alison hesitates. "I'm not sure what to say."

Meg writes out a little schedule on a paper napkin. "If you get your job back, we're okay. Tell her we can do two hundred each week. We can pay on Fridays. We'll be paid up for last month by the twenty-second of this month, and we'll be ready to pay in full next month."

Alison studies the piece of paper.

"If we get the other money we're supposed to get, we're *way* in the clear. We have to try. There are things we want, you know," she says, swallowing hard, "if we get in the clear."

"What?"

"Music players, clothes, books, a computer. Mostly a computer. Detective Potocki told us to make a list."

"Oh."

Meg doesn't want to overwhelm Alison with demands. She brings two cups of tea to the table. Teabags in the house, the kids calm and watching TV in the next room—it's all she wants, really. The wish list has made her nervous. She doesn't want to lose the feeling of wonder at having little things.

FRIDAY EVENING AND COLLEEN

is alone, sitting on her front porch, making notes. It's funny, come to think of it, because she's not likely to forget any of the items she's just jotted down: *check on Nick, check on Carl, check on Philips kids, check on*

Commander, write reports. Tomorrow or Sunday, she'll catch them all, the people she's pulling for.

The old-fashioned ice cream truck that comes by every evening pulls into the street, but the driver has to idle and then skirt wide because three teenage boys are tossing a football right in front of him and they aren't looking at anything else. In fact they're especially reckless. One of the boys keeps falling into Colleen's car. He clearly likes the big thumping sound his body makes when it hits metal.

The ice cream–truck driver starts his melodeon music-thing going. Kids of all ages start to appear from various doorways. It's going to be daylight for a while yet. She reads over her completely unnecessary list and laughs to remember a guy she once knew who wrote *rest* on his to-do list. She writes *rest*.

The boy who likes to smash himself into the fender of her old Accord does it again.

"Hey, watch it!" she yells.

Watch what? This old car? his outraged face says.

She levels him a look that makes him slink away. The car isn't worth much, but hey, she loves it anyway. She stretches her tired body and goes into the house to scrounge something to eat.